Prime Directive

By Alexander Geiger

Prime Directive (2013)
Flood Tide (2019)
Conquest of Persia (2019)
Immortal Alexandros (2020)
Funeral Games (2021)

Book One of the Ptolemaios Saga

Prime Directive

*An Epic Novel of the Rise of
Alexander the Great*

Alexander Geiger

Permissions Department
Ptolemaios Publishing & Entertainment, LLC
668 Stony Hill Road, Suite 150
Yardley, PA 19067

www.PtolemaiosPublishing.com

ISBN-13: 978-0-9892584-2-5 (pbk)
ISBN-13: 978-0-9892584-3-2 (ebook)

Library of Congress Control Number: 2019935856

Cover Design: Scott Schmeer, Prometheus Training, LLC

The author of this work is available to speak at live events. For further information, please contact the author at Alex@AlexanderGeiger.com

Revised Second Edition

Manufactured in the United States of America

To Helene, with love

Table of Contents

"Wherefore he resolved to have a moving image of eternity . . . and this image we call time."

Plato, Timaeus, 37[1]

---

[1] From *The Dialogues of Plato,* translated by B. Jowett (3rd ed., Oxford University Press, 1892)

Maps and Animated Battle Depictions[2]

Map 1 – Ancient Macedonia and its Environs

Map 2 – Mainland Greece in 336 B.C.E.

Map 3 – Lands Traversed by Alexandros in 335 and early 334 B.C.E.

Battle 1 – Chaironeia – August 338 B.C.E.

Battle 2 – Granikos – May 334 B.C.E.

List of Principal Characters

Alexandros Aniketos (356-323)[3] – King of Macedonia (336-323)[4]

Antipatros (397-319) – Macedonian nobleman; served as regent under both Philippos and Alexandros

Aristoteles (384-322) – Alexandros's teacher in Mieza

---

[2] In lieu of black-and-white maps and static battle depictions in this book, color maps and animated depictions of battles are available at AlexanderGeiger.com.

[3] Numbers refer to year of birth and year of death, respectively. All years are B.C.E. In some cases, the actual dates are either uncertain or in dispute. In those cases, the year in question is preceded by a c.

[4] Numbers refer to years of reign.

Attalos (390-336) – Macedonian nobleman; uncle and guardian of Kleopatra(2)

Audata (a/k/a Eurydike) (c.378-c.348) – Bardylis's daughter; Philippos's 1st wife; mother of Kynane

Bardylis (c.428-c.358) – King of Illyria (c.408-c.358)

Dareios (c.380-330) – Persian Emperor (336-330)

Hephaistion (356-324) – Alexandros's best friend

Kleitos Melas (c.357-327)[5] – A soldier in Alexandros's army

Kleopatra(1) (354-308) – Daughter of Philippos and Olympias; Alexandros's sister

Kleopatra(2) (355-336) – Philippos's 7th wife; mother of Europa and Karanos

Langaros (c.362-335) – King of Agriania (c.342-335)

Lanike (c.372-c.313)[6] – Alexandros's nursemaid; Kleitos's sister

Meda (unk-unk) – Philippos's 6th wife

Nikesipolis (unk-c.344) – Philippos's 5th wife; mother of Thessalonike

---

[5] The date of Kleitos's birth is uncertain, but he was probably several years older than depicted in this book.

[6] The dates of Lanike's birth and death are uncertain, but she was probably older than depicted in this book.

Olympias (a/k/a Myrtale) (377-314) – Philippos's 4th wife; mother of Alexandros

Parmenion (400-330) – Leading Macedonian general; served both Philippos and Alexandros

Phila (c.374-unk) – Philippos's 2nd wife

Philinna (unk-unk) – Philippos's 3rd wife; mother of Arrhidaios

Philippos Amyntou Makedonios (380-336) – King of Macedonia (359-336); father of Alexandros

Ptolemaios Metoikos (c.364-c.282) – One of Alexandros's bodyguards

Alexander Geiger

Additional Materials

Additional materials, including sources, illustrations, maps, battle depictions, an author's blog, and descriptions of upcoming volumes, are available at AlexanderGeiger.com.

Acknowledgements

The author wishes to express his gratitude to the following individuals who kindly read (and, in some cases, re-read) the manuscript of this novel and offered numerous helpful suggestions and corrections, ranging from fixing typographical errors to pointing out infelicitous phrasing to urging a restructuring of plotlines: Helene Geiger, Kathy McGowan, Aviva Schwarz, David Schwarz, and Alan Unsworth. Special thanks to Scott Schmeer of Prometheus Training, LLC, for the cover design.

Any remaining mistakes are attributable solely to the obduracy of the author.

Chapter 1 – Elastic Limit

A fleeting, inchoate thought crossed my mind: *Perhaps I should rescue the struggling boy.*

I banished the thought even before it had coalesced into coherent words. It was a dangerous, aberrant thought. All my training had been designed to condition me against such foolish, potentially catastrophic impulses. And besides, it wasn't in my nature to do stupid things with unforeseeable consequences.

From a tender age, I'd spent my life foreseeing disasters and avoiding them. *Remember,* I told myself, *don't fuck with the future!* Of course, saving the life of an obscure shepherd boy, who lived in a place that had never played much of a role on the world stage, wasn't likely to have any impact on the future course of history. But still, why take a chance?

I'd been sitting, more or less continuously, in the crown of a huge sycamore tree, at the edge of a highlands meadow, somewhere in the godforsaken reaches of ancient Macedonia, for the better part of a day. According to my briefing, the initiation rites were about to begin.

Having arrived way too early, as was my wont, I'd frittered away the idle hours indulging in my favorite pastime – imagining various horrible disasters that might befall me. You see, I believe in reverse premonition. I figure, if you can see it coming, it won't happen. It's what you don't anticipate that'll kill you.

I'd pictured myself falling out of the tree. I could just see losing my balance, my arms shooting out in a desperate but futile attempt to arrest my fall, the back of my head striking a branch as I tumbled backward, causing me to reverse my spin and strike the next branch with my face, breaking my two front teeth, an incoherent noise involuntarily escaping my lips, the skin on my arms sprouting a thousand welts and scratches as my hands slapped uselessly against each successive branch, my head making something like a woodpecker sound with each new impact. Finally, drifting into shock, my body cleared the lowest branch of the tree and I free-fell the rest of the way, crashing head first into the underbrush, breaking my neck but not losing consciousness, struggling to breathe, the world gradually turning purple, dark, and cold.

Whew, that was a close call, I'd told myself, carefully shifting my weight while I held on more firmly to the branch under my right arm. I was almost surprised to see no blood on my hands and feel nothing broken. But at least now I was safe from an unexpected fall.

Next, I'd envisioned betraying my presence to a group of peasants traversing the path beneath my blind. Perhaps my dagger, perversely slipping out of my belt, caused them to look up. They glimpsed my gray cloak, clambered up the tree, tried to pull me down. I ran, they chased, and we fought. Eventually I got away but not before two peasants lay mortally wounded on the forest floor. There was a definite, inescapable disturbance in local chronology. I told myself that it didn't matter, that the reverberations of this disturbance, traveling down the river of time, would dampen out before they reached my own era, but I knew I was only kidding myself. The Prime Directive is short and to the point: "Don't fuck with the future!" which was precisely what I'd done. The repercussions of my interference would echo all the way to my origination point, severing my temporal connection and stranding me then and there forever.

The fight sequence with the peasants, and its existential denouement, was so vivid in my mind I'd felt tears welling up in my eyes. Of course, being stuck up a tree for many hours was perhaps a more likely explanation for my depressed mood. Nevertheless, I'd made sure my dagger was still securely fastened to my belt. I knew that I was being irrational, that I could not simply daymare all risks away, but it helped to pass the time. Life, after all, is not a rational endeavor. When embarked on a journey fraught with unpredictable and uncontrollable risks, the temptation to indulge in a little superstition is almost irresistible.

I'd imagined falling asleep and missing the initiation ceremony I'd come to observe. When I woke it was completely dark. The forest was filled with the calls of nocturnal creatures. The moon was beginning to clear the treetops. My observation log for the day was as blank as the mind of a teenager in love, while I searched in vain for a plausible explanation for the utter failure of my expedition. My advisor was dumbfounded. I flunked out of the program and the disciplinary committee sentenced me to teaching philosophy to incoming cadets for the rest of my life.

Another disaster successfully avoided. I suppressed an inward smile, only to realize with a start that I was in fact still asleep, dreaming about the preventive benefits of imagining the consequences of falling asleep during my watch.

This time I'd awakened for real, shaken and sweaty, but also grateful for my knack, which I've had since childhood, of being able to tell, even while asleep, whether I'm dreaming or not and to wake from dream to reality at will. At least I fancied myself possessing such a knack. I was twenty-one then, callow and untested, and therefore brimming with self-confidence and self-regard.

Prime Directive

While I awaited the arrival of the worshippers of Dionysos, I'd spent the rest of the afternoon in contented hypnagogia, mentally careering from fanciful fiasco to fantastic failure. Unfortunately, during all that meandering through mindscapes of delicious, anxiety-inducing, faux-fatal near misses, I never did manage to imagine, and thus avert, the one actual disaster that was stealthily stealing its way toward me.

I'd rubbed my eyes, slapped my arms, pinched my thighs, trying desperately to maintain my focus. Finally, the sun began to paint the western sky with bold brushstrokes of vermilion and mauve. *It shouldn't be too much longer now. Maybe I have time to contemplate one more mishap.* But no, just as I'd begun to picture losing control of my bladder, the rustle of bodies through the underbrush impinged upon my reverie. A group of women, no more than eight or ten, were laboriously making their way toward the clearing below me. They ranged in age from adolescent to dowdy.

Although I should have known better, I couldn't take my eyes off the youngest of the women, ignoring her more mature companions in the process. Little did I appreciate, during that fateful moment of folly, the far-reaching ramifications of my first, lingering, libidinous gaze at this seductive avatar of endless heartache. She was festively dressed, wrapped in a sparkling white linen cloth pinned with a brooch over the left shoulder. The fabric was carefully draped and pleated, cascading over her bouncy, spirited bosom and down to a bright red belt, which held the pleats in place and accentuated her swaying hips. She wore black-eyed susans in her hair and was dragging a small, dusty gray goat behind her.

Reluctantly, I'd torn my attention away from the marvelous maiden and observed the rest of the women. They were similarly dressed but their clothes were not quite as sparkling nor their figures as alluring. Some were balancing baskets on their heads, while others carried amphorae in their arms. A few leaned on ivy-covered walking sticks. One was cradling something that looked a lot like an enormous wooden phallus to her bosom. There was a second, larger goat trailing behind, laden with cargo.

I'd pulled out my notepad and stylus, being very careful not to drop either one, and started a new entry in my log. For reasons known only to my subconscious, I'd decided to label the young woman Aphrodite, for research purposes only, of course, so as to keep myself from confusing her with the others. The remaining women I'd labeled female subject two, female subject three, and so on, except for female subject eight, whom I'd decided to call the penis lady in my notes.

Additional women and animals emerged from the opposite side of the meadow, adding their contributions to the stockpile of gear and provender growing in the lee of a large, flat boulder near the center of the clearing.

Much squealing, laughter, and communal hugging ensued. Then, while a few women set out in search of firewood, others got busy making preparations. They staked out the perimeter of the meadow with what I took to be torches. They tied the animals, two goats and some sheep, including a nursing ewe with a couple of tiny lambs, to a nearby stand of trees. They built an effigy of their god Dionysos next to the flat-topped boulder. All the while, additional celebrants kept arriving in twos and threes.

By nightfall, three dozen women were milling about, clustered in small groups, weaving garlands of flowers and ivy shoots, chatting and gesturing animatedly, waiting for the festivities to begin. As the last of the twilight faded, a woman in her thirties arrived, attended by an entourage of female servants. She radiated an air of authority.

Despite her advanced age (at least in the eyes of a twenty-one-year-old), she was gorgeous, in a scary sort of way. Her face was narrow, almost gaunt, with prominent cheekbones. I guessed she might have had dimples, had she ever smiled. Her eyes were a frosty pale blue, cold and hard. Her light brown hair, tightly braided and then woven and mounded, formed an impressive crown atop her head. Her carriage was regal, her gestures peremptory. In a stroke of prescience, I decided to call her Medusa.

Shortly after her arrival, and having acknowledged the greetings of the other celebrants, Medusa lit the bonfire in the middle of the meadow. At the same time, some of the other women started lighting the torches that formed a kind of peristyle at the outer edges of the clearing.

All this combustion did me little good. Without the warming rays of the sun, there was a chill in the air. I was trying to figure out how to stay warm and awake when an unexpected solution revealed itself. On a signal from Medusa, who appeared to be in charge of the proceedings, the women started to remove their garments. It was interesting to see that each elaborate dress, full of pleats and flourishes, unwound into a simple, rectangular piece of fabric, which the women carefully folded and placed on the ground.

Much to my disappointment, it turned out they were wearing another layer of clothing under their robes. Straining to see in the flickering torchlight, I realized their bodies were encased in spotted fawn skins, stitched together with string made of gut and sinew, barely large enough to conceal their torsos. Some of the celebrants had evidently gained weight since their initial acquisition of the vestigial vestments, judging by the rolls of flesh seeking to burst out into the brisk night air.

A drumbeat filled the meadow, joined by the sweet, plaintive cry of a flute. The women, barefoot now, formed a circle and, holding hands, started to dance around the fire. As the cadence of the drum increased its urgency, the dance became more and more frenzied. Soon the flickering fire was surrounded by a whirling cylinder of glistening skin, dappled animal pelts, and white flashes of bared teeth and bulging eyes.

The pace became unsustainable. Fidgeting in my blind, I wondered how long they could possibly remain afoot when the air was rent by a piercing shriek. The flying circle of dancers disintegrated, sending bodies tumbling and hurtling away from the fire. As the women, their chests heaving, gathered themselves on the cold, dewy ground, two celebrants made the rounds, pouring wine directly into their panting mouths.

They didn't look especially menacing, these entranced women, their faces and bodies dripping sweat and wine. They didn't appear bestial or bloodthirsty. I didn't see any Prime Directive violation lurking in their lassitude. Truth to tell, I was far too engrossed by the tantalizing tableau in front of my eyes to appreciate the peril bubbling below the surface of the sacred scene.

After a brief respite, and urged on by the insistent beating of the drum, the initiates of Dionysos roused themselves and resumed their dancing. Their pace slackened somewhat, while their movements became more sensuous and salacious. The large wooden phallus reappeared, planted right in front of the effigy of their god, and was soon mounted by one of the women. The rest clapped rhythmically, cheered, hurled vaguely obscene encouragement, and continued to dance in place, while the featured performer enjoyed her moment of deific copulation. When she sank to the ground, spent, another one took her place, until most of the women had had a turn. Aphrodite came last. She seemed hesitant and inartful, which made her all the more captivating to my inexperienced, starry-eyed, distracted mind.

My heart was beating faster and louder than the drum in the meadow and my mouth was parched as I watched Aphrodite's lascivious dance and eventual swoon. I felt an irresistible urge to jump down from my tree and share the wine the women were pouring straight down her throat but, luckily, I resisted. My perch, however, was growing more uncomfortable by the minute.

I'd expected the celebrants to bed down for the night but, after a momentary pause, they started to chant and then resumed their dancing, more jagged than ever. Several more rounds of chanting, dancing, and drinking followed, but I'm not sure how many. I'm embarrassed to admit that, at some point, with my eyes bulging and my penis permanently engorged, I'd stopped keeping an accurate count. Eventually, some of the women could barely move but, as they collapsed to the ground, they continued to twitch on the slick, wet grass in time to the relentless drumbeat.

Prime Directive

As far as I could tell, none of them had eaten anything since they'd first made their way to the meadow but now Medusa approached each one and gave them some kind of leaf to chew, which seemed to inject them with renewed energy. While they chewed on the leaves and drank wine, Medusa preached to them.

Well, it looked like Medusa but it didn't sound like any woman I'd ever heard. Her eyes were closed, her mouth wide open, and the words issued from deep within her chest. Her arms seemed to gesticulate of their own volition. It was as if she were a marionette, being manipulated by an invisible god, who spoke through her in an unearthly, resonant, musical voice. She was channeling Dionysos, I realized.

I could only catch snatches of her sermon, and my grasp of the Macedonian dialect was fairly tenuous, but I was able to make out the general drift of her comments. They were all disciples of Dionysos, except for the young one who was being initiated that night. They were told that, by believing in their god and following his commands, they could assure themselves of fecundity and sexual satisfaction. Most importantly, they were told, anyone who believed in Dionysos, worshipped him, and made the proper sacrifices to him, would never die. Not surprisingly, the women seemed riveted by Medusa's sermon, repeating some of her phrases in a kind of singsong refrain and generally interjecting words of assent, approbation, and allegiance.

At the end of the sermon, the women rose to their feet and surrounded their high priestess. The next time I spotted her again, she was holding two large snakes in her hands. I did a double-take when I realized Medusa's coiffure was squirming on her head; she had entwined several small snakes in her hair. It was indeed a vision capable of freezing one's blood. But the celebrants were unperturbed. They screamed and laughed while letting the larger snakes slither all over their bodies. One or two seemed delirious, foaming at the mouth, writhing on the ground. Some had lost their animal-skin coverings and were cavorting naked in the cold night air. I saw one woman pick up the two small lambs and suckle them at her breasts. An older matron disentangled herself from the group, tottered a few steps to the side, and voided where she stood, keeping her legs wide in order to avoid the steaming puddle forming between her feet.

I was so spellbound by the spectacle in front of me, I didn't even notice the arrival of a couple of fellow observers on the scene. It was only an unexpected, muffled cry from below which caused me to realize that, at some time during the night, two boys had crept to the edge of the meadow, not far from my blind, and were staring through the bushes with even more wide-eyed fascination than I was.

By now, the sky in the east had started to blanch and turn pink. With some effort, Medusa managed to call a halt to the frenzied dancing. The women gathered around the flat-topped boulder and dragged the larger goat with them. The goat was placed, bleating and thrashing, on top of the boulder, held there by a dozen hands. Aphrodite, floating on the edge of consciousness, found herself in a hollow beneath the rock. Medusa then recited a long and incomprehensible – at least to me – incantation and suddenly, with a swift flash of a dagger, slit the goat's throat. Copious quantities of blood squirted and poured from the still twitching animal straight onto Aphrodite, coating her in warm, steamy gore, as she squirmed on the ground, spreading the coagulating liquid all over her body.

When the torrent of blood from the animal slowed to a drip, some of the women came running around the boulder with a joyful shout and lifted Aphrodite to her feet. Medusa herself approached and, slashing savagely with her dagger, tore off one of the animal's hind legs. She offered the leg to Aphrodite, who grabbed it and started to munch on some of the exposed flesh. As if on a signal, the rest of the women fell on the remnants of the goat and, in the blink of an eye, tore it to pieces. Medusa carefully set aside a few choice cuts from the shoulder and flanks of the sacrificial victim for the nourishment of the god while the women devoured all the rest. Unlike the god, whose portion would have to be burned, the women consumed the animal's flesh raw.

There wasn't enough meat on the carcass for all of the women in the group. Some of them fanned out in the meadow, seized the second goat, and tore it apart with their bare hands while the poor animal bleated helplessly. Next, they descended on the sheep, according them the same treatment. Then they spotted the two boys hiding in the bushes.

A short moment of silence intervened. The women stared at the shivering boys and the boys peered at the crazed women. Then, simultaneously, each group let out a yell and the boys were off and running, closely pursued by half a dozen wild-eyed bipedal beasts. The boys never had a chance. They looked to be twelve to fourteen, wearing nothing but short tunics. They were running for their lives but their pursuers were adults, in their prime, nicely loosened up from their nocturnal exertions, and there were more of them.

On the point of being caught, the taller boy yelled to the shorter one to keep running toward the village. He then stopped and waited for the pursuit to wash over him. When two of the women grabbed for him, their hands slick with animal gore, he slipped through their grasp, ducked under their arms, and took off running in the opposite direction, back toward the meadow. The women turned and followed, ignoring the smaller boy who was able to make good his escape.

The boy was running directly toward me, his face clearly visible. He had a swarthy complexion, with pitch-black hair. His expression was remarkably calm, considering he was about to be torn to pieces by a pack of deranged predators. When it was clear his companion was out of danger, he actually slowed, perhaps because the prospect in front of him was more fearsome than the fast-approaching fate gaining from behind. The meadow was filled with more or less naked women, covered in blood, devouring chunks of raw meat, amidst dripping scraps of skin and sinew scattered about the grass and hanging from the surrounding trees and bushes.

The women behind the boy, although they might have been raving mad, pursued with more coordination. They formed a semi-circle, giving him only one avenue of escape, toward the meadow. The boy tried to slip through once again but this time the women closed in and held fast. There was an eerie silence, as the boy continued to struggle, without uttering a word, and the women simply growled and grunted as they went about their work.

Looking at this boy, who had saved his friend despite the terrifying prospect before him and who was continuing to struggle stoically in what was clearly a lost cause, I could imagine a man of courage, cold-blooded determination and, above all, unshakable loyalty. I was tempted to save him but I resisted the temptation.

Despite my relentless drive to succeed at the Academy, I had always avoided unnecessary risks. With an officer's commission almost within my grasp, with a simple observational jaunt into the past the last remaining obstacle between me and graduation, I could already envision the joyful ceremony, the pride and elation of my family, the cool, smooth, priceless feel of an Academy diploma in my hands. I was certainly not going to disobey my orders at this late stage, much less risk violating the Prime Directive.

So, I sat and watched impassively as a covey of crazed crones set about tearing a small boy limb from limb. I tried not to think about it. Instead, I focused my mind on the inertial tendencies of the temporal stream. Clearly, any trip into the past by a time traveler disrupted the fabric of the space-time continuum to some extent, yet the universe didn't blink out of existence the first time someone had traveled back in time. Theoreticians had determined that, up to a certain elastic limit, the stream of time would simply return to its original path after a disruption, much as a river continued to flow more or less unaffected by a pebble tossed from the bank. By the same token, it was equally clear that there was a breaking point beyond which the future would be irremediably altered by a traveler carelessly changing the past. The old chestnut about a traveler returning to kill the common genetic ancestor of our species, thus wiping out the human race as we know it, contained a kernel of truth.

The trouble was that the theoreticians didn't know exactly where the elastic limit lay and the practitioners were loath to find out. Hence, the repeated emphasis on rigid adherence to the Prime Directive.

Prime Directive

I knew all this perfectly well, but still I thought: *Surely, it couldn't possibly change anything, twenty-four hundred years from now, if I saved the life of this one boy.* I could see myself jumping down from my tree and dispersing the women. After all, six unarmed women, no matter how crazed, were no match for one highly trained twenty-one-year-old warrior. Plus, I had the element of surprise on my side. It would be a piece of cake. Then it hit me: *If you can see it coming, it won't happen.*

Whew, that was a close call. I had almost violated the Prime Directive. *Now let's pick up that pad and start taking notes!*

And then, without further conscious thought, I slid from my hiding place atop the tree, shedding my clothes in the process, and landed no more than five yards from the struggling clutch of women. "I am Dionysos!" I thundered.

Although I spoke with a heavy accent, they stopped dead in their tracks. *Dionysos is a foreign god,* I thought irrelevantly, *so it's okay that I have an accent.* Then the women lunged at me. Not with any evil intent, mind you, but rather, with a desperate determination to mate with me. *Resistance is futile,* I tried to tell myself but, nevertheless, I held up my arms and bellowed once again: "Go! Go!"

The women stopped, kissed my hands and feet and other parts of my body and then withdrew, eyes bulging, pupils fixed and dilated, expressions beatific, the absence of reason apparently total.

I puffed out my chest. *I am divinity manifest.* Then I looked over to the boy, still sitting on the ground, looking at me curiously. When our eyes met, I gave a little, embarrassed smile. He smiled back, got up, and prostrated himself at my feet.

"No, no," I said. "I'm not really a god."

He laughed. "I didn't think so but there's no sense taking any chances."

"It's a little late for that."

"Yeah, but it was worth it, wasn't it?"

Suddenly, the burden of what I'd done descended on me like the extra G's of a spaceship returning to Earth. "You'd better disappear before they come back looking for you."

"You too," he said, reasonably enough, and set off at a trot toward the village. "I'll see you around," he called back over his shoulder.

"What's your name?" I shouted by way of an afterthought.

"Kleitos," came the faint response, muffled by the intervening trees and brush.

Prime Directive

"Stop yelling," I muttered as I climbed back to my blind. Before I had time to collect my meager possessions, I saw the women returning. I jumped down and ran.

I could see getting caught by the aroused worshippers. First, they tore the little sack of supplies from my back. Next, they stripped my cloak and tunic, leaving streaks of blood on my shoulders. It was not clear whose blood it was. I could feel some scratches on my skin but without sufficient sting to produce any blood, leading me to conclude it wasn't mine. Next, they tore off my loincloth, reaching eagerly for my genitals. Their intentions were ambiguous. With a cry, I covered my privates with both hands and tried to turn away from the assault but there were too many of them and their grip was too strong. I tumbled to the ground; the women piled on top of me. I was getting crushed by a huge mass of squirming, panting female flesh, with hands and fingers clawing all over my body. I couldn't move, scream, or breathe; all I could do was whimper.

The entire vivid image took only a moment to flash through my brain. When I opened my eyes, I was still running, dodging tree branches, my genitals cupped protectively in my hands. I let go of the family jewels and redoubled my running speed.

It soon became clear I wasn't being followed but I kept running anyway. My rendezvous time was at noon of the following day, so there was no need to rush, but I persisted in maintaining my pace nevertheless.

I reached the abandoned rock quarry that was my designated pickup point well before noon, affording me more than twenty-four hours to complete preparations for my return. Having found a nice, flat spot near the quarry to rest and eat, I started by driving a stake into the ground to create a sundial. Then I scratched in the dirt the curve traced by the end of the shadow of the gnomon as the sun reached its zenith and started declining toward the west. I carefully marked the point where the curve of the shadow passed closest to the base of my stick. Next time the shadow reached that point would be tomorrow, high noon.

With that chore finished, my thoughts turned to food and water. I found a brook nearby, with tantalizing shadows of fish gliding beneath the surface. After a lot of unsuccessful tries and one lucky hit, I beheld a magnificent carp skewered on a make-shift spear. While the carp roasted, I pulled some arrowroots from the mud on the bank and boiled the tubers. Some delicious mushrooms and blackberries rounded out my repast with. A feast fit for a king.

After my meal, I organized and amplified my notes of the previous day and settled back for a quick nap. Judging by the stars, my nap lasted about seven hours. No matter, time wasn't an issue just then. With the sun well advanced above the horizon, I took a leisurely stroll through the woods, ate some leftover roots and berries, and packed my gear. I was ready for the portal to materialize with plenty of time to spare as I watched the shadow on my sundial creeping slowly toward its perigee.

Precisely at noon, nothing happened. I imagined the implications of being stranded without a portal but it didn't help. When I opened my eyes, there was still no portal. *Just a technical glitch*, I told myself as I settled down to await my rescue.

Chapter 2 – Lupika's Luck

I had plenty of time to contemplate all the calamities coming my way while I awaited my rescue but for some reason the implications of the unanticipated delay in the date of my departure never crossed my mind. Instead, I devoted all my energies to staying alive until the extraction party arrived. I grubbed for sustenance, avoided human contact, and struggled against the soul-sapping side-effects of solitude.

One morning, about a week into my involuntary stay, I awoke to the siren song of a human voice. The sound was too distant and indistinct to determine the gender of the caller, much less the content of the clamor, but my first instinct was to run toward it. Then I remembered the Prime Directive. Even as the ruckus drew nearer and resolved into the outcry of a young boy evidently calling upon his god – *it's amazing how prevalent the worship of Dionysos is in these parts* – I continued to cower in some bushes near the entrance to my cave. I didn't come out until the sound had safely faded into the distance. Then I spent hours listening anxiously, hoping to hear the youngster's sweet sonority again, but all I heard was the impersonal murmur of the brook nearby, the melodic gossip of the local avian population, the surreptitious rustling of the ubiquitous rodents, and the incessant background thrum of frogs, crickets, and other vermin.

I missed home, missed the comforts of civilization, missed human intercourse. Speaking of which, I also missed my girlfriend Paloma. She and I had been together for less than six months. She was my first true love and I was plagued by feelings of guilt. Didn't get a chance to say so much as a goodbye because Academy rules enjoined us from disclosing travel orders to anyone, including our loved ones. And besides, had the trip proceeded as planned, I would've been back in my own time within minutes of my departure. Of course, I still expected that to happen, once I was rescued, but, in my own personal chronology, here in this ancient era, time was beginning to drag. It felt as if I hadn't seen Paloma for many days, which, as far as my internal clock was concerned, was in fact the case. *You should have said something to her.* My mind kept returning to the same guilty groove.

After four weeks, I could no longer keep the creeping encroachments of doubt below the level of conscious thought. In that short span of time I had somehow managed either to catch or to scare away all the fish in my stream, to eat every bird's egg I could find, and to harvest all the obviously edible plants within easy walking distance of my cave. Still, there were plenty of other plants, fungi, and roots which might turn out to be edible, and there were lots of succulent critters all around me that I might be able to catch and eat. *It's lucky*, I thought, *that I had gotten stranded in such a secluded yet bountiful spot.*

Technically, this is known as Lupika's Luck. At the Academy, Lupika was a legendary cadet, said to have finished last in his class, a couple centuries ago, but fortunately for him, a war broke out shortly after his graduation and so many of his classmates were killed that, notwithstanding his evident lack of talent, he found himself promoted to general officer rank. "It's lucky," he allegedly said when presented with his first star, "that I was not called upon to serve in peacetime."

According to Academy lore, Lupika was not a very good officer but an extremely vain man. "It's lucky I have no tan lines," he allegedly said while being dragged naked through the streets of Tiraspol after his capture during the Battle of Three Rivers.

He was eventually ransomed and put back in command but his excessive zeal – during the very next engagement – resulted in the annihilation of two battalions of his own troops, while he himself sustained a superficial but humiliating wound. He was patched up, court-marshaled, and sentenced to several years at hard labor. During a subsequent escape attempt, he got shot in the rear by a prison guard and thrown back in the brig. "It's lucky," he confided to a prison visitor, "that they shot me in the same spot as the last time. At least I didn't get any new scars."

In the end, he was paroled, discharged from service, and fortunate enough to die in bed – killed by the jealous husband of a woman who had assured him her husband would be out of town for the entire week just before Lupika mounted her. "It's lucky," he allegedly whispered in her ear shortly before he expired, "that your husband waited until after I had climaxed before returning home." Lupika's Luck, indeed.

Ever the optimist, I decided – after four weeks had elapsed – that, with all these delectable animals hopping around practically within reach and given my extensive knowledge of mechanical dynamics, it should be a simple matter to catch my next dinner. It didn't quite go according to plan. At the decisive moment, there I was, sweaty, itchy, tired, trembling with anticipation and exhaustion, while this small insolent jackrabbit was laughing at me. I had labored for days to fashion a foolproof snare, had baited it with my last, precious bits of cattail hearts, and had been crouching for hours in my prickly, hot, humid foxhole. The impudent hare, its large, asinine, translucent ears cocked and perky, sidled up cautiously to my bait, threw a few timid glances in my general direction, then quickly nipped a healthy bite out of my delicious hearts. The huge, flat boulder, balanced precariously above the bait, designed to fall and crush any creature dumb enough to venture beneath and touch the trigger stick, remained implacably unmoved. Experienced hunter that I was, I bided my time, holding my breath lest I frighten my prey away. The hare continued to consume the last of my food supply, pecking occasionally at my bait, munching contentedly, its ears twitching, its eyes darting, a smile playing upon its lips. When all the food was gone, the hare licked the trigger stick one more time, looked directly at me, winked, and hopped out from under the boulder, bounding across the meadow, sated and smug.

With a prodigious screech, I leapt out of my hole, hurling my spear in the direction of the jackrabbit. The nimble beast executed three long hops before the spear arrived in the vicinity of where the bastard had been when I originally launched my weapon. Although I attempted to pursue the cheeky little thief, throwing rocks and imprecations in its direction, I had as much chance of catching the rabbit as any youngster has of grabbing immortality by the tail.

I returned to my trap to figure out why it had failed. The flat trigger stick, on which my precious bait used to sit, was still in place. I gave it the slightest tap with my foot, causing it to slip from under the small smooth rock that had been restraining it. Without the restraint, the stick flew upward, dislodging the tree branch supporting the huge, flat boulder, poised like the sword of Damokles above the trigger stick. Responding to the force of gravity, the huge, flat boulder promptly thundered to the ground, missing my hastily retreating foot by the width of a toenail. Evidently, my snare was incapable of bagging any game but it was more than adequate for maiming its designer. *It's lucky I still have my reflexes.*

I was tempted – but only for a moment – to consider my alternatives. *Is waiting here passively really my best plan?* I banished the thought. Things were not so bad, I told myself. Except for the gradual disappearance of obvious sources of nutrition and the imperceptible disintegration of my clothes and the steadily more frequent bouts of intestinal distress and the lack of any human contact, my life had settled into a grinding routine. I rose at dawn each morning or, more accurately, was forced to flee the cave in which I slept by the bats returning from their nocturnal hunt. For creatures with inaudible cries they certainly made a lot of noise. However, I didn't argue. They let me use their cave at night and I let them have it the rest of the time. And every once in a while, I managed to kill one of them with my club. Not exactly tasty, but better than a handful of worms. Unfortunately, as I became hungrier, either their sonar became more effective or my coordination deteriorated or perhaps I just found the prospect of eating any more bats revolting but, for whatever reason, my batting average declined over time.

****

The morning after the rabbit fiasco, I decided to turn my efforts from fauna to flora and launched another edibility test. I'd had my eye on some oversized parsley-like plants that grew near the creek. At this time of year, the plants supported starbursts of tiny white flowers looking like cauliflower from a distance. Up close, the stems were smooth and hollow, covered with purple spots. The leaves were fern-shaped and finely chopped. The taproot was large, thick, yellowish white. *Maybe it's a wild carrot,* the hungry part of my brain thought. *Or maybe it's hemlock,* my more rational prefrontal cortex answered.

I would find out soon enough but first my morning routine: Relieve my bladder; jump in the creek; splash some absolutely freezing water on my face and body; swear up a blue streak; run along the bank naked, yelling and screaming while trying to slap some circulation back into my arms and torso; revive my fire and brew some fake tea; wash my tunic and put it back on while still wet; and enjoy a leisurely breakfast of boiled pokeweeds. Not appetizing or nutritious but previously confirmed to be edible.

I ate seated on the ground, facing a large, moss-covered rock, which would have been perfect for sitting. The first few days in, I did in fact sit on it while eating but then one day I started talking to the rock and after a while it seemed disrespectful to sit on my breakfast companion while we indulged in extended discussions about the relative merits of boiled shepherd's purses versus roasted pine nuts. Of course, I did most of the talking but the rock listened amiably, seeming to nod its velvety dome once in a while, although it's possible that it was I who was nodding off.

One day, just to show off, I started reciting to my mossy mate all the useless knowledge I'd acquired in preparation for my trip. "Take Philippos Amyntou Makedonios, for example. Did you know he's the second Philippos to reign as king of Macedonia? That's why we call him Philippos Deuteros."

My mossy mate said nothing. He was, after all, dumb as a rock. Really, a perfect audience for my lectures.

"He's been the king of Macedonia for the past sixteen years," I continued, encouraged by my auditor's silence. "But he's led a tough life, both before and since becoming king.

"Do you realize how poor his prospects were at birth, considering he was, after all, a scion of the royal family?" It was a rhetorical question.

"The trouble was, you see, that in a land ruled by primogeniture, Philippos was born the fourth child, and third son, of a weak king. His father, Amyntas Tritos, reigned over a small, backward, impoverished kingdom that was, at the time of Philippos's birth, well on its way to extinction.

"Although Macedonia was a kingdom with a proud heritage, by the time Philippos's father had ascended to the throne, the ancient land was in chaos. In the six years before Amyntas assumed power, there had been six different kings, each of whom had met a violent end. That's one king assassinated or killed in action per year, in case you're keeping score."

I didn't think the rock was in fact keeping score but you never know.

"Amyntas managed to hold on to his diadem for about a year, precisely on par with recent Macedonian trends. Then, two of his cousins convinced the Illyrians, a barbarian tribe to the north, to overrun the country and put the cousins in charge of the remaining rump. Amyntas escaped to the Thessalians, a Greek tribe to the south, and induced the Thessalians to ravage Macedonia in turn. The Thessalians were only too happy to oblige. Amyntas did manage to regain the throne as a result of the Thessalian invasion but it was a much-diminished throne. The land and its people, having endured countless invasions and civil wars, lay in tatters. That was the low point."

I was beginning to warm to my subject. "Despite his dismal prospects," I continued, "Amyntas managed to rally. Through shrewd diplomacy and numerous marriage alliances, he not only contrived to survive but to salvage his kingdom as well. He held on to power for some nineteen additional years, before dying a natural death, thus breaking the suicidal streak of internecine destruction and regnant murder that had prevailed immediately prior to his reign. He left behind a daughter and six sons. His eldest son, Alexandros Deuteros, became king.

"Soon there was trouble in the family. Shortly before his death, Amyntas had married off his daughter, Eurynoe, who was his first-born child, to a scion of another branch of the family, one Ptolemaios, promising that, as his new son-in-law, Ptolemaios would follow immediately after his own son Alexandros in the line of succession.

"Ptolemaios waited the customary one year after the death of Amyntas before growing impatient. Civil war ensued. The warring sides appealed to Thebes, the leading military power in Greece, to mediate the dispute. A Theban general showed up with a company of Theban hoplites, disarmed the warring parties, entertained competing offers of tribute from Alexandros and Ptolemaios and, deeming Alexandros's offer more advantageous to Thebes, put him back in nominal charge, telling Ptolemaios to cool it. The general then retired back to Thebes, taking with him not only the initial installment of the agreed upon tribute and a solemn undertaking as to the rest but also some thirty hostages, as assurance of the good-faith performance by the Macedonians of their remaining obligations.

"One of the hostages was fourteen-year-old Philippos. You'll recall he was the third son of the late King Amyntas, younger brother of current King Alexandros, younger brother of would-be King Perdikkas, and younger brother-in-law of dying-to-be King Ptolemaios. In short, at that moment, the only things standing between Philippos and the kingship of Macedonia were the fact that he was being held hostage in a foreign land and the fact that there were at least three relatives with claims superior to his own in the line of succession. Of course, at the time, all of these obstacles might have been a blessing in disguise. Who in his right mind would have wanted to return to this strife-ravaged land to serve as an irresistible magnet for every passing assassin and invading barbarian?"

My mossy mate maintained his sagacious silence.

Undeterred, I continued. "As it happened, the dust had barely settled in the wake of the withdrawing Thebans before Alexandros was assassinated. Suspicion fell on Ptolemaios. Ptolemaios denied everything and demanded the diadem. The Macedonian Assembly, also known as the army, settled on a compromise. It elected Amyntas's second son, Perdikkas (the middle brother between Alexandros and Philippos), as the new monarch but, because Perdikkas was still a minor, it also named his brother-in-law Ptolemaios as the regent.

"There were other pretenders and more wars. The Theban general returned, reimposed order, and took more tribute and more hostages. Ptolemaios remained in charge, under the watchful supervision of the Thebans, for a couple of years, at which point Perdikkas attained his majority and Ptolemaios promptly died under mysterious circumstances.

"Perdikkas, now in nominal control, managed to convince the Thebans to release some of the hostages, including his younger brother Philippos, then seventeen years old, who was allowed to return home.

"Perdikkas sat on Macedonia's shaky throne for another five years or so. After that relatively benign stretch, his country was invaded once again by the barbarian Illyrians from the north. An epic battle ensued, in the course of which the bulk of the Macedonian army, some eight thousand men, perished. Among the dead left on the field of battle was Perdikkas, the young king. The rag-tag remnants of the army fled to lower Macedonia, stopping their headlong flight in the new capital of Pella only long enough to elect a new monarch. In their usual decisive fashion, they elected as king Perdikkas's infant son, who became Amyntas Delta. They appointed his uncle, Philippos, then twenty-three years old, as the infant's guardian and regent of the kingdom. With the

Illyrians in hot pursuit and half a dozen relatives plotting against him, Philippos's life expectancy, at that moment, was about two hours.

"Against all odds, he managed to evade doom and salvage his country. He spent his first year as regent putting into practice everything he'd learned, during his years of captivity in Thebes, about building a professional army. The Macedonian cavalry had always been a small but formidable force, but the infantry was little more than an enthusiastic fighting mob, and there was no coordination between the two arms. Philippos created state-of-the-art heavy infantry divisions and equipped them with standardized, up-to-date weapons and body armor. He then spent endless hours, days, weeks, and months getting his new troops in shape by forced daily marches of thirty-five miles or more and by constant training, exercise, and mock fighting. He also taught them the latest Theban phalanx tactics and made sure these tactics became second nature as a result of incessant drills, maneuvers, and dress rehearsals. Finally, he worked on honing the coordination between the infantry and the cavalry.

"Less than a year after the devastating defeat inflicted on Perdikkas by the Illyrians, the new Macedonian army took the field for a return engagement. This time, Philippos turned the tables on Bardylis, the Illyrian king. When the barbarians formed up in their usual hollow square, the young Macedonian commander dispatched his cavalry on a flanking maneuver, threatening to attack the Illyrian square from the back. Simultaneously, he deployed his phalanx in an echelon formation, placing the strongest and most advanced division directly opposite the left front corner of the square. As his slanted battle line attacked, he personally led the assault of the most advanced division against the Illyrian corner. The square inevitably deformed under the weight of the superior force concentrated by Philippos at a single point of the line of engagement. Eventually, as the Illyrian square began to crumble, the Macedonian cavalry wheeled and poured through the gaps in the sides of the square. The barbarians, not as well equipped nor as disciplined as the Macedonian troops, found themselves getting pounded by superior infantry in the front and scything cavalry in their backs. In a matter of minutes, they broke ranks and ran. The Macedonian cavalry then spent the remaining hours of daylight riding them down from behind and slicing any survivors to ribbons.

"Night fell on seven thousand dead Illyrians. Bardylis beat a hasty retreat and negotiated the best terms he could under the circumstances. Philippos emerged overnight as the first great Macedonian general, the savior of his nation, and the husband of Bardylis's daughter, Audata. He promptly dispensed with the pretense of regency and assumed full control of Macedonia, becoming King Philippos Deuteros. To his credit, he managed to assume royal power without having his little nephew, the nominal king, killed. In fact, a few years later, young Amyntas the Nephew, as he was called, became a commander in Philippos's Companion Cavalry. It was fairly risky leaving a potential rival to the throne alive but Philippos believed in his destiny and therefore occasionally turned a blind eye to personal safety.

"Having temporarily pacified the northern frontier, Philippos embarked on an almost unbroken string of military and diplomatic successes that, in addition to his unchallenged control of Macedonia, saw him named archon of Thessaly, head of the Amphiktyonic League, and husband to six more strategically important brides. Wife number four was Myrtale, a member of the Molossian royal family and niece of the reigning king of Epiros, the kingdom on the western reaches of Macedonia. It was said to be a love match but Philippos normally bedded, rather than married, the women he loved. He made an exception in this case in order to secure the western border. At the time of the marriage, Myrtale renamed herself Olympias, a name she considered more in keeping with her aspirations and the name by which she is still known here in Macedonia."

I lapsed into silence. My audience of one, used as he was to thinking in geologic time, undoubtedly dismissed my story as nothing more than a description of some insignificant pebbles carelessly kicked about on the highway of history.

Getting back to my feet, I left my companion with one final thought. "It's too bad I've gotten this close to Pella but will never get to see either the city or its inhabitants before I'm extracted out of here." Little did I realize, at that time, that King Philippos had become aware of my existence soon after my arrival in his kingdom and was doing his best to afford me an opportunity to visit his capital.

****

Less than forty-eight hours after my portal had failed to materialize, king Philippos had laboriously climbed, after a long night of drinking, arguing, fighting, and laughing, the steps to his queen's sleeping chambers, hoping to enforce his marital rights even before his wife number four had had a chance properly to wake up. Unfortunately, his efforts to slake his lust were temporarily stymied when, upon clambering into her bed, he discovered it to be empty and cold.

Philippos continued to pat all around the bed long after it had become evident the bed hadn't been occupied for some time. "Where in Haides is she?" he muttered, as he pole-vaulted himself back onto the hard, wooden floor. Feeling his way toward her inner sanctum in the semi-darkness of the gathering dawn, he crashed heavily into a large chest blocking the doorway.

"Go away!" a female voice commanded. "I'm busy."

Pushing the chest out of the way, Philippos barged into his wife's personal shrine. "Not too busy for this, I hope." He proudly revealed his state of arousal to Olympias, who had risen to meet his assault.

"You can just put that thing away." She waved her hand as if to flick away a fly. "In case you haven't noticed, I'm doing my devotions to Dionysos at the moment."

"Why bother worshipping a phantom when you can have me in the flesh?" He tried to grab her but, in his drunken state, he succeeded in clutching nothing but thin air as he sprawled to the floor. Even in his current condition, though, he was enough of a tactician to make sure, as he fell, that his prostrate body blocked the doorway behind him.

Olympias tried to jump over him in an attempt to make her escape, as he rolled to his back, but tripped and landed on top of him instead, a situation that suited his amorous purposes perfectly.

"I missed you at the symposion last night," he whispered into her ear as he held on tight.

"Well, I didn't miss you." She kneed him emphatically in the groin.

He stopped breathing for a moment but didn't let go. "Not a good move," he growled when he was able to catch his breath. Unfortunately, his ardor had subsided somewhat in the meantime.

"That was easy," she laughed, extricating herself from his embrace.

Watching him lying on the cold hard floor, panting and clutching his genitals, she had a sudden change of heart. "Come on, let me make it feel better." She tried to lead him to her bed.

Philippos did his best to hobble after her. His erection had magically returned.

"I saw Dionysos two nights ago," Olympias mentioned afterward, as Philippos lay next to her, spent and drifting off to sleep.

I'm glad you did, sweetheart," he murmured, practically asleep.

"We had an initiation ceremony for Lanike and Dionysos showed up."

Philippos, still warmed by the afterglow of their recent coupling, roused himself a bit. "Well, the ceremony obviously worked wonders. I take back all the bad things I've said about those foolish outings of yours."

"No, I mean the god himself was there."

"Yes, dear, of course he was."

"Hey loverboy, let go of your dick for a second and listen!" She was shaking him now. "Dionysos himself came to visit Macedonia."

"I'm not holding my dick," he protested. "And as I've told you a thousand times, gods exist only in children's tales and the fertile imagination of wizened old widows. You can't actually see them in real life."

"Well, I did see one with my very own eyes and so did every other woman at the Dionysia. So now we know for sure that your atheism is full of shit. It's only a matter of time, you know, before some god shows up to teach you a lesson. I'm sure you'll be good and sorry and all but it'll be too late by then."

She'd managed to badger him awake. "Tell me again exactly what happened," he asked. When Olympias finished, he asked her to describe Dionysos.

"There's something odd about this fellow," Philippos observed. "Let me talk to Lanike and the other ladies at court who allegedly saw him. Send them to my study after I've had my breakfast."

And so it was that, within two days after the portal had failed to materialize, Philippos dispatched a squadron of Companion Cavalry to capture and bring back to Pella the stranger who'd claimed to be Dionysos. There would be no mysterious apparitions roaming the countryside of Macedonia while King Philippos was in charge.

****

Luckily, it wasn't easy to find me. Oblivious to the search, I was hunkered down near my quarry, testing the carrot plant. I decided the taproot held the most promise. I ground it up in my makeshift mortar and then boiled it in the kettle until it turned into a thick, white mush. Setting the mush aside to cool, I embarked on my daily hunt. In order for the edibility test to be valid, I had to fast for at least twelve hours, before tasting my concoction.

I meandered through the woods and meadows surrounding the quarry, searching for signs of the extraction party, looking for footprints of any locals, and sniffing for spoor of edible prey, in descending order of palatability. My mind, in the meantime, wandered the winding trails of memory, reliving episodes of triumph from my prior life, recalling moments of sweet romance with Paloma, wallowing in self-pity, and fantasizing away dangers and disasters through prophylactic mental flagellation.

Once again on that day, I saw no sign of any people, either rescuers from my own time or locals from the current time. *The extraction team should have been here by now.* But then, four weeks wasn't a long time to organize a search and rescue mission. At least that's what I told myself. I imagined different explanations for the delay: Everybody might've been on vacation the week the portal malfunctioned; there might've been a big argument about who'd be in charge of the extraction team; they might've run out of snacks during the planning meeting and the delivery boy bringing more refreshments might've gotten lost. There could've been any number of reasons why it would've taken more than a couple of weeks to mount a rescue operation.

Of course, time travel doesn't work that way. Even if it had taken years in my native era to organize the search and rescue expedition, mission control should've been able to pinpoint the extraction squad's arrival time in my destination era to within a day of the portal's nominal appearance date. It didn't matter how long it took to launch the extraction team; the only thing that mattered was the expected margin of error in the pre-programmed arrival time. Normally, any error was limited to a matter of seconds. There had never been an error of more than twenty-four hours in the history of time travel. In short, my rescuers could've arrived in this era less than a day after the portal had failed, regardless of preparation time. Luckily, this particular idea had failed to infiltrate my conscious thinking while I struggled to stay alive, day after day, in my seemingly bountiful yet mercilessly disinterested paradise.

The phrase "Escape Hatch Corollary" did manage to surface briefly in my mind but I promptly suppressed it. Instead, I kept my eyes on the ground. While I'd never seen any human footprints, sightings of paw prints, broken branches, and an aromatic variety of spoor were a daily occurrence. However, over time, I'd become too phlegmatic either to chase after animals I might've been able to catch and eat, such as squirrels, hares, foxes, and deer, or to cower and hide from animals that might've been strong enough to catch and eat me, the boars, bears, and mountain lions. Gradually, my walkabouts had become longer and longer and successful finds farther and farther apart. At some point, the balance between energy expended in pursuit of food and energy gained from what I managed to catch and eat had slipped into a deficit posture.

I resolved to become a vegetarian. Plants, unlike animals, were still too slow to outrun me, although the gap was closing fast. Unfortunately, as I inexorably consumed all the edible staples within walking distance of my cave, I was forced to spend more and more time conducting edibility tests. My meditation on the relentless decline of my paradisiacal circumstances reminded me of the delicious mush awaiting me at my cave. It had certainly been long enough since my last meal to be able to tell, in case I poisoned myself, which meal was the culprit.

By the time I returned to the cave, the sun was quickly sinking beyond the surrounding mountain range. The whitish mush in my kettle had dried to the consistency of a horse patty but it had a pleasant, healthful odor, which was encouraging. I had a long list of unacceptable smells that would have required me to toss my patty without even tasting it, such as the smell of almonds, the smell of rotten eggs, the smell of decomposition, and the smell of feces.

Having progressed past the sniff test, I broke off a morsel of the patty and held it against my skin. Thankfully, it didn't raise a rash, enabling me to proceed to the next step. I held the morsel against my lip, to see whether it would burn or itch. After a few minutes, with my lip remaining cool and calm, I placed the morsel on my tongue, being very careful not to swallow it – a task made more difficult by all the saliva flooding my mouth. There was no immediate allergic reaction.

After a few more minutes, I started to chew my sample, letting it mix with saliva and permeate my taste buds, prepared to spit it out at the first sign of trouble, defined as numbness, itching, stinging, burning, difficulty breathing, thickening of the tongue, pain, nausea, malaise, or any other odd sensation. Considering I'd been ravenous for days, the sensation of food in my mouth was bound to feel odd but I tried to retain my objectivity.

Finally, after taking a deep breath, I swallowed the tiny mouthful of horse patty or, as I preferred to think of it, the tiny mouthful of wild carrot cake, keeping my index finger extended and my pot of boiled water close at hand, ready to induce vomiting, followed by copious gulps of water to dilute whatever poison the emesis failed to bring back up. In this case, all seemed fine, sparing me the ordeal of retching and drinking, retching and drinking, to the brink of oblivion.

It was getting dark by the time I'd finished. Feeling no ill effects, I ate a slightly larger portion of my carrot concoction, cleared the newly deposited guano from my sleeping quarters, and bedded down for the night. *Ironic, isn't it?* I was drifting off to sleep. *I got into the Academy, then into the Time Travel Corps, because I wanted to be an insider. Now I'm living out of doors, out of place, out of time, out of human contact. Couldn't have become more of an outcast if I'd tried.*

To fight off such gloomy thoughts and hasten the arrival of blissful sleep, I made a mental list of things to do the next day: Eat the rest of my delicious wild carrot cake in the morning; start working on a monograph describing ancient Greek Dionysian rites; make a plan for the trip to the escape hatch; somehow interact with any locals whom I might encounter en route without running afoul of the Prime Directive. I fell asleep dreaming of Paloma. Or was it Aphrodite?

****

Alas, the ardor of my dreams failed to keep my body warm. I awoke shivering, shit-covered, and sharp-witted. *The next predicted, naturally occurring time portal is a score of years away and located in Egypt! I can't possibly last that long and travel that far on my own.*

What had made time travel a practical tool was the ability of chronoscience to create artificial portals at predetermined space-time coordinates. But that didn't mean naturally occurring portals had ceased to exist. They just became irrelevant because it was so very difficult to locate their respective termini, either in space or in time, much less to predict their spontaneous appearance in advance with any degree of accuracy. But we had always been taught that they did exist and that, if all else failed, they could serve as an escape hatch for a return trip back to roughly our own time.

I for one had never considered the possibility seriously. I simply took it for granted that, if anything went wrong, which was exceedingly unlikely, an extraction team would be put together and would come and get me. My only job was to avoid violating the Prime Directive; the rest was up to the folks back at Time Command. Nevertheless, somewhere in my subconscious mind the idea of the Escape Hatch Corollary had taken root because everything I'd been taught about naturally occurring time portals came bubbling up to my consciousness while I slept.

Pay attention to the situation at hand, idiot. My brain was screaming when I roused. *You're still alive!* Better yet, I had awakened without any cramps or diarrhea. After forcing myself to carry out my usual morning routine, I sat down by my trusty old rock and ate the rest of my horse patty.

I started to vomit almost immediately. Between bouts of upchucking, I drank copious amounts of water straight out of the creek, fully conscious of the fact that I should've boiled it first. The pain in my stomach was excruciating. My leg muscles started to twitch and I was having trouble breathing. I could feel my thoughts slowing down. The entire world became bright, washed out, pastel colored.

Luckily, I still had my daydreams to keep me busy, while I waited for my symptoms to subside. I imagined my impending rescue in elaborate detail. I could clearly visualize members of the extraction team walking up to me, in their anachronistic outfits, moving briskly, silently, efficiently. No time for greetings, celebrations, or explanations. Just time enough to gather all my belongings, all the detritus of my stay, all trace of my existence in this era, and then, in a whoosh, a disappearing act.

As I lay in front of my cave, curled up in pain, my muscles simultaneously twitching, swelling, and weakening, I worked on my acceptance speech on the occasion of my elevation to the Sophokles Sophist Society. I imagined the honors bestowed upon me in light of my exemplary conduct as a castaway. I stared into my fire, thinking about the world and time I'd left behind.

After another bout of retching, I felt a little better. Somehow I dragged myself to a sunny clearing nearby, where I'd observed a family of marmots a couple of days earlier. I spotted the daddy marmot, standing guard in the early morning mist at the edge of the woods. He stood there, reared on his hind legs, motionless, looking almost like a little bear. Then he snapped his head in my direction, emitted a loud whistle, took two hops, and disappeared into a hole. On further reflection, he looked nothing like a bear; more like a cross between a prairie dog and a woodchuck. He looked, at least to me, good enough to eat.

In a moment of inspiration, I decided he was probably still hiding in that hole. I found a nice stout branch and started to dig. It took me a couple of hours of effort, interrupted by fitful retching and drinking, but eventually I managed to uproot the entire tunnel. It led to two other tunnels. I kept digging.

Every once in a while, as I worked steadily, hour after hour, trying to unearth the entire subterranean labyrinth, I would catch a glimpse of my marmot, looking at me curiously, with a friendly sparkle in his eyes, urging me not to give up. I decided to call him Martin.

As the sun reached its zenith, Martin continued to sit on his haunches, just across from my latest trench, peering at me with intent, unblinking eyes. Eventually, he introduced me to his family: a smaller, female marmot – Margo – and a clutch of tiny, adorable cubs. They spread out throughout the meadow, each one next to a convenient hole.

A few minutes later, as the sun's blinding rays continued their merciless assault, I collapsed to the ground and attempted to explain to Martin that, unless I managed to catch him and cook him for dinner, I would surely die. Unlike my breakfast companion rock, Martin actually made an audible response, although he spoke in a binary, whistling code. I was too slow-witted to decipher his response.

Luckily, just before I lost consciousness, I sighted another creature making its way toward me through the woods, walking on two legs. *It's Kleitos.* I immediately dismissed the idea as yet another hallucination.

"Eureka!" the creature cried out when it spotted me. My first instinct was to dive into the trench I'd been digging and join my marmot friends in their underground lair. Unfortunately, despite my emaciated state, I was still bigger than a marmot and therefore unable to fit into the trench.

The creature, in the meantime, broke into a run, whooping and hollering as it approached. I sat there, lacking the strength, physical or mental, to comply with the mandates of the Prime Directive.

Chapter 3 – Philippos

When I regained consciousness, Kleitos was cradling my head and pouring water on my face.

"Had me scared there for a minute, Dionysos," he said when I opened my eyes. "For an immortal, you looked surprisingly close to dead."

I sputtered, trying to cough out the water that had trickled down my windpipe. "It's a little trick we gods have. We can assume any appearance we wish, even look like shit warmed over if we want to."

Kleitos laughed. "Here, Dionysos, try eating some bread."

"You do realize I'm not really Dionysos."

"I wish you'd stop saying that," he replied with a straight face. "I'm gonna lose all my faith in gods."

I didn't respond immediately. First, I was amazed he could understand my broken Greek. Beyond that, I was too busy eating to respond. The bread and water were having a magical effect. In the space of a few minutes, the tribulations of the previous four weeks were wiped from my mind.

"What are you doing here anyway?" I asked when I had finished chomping the rock-hard but incredibly delicious hunk of bread.

"Oh, I've been looking for you for weeks. In fact, there are lots of people looking for you. It's lucky I found you first."

This alarming piece of intelligence – that there were people looking for me – immediately raised my hackles but I was too busy luxuriating in the presence of another human being to pay attention to my instincts. *Maybe it's the extraction party*, I thought.

"Got any more food?"

"How about some more water instead?" He nodded in the direction of a dead, brownish gray bird, lying on the ground behind him. "I killed it on my way here. We can roast it later but let's pace ourselves for now. You digest what you've eaten and I'll go pluck this beauty in the meantime."

****

Kleitos was down by the creek, washing his quail, when the Companion Cavalry came thundering out of the woods. He'd been more accurate than he'd realized. Apparently, while he was busy tracking me, a lot of other people had stayed on his trail, hoping he would lead them to me.

Suddenly, it all flashed before my eyes: We would be captured, tortured, and butchered. Well, at least I would be. They'd probably let Kleitos go. By the time the extraction party arrived, they'd be lucky to recover my remains. *Well, I'm sure they'll recover most of them. The odd scrap of flesh or pint of blood might have to stay behind.*

We tried to make a run for it but these soldiers were accomplished horsemen and I could barely move. They simply toyed with us, blocking our path with their animals whichever way we turned. In short order, we were trussed up, being led by ropes tied at one end to our bound wrists and held at the other end by our captors.

Yet it could've been worse. *It's lucky*, I told myself, *that the soldiers are not entirely sure how to treat me.* It was obvious they didn't believe for one second I was a god – these were level-headed, tough, practical men and I sure didn't look like a god – but, on the other hand, it was also clear they'd been ordered to collect me and bring me back unharmed. On their own initiative, they'd evidently also decided to bring Kleitos along, for fraternizing with a deity, I suppose.

Still, their instructions did leave some scope for individual enterprise. One solder in particular – his companions called him Battos – took special pleasure in tormenting me. While we were still getting ready to leave, but after my wrists had been tied up, he walked up to me, smiled, and then smashed a roundhouse right hook into my cheek, knocking me to the ground. Everyone stopped what they were doing and stared in astonishment. The silence lasted only a split second. Then Battos started to guffaw: "I knocked down a god," he finally managed to spit out. Most of the remaining soldiers joined in the general merriment. A couple stepped in and kicked me in the ribs as I attempted to get up.

"That's enough," their commander said. "Let's go."

He assigned another soldier, Kuniklos, to drag me behind his horse. Kuniklos dutifully carried out his assignment … for about an hour. Then he became bored. Every few minutes, just for the fun of it, he would let his horse break into a trot, forcing me to sprint for my life, the rope taut between us, my arms stretched painfully in front of me, my legs churning in a desperate effort to stay upright. Finally, he would rein in his steed and shrug in mock apology. "Sorry," he'd say, before bursting into laughter.

The other soldiers found this performance immensely entertaining. "When you gonna learn to control your animal, Kuniklos?" one would yell.

"He's just testing to see if Dionysos can fly," another would answer.

"Try tying a naked slut to the back of your horse, if you wanna see him fly."

"Nah, he'd trip over his dick if you did that."

It was all very witty and amusing to them, less so for me. We'd done wind sprints during training. We used to call them suicides, for some reason. *We should have called them survivals.* I would never have made it but for those suicides.

Finally, I'd had enough. As Kuniklos accelerated once again upon reaching a slight downslope, I stopped short, dug in my heels, and yanked on my end of the rope, hoping to dislocate my tormentor's shoulder or at least dislodge him from his perch. Unfortunately, my hopes outpaced reality. His shoulder withstood the sudden jerk without apparent ill effect. He simply jerked back, much harder than I had. The next thing I knew, I was lying prone on the ground, the dirt under my face beginning to turn red.

"A good one!" Kuniklos yelled. "Now get up before I start getting mad!"

Battos jumped off his horse to help me get up. When I was half way up, he let me fall again, kicking me in the abdomen before I hit the ground, causing me to tumble down the slope. "Keep on rolling to Haides or wherever you came from, you foreign fart."

"Maybe we can kick him all the way to Pella," someone suggested.

"Put him on your horse, Battos," the commander ordered. "He'll ride with you the rest of the way. And Kuniklos, you can carry the other one."

"Yes, sir." Kuniklos cut loose Kleitos's bindings, offered him his hand, and in one smooth motion lifted the boy behind his back.

Battos glared but said nothing. He cut the rope by which Kuniklos had been pulling me but left my wrists bound. Without much apparent effort, he lifted and threw me like a sack of oats across his horse's back. He then secured my wrists to my ankles under the horse's belly, before jumping on himself. No one else made a sound. When Battos was ready, we set off at a swift, silent canter.

With each stride of Battos's horse, I was lifted into the air and then smashed back down, abdomen first, against the horse's tough, bony, sweaty, bare back. It became a macabre waltz, the horse's hooves beating out the characteristic canter beat – one, two, THREE; one, two, THREE; one, two, THREE – with a powerful whomp into my solar plexus on every third beat.

I'm not sure how I was able to continue breathing. My brain was certainly not getting enough oxygen because I remember very little of the ride.

****

When we arrived at the palace complex in Pella, we rode straight to the stables. Somehow, Battos managed to get his horse to stop short, lifting his hind quarters off the ground, thus causing my inert body to tumble neatly over the horse's head and into a pile of hay, eliciting whistles of appreciation from his fellow riders. Frankly, I was just as glad to be off the horse.

The rope between my wrists and ankles had become entangled with the horse's forelegs. Battos cut the rope and dragged me into a rudimentary stall where he left me, with my wrists still bound. Two other men approached and shackled my ankles to a post. Kleitos was deposited, none too gently, two stalls over. In between, the soldiers tied up a couple of horses, their heads contentedly immersed in feedbags. The streams of steaming urine, which they released from time to time into our communal bed of hay, lent a warm, homey, pungent ambience to our new quarters.

"Sorry about that," Kleitos ventured after a moment.

"It's not your fault." I was mad as hell but it seemed ungracious to blame a boy who was only trying to help.

What are the chances, I thought, *that this snot-nosed, barefoot, 14-year-old hick would prove to be my undoing?* To be fair, the king's soldiers likely would've tracked me down sooner or later, even if Kleitos had not inadvertently led them to me first, but I kept thinking – incorrectly – that, but for Kleitos's efforts, I might've gotten extracted by our own search and rescue team before the soldiers had found me.

"The reason I tracked you down was to warn you." Kleitos kept trying to explain himself. "Your appearance at the ceremony was big news, you know. We don't get too many visiting gods around here. All the women were jealous when they found out that Dionysos himself had been there. Unfortunately, King Philippos apparently had his doubts about your divinity as soon as Olympias reported your cameo to him. He thought you were a Persian spy and dispatched his soldiers to find you."

"How would Olympias know I was at the rites?"

"She was there," Kleitos said, suspicion edging into his voice. "She's always there. Everybody knows that. How long have you been living in that cave anyway?"

"The queen was at the rites?" Now it was my turn to be surprised. I wondered which one she might have been. *Maybe the penis lady.* I laughed aloud at the image.

The soldiers returned before I could pursue my line of inquiry further. Without bothering to give us clean clothes or even a chance to wash up, they jerked us to our feet, managing to land a slap or two to our faces in the process. Then they frogmarched us into the palace, dumping us on the floor of the guardroom, and shackling our legs to iron rings embedded in the wall. But at least there were no urinating animals nearby and we could observe the comings and goings in the palace at our leisure.

Beyond the guardroom lay the atrium. It was a curious place. At first glance all marbled elegance and ostentatious artwork, upon closer inspection it turned out to be the central courtyard of a small but rugged fort, wearing a recent veneer of newly acquired wealth. In a corner, poking through the earth, were the tumbledown remains of an ancient well, now filled in and forgotten. In its stead, a fancy, ornamental pool in the center of the courtyard – marble-lined, with an intricate, inlaid pattern of black geometric shapes – lent an aristocratic air to the old mustering ground. The pool was much less useful in case of siege than a well but so much more refined.

"Of course Olympias was there." Kleitos resumed our conversation as if there had been no interruption at all. "Truth is, there were no Dionysian rites around here until our new queen arrived from Epiros a few years back. Now all the women at court are devotees, even my own sister."

Prime Directive

I absorbed this information in silence. On the one hand, Kleitos obviously had a lot of invaluable intelligence. On the other hand, despite, or perhaps as a result of, my weeks of solitude, I was beginning to find his chattering a little too intrusive. We settled down to open-mouthed, silent gaping.

Around the pool stood a peristyle of brightly painted Ionian columns but the ground between the edges of the pool and the surrounding pillars still showed signs of recent cultivation. The short axis of the courtyard – from the main entrance gate, across the pool, and to the reception hall doorway – was paved with colorful, finely detailed mosaics of hunting and war scenes but the rest of the courtyard was simply hard-packed dirt.

The ground floor walls surrounding the courtyard were covered in newly applied white stucco and decorated with beautiful, glowing frescos of mythological scenes, interspersed strategically between various doorways, stairways, and interior windows. A scene of dour-faced Haides snatching deep-bosomed Persephone into his golden chariot on one side of an arch was nicely balanced by a depiction of noble, tumescent Perseus rescuing a suggestively chained, achingly beautiful Andromeda on the other side. There was a whole series of frescoes depicting the twelve labors of a determined, muscle-bound Herakles and, of course, the obligatory scene of a glowing, exultant Achilleus dragging the tattered remains of doomed Hektor behind his chariot.

By contrast, the upper floor, where the women's quarter was located, was painted a dingy brown, devoid of any decoration. The staircase leading to the women's quarter, tacked onto a side wall, started out with three wide marble steps but then degenerated into a worn, wooden staircase the rest of the way up.

Soldiers, servants, maids, functionaries, supplicants, and courtiers hurried in and out of various doorways, trying not to step on the chickens pecking underfoot, while pigeons kept flying in from the outside and stealing the chickens' seed. No one paid the least attention to Kleitos and me.

****

The courtyard gradually descended into a twilight gloom. The parade of humanity eased to a trickle. A servant placed lit torches in sconces located at regular intervals on the atrium walls. And then, a woman came staggering into the yard, cursing up a storm. She didn't even notice Kleitos and me in the guardroom; she was too busy struggling with her recalcitrant snake.

It was an unusually large water snake. Even I could see that the woman's efforts to control it were doomed to failure. Her grip, with one hand just behind the snake's head and the other near its tail, was tenuous – her fingers not quite long enough to encircle the snake's thick body and her arms not quite strong enough to counter its robust muscular contractions. She was twirling and tottering around the columns, drifting in and out of the light cast by the torches. It took a moment before I finally managed a good look at her face.

She appeared to be about thirty years old. Even in her current predicament, she was strikingly beautiful, with prominent cheekbones and frosty blue eyes. I had to blink twice before believing the evidence of my own senses. It was Medusa, up to her old tricks again. *What were the chances?*

"Does Medusa live right here in the palace?" I whispered to Kleitos, who was staring wide-eyed at the struggle between woman and serpent.

Kleitos, in response, was barely able to control himself. He clapped a hand over his mouth, his face turned red, and his entire body shook, as he tried not to burst out laughing. "That's a good one," he finally managed to whisper. "No one has ever called the queen 'Medusa' before but, now that you mention it, the name really fits."

It was my turn to reel in amazement. I realized even before Kleitos replied that Medusa was simply the name I'd given to the leader at the initiation rites; the shocking part was that the head cultist would turn out to be the queen of Macedonia.

"That's the queen?" I was still incredulous.

Kleitos hushed me. "She's pretty strange, isn't she? Everybody is afraid of her. Even the king."

Inevitably, Olympias lost her hold on the snake's tail, which was instantly transformed into a self-actuated whip, lashing her about the head and torso, disheveling her carefully heaped hairdo and tearing off the top of her tunic.

For some reason, Kleitos let out a laugh. The queen, still holding the snake with her right hand, fixed Kleitos with a malevolent glare. Then, she glanced over at me ... and froze. She stared at me for a good minute. She must have tightened her grip around the snake's neck because even it seemed momentarily paralyzed.

After an endless interval and without uttering a single word, she threw the snake in our direction, gave her disheveled hair a toss and, with her head held high, her back completely erect, and her breasts jiggling in the open air, she walked upstairs into the women's quarter. The snake landed in the doorway of the guardroom, no more than a couple of steps from where we sat.

Now, it was my turn to let out a yelp and try to get out of the way. The snake, more frightened than I, quickly slithered away in the opposite direction and disappeared into the reception hall. Soon thereafter, a torrent of invective issued through the open doorway. Although I was unable to follow the individual words, the general import was clear enough. Someone was displeased with the intrusion.

The king, his face disfigured by battle scars and softened by laugh lines, emerged from the room, holding the front end of the snake in his left hand. A bloody sword was in his right. The snake's eyes were still open, its tongue was still flicking in and out of its yawning jaw, and the stump of its body was still twitching, spraying droplets of blood throughout the courtyard. "Olympias!" Although loud and emphatic, his tone was all sweetness and light. Then he noticed Kleitos and me.

"Who in Haides are you?" he asked amicably.

Olympias reappeared at the top of the stairs.

"You forgot something, dear." The king threw the remnant of the snake at her.

Ignoring the airborne carcass, Olympias came flying down the stairs. Her hands were on the king's throat before the dead snake thudded back to earth. "I'm going to kill you, you crippled old goat. I'm going to feed your balls to the hogs," she added on further reflection, "and then I'm going to kill you."

The king grabbed her by the wrists and restrained her. "Next time keep your boyfriend in your bedroom." He was grinning, but the curve of his compressed lips looked more like a scar left by an old sword slash; his eye was cold and unsmiling.

Olympias took one look at his face and stiffened. It was obvious to me that Kleitos had been wrong: The king was not afraid of the queen. It was all an act. She was terrified of him and it amused him to toy with her, to tolerate her tongue, even to egg her on, but only up to a point. If, in her vituperative flow, she inadvertently crossed some invisible line that existed only in his mind, then suddenly, in a blink of his one good eye, her life hung in the balance, protected only by the passion he had felt for her in earlier times.

She cast a hopeful glance in my direction. "Dionysos will have his revenge soon enough." To her apparent disappointment, I just sat there – dirty, smelly, emaciated, and utterly undivine. She looked back at the king's face, seeking to discern on which side of the invisible line she had landed.

"Dionysos can kiss my ass." His merry tone left her simultaneously relieved and outraged. "Take her upstairs!" he added to the two soldiers who had appeared in response to the commotion.

She shook loose of their grip. "Don't you dare touch me!" She twirled on her heels and walked back upstairs, unaided, her head still held high, but her shoulders shaking with rage.

****

"Now boys, back to you." The king returned his attention to Kleitos and me. "As I was saying, who in Lethe's name are you?"

Before we could answer, one of the soldiers whispered something in his ear. His eyebrow arched. "That one?" The soldier nodded.

"Oh, I beg your pardon, your worship." The king sank heavily to one knee in front of me. "I didn't realize Dionysos himself was honoring us with his presence. Welcome to my humble abode." A sardonic smile flashed across his face. "Although I must say, for a god you do look a bit unkempt."

He struggled back to his feet. "Clean them off," he said brusquely. "They stink. Try not to kill them though, because we need to have a little chat. Bring them around to the dining room when they're scrubbed," he added with a minatory smirk. For a moment, I thought he'd also winked at us but his right eye was missing and therefore the wink might have been simply a tightening of the scar tissue over his eye socket.

It was back to the stables with us, where buckets of cold water were unceremoniously dumped over our heads. I was sure they groomed their horses with more care but at least we were handed clean, dry clothes. Eventually, we were marched back through the main gate to the palace courtyard and into the reception hall. A doorway at the far end of the reception hall led to a second, more intimate courtyard, surrounded by a covered colonnade. On the opposite side of the second courtyard was the dining room, which is where we found ourselves sitting on the floor. A couple of grizzled veterans stayed behind, hovering over us, their hands resting menacingly on the hilts of their swords.

It was a warm, dim, stuffy room. Seven couches were arranged in a U-shape around the sides of the chamber, with three couches against each side wall and one larger couch against the wall opposite the entrance. A number of small tables holding platters of food and chalices sat within arm's reach in front of the couches. Each couch was occupied by one or two reclining men. The king was sprawled across the larger couch at the bottom of the U.

The smell of food and wine was oppressive, perhaps because I was famished. Evidently, the feast was well advanced. The king had finished his meal and was busy directing the preparation of diluted warm wine in a huge, elaborately decorated silver tub, located in the corner next to his couch. The dozen or so tough-looking men reclining on the side couches were finishing their meals and chatting among themselves. Several young girls bustled about, getting ready to serve the wine and perhaps provide entertainment as well. A couple of dogs saw to the scraps on the floor.

I found my thoughts adrift again. *Hey, what an opportunity – a bonus ritual to observe.* I withdrew further into the shadows, hunkered down against the wall, and felt for my notepad and stylus, only to remember that I no longer possessed any of my meager belongings.

"Feed them," the king ordered.

Suddenly, we were surrounded by food, diluted wine, and envious dogs. Without bothering to check what I was eating, I stuffed my face. *Someone else must have checked whether these were edible,* I thought.

After devouring the food in front of me and washing it down with some surprisingly sweet wine, I was beginning to nod off when a splash of liquid in my face, followed by the clatter of a cup hitting the wall next to my head, brought me back to reality. One of the guests, while reaching for a proffered cup of wine, had mistakenly grabbed the breast of the serving girl instead. She had pulled out of his grasp and interposed the cup between her body and her attacker's hand, in an attempt to parry his advance. He gave the cup a backhanded slap, sending the cup and its contents sailing in my direction. The man rose unsteadily from his couch, clearly intending to continue his pursuit, while the girl backed away, torn between her reluctance to give offense and her fear of being assaulted.

"For crying out loud, Attalos," the king growled, "can't you see she's new?"

"Oh, I can see it very clearly. You forget I still have two good eyes."

"I don't forget." The king's flat tone chilled the temperature in the room by several degrees. "Come here, hon, I need you to bring me something." She nodded solemnly as he whispered in her ear, then left the room, not to be seen again that night.

"I didn't mean that, Philippos," Attalos mumbled.

The king said nothing.

One of the other men tried to fill the awkward silence. "I hear, sire, the Illyrians are getting ready to mess with us again. Ever since Bardylis's daughter died, they've been on the war path."

"First off, her name was Audata." A brief gust of wistfulness swept across Philippos's face, only to be quickly replaced by his previous adamantine mien. "Second, as long as there's a single Illyrian alive, he'll be plotting our destruction. Third, after what we did to them last year, they're still trying to find their way back to their hovels. There'll be no attack from the Illyrians this year. I'm more worried about trying to negotiate something with the Persians right now."

"Ochos is a tough nut," another man put in. "He may be a butcher but he's the most capable butcher they've had since the original Xerxes."

They kept talking and drinking for hours. A couple of the guests had fallen asleep, most of them had availed themselves of the serving girls' charms, and all of them were falling down drunk, before the king deigned once again to acknowledge our presence in the room.

"Move 'em a bit closer." His speech was slurred.

Prime Directive

With a couple of well-aimed kicks from the soldier behind us, we were readily persuaded to scamper forward on our haunches, eliciting a wry, drunken smile from the king.

Philippos's face was difficult to read. His full, curly beard was luxuriant but neatly trimmed, with just the slightest hint of gray on either side of his chin. Beneath a mop of unruly, curly, pitch-black hair, and riding a pair of curious, nimble eyebrows, sat a high, deeply-creased forehead, radiating a shrewd intelligence. His skin had the suppleness and elasticity of a young man, yet it bore the scars, creases, and wrinkles of an elderly sage. His nose might have started out straight but had acquired a bump or two along the way, with nostrils capable of flaring from tranquil repose to ruthless rage without any stops in between. A soft, sensuous, sybaritic mouth, with one corner upturned in wry amusement, the other descended in perpetual contempt, lent his expression a Janusian tinge. But it was the eyes that gave me the most trouble. The left eye was wide open, twinkling, full of life, while the right eye was merely scar tissue over an empty socket, yet it too was somehow animated, the way the shades in Haides are animated. There were deep crow's feet at the corners of both eyes, the left one crinkled into a warm, conspiratorial embrace, the right one incised with the cold, cruel, contemptuous crevices of a corpse. And yet, both sides of his face, above the curls of his mustache, were edged by well-worn, friendly laughlines.

A hard man, I thought, *with whom one shouldn't cross swords lightly.* I tried to guess his intentions. Was he planning to kill us or was he just pawing at us, the way a cat might toy with a cornered mouse? I hoped he'd refrain from doing us harm but, in all honesty, I couldn't tell.

A quick, sidelong glance at Kleitos was not reassuring. Although admittedly still only a youngster, he had displayed such self-possession and poise in the face of the crazed crones that I was surprised to see him quailing now, cowering under the force of Philippos's personality.

Philippos motioned to the girls to serve us some more wine. "I understand you're a Persian spy." His tone was conversational, his words no longer slurred.

Kleitos jumped in before I could say anything. "No, Your Highness, never. I've never even been to Pella until now, much less Persia."

The king stood with unexpected celerity, his knee making solid contact with Kleitos's jaw in the process, knocking my friend to the floor. "Oh, I'm sorry," he apologized. "Did I bump into you? I was actually speaking to your companion here, if you don't mind," he continued. "Don't worry, we will get around to you soon enough."

He turned to me. "Now, tell me who you are. And try to be quick about it. I have my marital duties to attend to."

Prime Directive

"My name is Ptolemaios, son of Lagos. I was born right here, near the village of Kyrrhos. My father took me to live among the Bottiaioi, in Stagiros, when I was an infant. After he died, I decided to return to my homeland. Our ship was wrecked in a storm as we were rounding Cape Kanastraion. As far as I know, I was the only survivor. I was making my way back to Kyrrhos when your men captured me."

Rote memorization has its uses. Notwithstanding the stress of the moment, I could've recited that capsule bio in my sleep. It was an important part of my tool kit, my cover story, in the event I had the misfortune somehow to run into any locals and needed to account for my whereabouts.

The king smiled. "Let's start again. Tell me who you are before I lose my patience." There was that subtle shift in his face. "Trust me; you don't want me to lose my patience." I couldn't quite figure out how there could be so much menace in such an ordinary sentence.

Luckily, Olympias entered the room just then. "Don't be too harsh on them." She was practically crooning. "They're just youngsters."

Philippos appeared puzzled for an instant but then his countenance brightened. "Oh, I get it. They pissed you off somehow, didn't they?"

Olympias said nothing.

"Kind of pathetic, this Dionysos here, isn't he?"

Olympias sneered. "Don't be too pleased with yourself. This character may be a fake but there's one thing I know for sure: Your hubris will catch up with you eventually. The gods always get even."

Philippos was unperturbed. "Tell you what. I'll make you a deal. If this fellow doesn't tell me what I need to know, I'll place both of them into your tender care, to do with as you wish. In the meantime, why don't you get yourself ready in your bedchamber. I'll be along momentarily." He gave her one of those disconcerting winks of his hollow eye.

"Now boys," he turned back to us. "You heard what the lady wants. And generally speaking, what the lady wants, the lady gets. I'd start talking if I were you."

I glanced at Olympias. She was staring intently at me, a viperous smile playing on her lips.

"We'll tell you anything you want to know," Kleitos interjected again. "Just send for Lanike first."

"Listen, boy … ," Philippos started, dropping any pretense of patience. "What's Lanike got to do with this?"

"She's my sister," Kleitos blurted out.

"You're Lanike's little brat brother?" The king was incredulous. "Go get her," he finally ordered one of the serving girls.

"Stop!" Olympias countermanded. "Lanike is busy just now. I'll take them to her after you're finished, dear."

"That's fine, sweetheart, but I still give the orders around here. So please, leave them with me. I'll see you soon." Maybe it was my lack of language skills but when he said, "I'll see you soon," it sounded very much like, "One more word and you won't make it out of this room alive." Olympias executed one of those pirouettes on her heel, with the simultaneous head toss and breast jiggle, and was gone.

Philippos nodded to the serving girl, who left on the double to look for Kleitos's sister. He then turned to me. "In the meantime, 'Ptolemaios,' let's consider your story. There's no one by the name of Lagos in Kyrrhos. There was a Lagos who lived at Edessa but he died during the siege of Olynthos, leaving no heir. I know, because I inherited his lands. We've had several trade missions to Stagiros but, believe me, no one goes on such a mission without my knowledge and leave. Our mission last year returned safe and sound, with the loss of only two men. Our mission this year is not scheduled to return until the middle of Hyperberetaios. There've been no shipwrecks in the Thermaic Gulf this season. Not much happens in my humble little kingdom without my knowledge.

"So, you could say there wasn't a true word in your entire story, except possibly for the part about being captured by my men. However, the fascinating thing wasn't the complete dishonesty of your story; the thing that got me was that you recited your story as a child would recite a poem written in a foreign tongue. Which reminds me, you didn't even get the accent right. You don't sound like a Macedonian, you don't sound like a Persian, you don't sound like an Illyrian trying to speak Greek, you don't sound like anybody I've ever heard.

"Now, if I were making up a horseshit story, I'd try to avoid assertions that are easily checked. I think you were on the right track claiming you were Dionysos but then you blew it by letting yourself get captured by a handful of mortal soldiers. No self-respecting god would ever countenance such a thing. I must say, though, I'm grateful to you for embarrassing my wife. But that's not enough to get you off the hook right now. So, how about you start telling us the truth, before we start cutting off little bits of you, just to see which language you choose to scream in?"

"I'm not a Persian spy."

"That may be true. You don't look, sound, or act like any Persian I've ever met before, but then again, you don't have to be Persian to spy for them, do you?"

"You have a point there, sire," I had to admit.

Prime Directive

"I almost wish you were a Persian spy. Then we could extract some useful information out of you before we put you out of your misery. So how about it, tell me something useful before I let these guys get on with the business of killing you."

For the life of me, I couldn't think of anything useful to tell him.

"Or should I send you to Olympias instead? Trust me, being tortured to death by my men is a far better alternative." He laughed at his own joke. I noticed no one else in the room was laughing.

The king abruptly changed tacks. "Tell me, young man, why did you decide to impersonate Dionysos?"

"It was just a spur of the moment impulse," I answered truthfully.

"I understand." Philippos nodded thoughtfully. "Let me see if I've got this straight. You traveled an enormous distance from some unknown country to arrive here in Macedonia at just the right moment to be at a Dionysia; you then concealed yourself for hours in the bushes watching the ceremony; and then you jumped out at the height of the proceedings, after all the women were naked and drunk, yelling that you were Dionysos. Is that what you mean by a spur of the moment impulse?"

I had to smile. "That's not exactly what happened, sire. I was at the ceremony on purpose, and I was watching the proceedings on purpose, but I had no intention of revealing myself to the women and claiming to be Dionysos. That part of it was spur of the moment."

"You just felt inspired by what you saw, I guess."

"No, that's not it, either. They were about to tear Kleitos to pieces and claiming to be Dionysos in order to stop them was the best I could do on short notice."

"Wait a minute! You and Kleitos went to the ceremony together?"

"No, we met there."

"Oh, of course you did. That's the perfect place for a get-together." He smacked his forehead in mock realization. "You must've said to each other: 'Where should we meet? I know, let's meet in the middle of the night, in the middle of nowhere, at a Dionysia. See you there, buddy.' That's exactly what happened, right?"

There were guffaws in the room.

"I had no idea Kleitos was there, sire," I resumed, after the laughter had died down. "I had never met him before. The first time I became aware of his existence was when the women started chasing him. They were going to kill him, sire."

"So, you jumped in front of these crazed women to save this complete stranger's life. Did it occur to you they might kill you as well, while they were at it?"

"I really wasn't thinking at that moment, sire."

"You just jumped out and yelled, 'I'm Dionysos,' is that what happened?"

"Pretty much."

"And did that work?"

"Long enough for us to get away, yes."

Philippos thought about this for a moment. "I like it," he finally said. "I like your style, young man." He paused. "I don't believe you but I like your style."

I was considering my response when Lanike appeared in the doorway. She shrieked with delight and threw herself at Kleitos.

I was too stunned to utter a sound. Kleitos's sister was Aphrodite of the initiation ceremony. *What were the chances*, flashed through my mind for the third time that day. But at least now Kleitos's clandestine presence at the rites made a little more sense.

"So, you two are siblings?" Philippos's voice dripped with sarcasm. "I can see the family resemblance."

He turned to the guards, maintaining that same expression of surprised wonderment. "Tie her up too!"

"But, sire, I've been Alexandros's nursemaid since he was six."

"I know that, Lanike, but Alexandros is not here at the moment and now I've found a better role for you – you can be a hostage. If I don't miss my guess, both of these young men like you, one as a sister and the other as something more than a sister."

Did Philippos understand my feelings about this girl better than I did?

Philippos beckoned one of the soldiers to his side and then whispered at length into his ear. The next thing I knew, Kleitos and Lanike were being removed from the dining room.

The king waited until they were gone before rounding on me. "If you want to see either one of those two alive again, you'll start telling me the truth right now."

I nodded.

"Ptolemaios isn't your real name, is it?"

"No, sire, it isn't."

"So, what is it, then?"

"I can't tell you, sire."

"Where're you from?"

"I can't tell you, sire."

"Why are you here?'

"I can't tell you, sire."

"Why not?"

"Because there is a risk that many people would be adversely affected if I did."

Philippos shook his head. "All right, I've heard enough. Take him to the armory. The rest of you, go on as you were. I'll rejoin you after I'm done."

I didn't resist as they dragged me out. *What's the point?* Out of force of habit, I tried to imagine all the things they'd do to me, in order to avert any unpleasantness from actually coming to pass, but all I succeeded in accomplishing was to make myself nauseous.

"Leave us," Philippos ordered the soldiers when he arrived in the armory. "And untie him before you go."

"But sire … ," one of the soldiers started to protest.

"Don't worry," Philippos interrupted, "I can still take care of myself."

I stood in the room, rubbing my wrists, surreptitiously eying the large table in front of me, covered with scrolls, maps, tablets, sheets, and writing implements. There was a chair behind the table, which Philippos appropriated for himself. The walls were lined with cabinets and racks laden with pikes, swords, shields, and other armaments. Otherwise, the room was apparently empty and mostly hidden in shadows, illuminated by a single brazier positioned next to the table.

"Sit down!" Philippos's demeanor had changed, as if he no longer had to play to an audience, now that we were alone.

I looked around but the only chair in the room was already occupied by Philippos.

"On the floor – there should be a rug there somewhere."

There was no rug but I sat down.

"You're a strange fellow, Ptolemaios, or whatever your real name is," Philippos started. "I've never met anyone like you. And I've met a lot of people, from a lot of different places." He lapsed into pensive silence.

"I've got a pretty good idea what happened at the Dionysia," he resumed after a moment. "I've spoken to a number of the women who were there and their accounts are as consistent as you'd expect under the circumstances.

Of course, they all think they saw Dionysos but, aside from that delusion, their reports are fairly rational. What you did to save that boy was pretty courageous and it showed some quick thinking. It also showed me you're not from around here. Nobody around here would've pulled a stunt like that."

I said nothing.

"What I don't get," he continued, "is why you'd risk your life to save a child you didn't know but why now, when you've gotten to know him better, you're willing to let him get killed, rather than answering my questions truthfully. Not to mention getting yourself killed. Not to mention getting Lanike killed."

"Sire, believe me, I wish I could be more forthcoming but I simply can't. I have orders I cannot violate."

"Whose orders?"

"I'm not permitted to say, sire."

The king thought for a moment. "Do you have any military training?"

"Yes, I do, sire."

"But you didn't come here to attack me, did you?"

"No, sire."

"So that leaves only spying, doesn't it?"

"Not in the sense you mean, sire, no. I did come here to observe but only in order to learn. Not to prepare for an attack."

"So, where's the rest of your squad?"

"There's only me."

"You're kidding. You expect me to believe you traveled all this way alone?"

"Yes, sire, I did."

"And you have been hiding out in our forests alone?"

I nodded ruefully.

"For how long?"

"Too long," I said.

"Must've been tough. I don't mean physically surviving on your own but having no one to talk to."

"Yes, sire." I fought back an unexpected lump in my throat.

The king fell silent. "You must've traveled through many lands." He seemed to be ruminating, more than addressing me.

"Not as many as you'd think."

"What do you know about Persia?"

"Very little, sire. I'm sorry."

"That's too bad. I need to learn more about Persia."

He rummaged through the rolls on his desk. "Yes, here it is." He picked up a scroll. "Have you ever read this?"

I took the roll cautiously from his hands, expecting it to be extremely fragile. I had never seen an ancient papyrus roll in my life, much less held one in my hands. To my surprise, it felt pleasant, smooth, supple, not at all brittle.

Philippos seemed surprised by my hesitation. "You do know how to read, don't you?"

"Yes, sire, I can read an ... , I can read Greek but not very well." I'd almost said 'ancient.' I took a moment to compose myself. "What's this?" I asked, to cover my distress.

"It's the first book of Xenophon's Anabasis."

"I'm sorry but I've never heard either of the author or the book."

"Really? This is a well-known work and you strike me as an educated man."

"I've read some other books but not this one."

Philippos lowered his voice. "Not a lot of people know this but this work has shaped my thinking ever since I first read it as a youngster, living in Thebes." He continued after a moment. "I actually met Xenophon once. He was living in Korinthos at the time. A pompous ass, not very insightful. But he had led an interesting life and he wrote some fascinating histories about it. He died about ten years ago but this particular story is never far from my mind." He paused again. "You should really read it. It's easy reading and I think you'd enjoy it. If I decide not to kill you, maybe I'll lend it to you to read," he added with a disconcerting wink.

"I would like that very much, sire."

He made a decision. "Tell you what. I'll keep you alive long enough to let you read this work. Then we can discuss what you think. And then we'll have plenty of time to kill you."

"I'm a slow reader, sire."

Philippos laughed. "But I'm an impatient man."

"I'll do my best."

"Well, we'll see."

He summoned the guards again. "Tie him up and take him back to the stables. And make sure he's still there in the morning!"

Back to the stables I went, dumped into the same aromatic bed of hay. I was pleased to see that Kleitos was shackled right next to me, sound asleep. But there was no sign of Lanike, which I found oddly disappointing.

I went to sleep well-fed, warm, and relaxed. *Luckily, the king is a lonely man,* I thought as I fell asleep.

Chapter 4 – Kassandra's Dilemma

I was still in a hypnopompic stupor, warm and secure and delighted with the world, my penis rigidly distended, my thoughts back at the Academy, when a jolt of adrenaline suddenly jarred me wide awake. *They're not coming,* I realized. *There'll be no extraction party.*

I tried to jump to my feet, only to be rudely reminded, as I thudded back into the stinking straw, that I was bound and shackled. But at least I managed to wake Kleitos in the process.

"Get over here!" I found myself in an inexplicable rage. "Give me your hands!"

I started to tug furiously at the knots that kept his wrists bound. Within minutes I managed to get his hands untied, although his ankles were still shackled and chained to one of the posts at the end of our stall. My chain ran to the opposite post.

Kleitos massaged the angry red welts on his wrists. "What's got into you?"

"We're getting out of here," I yelled. "Now untie me!"

"Not 'til you calm down. Besides, where we gonna go?"

"I'm going to Egypt. I have a rendezvous to keep."

"Whatcha talking about?" He proceeded to untie my wrists without waiting for an answer. "Lemme know when you figure out how to get these shackles off."

"Don't worry about it. They haven't built the prison yet that could contain me." I attempted to strike a note of defiance but in the end simply slumped back into the straw.

I was reasonably sure that we could get our chains unhitched and then pry the shackles open later. My problem was a bit more fundamental. *If there is no extraction party coming, then I must find my own way back.* But that was more easily thought than done. Although I had pretended otherwise, I remembered in detail every single thing I'd been taught about the Escape Hatch Corollary. None of it was terribly encouraging. The next naturally occurring time portal was predicted to materialize on the Mediterranean coast of Egypt, near the Nile delta, about two decades from now. Somehow I would have to make my way there, determine the precise location of the portal's appearance, and make sure I was in place, at the right moment, ready to chronoport. *It's going to be a long journey,* thought my rational self. *In that case, it's lucky you've got plenty of time to get there,* the spunky me replied.

Unfortunately, getting there, which necessarily also required staying alive long enough to complete the journey, was only half the problem. The other half was adhering to the Prime Directive in the meantime. Otherwise, when I finally made it through the portal, I might find myself in a whole new world. The trick was to make it back to the future without altering it in the process.

I sat in the hay, pondering the dilemma. One thing I'd learned about myself for sure: I was neither willing nor able simply to lurk, somewhere in an uninhabited wilderness, waiting for the extraction party to arrive. Even if I'd managed to figure out how to survive physically under such circumstances, I lacked the mental toughness to live without human contact. One way or the other, I had to make my way in this world, amid these people, without violating the Prime Directive, until I was either rescued or succeeded in rescuing myself. Passivity was never my strong suit. I was determined to fight my way to the escape hatch no matter the cost – short of permanently altering the future. If I was rescued in the meantime, all the better. But I wouldn't sit still; in fact, I would start on my journey right here and now.

While I was having this internal debate, Kleitos was busy throwing dried turds at the horses. I tried to dissuade him but to no avail. Having spent the night in close proximity not only to me and the horses but also to cats, dogs, chickens, rats, and assorted insects, he was literally itching to get going. I favored calling out to our guards instead and asking them to bring us some breakfast. Kleitos's idea was to spook the horses in order to create a commotion in the stables and then make our escape during the ensuing chaos.

"All that's going happen is that the horses will turn on us," I repeated.

"Don't worry," Kleitos assured me, "I know horses. They're scared of people." And he proceeded to irritate the horses by tossing feces at them, trying alternately to hit their eyes and their genitals. The horses didn't mind their own feces too much but they became increasingly more agitated when Kleitos started throwing the dung of one stallion into the stall of another.

When he finally succeeded in hitting the horse next to us right in the eye, the poor animal had had enough. His ears pinned back, his eyes rolled white, his teeth bared, he lunged for Kleitos, trying to bite his arm off. Kleitos barely managed to jump out of the way before the teeth clamped shut.

The rest of the horses, empathetic with their enraged herdmate, started milling about, pawing the ground, snorting and whinnying. Unlike the two of us, the horses weren't shackled and were thus free to roam the stables. However, until their equine equanimity had been disrupted by Kleitos, they seemed confined to their own stalls by invisible ropes. Now those invisible ropes snapped and the horses started closing in on us. The raging stallion reared up and attempted to stomp on Kleitos, who rapidly backed away as far as his chain would permit. I, of course, was cowering right behind his back. Several of the other horses attempted to invade our stall all at once. Luckily, the opening between the poles was too narrow and two of the horses got caught in the strait between the posts. As they continued to struggle forward, the wooden poles groaned, bowed, and finally snapped, releasing our chains.

"You see!" Kleitos cried out triumphantly, just before the roof collapsed on our heads.

It took the soldiers a couple of hours to dig us out. Fortunately, neither one of us was hurt but two of the horses sustained broken legs. We all stood around and watched as a large, muscular man knelt behind each in turn, looked at the sky, almost in supplication, and then slit their throats. The soldiers spat, sniffled, wiped away a tear or two, muttered a few imprecations, and then glared at us with homicidal intent.

The watch commander summed up their views. "You're lucky the king's out. Otherwise, you'd be dead by now. Those two horses were worth a hundred drachmas each. You two aren't worth a Thrakian obol right now." After a moment, he added, with a venomous gleam in his eyes. "But he's coming back tonight. And nobody loves his horses more than Philippos. Well, except maybe Alexandros."

"What did we do?" Kleitos protested.

"Save it for later, punk." The commander shoved him to the ground. "Get down on your ass and stay there! You too, you foreign fart."

****

Lanike's morning was no less challenging. Her charge, unruly under the best of circumstances, had decided it would be a fine day to invade the women's quarter, from which he'd been expelled the previous year, when he'd turned twelve. He should've been sent to live on the first floor of the palace much earlier, as soon as he started to show the first signs of puberty, but his mother insisted on doting upon her only son well beyond the point of seemliness.

Alexandros was not exactly a mama's boy. Far from it. He spent his days with his father's soldiers, practicing his horsemanship and all the martial arts and listening to tales of derring-do. In the evenings, he enjoyed reading about the exploits of ancient heroes, especially in Homeros's Song of Ilion. However, he was also a dutiful son, who loved and feared his mother in approximately equal measure, as most people who were close to her did. He picked this particular morning to stage his invasion, precisely because he knew his mother would be away.

The girls squealed with mock terror and undisguised delight as Alexandros raced from chamber to chamber, upending trunks filled with clothes and using them to erect jerry-rigged barricades. The youngest of the chambermaids and servant girls were the same age as he was and still remembered playing innocent childhood games with him. But suddenly, almost overnight, swept along on tidal waves of raging hormones, their game of siege, sack, strip, and plunder lost some of its innocence.

The older women watched with bemusement and stayed out of the way. They had neither the authority nor the inclination to put a stop to the depredations of their queen's favorite offspring. As a result, it was left to Lanike to bring the mayhem under control.

At nineteen, Lanike was considered a member of the senior staff. She was the daughter of a minor provincial officer, the unelected head of a village in the backward, barely-civilized, mountainous reaches of Upper Macedonia. As a young girl, she excelled in all the domestic arts, acquiring a proficiency with the distaff and the spindle before the age of six; learning quickly and easily the usual techniques of weaving, knitting, felting, braiding, and plaiting of fabrics and cloths; willingly taking her turn in the care of the family herds and flocks; displaying a particular affinity and aptitude around the kitchen; and, as the eldest child in the family, lending a hand with her younger siblings. She was her mother's favorite daughter and the apple of her father's eye, even before she started to show early signs of curvaceous pulchritude to come. By the time she was twelve, she had become, as far as her father was concerned, the family's most valuable asset.

In a burst of unexpected and atypical ambition, her father decided, on the twelfth anniversary of her birth, that Lanike should be sent to the court to do what she could to advance the status of her family. No one from the village had ever been taken on as a servant at the palace but her father was confident his daughter's talents would shine through and she could gain a suitable position, followed quickly by a desirable marriage to some important courtier, thus securing the future of her entire clan. No one thought it necessary to consult Lanike's views on the matter.

By coincidence or fate, the day before Lanike and her father arrived at the palace, a sudden vacancy occurred in the women's quarter when Alexandros's nursemaid was discovered to be pregnant. The unfortunate girl was dismissed on the spot and the queen launched an immediate search for a suitable replacement. For reasons that remained forever shrouded in the mists of the queen's devious mind, Olympias chose an unknown twelve-year-old commoner, without recommendation or family connection, as the new nursemaid for her six-year-old son. The betting among the staff in the women's quarter was that the new girl would not last out the month.

Somehow, seven years later, Lanike still occupied an important position in the gynaikonitis, notwithstanding the initial hostility of the entire staff to this outsider without credentials who'd usurped a position that by all rights should've gone to a daughter of one of the leading noble families of Macedonia and notwithstanding the queen's well-deserved reputation as an impossible taskmaster. In due course, Lanike had not only become accepted by the other servants in the palace but she had also managed to earn their respect and even affection. The queen, of course, was another matter. She didn't waste her affection on her staff but she did develop a grudging tolerance for the young woman who performed all her tasks faithfully and with meticulous precision. Alas, Lanike's days of service to the prince had come to an end a year earlier but a close bond of friendship still remained between them.

"That's enough," Lanike yelled at Alexandros when she finally caught up to him.

"You can't tell me what to do. You're not my nursemaid anymore."

"Yes, I am. And I'm older than you."

"So what. I'm stronger than you, so you can't stop me."

"No, I can't, but you're going to stop yourself and you'll do it right now."

"Why should I?"

"Because you're embarrassing yourself. This is not how a future king behaves."

Alexandros broke off his invasion of the women's quarter, gave his former nursemaid a sheepish smile, and withdrew to his soldier friends in the barracks.

****

Kleitos and I were left to marinate in the cold rain atop the remnants of the stable for the better part of the day. Eventually, Lanike came to her brother's relief. Hiding beneath a makeshift cowl of sackcloth, she braved the inclement weather and vindictive guards to bring him some bread, cheese, and wine. Kleitos, taking it for granted that the food was for both of us, broke the small loaf in two, passing the bigger portion on to me, along with some of the cheese.

"He's Dionysos, you know," he told his sister with a wink.

She kept a straight face. "Yes, I remember him from the initiation ceremony."

"I'm not really a god," I said modestly.

"We know."

Their intertwined laughter was cut short by a sudden commotion. The king had returned. Lanike vanished from sight but not before a quick peck on her little brother's cheek and a friendly wave to me.

"What in Haides happened?" Philippos demanded when he reached our scene of devastation.

"The roof collapsed, sire." Kleitos was innocence personified. "We were almost killed. You should take better care of your prisoners."

"Horseshit!" the king spat.

"You have no idea how right you are, sire," I mumbled under my breath.

He walked away in disgust but we were eventually picked up, fed, given dry clothes, and placed in a small, barren room adjoining the soldiers' barracks. The soldiers were evidently under orders to leave us alone because we had no human visitors that night, only local vermin – teeming, ravenous, unhampered by any royal decree. Luckily, there was no source of light or heat in our room, not even an oil lamp, making for a rather frigid ambiance, but at least the cold rendered some of the bugs too sluggish to bite. Others, however, soldiered on notwithstanding the cold. Instead of dreaming about Paloma or Aphrodite or Lanike, I dreamt of stepping on a giant anthill, breaking through its roof into an enormous cavern filled with millions and millions of teeming sterile worker ants, and struggling futilely to climb out of my hole.

A soldier kicked me awake shortly after dawn. My first instinct was to brush all the ants off but there were no ants, only a tingling sensation associated with blood circulation gradually returning to my stiff and frozen extremities and an itching sensation associated with sleeping with lice, fleas, and bedbugs. The soldier handed me a scroll. "The king wants you to read this. Lemme know when you're done. I've got six more to give you." As promised, it was the first scroll of a work entitled Anabasis, evidently written by someone named Xenophon.

"What about me?" Kleitos asked.

"You know how to read?" There was a touch of surprise in the soldier's voice.

"No," Kleitos admitted.

The soldier laughed. "Well, in that case, come and help us rebuild the stables."

******

I wished I had a pair of white gloves. The idea of touching a genuine, ancient papyrus scroll with my grimy, sweaty, oily hands seemed practically sacrilegious. Maybe other time travelers had handled such rolls during their trips but I doubted it. There had been relatively few visits to this era, always to remote, unpopulated areas, and always carried out under orders to avoid contact with the local population. No one had ever brought a scroll back because, among other things, the design parameters of time portals rendered it physically impossible to bring anachronistic artifacts back into the future. The only ancient papyrus or parchment scrolls that anyone in my time had ever touched were tattered, incredibly fragile fragments of mostly unimportant documents. And here I was, being handed a perfectly fine, albeit somewhat scuffed, scroll without so much as a second thought.

Before I'd finished reading the first scroll, there was a rustling in the doorway. I looked up and saw Lanike, bringing more food.

"I'm afraid Kleitos is not here." My real fear was that she might turn around and leave.

She repaid me with a shy smile. "Yes, I know. That's why I picked this time to come."

After we set aside Kleitos's portion, she watched me eat. I wanted to tell her that she was beautiful. "This tastes great," I said instead.

She blushed and changed the subject. "Where're you from?"

Prime Directive

I told her little about myself, preferring obfuscation to outright prevarication. She was similarly reticent in describing her own background. It was clear, however, that her position as nursemaid to the prince represented a huge change of fortune for her family.

We talked for a while. The more evasive my answers, the more fascinated she seemed to be. The more I listened to her, the more worried I became. It was bad enough I was being mentally unfaithful to Paloma but, far worse, I was inching perilously close to the dangerous penumbra of the strictures of the Prime Directive. Nevertheless, I found it difficult to resist the allure of her interest.

Finally, my training broke through her enchanting spell. I thanked her for the food, my tone putting an implicit end to our chat. She picked up immediately on the subtext of my expressions of gratitude and rose to her feet. As I escorted her to the door, she surprised me with a quick peck on the cheek, like the one she had bestowed on her brother, before running out of the room. As I sat down, trying to return my mind to reading Xenophon, I recalled ruefully the words of our behavioral protocol instructor: "The more beguiling the maiden, the greater the risk of a Prime Directive violation."

******

I read feverishly, trying to keep my mind out of trouble and my hands occupied. I finished the seven scrolls in less than two days. That night I was once again dragged to the armory. Philippos was seated at his table. I was dumped on the ground in front of him.

"Take off his shackles." Philippos dismissed the guard. "Did you read it?"

"Yes, sire."

"All seven books?"

"Yes, sire."

"In less than two days?"

"It was a fast read."

"Might have been wiser to take a bit more time."

The king's tone was friendly, relaxed, and infinitely menacing. I felt like a lion tamer, standing in the middle of a cage, being casually stalked by a huge, wild beast. But unlike most animal trainers, I had no tools, except possibly my wits, with which to tame this beast, and he, unlike most lions, was certainly a match for my wits. Plus, he was the one holding the whip in his paw.

Philippos winked his dead eye. "Weigh carefully what you say next."

I nodded.

Prime Directive

"Tell me the single most important thing you learned from this story."

I tried to put myself in his boots. I figured he couldn't care less what was important to me. My challenge was to hit upon some salient point of interest to him. I quickly ran through the entire work in my mind. The basic story was quite simple:

In the wake of Sparta's victory over Athens in their long and fratricidal war, Greece was overrun by hordes of landless, suddenly unemployed men, possessing few skills beyond the ability to engage in organized mayhem. Many of these men found gainful employment in the service of various ambitious Persian lords.

When the book opens, around 185 Z.E.[7], the old Persian king, Dareios, had died, leaving his two sons, Artaxerxes and Kyros, contending for power. The elder of the two, Artaxerxes, became the emperor. He promptly seized his brother, intent, in the usual Persian fashion, on putting to death all potential rivals to his throne. However, their mother, Parysatis, managed to persuade Artaxerxes to refrain from killing his brother and to appoint him satrap of

---

[7] Zoroaster Era, calculated from Zoroaster's purported date of birth. It is interesting to note that this calendar convention, introduced early in the history of the Persian Empire, remains in use in my native era to the present day. I arrived in ancient Macedonia in 243 Z.E., or some fifty-eight years after the events recounted in Xenophon's Anabasis.

one of the Persian provinces instead. Kyros took up his new post and immediately began plotting an insurrection against the emperor.

As part of his plan, Kyros assembled several small armies, each including a significant component of Greek mercenaries, under the pretext of attempting to pacify, more or less at the same time, various far-flung savage tribes threatening Persia's borders in the west and north of the empire. When he deemed himself in command of a sufficiently large force, he ordered the various divisions to meet him in Sardeis, the capital of Lydia, on the western coast of Anatolia.

Among the Greek mercenaries who arrived at Sardeis for this muster was an Athenian adventurer named Xenophon. He, like all able-bodied citizens of Athens, had fought in the Peloponnesian War and was searching for some occupation now that the long struggle had ended. He came at the invitation of a friend of his, Proxenos, who commanded one of Kyros's Greek mercenary brigades, but without any clear conception of what his role was to be. At a minimum, he hoped to benefit from making the acquaintance of the enterprising Kyros.

Once all his forces had assembled at Sardeis, Kyros ordered his combined army to start marching toward the interior of the country. At this point, it became obvious to some of Kyros's intimates, although not necessarily to the rank and file troops, that the ultimate objective of Kyros's maneuvers was not the conquest of some obstreperous savages but, rather, the overthrow of the Persian emperor himself. Someone promptly informed Artaxerxes.

It took Kyros's army more than four months to cover the fifteen hundred miles from Sardeis to the vicinity of Babylon, more than adequate time for Artaxerxes to make the necessary preparations. The two armies met at Kounaxa, on the eastern bank of the Euphrates River, perhaps thirty miles north of Babylon.

When Kyros received word that Artaxerxes's army was approaching, in battle formation, he ordered his own troops to prepare for battle. The Greek mercenaries, numbering some 10,400 hoplites and 2,500 peltasts, were arrayed on the right, next to the Euphrates, under the command of Klearchos, Proxenos (Xenophon's friend), and Menon. The center was occupied by a cavalry force of 600 Persians, under the personal command of Kyros. The left wing consisted of a large number of poorly trained native infantry troops under the command of a Persian nobleman named Ariaios.

The arrival of Artaxerxes's army was heralded by a dust cloud on the horizon, which gradually became darker and darker until eventually the dust blotted out the entire field of view. It took some time before it became possible to make out the outlines of the approaching hordes of massed troops in the haze.

According to Xenophon, there were perhaps a million soldiers arrayed across the line from Kyros's army. Apparently, Xenophon's count was obscured by the dust, by his excitement, and by the understandable tendency of military writers of all eras to exaggerate the strength of the enemy. Nevertheless, it was clear that Artaxerxes's army was sizable. In fact, drawn up in battle order, the line of Artaxerxes's forces was twice as long as Kyros's opposing line.

Artaxerxes himself was stationed in the middle of his line, amidst a cavalry force some six thousand strong, and shielded behind a screen of several thousand select infantry soldiers. As the two lines began to close, it became evident that, because Artaxerxes's army was so much larger, the middle of Artaxerxes's line, where he himself was stationed, was actually beyond the extreme left edge of Kyros's entire combined line. In other words, all of Kyros's troops, if they charged straight ahead, would engage less than half of Artaxerxes's line, leaving Artaxerxes in the middle and his entire right wing unopposed. Such a clash would in effect invite Artaxerxes to pivot his right wing and outflank Kyros's line.

Seeing this state of affairs, Kyros asked Klearchos to order the Greek mercenaries to attack on a slant, so as to engage Artaxerxes's cavalry in the middle of the line, presumably on the theory that, by decapitating the enemy, the numerical superiority of the opposing army would be neutralized. Klearchos declined Kyros's request, pointing out that by moving across the battlefield on a slant, the Greek mercenaries would lose the protection afforded to their right flank by the Euphrates River, making them vulnerable to being outflanked by the entire left wing of Artaxerxes army, which was at that moment directly across the line from them.

Rather than pivoting toward the center, the Greek mercenaries charged straight ahead and easily routed the much larger Persian force opposing them. Kyros, in the meantime, personally led a cavalry charge of his select Six Hundred against the center occupied by Artaxerxes himself. He succeeded in piercing the covering infantry screen in front of Artaxerxes's cavalry, engaged the cavalry, and penetrated through them far enough to inflict a superficial wound on Artaxerxes himself. However, at that point, the numerical superiority of Artaxerxes's cavalry began to tell. Kyros's Six Hundred lost all semblance of cohesion. They disintegrated into small squadrons, each engulfed in a sea of opposing knights. Although fighting gallantly, Kyros's cavalry was systematically cut to shreds and he himself mortally wounded. Once all of Kyros's cavalry companions were dead, someone severed Kyros's head and right hand and presented them to Artaxerxes. When the native troops, under Ariaios, realized that Kyros was dead, they turned their backs and broke into headlong flight.

In the meantime, the Greek mercenaries, ignorant of Kyros's fate, continued to press their advantage against the retreating Persian left wing. Artaxerxes and his cavalry, no longer opposed by anyone, galloped beyond the battlefield, looted the Greeks' camp, then wheeled and attacked the Greek foot soldiers from the rear. The Greeks easily withstood this charge as well. At that point, Artaxerxes, satisfied with the day's accomplishments, withdrew from the field of battle.

The small Greek force, in the meantime, storming from victory to victory, continued its pursuit of the withdrawing Persian forces. It was not until well into the evening that they were informed that, notwithstanding their own successes, their commander-in-chief Kyros was dead and their mission thus ended. Worse yet, upon returning to camp, they discovered that, in addition to losing the purpose of their expedition and losing any chance of being paid, they had also lost all of their baggage and provisions.

An uneasy truce settled in over the next couple of days. The Greek mercenaries, although no longer having an employer nor any reason for being in Persia, had no way of returning back to Greece. The victorious Persians, although they had carried the day, were hesitant to take on the Greeks in a direct confrontation.

After extensive negotiations, the two sides worked out a deal. The Greeks agreed to march out of Persia the way they had come, without inflicting any damage or casualties on the Persians or their subjects, and the Persians agreed not to oppose the Greeks' withdrawal and to provide them with opportunities to purchase necessary supplies along the way. The chief negotiators for both sides clasped each other's right arms, all participants swore elaborate oaths to their respective deities, and the Greeks set out on their journey home, closely followed by a large Persian force under the personal command of Artaxerxes's right-hand man Tissaphernes.

As the Greeks slowly made their way out of Persia, they continued to be harassed by the Persian forces, which repeatedly threatened to attack and annihilate them. Eventually, Klearchos, the overall Greek commander, requested a parlay with Tissaphernes in an attempt to lower tensions between the shadow-boxing opponents. They met on neutral ground and agreed that it made no sense for the Greeks to do anything but peaceably withdraw and for the Persians to do anything but let them do so.

Such was the glow of mutual good feeling between the two commanders that Tissaphernes invited Klearchos, along with all of his commanders, to a feast at the Persian headquarters to celebrate their enduring friendship. Despite the misgivings of some of his commanders, Klearchos persuaded most of his officers to attend Tissaphernes's feast. In addition, Klearchos brought along a force of two hundred of his best troops, ostensibly to purchase provisions for the rest of the Greek army, but in fact intended to serve as a security force, just in case.

The five Greek generals, including Klearchos, Proxenos, and Menon, were welcomed into the large tent with elaborate courtesy, while the remaining officers waited outside the entrance. On a signal, the Greek generals were seized, disarmed, and beheaded. The remaining officers outside the tent were surrounded by a large cavalry force and massacred. The Persians then fanned out across the countryside between the two camps and murdered every Greek soldier, camp follower, and slave they could find. One injured Greek soldier managed to escape to the Greek camp and raise the alarm.

The Greeks found themselves in an awkward position. They had no commanders to lead them; they had no idea which route to take home and no guides to show them the way; they were once again without provisions; and they were deep in the heartland of the Persian Empire, more than a thousand miles from the nearest shore, surrounded by a hostile population and by several hundred thousand enemy troops bent on their destruction.

The Persians invited them to surrender their arms, with promises of safe conduct out of the country, secured once again by the most solemn of oaths and undertakings.

The Greeks declined the invitation to surrender. Instead, they met in assembly and elected a new set of leaders from among the rank and file soldiers. One of the leaders to emerge was Xenophon. In addition, they chose a route out of Persia that seemed to them to offer the best hope of survival and escape. The adventures of the Ten Thousand, during the next eight months and across some three thousand miles of parched deserts, forbidding mountains, primordial forests, and unfordable rivers, during insufferable heat, lethal cold, and monstrous blizzards, in the face of unremitting opposition from the organized military forces of the Great King, from the local militias of his subject tribes, and from the untamed savages on the periphery of the empire, as the Greeks made their way out of Persia, make up the rest of the narrative. Almost all of the Ten Thousand made it home and one of them – Xenophon – wrote it all down for posterity.

"Tell me the single most important thing you learned from this story." Philippos's question still hung in the air.

I cleared my throat.

"You did read it, didn't you?"

I'd read it, all right, but I was still working out my answer. On the one hand, I had a tactical advantage in trying to answer Philippos's question because I knew more about the king than he knew about me. On the other hand, in a way I knew too much about him because I also knew what the future held in store for him. And I was determined to avoid influencing that future in some way by inadvertently letting Philippos in on what lay ahead.

It was taking me too long to answer. "Well," I finally said, "Kyros made the correct choice in attacking Artaxerxes's strongest point, in the center of his line, and in leading the assault personally, but he made a mistake by failing to bring overwhelming force to bear at the point of attack."

Philippos gave me a long, thoughtful look. Of course, he had no way of knowing I had learned, during my study of ancient military history, that Philippos's own favorite tactic was to pick out his adversary's strongest point and then to bring overwhelming force to bear against that point, even if this meant temporarily neglecting the remaining line of battle. Once the enemy soldiers saw that their strongest point was crumbling, the entire enemy line invariably broke and ran, despite the fact that, had they persisted, they could have easily prevailed everywhere else, except at the point of the initial clash.

In reading Xenophon, I was struck by the fact that Kyros had applied only half of the Philippos approach. Kyros did attack the enemy's strongest point but he did so with insufficient force. As a result, his attack was repelled and he himself killed. In trying to guess what Philippos might have found significant in Xenophon's account, it seemed to me the failure of Kyros's attack was as good a place to start as any.

Philippos finally cleared his throat. "Yes, I agree. Kyros made a mistake. But surely, that's far from the most important thing in this book."

Uh-oh, I thought.

"This was one bunch of Persian cavalrymen beating another bunch of Persian cavalrymen, right? Why would I care about that?"

I decided to venture another guess. "The Greeks easily beat both Persian infantry and Persian cavalry, even though there were many more Persians fighting against them. In fact, if Kyros hadn't foolishly gotten himself killed, the Greeks would have carried the day for him."

Philippos smiled. "You're right. The Greeks come off looking like the winners at Kounaxa, even though they ended up on the losing side of the battle." He paused. "However, we must keep in mind that Xenophon was a Greek. I wonder what the Persian version of the battle looks like."

"I understand that, sire, but Xenophon's account has the ring of truth about it."

"I think so too, but surely that's not the most important point of the story. The battle of Kounaxa was just a sideshow, wasn't it?"

"Yes, sire, you're right. This is a story about ten thousand Greeks fighting their way out of Persia."

"Go on."

I decided to stop trying to guess what Philippos might find interesting. "To tell you the truth, sire, what I found most remarkable was that the Greeks, after all their commanders had been killed, refused to surrender. Instead, they elected new commanders and then they united behind them. What's even more amazing, the new commanders proved to be competent leaders."

"Had the tables been turned, wouldn't the Persians have done the same?"

"No, I don't think so, sire."

"Why not?"

"I've given that a lot of thought, sire. The Greeks were volunteers and the Persian soldiers, who were mostly not Persians at all but members of various subject nations, were conscripts. But there's more to it than that. Every Greek soldier was somehow a free, independent actor, willing and able to make decisions for himself, while the Persians were just interchangeable cogs in a giant machine, expected simply to follow orders."

"Every soldier must follow orders, even Greek soldiers."

"That's true, sire, but it's not the same. The Greek soldiers had more initiative and autonomy. It's hard to explain."

"You might be onto something, divine Dionysos, but you're not explaining it very well."

"I know, sire." I tried to suppress a rueful smile. "I'll have to think about it some more."

"You do that. In the meantime, let me tell you the single most important thing in this book."

He reached for one of the scrolls. "Better yet, let me show you."

While the king was rolling through the scroll, looking for his place, there was a sudden commotion just outside the room, climaxed by a loud crash. A woman burst through the door, followed by a frantic soldier. Even in the dim light of the armory, the woman was unmistakably Olympias.

The queen made a beeline for her husband, brandishing a wad of what looked to be women's undergarments. "Your son is out of control."

The guard, who'd been stationed outside the door, was hovering behind her, not quite sure whether to grab her or throttle her, an apologetic look on his face.

"Not now," Philippos said.

Olympias was undeterred, getting even louder. "While I was traveling outside the city, he staged a raid on the women's quarter, wreaking havoc, toppling furniture, and stealing the women's clothes." She paused for dramatic effect. "While some of them were still in them!"

"That's my boy," Philippos laughed.

"It's not a joke. He obviously has too much time on his hands and is getting restless here at the palace. Plus, he's your heir, isn't he? He needs to start his preparations to take over the kingdom at some point."

"Nobody is taking over my kingdom anytime soon." Philippos cast a meaningful look at the guard. The soldier immediately seized Olympias by her shoulders and started to steer her out of the room.

"Let go of me, you goon!" The queen was having none of it but the guard was stronger and the two of them started to back out of the room. Then Olympias tripped over me. Had the guard not been holding her, she probably would have fallen to the ground.

"Who the hell is this worm?" She struggled for balance. It was evident she hadn't seen me sitting on the ground until I had caused her to stumble.

"That's your Dionysos, dear." The king couldn't have been more pleased.

The queen regained her equilibrium. "You will pay for that." It was not clear which one of us she was addressing. "You don't want to test me." And with that minatory observation, she left the room.

As soon as she was gone, the king burst out laughing. "You're worth your weight in gold, young man. Now, what were we talking about?"

"You were going to tell me the single most important thing."

"Oh yes, that's right." He returned to his scroll.

"Do you remember, in Book Four, as the Greeks were marching to the Black Sea, they had to cross the land of the Chalyboi, who proved to be particularly pesky opponents? They had the endearing habit of cutting off the heads of any enemy soldiers they'd managed to overpower in a fight and then joyfully waving the severed heads at any enemy soldiers still remaining on the battlefield."

"Yes, I remember them."

"But that wasn't the interesting part. What caught my attention was that the Chalyboi carried a single twenty-foot-long pike into battle. The Greeks have always carried seven- or eight-foot-long pikes. Do you know why?"

"Because of tradition?" I guessed.

"Tradition's got nothing to do with it. Everybody knows that if you have a longer pike, you can strike your opponent before he can strike you. The trouble is that it's not humanly possible to wield a pike longer than seven or eight feet with any degree of control. Yet, here is

115

Xenophon, telling us that the Chalyboi used twenty-foot pikes and also telling us they were the most difficult adversary the Greeks faced during their entire journey. When I read Xenophon, as a youngster living in Thebes, I kept returning to this passage. 'How could the Chalyboi effectively control twenty-foot-long pikes,' I kept asking myself. Do you have any idea how such a thing was possible?"

I actually knew the answer to that question, having studied Philippos's military innovations in some detail. *Should I hazard a correct guess?* I asked myself. *Oh, go ahead!*

"Because they used both their hands?"

"That's exactly right," Philippos exclaimed. "How did you know? Xenophon never says anything about it."

"I reasoned it out," I lied. "He also never says anything about the Chalyboi carrying shields. The Greeks could wield pikes no longer than eight feet because they held their pikes in their right hands only, their left hands being occupied holding their shields. Because the Chalyboi carried no shields, they had both hands available to control their pikes. As a result, they could use much longer pikes."

The king gave me a long look. "That's what I thought, too, when I was fifteen years old, living as a hostage in Thebes," he finally said. "Do you know what I did next?"

I did know but I decided I'd pressed my luck far enough. "I have no idea, sire."

"That passage in Xenophon set me thinking. 'What would happen,' I asked myself, 'if we combined the best features of both approaches? Suppose we kept the shields but made them a bit smaller and attached them to our soldiers' left arms with leather loops, thus freeing their left hands to assist with the pikes. Then, having two hands available for wielding their pikes, they could manage to control longer pikes.' As soon as I became king, I started to experiment with attached shields and longer pikes. Eventually, I settled on a fourteen-foot sarissa as the ideal length and we haven't lost a battle since."

I nodded my understanding, with what I hoped was an expression of frank admiration on my face. "That was a brilliant innovation, sire."

He looked at me sharply, clearly doubting the sincerity of my response. Then, for the second time, he decided to let it go.

But two warning signals were enough even for someone as obtuse as I was pretending to be. *Be more careful playing games with the king. This guy is a sharp judge of character.*

"There is another thought that's been on my mind ever since I read Xenophon as a youngster," he continued after a while. "I've been thinking that, if ten thousand Greeks could hold off the entire might of the Persian

Empire, imagine what a unified army of all Greek states, armed in the Macedonian fashion, drilled by Macedonian commanders, and led by me, could accomplish."

"It's hard to imagine." I was stalling for time. It goes without saying there was nothing for me to imagine. Every school child in my era knew exactly what was going to happen. The Greeks, led by the Macedonians, would indeed invade Persia and would be comprehensively defeated by the Persian armies. Then the Persians, taking advantage of the resulting defenselessness of the Greek mainland and riding a wave of unprecedented confidence and euphoria, would counterattack with a vengeance, completing the conquest of Greece that had been thwarted – temporarily – at Marathon and Salamis.

Viewed from a distance of some twenty-four hundred years, the eventual triumph of Persia, leading to the first truly global empire, was considered foreordained and inevitable by the historians of my day. As explained in every grade school history textbook, in the long run, the loosely affiliated but constantly fighting Greek cities and small states simply had no chance against the vastly superior material and human resources and unified command structure of the Persian Empire. Even before their conquest of the Greeks, the Persians already controlled not only their ancestral Iranian plateau but also the southern reaches of the Black and Caspian Seas, portions of central Asia, the northern third of the Indian subcontinent, the entire Levant, and most of North Africa. With the bulwark of the Greek civilization out of the way, nothing but primitive tribes stood between the Persians and the Atlantic Ocean. In due course, the Persian Empire completed its subjugation of all of Europe, half of Africa, and most of Asia, and then maintained its control for more than a thousand years.

The king intruded on my musing. "Let me ask you directly: Do you think we should invade Persia?"

And here we'd made our way to the crux of the matter. *Should I tell him everything I know about his personal future, about the future of his kingdom, and about the future of the Greek civilization?* I asked myself.

Well, if you do, it will be the most sweeping violation of the Prime Directive ever attempted. In fact, just your thinking about it has set all the chronobars of the space-time continuum aflutter, my more sensible conscience answered.

But if I can avert this invasion, it will save countless lives and might even preserve Greek civilization for a couple of centuries.

Do you remember Kassandra? my conscience asked.

In fact, I did. In Greek mythology, Kassandra was the beautiful daughter of Priamos, the last king of Troy. She caught the eye of Apollon, who uncharacteristically asked for her permission, rather than simply raping her. He promised her the gift of prophesy if she complied with his wishes. She accepted the god's proposal and he bestowed upon her the ability to see the future. But, once she had received the god's gift, she changed her mind and refused to go through with the bargain. (I always wondered how, if she was able to foresee the consequences of her breach, could she have made such a foolish choice.) Apollon was disappointed. But, rather than killing her or forcing himself on her or taking back the power of prophesy, he devised a much more cunning punishment. He let Kassandra keep her newly gained ability (and her putative virginity as well). He simply decreed that, while she would always know what was to come, no one would ever believe any of her predictions. Only now did I appreciate the full dreadfulness of the god's revenge.

The king persisted. "Well, do you think we should invade Persia?"

"I don't know."

Another sidelong glance from Philippos.

This man understands me better than I gave him credit for.

The king summoned the guard. "That's enough for now. Take him back and make sure he's still there tomorrow."

Chapter 5 – Alexandros

He was, much like his idol Achilleus, a swift and steadfast runner and he enjoyed making others run faster and farther than they ever thought themselves capable of running. To Alexandros, everything was an opportunity for a contest and every contest was a test of wills.

Thus, when Leukonides announced, shortly after our scanty breakfast, that our training that morning would consist of a light run through the woods, Alexandros immediately insisted we turn the training run into a race. "We'll run to Lake Bokeritis and back," he announced, naming a destination some sixty stadia away. "And the winner will be in command of our group all day tomorrow; the loser will be everybody's slave for the day."

Not much of a penalty for me, I thought. *I'm already everybody's slave.*

In fact, what my role was supposed to be was something of a mystery. I'd managed to inveigle Philippos into sending Kleitos and me to the Precinct of the Nymphs in Mieza, the home base of the most exclusive boarding school in the Greek world – a school recently created specifically to further the preparation of Philippos's son Alexandros for his anticipated role as his father's successor.[8] But now that I was here, nobody could quite figure out what to do with me. I was certainly not going to be a part of the exalted little group that was Alexandros's study and training cohort but I wasn't exactly one of their servants or bodyguards or instructors, either. No, my position, as best as I could tell, was to be the outsider, the one guy who didn't fit in. Luckily, this was a role for which I'd been training all my life and was therefore quite adept at tolerating.

It hadn't been Philippos's intention to make me miserable. On the contrary, in the course of our conversations, his attitude toward me had gradually changed. He'd turned from a brusque, suspicious interrogator into an amicable, inquisitive, animated, and discursive interlocutor. In acceding to my wish to be sent to Mieza, he probably thought he was making a generous gesture toward me, while at the same time advancing the cause of his son's education. He must've figured I could serve as an object of study for the boys and their headmaster Aristoteles – an exotic specimen, like a chambered nautilus or a fire-breathing Chimaira, which

---

[8] For the location of Mieza and other places mentioned below, see Map 1 at AlexanderGeiger.com.

they could discuss, analyze, dissect, and catalogue. He'd simply forgotten how he'd felt when he was held hostage in a foreign city by people who were strangers to him.

Kleitos, by contrast, had no trouble integrating into the group. While he was not the scion of one of the noble families of Macedonia nor even the son of one of Philippos's close friends or allies, he was the brother of Alexandros's nursemaid. More importantly, he was about the same age as the rest of the boys, he was bright and enthusiastic, and he had a gift for getting along with people.

No sooner had we arrived at camp than the boys bestowed one of their highest accolades on him – they gave him a nickname. He became known as Kleitos Melas, the Black Kleitos. Of course, the fact that there was already another Kleitos in the class may well have accelerated the process. The other Kleitos was a blond, practically an albino, making my friend Kleitos look quite dark in comparison. And these boys, as kids everywhere, were unerring in plucking out their victim's most salient characteristic when bestowing their chosen sobriquet.

Truth to tell, everybody acquired a nickname sooner or later. The Macedonians were remarkably parsimonious in their menu of children's names, recycling the same handful over and over again. Chances were good that, if a dozen boys gathered in a group, there would be more than one Alexandros, Attalos, or Antipatros. To distinguish one Alexandros from the next, it was customary to add the name of the boy's father and his place of origin. Thus, our Alexandros was formally known as Alexandros, son of Philippos, of Macedonia. However, in practice, it was much easier just to give everyone a distinctive nickname.

Even I was given a nickname eventually. The boys called me Ptolemaios Metoikos. I thought I knew what the word meant but, unfortunately, my command of the language back then was not good enough to appreciate all the secondary connotations of my nickname. Nevertheless, I was flattered just to have received one.

The run was fun, at least at the beginning. It was pure pleasure to be able to stretch out my legs, after weeks of confinement in a dingy, smelly, damp, and pest-infested cell, with my ankles shackled much of the time. I was twenty-one years old, healthy, physically fit (notwithstanding my recent ordeals), and irrationally exuberant about life. The path on which we were running, through the woods between the village and the lake, was soft, pleasantly shady, and mostly clear of obstacles. The air was the fresh, clean, pine-scented, ethereally liberating. There was an implicit camaraderie among the boys. It was a fine day to be alive.

Leukonides and I were the only adults in the group. The old drill sergeant from Epiros was not actually running. He rode behind the pack, making sure we didn't lose anyone, and encouraging – with a stout stick – any laggards to catch up. I, on the other hand, was not only permitted to run but was actually singled out for the special honor of carrying a couple of waterskins, in a sack tied to my back. I guess it was only fair; I was, after all, a man running among boys.

We were running single file, with Alexandros in the lead, of course. He was thirteen years old at the time. He struck me, upon first meeting him, as an arrogant little turd. Still, there was something perplexing about him, some inexplicable quality I couldn't quite pin down. Was it his preternatural maturity; was it his apparent, if unfathomable, self-confidence; was it some intimation of greatness; or was it simply the impudence of a spoiled brat? Here I was, flattering myself on my ability to judge a person's character at a glance and yet unable to figure out what made this slight, physically unprepossessing kid tick or, should I say, run.

Actually, as I thought about it, he was not exactly unprepossessing. Although short for his age, he was put together well, surprisingly muscular for a kid, and setting a diabolical pace at the moment. Despite his relatively short stride, his legs were churning, his arms were pumping, his blond mane was billowing, and the rest of the group was panting.

I heard Alexandros yell "Root!" as he flew over an obstacle.

"Root!" yelled Hephaistion, the next kid in line.

"Root!" yelled the next eight runners in front of me.

"Ouch!" I yelled, as I tripped over the thick tree root and went sprawling.

"Ptolemaios!" yelled Kleitos, who was running immediately behind me, as he neatly jumped over my prostrate body.

"Root and Ptolemaios," yelled the next few runners in the line, as they hurdled both the root and me without breaking stride.

For a minute, I thought they were going to leave me there, which was just as well, as far as I was concerned. I really didn't feel like getting up and chasing after them. *Maybe a little nap and then I'll stroll back to Mieza at my leisure.*

Leukonides had other thoughts. He managed to rein in his horse just before it trampled me. Or possibly the horse stopped itself because Leukonides, far from exercising any control over his mount, was in some danger of being unhorsed, as a result of an uncontrollable fit of laughter. He finally managed to catch his breath long enough to emit a piercing whistle, which brought everyone back to us. They had all heard my fall and they were all tremendously amused but discipline was discipline and they didn't laugh and didn't stop running until given permission to do so by Leukonides's signal. At which point they made up for lost time. They all stood around, pointing and laughing uproariously. The worst part was that they had all managed to catch their breaths within seconds of stopping, while I lay there, panting.

Finally, the merriment proved too contagious to resist and I started to laugh as well. That signaled the end of the break. Alexandros reached down and helped me to my feet. "Say a prayer of thanks to Artemis," he instructed.

I was genuinely puzzled. "Thanks for what?"

"For not breaking your neck, you clubfoot," he laughed. "Or perhaps it was divine courtesy. You are Artemis's half-brother, aren't you?"

Evidently, the story of my Dionysos impersonation had reached all the way to Mieza. "I think it was more a matter of luck." Having no idea what prayer I was expected to recite, I was temporizing.

It was now Alexandros's turn to be baffled. "What does Tyche have to do with this? This precinct is clearly the domain of Artemis."

I didn't understand what he meant, having momentarily forgotten that Tyche was the goddess of luck.

Leukonides came to my rescue, diplomatically bridging the apparent jurisdictional conflict between the two deities. "Thank you, Goddesses, for sparing this fool from a broken neck. We will remember your kindnesses at evening sacrifice," he chanted, looking suitably worshipful and gazing slightly upward and to his left, presumably in the general direction of Mt. Olympos.

Then, looking back down at us, his next command arrived with the suddenness of a summer squall. "How long are you wheezers planning to stand there?" His pious expression and tone were abruptly gone. "Help him pick up his gear and let's get a move on!"

I grabbed my skins, which were miraculously intact, and took my place at the tail end of the line. Soon we were flying again. Alexandros was back in the lead. Hephaistion, same age as Alexandros and his closest friend, was once again glued to his leader's shoulder. He was taller than Alexandros, more slender, more elegant, a natural runner. It wasn't clear whether he was running in second place because he was unable to pass Alexandros or because he was unwilling to do so.

There was a little gap after the first two and then a group of slightly older boys, Kassandros the Frog Killer, 15, Fast Philotas, 17, Lysimachos the Bear, 17, Nuts Nikanoros, 15, and Squeaky Attalos, 13. Kassandros was the son of Philippos's favorite general, Antipatros. He was big for his age, bulky, a redhead, and a bully. Philotas and Nikanoros were brothers, the sons of Philippos's best general, Parmenion. They were smart, friendly, and devoted to each other. Attalos, same age as Alexandros and Hephaistion, was a dark horse. He was young, small for his age, and his voice often broke (hence his nickname Squeaky). Yet, he was smart, athletic, and seemed to enjoy Alexandros's friendship. As far as I knew, he was unrelated to Attalos the Adder, who was one of Philippos's senior commanders, but he was certainly descended from noble Macedonian stock. Finally, Lysimachos, another big kid, was a bit of an outsider himself because he was Thessalian, but his father was a great friend of Philippos's, which made Lysimachos almost accepted into the Macedonian clique of Alexandros, Hephaistion, Kassandros, Philotas, Nikanoros, and Attalos.

Running a little farther back were White Kleitos and Seleukos from Orestis, both 15. Then came a few more boys whose names I hadn't learned yet, followed by Leonnatos, also 15, from Lynkestis, Perdikkas, 16, from Orestis, and the local boy, Peukeotas. Finally, Kleitos and I were bringing up the rear, mostly because, after my fall, I decided to take it easy for a bit and Kleitos loyally hung back to make sure I was all right.

I was no longer enjoying the run quite as much. For one thing, there was an ugly gash on my right shin and my right ankle was rapidly growing to twice its normal size. Beyond that, it dawned on me that these boys were better conditioned than I was. *But I'll be damned if I'm going be a slave to anyone,* I thought, which was a funny thing to think, considering I'd been treated worse than a slave by everyone, with the possible exception of Philippos and Kleitos, ever since my 'rescue' from the quarry. But it did cause me to redouble my effort.

I started passing some of the boys. After another half hour of suicidal speed, I found myself running directly behind Alexandros and Hephaistion, entertaining thoughts of passing them both and becoming king for a day. But, as I drew abreast of Hephaistion, our eyes met and he gave me a little shake of the head. I decided not to pass them after all and settled back into third place.

By the time we reached the lake, I was beginning to fade. We had been running for almost an hour and I was ready for a break. When Alexandros veered toward a majestic oak right by the shore, I assumed we were going to sit in its shade, drink some of the water I'd been lugging, and catch our breaths. Instead, Alexandros, without slacking his pace, simply rounded the tree and started heading back to Mieza.

It's going be a long day. To think I'd spent several weeks in Pella doing everything in my power to secure an assignment to this post. After my epiphany – that passively awaiting my rescue was futile – I'd decided my chances of getting to Egypt in one piece and in time for the appearance of the escape hatch would be better if I could manage to ingratiate myself with Philippos, rather than trying to make my way in the teeth of his opposition. He'd already demonstrated an ability to track me down and Egypt was a long walk from Macedonia.

In addition, Egypt was controlled by Persia. At the moment, I was a "guest" of the Macedonian monarch who kept insisting to me – in all confidence, of course – that he was going to lead a great invasion of Persia one of these days. Tagging along with the expeditionary force and then defecting to the Persians once we got there seemed as good a way of progressing toward my goal of Egypt as any. And, knowing what I knew about King Philippos's future, it seemed a good idea also to insinuate myself into the good graces of his son and heir apparent, just in case it was Alexandros and not Philippos who ended up leading the invasion. In short, inexorable logic led directly to the conclusion that I ought to finagle a posting to Alexandros's boarding school in Mieza.

It was a balancing act, of course. I was as intent on avoiding any possible violation of the Prime Directive as ever but, at the same time, I was also determined to give fate a hand and make sure I was on the coast of Egypt, near the Nile delta, when 264 Z.E. rolled around. The only problem was dreaming up some plausible role that I could conceivably play in Mieza and then convincing Philippos to assign me to it.

It helped that Philippos seemed to like me, for reasons I couldn't quite fathom. Perhaps he found it reassuring that I was a total outsider. Although he couldn't determine from where I'd come, he was pretty sure I didn't belong to any clique at the court. That made me unique in a palace where wife intrigued against wife, commander plotted against commander, and diplomat maneuvered against diplomat.

Take the wives, as an example. Although Greeks in general believed in monogamy and had nothing but scorn for those barbarian potentates who married multiple wives, Philippos decided early in his reign that marriage was too useful as a diplomatic tool to be subjected to any arbitrary numerical limits. While ostensibly honoring Greek (and Macedonian) moral strictures by indulging in the pretense of being married to one woman at a time, he treated his ex-wives as his "honored guests," entitled to occasional conjugal visits for the remainder of their lives.

As he liked to explain: "As long as I have many enemies, at least some of whom can be turned into allies through the simple expedient of a marriage, why jeopardize the lives of thousands of soldiers on the battlefield if I can achieve the same objective simply by redoubling my own connubial efforts? And, by the same token, why waste all that feminine talent I have already acquired, just because my patriotic duty requires me to contract another marriage?"

He negotiated his first marriage in the aftermath of his first, and possibly most important, victory – the one over Bardylis, king of the Illyrians – which secured his hold on the Macedonian throne. As part of the armistice arrangements, Bardylis's daughter Audata became Philippos's first wife. It's a measure of how modest Philippos's aims were in those early days that, for a short time, he considered Audata his official queen, renamed her Eurydike (after his own mother), and labored mightily to sire an heir with her. Unfortunately, their only offspring was a daughter, Kynane. By the time she was born, other pressing matters of state intervened and Philippos moved on.

There was unrest among the nobles of Upper Macedonia and their loyalty to the king appeared shaky. Philippos therefore married Phila, the daughter of the leading family of Elimeia, the most important of the many fiefdoms in Upper Macedonia. However, she wasn't as attractive as the barbarian Audata and her relatives not as important in the greater scheme of things. Philippos never had a child with Phila but he never divorced her either. She was permitted to live out her life at court in chaste and contented obscurity.

Phila was followed almost immediately by Philinna of Larissa, presumably to keep the chieftains of Lower Macedonia happy. Philinna gave birth to a boy, Arrhidaios. Unfortunately, the boy turned out to be a half-wit but both mother and child were allowed to live in peace at the palace and the chieftains remained, for the most part, loyal to Philippos.

The next most immediate threat came from Epiros, the kingdom on the western border of Macedonia. Therefore, Philippos married Myrtale, a niece of the reigning king of Epiros. As with Audata, this was again a match simultaneously useful to Macedonia, from a diplomatic point of view, and stimulating to Philippos, from a concupiscent point of view. (When it came to his marriages, Philippos was a lucky man. He found, on several occasions, the requirements of state coinciding with his own preference for young, beautiful, intelligent, and sensuous women. Alas, these same women also tended to be headstrong, proud, and ruthless, but those were qualities that didn't manifest themselves to Philippos until after the honeymoon.) Myrtale displaced Audata, becoming the next official queen of Macedonia. She renamed herself Olympias and within the year gave birth to a son, whom they named Alexandros, after Philippos's older brother and short-lived predecessor on the throne. (Philippos's brother had been the second Alexandros to rule Macedonia and therefore known as Alexandros Deuteros. If Philippos's son ever became king, he would be known as Alexandros Tritos.)

Alexandros was Philippos's second son, after the half-wit Arrhidaios. From shortly after his birth, it became clear that Alexandros was the opposite of a half-wit. Thus, at a tender age, he was perceived by all as Philippos's heir apparent.

Philippos and Olympias had one more child together, a daughter born a year after Alexandros. They gave the child the venerable Macedonian name Kleopatra. Alexandros and Kleopatra were warm and loving siblings but their paths diverged drastically after they each reached puberty, reflecting the deeply ingrained misogyny of Macedonian society.

Having a viable heir apparent wasn't enough to induce Philippos to rest on his matrimonial laurels, much to Olympias's distress. Macedonia's alliance with its neighbors to the south, the Thessalians, required reinforcement with that special bond that only another marriage could supply. In came wife number five, Nikesipolis, niece of Iason of Pheron, ruler of Thessaly. Olympias, hearing reports of Nikesipolis's magical ability to cast spells over men, insisted on meeting this new rival. Surprisingly, the two women, who shared much in common – beyond a husband – including ambition, ability, and dazzling beauty, became friends and formed an improbable alliance at court. Of course, Olympias held the trump card, because she had a son, while Nikesipolis only had a daughter, Thessalonike. After Nikesipolis's unexpected, early death, Olympias raised Thessalonike as her own child.

Nikesipolis's premature death prevented the king from cleaving to her cleavage for long but, even though still in mourning, the marrying monarch marched on. To the east, controlling the territory between Macedonia and the Hellespont, lay numerous Thrakian tribes. Perforce, princess Meda of Odessa, daughter of King Kothelas of the Getai, the Thrakian tribe that controlled both banks of the Danube River, soon lay in Philippos's bed. How often the king lay in the bed with her is hard to tell, what with all his other obligations. The only thing that is certain is that Meda failed to produce an offspring.

After all these women, with their many demands, complaints, and quarrels, it was apparently a relief for Philippos to deal with me. I didn't ask for much, so when I asked to be sent to Mieza, Philippos gave in to my request. At least, that was my best guess for his decision, as I kept on running, struggling toward the finish line, trying to think about anything but the sweat pouring down my back, the burn in my thighs, the labored breathing scouring my windpipe, the oxygen debt getting ready to bankrupt my entire cardiovascular system.

I thought about Lanike. That was my one regret in leaving Pella. *You had to do it*, I told myself. *You can't permit yourself to get involved with anyone in this era.* On a rational level, it made sense to put some distance between Lanike and me but who ever thought rationally about attractive members of the opposite sex?

During the few short weeks of my stay in Pella, we had become friends. We spent hours talking. She told me about her family, about growing up in rural Macedonia, about life at court, about Alexandros as a little boy, about Dionysian mysteries, about her hopes for the future. I told her about my philosophy of life, about the vicissitudes of existence, about the role of random chance in the universe.

When she pressed me about my childhood, I changed the subject. When she asked me about my journey to Macedonia, I tried to distract her with a stolen kiss. When she asked me from where I'd come, I remembered Paloma and the Prime Directive and ran away from her, pleading another commitment.

It was an exquisite torture for both of us. She was eager to get to know me; I longed to confide in her; and we both yearned to progress beyond mere friendship. But I knew that any intimacy, with anyone living in this epoch, was precluded by the dictates of the Prime Directive. Our parting was filled with sadness, regret, and perhaps a touch of bitterness. We both knew that, even if I returned to the palace at some point, we would go out of our way to avoid each other. It was too perilous and frustrating to carry on a relationship doomed to wither on the vine.

Still deeply immersed in thought, I barely noticed that we'd run all the way back to the Temple of the Nymphs. I finished the race in third place, close on the heels of Alexandros and Hephaistion, and immediately collapsed to the ground. The boys, as they arrived one by one, looked at me contemptuously. They might've finished behind me and they might've been practically comatose but they weren't going to sit down. They stood around, joking and laughing and pretending they weren't in terrible pain.

"Hey Metoikos," Kassandros the Frog Killer yelled down to me. "Pretty pleased with yourself, aren't you? Beating a bunch of kids. Why don't you stand up and act like a man, instead of sprawling around like some kind of Persian satrap?"

I handed him one of my skins. "Here, have a sip of water, big boy."

The more aggressive among the boys, sensing an opportunity to improve their standing in the group, began to gather around us. "Did you just call him a boy?" Fast Philotas asked. "The mute moron speaks," was the insightful observation of Lysimachos the Bear. "What's he doing here anyway?" Nuts Nikanoros wanted to know. Kassandros, not wishing to lose the initiative, brought the repartee back on point. "Let's kick his ass."

I put the skins down and rose to my feet. I kept my hands dangling at my sides but my nose was only inches away from Kassandros's face. "Don't push me," I said quietly.

Kassandros continued to glare, while the other boys crowded in around us. "Fight, fight," a couple of them started to chant.

Alexandros stepped in and picked up one of the skins. "Time for a drink." After a good long swig, he passed it on to Hephaistion. Seleukos picked up the other skin. Taking advantage of the momentary disruption, I surged into the gap between Kassandros and Lysimachos, delivering a little shoulder shiver to the chest of each boy, and walked away. They chose not to follow.

By the time Leukonides rode in, just behind the last of the stragglers, things had settled down. The boys were standing in several small groups, chatting amiably. Kleitos and I were off to the side, watching.

"That was fine, boys," Leukonides said, "but tomorrow we'll try to work up a little sweat."

Before Leukonides could favor us with any further words of encouragement, a man draped in a sheet emerged from the modest temple in front of us. The contrast between the two couldn't have been more pronounced. Leukonides was past fifty but his muscles rippled every time he moved. He wore a coarse, stained, and torn tunic, stretched taut across his broad shoulders and powerful chest, but flapping loosely over his flat belly. His graying hair was short and unkempt and his beard haphazardly hacked. His stride was as energetic as his speech was laconic.

The other man looked to be about forty. He was tall, thin, and soft. His pristine white linen robe, pinned over one shoulder and tied at the waist, cascaded down his body in careful drapes and folds. The fabric, conspicuously luxurious and expensive, failed to conceal his incipient paunch. Numerous rings adorned the fingers of both hands. He was easily the flashiest dresser I'd seen since my arrival. In fact, he made me look like a native Macedonian by comparison.

His thinning hair was carefully trimmed, curled, scented, and combed forward, in an attempt to conceal his encroaching baldness. The eyes, although small and closely set, were unflinching and penetrating. His beard, which still retained some of its original auburn sheen, was a masterpiece of the barber's art but it was the tall, heavily lined forehead that dominated his agile and expressive face. To my mind, there was an aspect of kindness in the wrinkles of his face but I already realized that such a mien might come across as weakness in these parts.

He spoke in a high-pitched, effeminate voice, with a trace of a lisp, and he spoke a great deal. Yet everything he said sounded sensible, occasionally even profound. He had an inexhaustible store of knowledge about any subject that might come up and his ability to absorb, internalize, interpret, and classify information was dazzlingly fast and invariably accurate. The muscles on this man were all inside his head.

When he noticed me standing at the periphery, he ambled over. "Ah, young man, you must be my new specimen."

"Ptolemaios." I extended my hand.

He was startled at first by my unexpected gesture. Clasping of hands was evidently not customary around here. But he adjusted quickly, taking my hand in both of his, turning it palm up, and examining it closely. "You haven't made your way through life by physical labor, or

140

even by wielding weapons of war, have you? But it does look like you've been abusing your hands quite a bit lately."

Letting go of my hand, he thanked me for letting him take a look. "My name is Aristoteles. Please join us for our next discussion."

He stepped up to a narrow stone bench on which a small but intense fire was burning. "All right men, let's get started. Who will pronounce the invocation?"

The only person to move was Alexandros. He reached into a box next to the bench, grabbed a handful of incense, and cast it into the fire, causing it to blaze brilliantly and aromatically for a few moments.

"Whoa," Leukonides called out from the back. "Did you boys sack a spice-bearing caravan while I was asleep or are you just wasting expensive myrrh?"

Alexandros turned crimson. "You shouldn't stint the gods," he muttered. Hearing no response, he proceeded with the ritual prayer, intoning each phrase as if it actually meant something. The rest of the boys stood around paying no attention whatsoever.

At the end of the invocation, Aristoteles reasserted his control. "Let's get started. Who can tell me our topic for today?"

I'd expected a classroom filled with desks and chairs, I suppose. There was no classroom, there were no desks, and there were no chairs. We strolled the temple grounds instead, with Aristoteles in the front, and the rest of us forming an ever-shifting swarm around him. But his high-pitched voice carried well. It was easy to hear him and relatively easy to follow the thrust of his argument.

"Who can tell me what arete means?" Aristotle asked.

"It means excellence," one of the boys replied.

"No, it's virtue," said another.

"Well, which is it?"

"It means both."

"Excellence in what?"

"Excellence in war."

"Can you achieve arete in a time of peace?"

"Only in the sense of doing a good job preparing to become a warrior." This from Alexandros.

"Can someone who never fights in a war ever achieve arete?"

"No ... never ... not too likely," several of the boys called out.

"But isn't there a little more to it than just being a good fighter?"

Silence.

"Look at Achilleus," Aristoteles continued. "Was he a good fighter?"

"Absolutely."

"Did he honor his father and mother? His ancestors? The gods? Yes, he did. Was that part of what made him great?"

"Definitely."

"So, is there more to arete than just prowess on the battlefield?"

"I guess so."

"Wasn't he also loyal to his friends? Is loyalty a virtue?"

"Sure."

"Was he a good musician?"

"Beyond a doubt."

"Is that one of the things that made him virtuous?"

"Yes."

"Was he good at athletic contests?"

"The best."

"Is that part of arete?"

"Sure."

"Was he good at controlling his temper?"

The boys laughed. "No, he raged all the time."

"Was his tendency to rage part of his virtue?"

"Definitely," said Alexandros. "It was his fury in battle that made him such a great warrior."

"But wasn't he outraged when Agamemnon stole Briseis from him?"

"Sure."

"And what did he do as a result?"

"Nothing. He just sat there refusing to fight."

"And what happened to the Achaioi as a result?"

"They lost several battles and many men."

"When Achilleus saw that the Achaioi were in danger of losing the war because of his refusal to fight, did he control his rage and rejoin the fight?"

"No, he didn't."

"So what happened?"

"His best friend Patroklos stole his armor and went into battle pretending to be Achilleus."

"And did that work?"

"For a while, but then Hektor killed Patroklos."

"So, you could say that Achilleus's rage caused the deaths of many Achaian warriors, including the death of his best friend. Do you still think, Alexandros, that rage was one of the things that made him a great warrior?"

"When you fight, you have to be outraged, but the rest of the time, you've got to control your temper."

"But to be effective in battle, don't you have to keep a cool head? Remember all the things you learned in training? Put them into effect in the heat of battle? Carefully control and calibrate your movements, weigh your tactics?"

"Yeah."

"And doesn't being outraged interfere with your ability to do all that?"

Silence.

"So, can we agree that Achilleus was not a virtuous warrior?"

"No, we can't!" Alexandros was vehement. "He was the greatest warrior of all time."

"But he was prone to paroxysms of passion. Surely, that was a liability for a warrior and not an asset."

"Maybe," Alexandros conceded.

"Maybe there is more to arete than simply a list of virtues that a person possesses. Maybe you have to take into account the person's vices and shortcomings as well. Maybe it also matters what the person's motives and objectives are."

"What do you mean?" one of the boys asked.

"It matters what the person is trying to accomplish in life, doesn't it?"

"Like what?"

"Well, what are you trying to achieve in life?"

"I want to be happy," the boy said.

"Is that all?" Alexandros scoffed.

"What do you want to achieve, Alexandros?" Aristoteles asked.

"I want to be immortal."

"That, alas, is not an option available to us humans."

"Achilleus is immortal."

"But he died, didn't he? When Paris shot him in his heel?"

"Well, his body may have died but his name's lived on."

"Would you rather be famous or lead a happy life?"

"How could I be happy if I didn't achieve fame?"

Aristoteles shook his head. "Let me ask you a different question, Alexandros. Do you believe we are all born with certain talents and capabilities?"

"Sure."

"And some people are born with greater talents and capabilities than others, right?"

"Obviously."

"So, take two men: One has all the talent in the world but mostly squanders it. However, because he's of good birth and he's lucky and he does after all have a great deal of talent, he ends up living on a sizeable estate in the country, with a large family and many servants, leading a quiet but happy life. The other man is not particularly gifted in any way but he's extremely ambitious, hard-driving, and determined. He makes the maximum use of the limited talents with which he was born. He still ends up as a poor potter, living with his wife and two children in a small house that is his workshop, store, and living quarters, all in one, but he's come much closer to fulfilling his potential than his rich and slothful cousin in the country. Which of these two men is more admirable?"

"The man who makes the greatest use of his talents."

"Would you say that living up to one's potential is part of arete?"

"Sure."

"So, to determine whether someone is an admirable person, it is not enough to look at what he has accomplished. We have to look at his shortcomings and vices. We have to know what his goals in life were. We also have to know the circumstances from which he started, the talents and capabilities with which he was born, the opportunities that were afforded to him, and the use that he made of these talents and opportunities, right?"

"I see what you're getting at."

"So, let me ask you again. What does arete mean?"

"Living up to your potential," one of the boys said.

"And I guess that's as good an answer as we're going to get today," Aristoteles concluded.

I hadn't even noticed that we'd completed our circuit and were once again standing in front of the temple.

"Go have your dinner boys. Tomorrow we'll talk about justice."

The next morning, I was awakened by a sharp kick to the ribs.

"Time to wake up, dickhead," Kassandros the Frog Killer was saying.

I rolled over to my hands and knees. The pain in my chest was subsiding gradually but I was still finding it hard to catch my breath. I looked up at the tall, skinny youngster. He looked sturdier than he actually was in the semi-darkness of the arriving dawn. Maybe it was the armor he was wearing – a metal breastplate, leather skirt, greaves, studded sandals. There was some kind of cudgel in his right hand; definitely not a sword. Otherwise, he was unarmed.

I caught a movement out of the corner of my eye: Two more boys circling behind me, Philotas and

Nikanoros, holding sticks. Three more boys arriving from my right. Improvised weapons in every other hand.

Finally, I caught my breath. It must have taken a second or two. Sufficient time for the Frog Killer to kick me again.

I used the momentum of his kick to shift my weight from my knees to the balls of my feet, ending in a coiled crouch. Then I launched myself with all the power I could muster at Kassandros, hitting him flush on the hips with my shoulder.

The impact lifted him off his feet. When he returned to earth, he landed on his back, with a satisfying thud. I landed on top of him but pushed myself to my feet before he could hit me with his stick. Instead, I felt a solid blow across my temple from one of the others.

I whirled and struck Philotas in his Adam's apple with the edge of my hand. He crumbled to the ground, gasping, while I snatched the club from his grasp. For a beat, the rest of the boys simply stood there, gaping. Then, as if on a signal, they all converged on me simultaneously, swinging their truncheons and snapping their whips. Fortunately for me, they closed in too tightly, not leaving enough room to deploy their weapons effectively.

I sidestepped one swinging stick by moving my head an inch while parrying another thrust with the club I was now holding. The tip of a lash whistled overhead, striking one of the attackers instead of me. The snapper and the snapped were soon embroiled in a peripheral fight of their own.

In the meantime, I slipped through a gap between two onrushing boys. For a moment, they all stood in a circle staring at one another, flummoxed by my sudden disappearance. I pounded the nearest boy on the head, putting him down for the count, but the rest of them turned and attacked again.

This time, I feigned a left jab at the head of the boy directly in front of me, while kicking him in the groin. He sank to the ground, grabbing the nearest boy by the ankle. When that boy looked down, I kneed him in the mouth, causing him to topple backward on top of the first boy, who was still clutching his leg.

The flow of time slowed to a crawl. I saw distinctly the knotted tip of a lash make its way laboriously through the air toward my head. With plenty of time to spare, I grabbed the coarse rope with my left hand and snatched the whip out of the fist of the boy wielding it. Then, grabbing the handle sailing through the air, I snapped the lash across the shoulders of its prior owner, paralyzing him into inaction.

At this point, I was holding a truncheon in my right hand and a whip in my left. Believing that I was better served fighting with my bare hands, I tossed my weapons at the heads of a couple of onrushing boys, then pirouetted to face the boys behind me, who immediately backed away. *This is a lot easier than our martial arts training ever was.* I decided to really show off by hitting one of the boys with a flying kick to the face. My feet struck him flush on the jaw, rendering him hors de combat, while I gently floated back to the ground.

Lying supine, I executed a kip that even my gymnastically inclined friends at the Academy might have envied. With my hands pushing off against the ground, my back arched, and kicking my feet energetically, I snapped myself back to a standing position, ready to fight again, to the general amazement of all present. A couple of boys smiled and nodded appreciatively. I smiled backed and winked. In the meantime, some spoil-sport, missing out on all this by-play, conked me on the head from behind. Although my knees buckled a bit, I spun and delivered a two-handed smash to the bridge of his nose, knocking him out. There were no further attackers able, or willing, to continue. The fight was over.

And that's how I finally gained my assignment. I became the hand-to-hand combat instructor at Mieza. And the boys who fought me? Well, none of us had any inkling of the adventures fate had in store for them.

Chapter 6 – Chaironeia

Why didn't they just run away? As I surveyed the tight-knit clusters of corpses, I was struck by the remarkable cohesion of the Sacred Band. They had died as they had fought – side by side, shoulder to shoulder, shield to shield. Of the three hundred men in the battalion, two hundred and fifty-four died, forty-six lay grievously wounded, and zero men deserted. For our part, none of the horsemen in the Companion Cavalry squadrons had deserted either. But then, on this day, we had fought on the winning side and suffered very few casualties.

Five years had elapsed since my arrival in Macedonia. I'd spent the first three years in Mieza, trying desperately to balance the imperatives of the Prime Directive against the need to become a part of, and fit into, this brave old world in which I'd found myself and from which I might not be able to escape for a good many years. I befriended some people, won the respect of others, and made enemies among a few. It remained unclear to which of those camps Alexandros belonged.

When Alexandros had reached the age of sixteen, his father had decided to end the halcyon days of learning, training, and bonding at Aristoteles's version of Platon's Akademia. It was time for the next stage in Alexandros's preparations for his eventual accession to the throne. That year, 246 Z.E., Philippos was ready to launch yet another campaign in Thrake. Before leaving, he named Alexandros regent and told him he was responsible for protecting the home front while Philippos and the army were away, fighting one of the many proxy skirmishes in the ongoing conflict between Macedonia and Athens. Of course, Philippos left sufficient forces behind to safeguard the homeland and, more importantly, he left senior officers behind, led by Antipatros, to make sure the young regent didn't get himself into too much trouble. Nevertheless, the fact remained that Alexandros was nominally in charge in Pella while his father was away in Thrake.

Alexandros acclimated himself to his new role rather quickly. No sooner had Philippos left town than a report arrived from the northern frontier that one of the more intractable neighboring tribes had revolted. Alexandros duly forwarded the report to his father but he didn't wait for a response before acting. After all, it might take a couple of weeks for a messenger to make the round trip to the king and back, more than enough time for Alexandros to clean up the situation himself.

Deploying the home guard left under his command, Alexandros made a flying excursion to the northern border, subdued the rebels, sacked their principal city, turned it into a Macedonian outpost, and was back in Pella in time to receive his father's instructions to do nothing for now.

He responded to the message the day it arrived, reporting to his father that, unfortunately, by the time the instructions were received, the rebellion had been crushed. On the other hand, he assured his father he'd followed his example in every particular, including naming the newly established Macedonian outpost Alexandropolis. Of course, Philippos was a lot older than sixteen, and actually a king, before he had founded Philippopolis. Alexandros was showing early signs of decisiveness, speed of execution, ruthless efficiency, and a gift for self-promotion and propaganda.

****

Lanike and I lived in close proximity for two years. I'd returned to Pella after my three-year stint in Mieza and she'd never left. After relinquishing her responsibilities as Alexandros's personal servant, she simply started back at the bottom as an ordinary chambermaid and once again worked her way up. We were each acutely aware of the other's presence in Pella. When I returned from Mieza, I was twenty-four and she was twenty-two and we were both still unattached. For a young woman to remain unmarried at the age of twenty-two was a sure sign of some grave physical defect or irredeemable imbecility. Lanike suffered from neither condition and yet, here she was, wholly dedicated to her service in the palace, while I remained completely committed to getting back to my own time and place. As a result, we studiously avoided each other – until the day we literally bumped into each other just outside the palace walls.

She was carrying a heavy hydria from the communal fountain. I was striding briskly from the main gate of the palace to the barracks, my eyes on the ground and my mind in the clouds. She must've seen me approaching but didn't utter a sound. She also may have moved out of my way in order to avoid a collision but, if so, she didn't move far enough. My hip grazed against hers, which was all it took. Although she was steadying the hydria on her head with a hand on one of the handles, our slight contact was sufficient to unbalance her and start the vessel on its inexorable trajectory to the ground. She tried to grab the other handle with her free hand but it was too late. She did manage to arrest the fall long enough to spill most of the water from the hydria all over my clothes but couldn't stop the jar from hitting the ground. Miraculously, the pottery vessel didn't shatter upon impact, perhaps because the path had been softened by recent rains or perhaps because the walls of the hydria were quite thick or, most likely, because she was agile enough to dissipate the hydria's momentum before touchdown.

"You're all wet," she observed, laughing. Then, seeing the consternation on my face, she quickly added,

"I'm so sorry about the water. But I'm glad to see you're looking well, aside from being drenched, that is."

"It'll dry out quickly enough," I assured her, "especially if I continue to stand here in the warmth of your presence." Then I recalled the Prime Directive. "Shouldn't we refill your jug before they start wondering what's happened to you?"

"Or even worse, begin to suspect I stopped to speak to a man."

"Why are you out here anyway? Isn't this the job for a junior servant?"

"The great thing about being in charge," Lanike laughed, "is that you get to do everybody's job. If somebody is sick or absent without explanation, guess who's ultimately responsible for all the chores getting done on time. Speaking of which, I suppose you're right. I'd better go and refill this jug."

"Let me help you with that. After all, it's my fault you spilled the first load."

"No, it's my fault. And besides, shouldn't you be getting a dry tunic before you catch a cold?"

We bickered playfully as we walked back to the fountain and refilled the hydria. Then we fought for the honor of lugging it back. It turned out I was really bad at carrying a heavy jug on my head, even when holding both handles for better balance. After amusing Lanike no end, I let her carry it the rest of the way.

"Wait here," she instructed me when we reached the staircase leading to the women's quarter. "I'll be back in a minute with some dry clothes."

She came back carrying not only a dry tunic, which unfortunately was clearly meant for a woman but also some fabric to use as a towel. "Let's duck into the dining room and get you changed. Nobody's going to be there at this hour of the day."

The dining room was indeed deserted and quite dim, once we closed the doors. Lanike removed my tunic and dried my hair, face, and torso with her towel. With her eyes focused on the task, she continued wipe my chest long after it was dry. Soon enough, I was forced to turn my back to her to conceal my rising embarrassment. Without missing a beat, she continued to caress my back.

"Better give me that dry tunic," I said. "Someone might come in."

After she pulled it over my head, I hurriedly took a seat on one of the couches, hoping that the dim light and my crouched postured would be enough to conceal my true feelings about her.

She sat down next to me, careful to leave sufficient space between us to preserve some vestige of decorum. "Have you been trying to avoid me since you got back?"

I was tempted to deny it but then just shrugged. How could I explain the conflict raging within me? "I've longed for you since the day I first saw you," I finally said. "But now you'd better run, before somebody catches us. Meet me in the armory during the second watch tonight, so I can return your tunic to you."

She nodded and left without a further word. After that, we stopped avoiding each other.

****

Although I wasn't there when Philippos received his son's report about the crushing of the revolt by the northern tribes and the founding of Alexandropolis, I suspected his reaction was a mixture of paternal pride and cagey concern about a nascent royal rivalry. Not that Philippos had a lot of time to contemplate the ramifications of his offspring's precocity. The proxy war against Athens was heating up.

Ever since Philippos had arrogated the Macedonian throne, some twenty-one years earlier, he'd been attracting the attention of the Athenians. It was a complicated relationship.

On the one hand, there was an ongoing, slow-motion collision between the expanding sphere of influence of Macedonia and the remnants of the Athenian empire on the southern coast of Thrake and the shores of the Black Sea. Philippos's aggressive, expansionist policies were undermining Athens's traditional relationships with its allies and threatening the vital shipping lanes between Athens and the Black Sea, through which Athens obtained much of its grain. Athens attempted to maintain its control by diplomacy, if possible, and by armed force, if necessary. Unfortunately, diplomacy failed on a regular basis, resulting in an endless series of military engagements between Macedonia and Athens. These conflicts were fought mostly by Athenian surrogates and mercenaries and it was the Athenian allies who bore the brunt of the losses; nevertheless, the average Athenian wasted little affection on King Philippos of Macedonia.

On the other hand, there was also a mutual attraction between the leading lights of Athens and the reigning monarch of Macedonia that appeared counterintuitive at first. For his part, Philippos genuinely admired Athens, and especially the legacy of Athens, no matter how much trouble the current version of the city-state was causing him. Some Athenians, for their part, also felt a reluctant tug in the direction of the uncouth upstart up north, which came about as follows:

The greatest days of Athens lay behind it, those heady decades after the twin victories at Marathon and

Salamis, when Athens was the unquestioned military, religious, cultural, and intellectual leader of the Greek-speaking world. Sparta had never accepted the preeminence of Athens and the rivalry between the two cities eventually resulted in the epic thirty-year struggle known to subsequent historians as the Peloponnesian War. Neither Athens nor Sparta ever fully recovered from the devastation of that fratricidal conflict. With the military power of Athens and Sparta waning, other cities rose to prominence, Thebes foremost among them. But no Greek city ever recaptured the glory that had been Athens.

Despite the self-evident ebb tide in the fortunes of Athens, no right-thinking Athenian was willing to accept the gradual, but inevitable and irreversible, decline of their beloved city. The question debated endlessly in the Athenian Assembly, in the Athenian agora, and during countless symposia held in Athenian private homes, was not the best way forward given the reality of current circumstances but, rather, the best means of recapturing the greatness that had been lost. And the most frequent answer, which kept occurring to the symposiasts, especially after liberal consumption of wine had sufficiently lubricated their tongues and dulled their faculties, was the need for another glorious military campaign against Persia, led by Athens, of course, resulting in the liberation of all Greeks currently suffering under the Persian yoke, the restoration of the Athenian empire, and the long-overdue retribution for the sack of Athens by Xerxes in 106 Z.E.

All of these discussions ignored the reality that the hegemony of Persia was unassailable. Among other factors, Persia's potential military, financial, human, and material resources exceeded the combined resources of all the Greek cities in the aggregate. Beyond that, there was no chance the Greek cities would combine their efforts and resources in a joint venture against the Persian Empire. Never mind the age-old hostilities, rivalries, and incessant internecine wars among the Greek cities. The Greek cities would never combine in a war against Persia because Persia directly controlled all of the Greek cities on the Aegean coast of Anatolia and because it indirectly controlled the external policy decisions of most of the remaining Greek cities, through treaty obligations, commercial ties, diplomatic pressures, and the outright bribing of kings, tyrants, oligarchs, and leading politicians. And nowhere were there more politicians and public officials on the Persian payroll than in Athens.

But the inebriates at the symposia and the hagglers in the agora and the demagogues amidst the Assembly were not detained by these pesky details. Instead, they focused on the one missing ingredient – the need to find a leader to organize and command such an expedition. An Athenian gadfly named Isokrates spent a good portion of a long life trying to identify and then enlist one likely candidate after another. After exhausting the list of Athenian possibilities without success, he turned to Archidamos Tritos, the bellicose king of Sparta. Although this formidable commander seldom passed on an opportunity for military adventure, he managed to turn down the little Athenian's appeal. Isokrates next turned to the Syracusan tyrant Dionysos Deuteros, whom Platon himself had tried, but failed, to turn into a philosopher-king. Having had his fill of Athenian thinkers, Dionysos also declined Isokrates's entreaties.

Finally, having approached every possible candidate in the entire Hellenic world, without the slightest success, Isokrates eventually hit upon the idea of nominating Philippos, the young but rising monarch of Macedonia, to lead the sacred, pan-Hellenic expedition against the Persian Empire and incidentally to restore Athens to her former grandeur in the process. Perhaps to Isokrates's surprise, the shrewd and ambitious Philippos was quite receptive to the idea. The thrilled Isokrates set to work trying to persuade his fellow Athenians to accept the king of Macedonia as the commander of what was to be essentially an Athenian war against Persia.

Isokrates, while quite naive, was nevertheless an energetic speaker, proselytizer, and pamphleteer. He succeeded in persuading a number of his fellow Athenians to become Philippos's proponents. Philippos, for his part, was sufficiently adroit and cynical to use Isokrates for his own purposes. He had conceived a plan for a Macedonian invasion of Persia long before Isokrates had approached him with the notion of a pan-Hellenic expedition. If Isokrates and his ilk could obtain the cooperation of the Greek cities in this endeavor, all the better. If they could simply keep the Greek cities from invading Macedonia while Philippos was away fighting in Persia, that alone was of some strategic value. In short, there developed a warm, albeit short-lived, dalliance between Philippos and a faction of Athenian thought leaders.

There were other Athenian demagogues, however, who saw Philippos more clearly than Isokrates and his followers. One of the first to recognize the threat that Philippos posed to the freedom and independence of Athens was an agitator named Demosthenes. He worked tirelessly to squelch the budding love affair between Athens and King Philippos of Macedonia.

By 248 Z.E., when Philippos was forty-four and Alexandros eighteen, the brilliant military and diplomatic house of cards that Philippos had assembled was beginning to totter. Partly, he was the victim of his own success. When one pack of wolves begins to dominate and expand its territory, there is a natural tendency among the remaining packs to coalesce in opposition to the preeminent power. By this point, Philippos had built the finest military machine this side of the Hellespont. He had been named leader of the Amphiktyonic League and defender of Apollon's oracle at Delphi. He was called in to mediate disputes among contenders for government leadership of Greek cities and to check aggressors threatening weaker neighbors. His country served as the bulwark against barbarian invasions. He controlled and exploited the most abundant gold and silver mines in

Prime Directive

Greece and some of the most productive forests and fertile agricultural resources of Thrake. He dominated trade routes and sea lanes. His horses won at the Olympic Games. And, most importantly, he had managed, with varying degrees of success, to make allies of the remaining powers in Greece – Athens, Sparta, Thebes, Korinthos, Megara, and all the rest. But his incredible run of successes was beginning to show some chinks.

The year before, he had besieged two cities in Thrake, Perinthos and Byzantion, which controlled his expected invasion route across the Hellespont. Incredibly, despite his vaunted military might, both sieges had failed, thanks mainly to the fact that both his targets were seaports and both continued to receive supplies by ship from Athens throughout the sieges. Even worse, Philippos's navy, such as it was, was powerless to stop the Athenian resupply operations, highlighting the continued superiority of the Athenian navy. And worst of all, on the way home from the unsuccessful sieges, Philippos's army was ambushed by one of the primitive, ferocious tribes from north of the Danube. Philippos managed to extricate his forces with relatively few casualties but all the booty they had managed to accumulate during the expedition was lost and, to add injury to the insult, an errant enemy spear found its way into Philippos's right thigh, leaving him with a nasty scar and a permanent limp.

On the diplomatic front, and perhaps not entirely by coincidence, some of the many balls Philippos had managed to keep in the air simultaneously were beginning to hit the ground. The Athenians had in effect waged war against Macedonia at Perinthos and Byzantion. The Boiotian League, led by Thebes and nominally allied with Macedonia, expelled a Macedonian garrison from the strategically important strongpoint of Nikaia, just to the south of Thermopylai. The Amphiktyonic League, acting at Philippos's behest, declared war against Amphissa for an act of sacrilege and the Boiotian League promptly came to the assistance of Amphissa.[9]

Philippos greatest fear was an alliance between Athens and Thebes, thus uniting Attika and Boiotia against Macedonia. Yet, that's precisely what happened at this point. When the Macedonian army marched south, ostensibly to enforce the dictates of the Amphiktyonic League against Amphissa, it found itself opposed by the combined land forces of Thebes and Athens. Thebes was acting contrary to its explicit treaty obligations with Macedonia. Athens was probably acting contrary to its own strategic interests but had been whipped into a patriotic frenzy by Demosthenes who saw an opportunity finally to check the uncouth upstart from up north.

Philippos tried one more time to employ diplomacy, rather than military force. He sent envoys to both Athens and Thebes, asking each to assist him in the campaign against Amphissa or at least to allow him free

---

[9] See Map 2 at AlexanderGeiger.com for some of the locations discussed in this chapter.

passage and maintain neutrality. Both Athens and Thebes declined Philippos's request and joined forces against him instead. Korinthos joined the new coalition, as did Achaia, Megara, Akarnania, Euboia, and a few others. The coalition also retained the services of a substantial number of mercenaries.

Philippos didn't entertain any illusions about the reception likely to be accorded to his emissaries. While they were negotiating, his army was marching. Before the new anti-Macedonia coalition could act, Philippos's army had crossed Thermopylai and recaptured Nikaia. However, instead of continuing on toward Amphissa, Philippos then turned east and invaded Elatia, threatening both Boiotia and Attika. The Athenians, now in a genuine panic, hesitated no longer. Ten thousand Athenian hoplites marched out of the city, amid tumultuous cheering from the old men, children, and non-citizens whom they were leaving behind. Their wives and mothers were noticeably less ebullient in their celebrations. The Athenians were soon joined in the field by contingents of Boiotians, other allies, and mercenaries.

The coalition forces successfully occupied all of the passes into Boiotia and Attika, thus blocking Philippos's possible routes of attack. Philippos was undaunted. Finding his route stymied, he ordered his army to turn around and start marching – ever so slowly – back toward Macedonia. He also arranged for a secret dispatch to be captured by the enemy. According to this spurious message, a rebellion had broken out in Thrake and the Macedonian army had been ordered to return home with all possible haste.

There was rejoicing in the Athenian Assembly that night. Demosthenes was awarded a gold crown for his services to the city. Unfortunately, the Athenians had failed to take into account Philippos's cunning.

The next night, while the mercenaries guarding the Gravia Pass were sleeping off their celebrations, the Macedonian army returned – unobserved – and attacked under cover of darkness. They easily dislodged the sleeping and drunken mercenaries from the pass. By the next morning, the entire Macedonian army was pouring into the Kephisos River valley.

The coalition commanders had little choice but to abandon the passes which they had occupied previously and to consolidate their forces in the valley, near the small village of Chaironeia. Although outwitted by Philippos, the coalition still enjoyed superior numbers and occupied a highly defensible position. Philippos once again dispatched negotiators to urge an end to hostilities and to invite coalition forces to join the Macedonian army in a pan-Hellenic expedition against Persia instead. These last-ditch overtures were once again summarily dismissed and the opposing armies made preparation for what, as everyone realized, would be the battle to decide the future course of Greece.

****

Prime Directive

The night before the battle, Philippos assembled his commanders. Thirty or so men crowded into the king's small, plain tent. For reasons I couldn't quite fathom, I was one of those invited to attend. I made sure to stay out of the way, my shoulders pressed against the back flap of the tent.

In the center of the tent, floating in a puddle of light, was a small table, covered in its entirety by a crude map of the prospective battlefield. On the map were several colored wooden counters. There were also some writing implements and pointing sticks scattered about. Standing behind the map was Philippos, flanked by his two senior commanders, Parmenion and Antipatros. Attalos the Adder was hovering just behind their backs.

Parmenion, at sixty-two, was the oldest man in the tent. A dapper little man, with a neatly-trimmed beard, soft face, hard eyes, a surprisingly straight back, and an air of authority about him, he was Macedonia's most experienced and successful military commander.

Antipatros, fifty-nine, looked completely different – tall, bearded, aristocratic – but was just as tough as, and possibly even shrewder than, Parmenion. He was Philippos's foremost diplomat and had served on several occasions as Macedonia's regent in Philippos's absence.

Attalos, fifty-two, was not nearly as accomplished a field commander as the other two but exceeded them both in ambition and sycophantism.

Philippos himself, at forty-four, looked almost as old as his senior commanders. He was stooped under the weight of responsibility, his face creased with concentration, his empty right eye socket encrusted with a yellowish discharge, the massive new scar on his right thigh a livid maroon in the shadowy light of the tent. Yet, he seemed strangely serene.

Standing across the table were two men of roughly the same age as Philippos, Antigonos (he still had both his eyes back then) and Aeropos of Lynkestis (who had not yet been banished), two men of limited military accomplishments as yet but outsized egos.

Finally, standing at the head of the table, even though the table was square, and looking absurdly young at eighteen years of age, was Alexandros. Somehow, he managed to give the impression of actually belonging at the forefront of the discussion. No one stood across the table from him.

Arrayed in loose and shifting chevron patterns behind each of these leaders were their respective aides and adjutants. The group behind Alexandros included his clique from Mieza – Hephaistion, Perdikkas, Philotas, Nikanoros, Kassandros, Squeaky Attalos, Lysimachos, Seleukos, and a few others – all looking like children who wandered into a grown-up party by mistake. Kleitos and I were standing at the back of this group.

Prime Directive

Philippos was moving counters on his map, chatting with Parmenion and Antipatros in a voice too quiet for me to hear. Finally, he was ready to start the briefing. "Well, men, Antipatros has just returned from his talks with the Athenians and Thebans. He's lucky they let him go. There'll be no peace between us. We fight at dawn."

"Bring 'em on!" somebody shouted.

Philippos looked up with a rueful smile. "There're an awful lot of them out there, you know, and they're holding a position that's going to be tough to turn. Parmenion, why don't you give us their dispositions."

Parmenion picked up one of the sticks and started to point to some of the counters. "These blue blocks are the Boiotians; the purple ones are the Athenians; the yellow are mercenaries. These round ones are cavalry and the little sticks are light arms and auxiliaries. It's clear from their numbers and from where they're camping tonight that they'll line up across the entire plain tomorrow, from the Kephisos River on the right to the Chaironeia akropolis on the left." He pointed to the neat row of blocks stretching all the way across the width of the map. "Yes, they have enough troops to block the entire valley." He paused to let the import sink in.

"According to our spies, there are 12,000 Boiotian hoplites, led by the Thebans, all heavily armed. They're camped near the Kephisos River and our guess is, that's

171

where they'll line up tomorrow, holding the right end of the front. My assumption is that their best company, the Sacred Band, will anchor the line, flush against the river.

"The Athenians are camped beneath the akropolis. They'll be manning the left end of the front, extending from the akropolis to about here." He pointed to a row of purple blocks covering the left third of the enemy line. "There are 10,000 Athenian citizen hoplites ready and eager to fight.

"In the middle will be the mercenaries, maybe another 10,000 heavily armed foot soldiers, right over here, plus another 8,000 hoplites provided by their allies. All told, we'll be facing about 40,000 heavies."

I was staggered by these numbers. It was dawning on me that the size of the army arrayed against us was bigger than the population of any city in the Greek world. This was going to be a big battle.

Parmenion, in the meantime, continued his enumeration of the enemy forces. "They've got a few thousand light troops in addition and I suspect they'll use those to shield their front just before the two lines engage, per standard practice, but I doubt those troops will play a major role once the battle starts in earnest. Still, we'll have to account for them.

"And finally, there is the cavalry. They're the wild card. There are more than 4,000 of them and, because they're cavalry, they're liable to show up anywhere on the battlefield."

"They're not as good as us," Alexandros interrupted.

"That's true," Philippos agreed, "but we've got a special job reserved for our horseboys. But why don't we let Parmenion finish first?"

"Yes, let's talk about our side of the battlefield," Parmenion resumed. "We have 30,000 heavy infantry, 2,000 cavalry, and no auxiliaries to speak of. So, they've got us outnumbered."

"Yeah, but we're Macedonians," somebody said.

"True enough," Parmenion continued, "but numbers matter. The weight of the files behind the front rank matters. There's no doubt our troops are tougher, better trained, more experienced, and better equipped than most of their troops but let's not be overly confident. Let's remember that the Thebans haven't lost a battle in thirty years. They're the army that broke the hegemony of Sparta. And the Sacred Band, although numbering only 300 men, is the cream of that army. The Sacred Band will be anchoring their line. If we can't dislodge them, it'll be tough to rout the rest of the enemy."

The tent was silent.

Hearing on objections, Parmenion continued. "The reason we're here tonight is so we have a plan for tomorrow. Without a plan, I don't think we can beat them. On the other hand, our king has come up with a superb plan and if we each do our job tomorrow, then we can't lose."

"What's the plan?" a voice from the back called out. "Let's get on with it," another one added.

"I'm almost there." Parmenion, undeterred from his patient exposition, smiled patiently. "One last thing that we need to consider is the ground itself. As you know, every commander wants to fight on good ground. Unfortunately, you don't always get what you want."

"In this case, they picked the ground," Philippos interjected, "but we helped steer them into the right location." He gave us a wink with his empty eye socket.

Parmenion resumed. "We'll be fighting on level ground, which doesn't favor anybody. That's actually a point for us because they could've chosen ground a little farther back, over here, and come down at us from the foothills of the mountains behind them. But I guess they're traditionalists and so they like to fight on level ground.

"Aside from that, however, they did choose pretty wisely. As our king already mentioned, we can't turn their flank on either side of their line. At the right end, they're flush against the river; on the left end, they're flush against the Chaironeia akropolis. So, we're not getting around them."

"We'll just go through them," somebody yelled, to appreciative laughter all around.

Parmenion didn't join in the merriment. "Those of you who've been through a few of these know very well that it's impossible to break through a disciplined line of hoplites, especially when they have adequate numbers to line up at least eight men deep across the entire field of battle. And as I just told you, they've got more than enough heavies to do just that tomorrow.

"Anyway, even if we managed to push them back, they'd just retreat in an orderly manner through the Kerata Pass, which happens to be right behind their backs, and then where would we be?"

"We didn't come here to push them back," Philippos said. "We came here to destroy them, once and for all."

He had clearly lost patience with Parmenion's systematic exposition. "Here is what we'll do tomorrow. I'll be leading the right wing, which will be opposite their left end; in other words, we'll hit the Athenians first. They still think they're at Marathon but that was a very long time ago and that was against the Persians. Against our modern army, they don't have a chance.

"We'll echelon our troops from right to left. The point of our attack will be the right-most end of our line. We'll have the most depth, and the best troops, at the tip of the spear that will engage their line first.

"Our job will be to disrupt their front. And I guarantee you, their front will be disrupted, sooner or later. That'll be my job. The rest of you will be responsible for gradually engaging their line, one company at a time, and fighting them to a standstill. All you guys will be the anvil; the cavalry will be the hammer.

"The cavalry will hang back, behind our infantry. When a gap develops in the enemy front, the cavalry will attack the gap, in a flying wedge, and drive through their line. And that's how we will outflank them."

There were quiet whistles in the tent. It was a good plan, that much was obvious to everybody, but not an easy one to execute. There was one crucial detail remaining: Who would lead the cavalry attack?

As if reading our minds, Philippos said, in the most matter-of-fact manner possible: "Alexandros will lead the cavalry charge."

The silence was deafening. Philippos was entrusting the key element of his plan to an untested eighteen-year-old youngster.

"Don't worry, my friends." Philippos hastened to counter the implicit disapproval. "By nightfall tomorrow, all Greece will be united behind us. Now, go get a good night's sleep. Make sure your sentries are alert and make sure everybody is fed, geared up, and in formation at the start of the last watch of the night. We'll take the field at dawn. And give the boys an extra ration of uncut wine with their breakfasts!

"That's it; you're dismissed. Get some rest!"

"Aren't we forgetting something?" Alexandros spoke up. "Have we consulted the soothsayers to make sure the auguries are propitious?"

"You're right, son, I did forget. We have consulted all appropriate oracles, seers, diviners, and soothsayers, and they all agree there couldn't be a better time than tomorrow to whip their asses. Now, get out! I need to do some last-minute planning."

There were no stirring speeches, no discussion, no debate. Every man (and boy) kept his thoughts to himself as we stumbled back to our own squadrons through the darkness of a moonless night.

****

I thought about Lanike. It had been two years since I'd bumped into her outside the palace walls in Pella. During that time, we met almost every night I was in town, which unfortunately wasn't all that often. Philippos kept us on the move, training, campaigning, and supporting various diplomatic missions. And even when I was in Pella, finding a private corner was well-nigh impossible. Privacy was the preserve of royalty and nobility. Ordinary folks like us led lives surrounded by teeming multitudes day and night. Nevertheless, we did manage to sneak away and steal a few quiet moments in secluded, secret spots known only to the two of us.

We spent our time discussing the quotidian details of our lives and became the best of friends – friends who spoke for hours and surreptitiously touched each other on a shoulder or a thigh from time to time and on a few occasions parted with a quick kiss or a passing hug but nothing more. And it was all my fault. Lanike was more than willing, even eager, but there was always an invisible presence between us, a force field that kept us apart, an article of religious faith on my part called the Prime Directive. The fact that Lanike persevered through all those frustrations is a source of ongoing wonder to me.

A rueful thought kept coursing through my mind. *If I die tomorrow, what a waste that'll be.* I was struck by the absurdity of it all. *I'm not even supposed to be here. I'm not a part of this. I'm just a castaway, caught up in a maelstrom.*

Yes, but you might as well enjoy the spin, a more optimistic region of my brain interjected. *You've got the makings here of the best travelogue of all time, if you ever get to write it.*

My reverie was interrupted by a sharp pain in my right big toe, as I kicked a rather large rock in my open-toed sandals. *Pay attention to the here and now,* was the message communicated all the way from the tip of my toe to the top of my cranium.

Surprisingly, the possibility of dying didn't exercise me too greatly. What really concerned me was the fear of embarrassing myself.

****

The first pink streamers of dawn unfurled above two armies, drawn up and ready for battle.[10] My buddies and I were sitting on our horses, beyond the left end of our line. Directly across the field from us, not more than three stadia away and standing in rigid battle order, was the Sacred Band. Next to them stood another company of hoplites, and another, and another, and a hundred more. For more than a mile across the barley fields of Chaironeia, disappearing into the listless early light, stretched an uninterrupted wall of men, standing shield to shield and bristling with spears, like an endless, menacing, mutant millipede.

Standing next to us and extending out of sight to our right was the Macedonian line, undoubtedly looking just as alarming to the other side as they appeared to us.

---

[10] For an animated depiction of the Battle of Chaironeia, see Battle 1 at AlexanderGeiger.com.

What the enemy probably couldn't see was the uneven depth of the Macedonian line. At its extreme right, our line was sixteen men deep but it gradually thinned out. At its left end, immediately next to us, the Macedonian line was only four men deep, not really effective enough to fight against a full phalanx of enemy hoplites.

It was still early in the morning. A mellow mist rose toward the mostly overcast sky. Some breaks developed in the clouds, through which came streaming shafts of brilliant sunshine, looking like huge columns of light supporting the billowing canopy above. For a moment, the two armies facing each other reminded me of worshippers gathered to pay homage to their favorite deity in a gigantic temple of Ares. But the columns of light were leaning precipitously. The ceiling of the temple was ready to fall. The deity had left the building some time ago.

Pandaros, my horse, was restless. He could sense my uncertainty and alarm. Although I was protected by a breastplate, helmet, and greaves, I felt practically naked. The reins in my right hand were slick with sweat; the two short spears in my left were in constant danger of slipping through my fingers; my sword and dagger, strapped to the outside of each thigh, burned against my skin.

We had practiced our maneuvers a thousand times but all my training had seemingly evaporated with the morning dew. I looked at Alexandros. His Boukephalas was prancing, confident and carefree, in the vacant space between the two lines. The identity of the horse and rider was unmistakable. Boukephalas was the biggest horse on the field, with a distinctive white blaze on its forehead. Alexandros was the brightest warrior, his polished armor flashing beacons of reflected sunlight at the enemy. His helmet sported his signature white plume, matching the marking on the head of his horse. His erect seat, atop the giant animal, made him look preternaturally tall.

It's hard to believe that inside that shiny armor, coiled like a spring, sits an eighteen-year-old boy, I thought. *He looks superhuman, compared to the rest of us.*

As if reading my thoughts, Alexandros turned to face us. "Men, today's the first step on the road to our ultimate destination. We're an unstoppable force and together we will conquer the world." He spoke in a clear, calm, carrying voice. "Keep a close eye on my movements. I don't want to spend time giving orders. Just follow my lead; protect my rear; and kill any bastards who get in the way. Remember, Zeus, Tyche, and Nike are riding with us this day. As long as they remain on our side, we're invincible. Stick with me and I'll lead you to our destiny."

That was the stupidest pep talk I've ever heard, I thought. *Am I being commanded by another General Lupika?* But as I looked around, the rest of my mates were staring at the enemy, their jaws set, their eyes blazing, their confidence unbounded. *This guy's got some charisma*, was my revised opinion.

There was a brief pause on the battlefield, with each side seemingly reluctant to make the first move. Then the Macedonians started marching. An eerie silence descended on the fields of Chaironeia, hushing even the twittering of the birds. The only sound was the rhythmic, relentless thud of thirty thousand phalangists, advancing in unison.

We, the cavalry, got out of the way. Our job was to wait until ordered into action by Alexandros. In the meantime, we had an excellent vantage point, at the edge of the battlefield and on top of our horses, from which to observe the action.

Our right wing, consisting of several battalions of Foot Companions, was directly across the field of battle from the Athenian brigade. With the rest of the Macedonian line angled farther and farther back, it was clear the battle would begin with the clash of the Foot Companions against the Athenians.

When the leading rank of the Foot Companions reached within a stadion of the Athenians, Philippos halted their advance and a company of Agrianians materialized from among their midst. The semi-barbarian Agrianians, armed only with slingshots, unleashed a volley of rocks at the Athenians, which the Athenians deflected harmlessly with their shields. However, while their attention was fastened on the incoming missiles, the Macedonian trumpets sounded and the Foot Companions charged on the double into the narrow strip of land between the armies, closing the gap in a matter of seconds.

The sight of the onrushing phalanxes must have been unnerving to the Athenians. Once the silence had been shattered by the trumpets and the Macedonians had broken into a run, they raised their voices into a deafening roar of shouts, songs, and exhortations. Yet, despite the speed and noise of their approach, the discipline of their ranks never wavered. As they ran, each man continued to occupy exactly a two-foot width of the line; each line remained exactly three feet behind the line in front of them.

The men in the first row held their sarissas level with the ground. The Macedonian pikes, which were almost twice as long as the Athenian spears, reached some twelve feet in front of the men. The second row held their sarissas angled slightly upward, with the result that the points of their weapons were some three feet behind and about a foot and a half higher than the points of the first row. The third rank held their sarissas angled higher yet.

The overall appearance of the Macedonian phalanx, from the viewpoint of the Athenians, was of an irresistible tidal wave of sharp points about to break against the Athenian shields, cuirasses, and helmets.

To their credit, the Athenian hoplites, most of whom had never worn their armor in anger before, stood their ground. Although the point of a sarissa found its mark here and there, penetrating the armor and flesh of an

Athenian soldier, most of our men's thrusts were parried and deflected by the sturdy shields and the more mobile spears of the Athenians.

The two lines gradually closed in on each other. The men in the front ranks dropped their spears and started hacking at the enemy with their swords, while being pushed forward by the weight of the men behind them. Screams of pain mingled with cries of triumph as countless little skirmishes developed all along the line. Chaos seemed to reign supreme.

At precisely that moment, Philippos ordered his Foot Companions to retreat, even as the other Macedonian units, gradually moving down the line, began to engage the enemy units opposed to them one by one.

The Athenians opposed to Philippos's Foot Companions raised a joyous shout, assuming that they had won, and they started to pursue their enemy. "Let's chase them all the way back to Macedonia!" was one of the things they were screaming as they ran.

Had the Athenian strategos, Stratokles, been a more experienced commander, he would have noticed that the Macedonians' retreat was anything but a disorderly rout. The phalanxes continued their rigid discipline, their ranks unbroken, still facing the enemy, with men in the rear ranks stepping forward to fill any gaps resulting from casualties. The Foot Companions were simply withdrawing, step by disciplined step.

In their enthusiasm to charge, the Athenians' order broke down. Also, as Philippos had anticipated, the entire enemy line started to shift to the left, because that was where the Athenians were so vigorously pursuing their Macedonian counterparts.

The Athenians drifted to the left, and the allies and mercenaries in the middle drifted to the left, and the Boiotians on the right drifted to the left. Everybody but the Sacred Band drifted to the left. Ironically, because of their superior discipline, the Sacred Band did not drift and soon a gap developed between them and the rest of the enemy line.

As soon as Alexandros saw the gap, his eyes narrowed and a tense smile curled his lips. "It's time for us to go." Without another word, he heeled Boukephalas into a gallop, leaving the rest of us momentarily behind.

There were hurried shouts from squadron commanders as we set out in pursuit of Alexandros. Although galloping as fast as Pandaros would take me, I was struggling mightily to stay aboard. Saddles and stirrups hadn't yet been invented. We were riding bareback, seated all the way front, against the necks of our horses, using our legs and knees both to control the animals and to maintain our balance. My fellow horsemen had learned to ride before they knew how to walk. They spoke to their animals with subtle body shifts, with a bit of pressure here, a tiny kick there. Using their voices, much less their reins, was beneath contempt. Despite all my training, my horse language was even more deficient than my Greek. When it came to equitation, I was a deaf-mute in a land of telepaths.

On the plus side, I was concentrating so hard on not falling off my horse and on not losing my javelins that I completely forgot I was about to engage the enemy. When I finally looked up, Alexandros was far ahead. He had evidently already thrown one of his javelins because there was only one left in his left hand. In his right, he was now holding his sword, waiving it wildly overhead as he headed straight for the front rank of the Sacred Band. He still had a four-length lead on the fastest of the riders in our squadron. The rest of us were trailing even farther behind. Without bothering to look, I could hear the entire Companion Cavalry, two thousand men strong, thundering across the field, in pursuit of our leader.

For a moment, I thought Alexandros would reach the Thebans before we could catch up to him. I half expected them to surge forward and envelop him. If they'd done so, they would've disrupted the cohesion of their ranks and made themselves vulnerable to our attack but they would've also hacked Alexandros to pieces before anyone could've come to his rescue.

The Sacred Band was too well trained to indulge in such a foolish move, even if it would've meant the destruction of the Macedonian prince. Instead, they were desperately trying to close ranks with their fellow Boiotians farther up the line who were rapidly drawing away from them. They were caught in a dilemma. If they moved as a unit to the left, they would lose contact with the river, thus permitting our infantry to turn the flank of the entire enemy line. On the other hand, if they maintained contact with the river, then, no matter how much they thinned their lines, they couldn't stay in touch with the next Boiotian company up the line. They chose to carry out their orders and hold their end of the line.

When Alexandros was almost on the points of their spears, he suddenly veered to his right, and plunged into the gap between the Sacred Band and the rest of the Boiotians. A man on a horse, armed to the teeth, shooting fire from his eyes, and bearing down on the enemy, is a scary sight to a foot soldier, even one who is heavily armed. However, as long as the foot soldier is part of a phalanx, hunkered down behind a wall of large shields, touching edge to edge, with a tight matrix of spear points protruding beyond the shields, and files of men pushing and supporting him from behind, he has a good chance of repulsing the onslaught of a charging cavalryman. But if the assault comes from the side, before the phalanx can execute a ninety-degree turn or, worse yet, if the assault comes from all sides simultaneously, then the foot soldier has no chance. The phalanx is like a hedgehog. As long as it is nicely balled up, with its spines radiating outward, it can be a tough adversary. But if one can unroll it and get to its soft underbelly, it has no defenses at all. Alexandros had managed to attack the soft underbelly of the Sacred Band.

At that moment, the rest of us, pouring into the gap right behind our leader, started tossing our javelins. Once again, this presented an extra challenge to me. I had to let go of the reins and control my horse solely through the pressure of my knees and legs. I had to transfer one of my javelins from my left hand to my right hand and then throw it, as hard and as accurately as I could manage, without falling off my horse. While I was busy doing all that, I had to keep track of Alexandros's movements and I had to dodge any arrows, stones, and spears that might come flying my way. I was in such a hurry to get my hands free of the irksome spears that I threw the second one immediately after the first and proceeded to draw my sword, without bothering to check whether my missiles had reached their targets.

In the meantime, Alexandros, not waiting for reinforcements, kept plunging deeper and deeper into the gap, enlarging the breach in the enemy line as he went along. It was imperative for the rest of us to stay with him; otherwise, he could easily have been cut off, engulfed, and destroyed. On second thought, maybe it wouldn't have been all that easy. As I struggled to make my way to his side, parrying spear thrusts with my sword, I realized, with some wonder, that Alexandros was perfectly capable of fighting off a dozen foot soldiers simultaneously. Unlike me, he still had his second javelin and was using it to thrust at random attackers on his left side, while at the same time smashing heads on his right with his sword. His horse, either responding to subtle guidance from Alexandros's legs or acting of its own volition, was dancing and twirling, seemingly positioning its rider for each new attack. If all else failed, Boukephalas simply trampled soldiers that got in its master's way.

I actually stopped to watch this lethal ballet. Alexandros's reflexes were so fast that everything else seemed to be moving in slow motion. A spear thrust at him by an enemy soldier was splintered by his slashing sword before its tip came anywhere near its target. At times, sliced off spear tips were raining down all around us like hailstones. He used the tip of his javelin to dislodge an enemy soldier's helmet and then, almost in the same motion, swung down his sword hand, cleaving the man's skull in two. One enemy soldier managed to leap up on his horse and started to pull him down by the neck. Alexandros hacked off the man's arm with one swing and then thrust his javelin under the man's breastplate, lifting him off the horse and into thin air, where the mortally wounded soldier flailed for a second, liked a speared newt, before sliding off the javelin. He was no longer moving by the time he hit the ground.

My admiration of this macabre dance of death was interrupted by another Theban soldier who had the bad manners to attack me. Fortunately, he let loose with a mighty yell at the same time as he threw his spear, giving me plenty of time to duck. I think the spear ended up hitting one of his fellow soldiers on the other side, although I didn't have time to check; the cheeky Theban kept coming. Before he could get within slashing distance, Pandaros reared up and threatened to trample the man. Of course, he also threatened to spill me to the ground but I managed to maintain my seat by grabbing onto his neck. My horse's flailing hooves brought the Theban to a temporary halt. When Pandaros returned to earth, I was looking down into my attacker's face. He was just a boy, no more than nineteen or twenty years old. We looked at each other. Then I swung my sword, missing him by a wide margin, and at the same time urged Pandaros away from the scene of the confrontation. I don't think the Theban lad ever swung at me at all.

It all became a blur, almost like a really fast game. My training kicked in and I executed what I'd practiced, more or less without the intervention of conscious thought. Certainly, I had no time to be frightened, much less to contemplate the possibility of getting hurt or killed. I was just doing what I'd been taught to do.

When I was next able to locate Alexandros, I saw that the circle of soldiers attacking him had drawn back a little, reminding me of a pack of wolves shrinking away from a flaming branch. Before they could surge forward again, several of my squadron mates and I joined Alexandros in the circle. He gave us a smile. "It's fun, isn't it?"

After a while, we succeeded in fighting our way to the back of the Theban phalanx. As soon as we were in the clear, Alexandros immediately wheeled us to the left, so that we could take the Sacred Band from the rear. We had them isolated from the rest of their forces and hemmed in on three sides. The Kephisos was on the fourth side.

They retreated slowly toward the river. Or more accurately, the perimeter of their square contracted slowly as their men fell, for they didn't step back, choosing instead to die where they stood.

Alexandros was tireless and so were the rest of us. It's easy to be enthusiastic when one is winning and it was clear to us we were winning. Almost the entire Companion Cavalry was engaged in destruction of one battalion of Theban infantry, consisting of three hundred men, fighting against two thousand mounted warriors.

At long last, there was but a single Theban soldier left standing. He wavered for a moment, looking uncertainly at the eight or ten horsemen surrounding him and at the dead comrades at his feet. Our men stopped, waiting for the Theban's next move. After what seemed like an eternity, the soldier gathered himself and, with a loud yell, thrust his sword at the nearest horse, wounding it in the shoulder. In an instant, he was hacked to death, his arms and head cleanly severed from his torso.

No more Thebans remained on their feet, although there were a few still writhing and moaning on the ground. We all stopped and stared for a long, silent moment. Not one member of the Sacred Band had attempted to surrender. They had a one hundred percent casualty rate: More than eighty percent dead, the rest grievously wounded. There would never be another Sacred Band.

"That's enough resting," Alexandros yelled. "Let's get back to the fight."

We wheeled again, trying to see how the rest of the battle was going. It turned out that, as soon as Philippos had seen that we had secured the gap, he'd halted his retreat and renewed the attack against the Athenians. The entire line engaged in a furious battle, except there was no longer any cohesion in the Athenian ranks, which had lost their shape during their enthusiastic pursuit of the retreating Foot Companions. In addition, there was now no anchor on the right end of the enemy line, making it possible for our cavalry to flank them and take them from the rear.

The two prongs of the Macedonian attack started to roll up the enemy line from each end. Philippos's Foot Companions were devastating the foolhardy Athenians; the Companion Cavalry were trampling the Boiotians, who were also being pressed in the front by Antipatros's Guards; Parmenion's Silver Shields were holding their own in the center. The enemy was being gradually ground up. Eventually, led by the Athenians, they all turned tail in a disorderly rout.

Of the ten thousand Athenian soldiers present that day, about a thousand died and more than two thousand were captured. Although the losses of the rest of the enemy were not quite as heavy, it was an overwhelming victory for Macedonia.

Alexandros, having regained the vanguard of the Companion Cavalry, and Philippos, at the head of his Foot Companions, met on the battlefield at about the point where the mercenaries had stood earlier in the day. Alexandros was euphoric. He was screaming and shouting and laughing. Even Philippos was uncharacteristically ebullient, smiling ear to ear and waving his arms. They dismounted and embraced. But before they celebrated, there were mopping-up operations to organize.

Philippos wanted to make sure all the injured Macedonian soldiers were being treated in the field hospitals and all the dead ones collected and prepared for cremation. He also appointed commanders and organized detachments responsible for rounding up the captured prisoners and establishing prisoner camps. He dispatched other groups to secure the enemy camps and baggage trains and to collect the captured loot. He placed Attalos in charge of several squadrons of the Companion Cavalry and ordered them to chase down and round up as many enemy stragglers as possible. He made it clear, though, that he didn't want to suffer a single additional casualty. "We've got plenty of prisoners already. It's not worth losing a single man in trying to capture a few more. And make sure to break off the pursuit at dusk. We don't need you guys stumbling into any ambushes in the dark." And then he proceeded to organize that evening's festivities.

After he'd finished taking care of all the details, Philippos turned his attention back to Alexandros. "That was a hell of charge, son."

"I know."

"Walk with me as I inspect the field."

The two of them, trailed by a large entourage of commanders, subalterns, and aides, walked from one scene of carnage to the next, reliving the highlights of the battle. When they noticed someone alive under a pile of enemy corpses, Philippos arranged for transportation to the nearest field hospital. "Just make sure our boys get taken care of first."

They paused near the river bank, gazing at the remnants of the Sacred Band. "It's a shame," Philippos said.

"Yeah," Alexandros agreed, "but they died glorious deaths."

"Good for them," Philippos nodded. "I'm glad they got the glory and our guys got to stay alive. Just remember, son, the secret to victory is to make sure it's the other guy who gets to die a glorious death." Philippos laughed. He was in a remarkably good mood. Alexandros had become strangely subdued and pensive at some point during their inspection tour.

"Still," Philippos added, "it's a shame we couldn't get them to fight on our side. But the good news is that neither Thebes nor Athens nor anyone else in Greece will ever rise against Macedonia again." Although frequently a sage prognosticator, in this instance Philippos would prove to be less than clairvoyant.

"How d'ya like that plan?" Philippos asked no one in particular. "A hell of a plan, wasn't it? We sure did sucker them. They came charging at us like madmen and we just continued our slow retreat, never breaking ranks. And then, when they were totally disordered, we stopped, turned, and gutted them. You should've seen it."

"I was busy elsewhere," Alexandros replied.

"That's true. And by the way, your guys did a terrific job, charging into the breach. I'm proud of you, son."

I could tell, looking at Alexandros, that wasn't quite sufficient praise. At a minimum, he expected some favorable comparisons to Achilleus. I think Philippos could tell as well but he had exhausted his quota of compliments for one day.

Just then, a ragged column of Athenian survivors was being marched by us, on their way to the prisoner camp. The men had been stripped of their weapons and armor. Most wore only torn and dirty tunics. Some had only rags. One or two were naked. Many were bleeding.

Here and there, the men carried one of their more seriously wounded comrades.

Philippos was clearly enjoying the sight. "You know, son, I believe this is my best victory yet. There'll be a hell of a party tonight. Make sure you're there. We might have an award or two for your men."

****

It proved to be a memorable feast. The wine that evening flowed like the blood had earlier in the day. Philippos was generous with his praise and lavish in his gifts. Dozens of men were singled out for their heroism during the battle, including Alexandros, who received the captured standard of the Sacred Band as his gift.

My comrades and I were sitting at the periphery of the festivities, laughing and yelling and drinking. I'd received no awards but was perfectly content. For the first time since my arrival, I felt included. I was part of the group. During the battle, after the initial shock had worn off, I'd fought in a trance. I could only hope I'd managed to avoid killing or wounding anyone. Undoubtedly, I'd evaded a few potentially lethal attacks by the enemy as well but I had no recollection of those either. All I remembered was the exhilarating feeling of physical well-being, of martial competence, of dodging death, of belonging to a team. Even hours after the end of the battle, lounging around the campfire, that feeling of camaraderie was still with me. *This could be addictive*, I thought.

After the speeches, Philippos and his senior commanders settled down to some serious drinking. Alexandros and his circle of friends did their best to keep up with their elders but it soon became clear that the ability to absorb vast quantities of alcohol was an acquired skill, requiring years of training.

I noticed Alexandros had slipped away at some point, probably to perform some oblations or other religious rituals. Soon enough, though, he'd returned, more sober and more subdued.

As most of the inner group was gradually slipping to a point somewhere between stupor and coma, a soldier made his way to Philippos and whispered something in his ear. Philippos let out a joyous shout and sprang to his feet. More whispering followed, after which Philippos broke into a guffaw, slapping his thighs.

"Listen up, everybody," he yelled. "We've captured Demosthenes!" Although most of the men were too drunk to care, a few raised their cups in a toast. "Long live the captured Demosthenes. May he rot a slave forever."

"Who captured him?" somebody wanted to know.

"That's the best part," Philippos yelled with great glee. "Tell you what: I'll give a talent of silver to the man who forced his surrender." The men suddenly sobered up. A talent of silver was roughly equal to twenty years' wages of a rank and file soldier. When Philippos had everyone's attention, he turned to Antigonos: "Well, Antigonos, who captured him?"

"A bramble," Antigonos said.

"Who?" several people yelled.

"He was captured by a bush," Antigonos repeated. "He was running for his life from the field of battle, having already abandoned his sword and shield, when his cloak caught on a bramble. Feeling the tug, and without looking around, Demosthenes threw up his hands and cried: 'Take me alive; take me alive,' thus surrendering to a bush."

As the story progressed, Philippos turned more and more flushed, trying to contain himself. Finally, when Antigonos reached the climactic end, Philippos collapsed to his back, laughing uncontrollably and beating the ground with his feet and hands. "He surrendered to a shrub!" he screamed. "The great Demosthenes surrendered to a stinking shrub!"

The intoxicated king jumped to his feet and started to dance around the field, singing, over and over again: "Demosthenes proposes and Philippos disposes; Demosthenes proposes and Philippos disposes." Attalos, who was even more drunk, joined his commander, grabbing him by the waist and dancing along behind him. Other men joined in, forming an ever-lengthening line of dancing, singing, inebriated men. They snaked their way in the darkness around tents and trees and across the battlefield, tripping now and then on the bodies of dead men.

When they spotted a group of Athenian prisoners huddled around a campfire, the noise and enthusiasm of the long line of revelers, led by Philippos, redoubled. They were hurling contemptuous epithets at the Athenians when a short, fat, balding man stepped into their path. He spoke directly to Philippos. "Tell me great king, when the gods have cast you as Agamemnon, why do you insist on acting the part of Thersites?"

Philippos pulled up short and looked at the little fat man. "You look familiar."

"Don't you recognize me? I'm Demades, a captured Athenian soldier." The little man defiantly thrust out his large belly.

"Demades, my friend, the great Athenian orator!"

"Yes, sire."

"Demosthenes's great opponent!"

"At your service."

"Come and join us." Philippos put his arm around the smaller man. "And bring the rest of your men along. There is wine enough for everybody."

Remarkably, Philippos was sober and engaged in discussion with Demades when I awoke, feeling exceedingly ill, the next morning. Instead of punishing the captured enemy soldier for his bold and cuttingly apt rebuke, Philippos had apparently decided to utilize the good offices of the venal Athenian politician to secure the preliminary approval of the Athenian Assembly for his proposed peace terms.

Philippos's terms to Athens were significantly more lenient than his terms to Thebes. He considered Thebes, which had breached its treaty obligations to Macedonia in taking the field at Chaironeia, to be a city of traitors. By contrast, he'd always harbored a secret admiration for the military and intellectual history of Athens and, even after the battle, didn't relinquish his hope of persuading, rather than forcing, Athens to support his sacred war against Persia.

Accordingly, he insisted that captured Theban soldiers be ransomed at the going rate of thirty drachmas each in order to escape being sold into slavery, while he agreed to release captured Athenians – including even Demosthenes – immediately and unconditionally. He also installed a permanent Macedonian garrison on Kadmeia, the akropolis of Thebes. In Athens, he didn't attempt to station any Macedonian troops. On the contrary, in an effort to reassure the panic-stricken Athenians, he voluntarily agreed to keep his army out of Attika altogether. He also dismantled the Boiotian League, the small empire controlled by Thebes, while contenting himself with simply crippling the empire of Athens, which was crumbling of its own accord in any event.

Demades returned to Chaironeia within days, having persuaded the Athenian Assembly to accept Philippos's terms. Presumably, he had pointed out to his fellow Athenians that they were not in a position to quibble. In fact, the Athenians, at least according to Demades, had expressed a great deal of gratitude for the lenient treatment accorded to them.

The Athenian dead had been cremated in the meantime, this being the middle of Metageitnion. In a final show of good will, Philippos, having received word of the acceptance of his terms from Demades, dispatched the ashes of the fallen Athenians back home with full military honors. He even sent a delegation led by Alexandros and Antipatros to accompany the wagon train carrying the ashes and to conclude the agreed-upon peace treaty.

The Thebans, who were much closer to home, were able to bury their own dead, most of whom they carted back to their native city. However, they decided to inter the fallen members of the Sacred Band in a common grave, right there on the battlefield, hard by the Kephisos River, laid to rest as they had fought and died – in the disciplined, orderly formation of a phalanx. Eventually, a statue of a winged lion was erected over their common grave, as a guardian of their memory and a symbol of their bravery. When I visited the Greek Peninsula during the summer before my trip to ancient Macedonia, some 2,400 years after the battle of Chaironeia, the monument was still there.

Chapter 7 – Athens

Alexandros had proven himself on the field of battle but, as far as his father was concerned, he had a long way to go before he was ready to inherit the mantle of leadership. Physical prowess was fine, Philippos believed, but it was cerebral dexterity that kept a ruler in power. And what better way to hone Alexandros's wits than by sending him on a diplomatic errand to that vipers' nest of canny politicians, corrupt demagogues, conniving conspirators, cunning assassins, and contemptuous snobs that was Athens. If Alexandros survived his dicey mission to the violet-crowned city, he would be one step closer to completing the demanding royal curriculum devised for him by his father. Accordingly, Alexandros's next royal commission was to head the Macedonian delegation accompanying the cremated remains of the fallen Athenians back to their home city.

Before the wagon train carrying the ash-filled urns set out on its slow journey, Philippos called me into his tent. "You're going to be part of the cavalry squadron accompanying the wagons, Ptolemaios," he said, by way of greeting. "But the dead don't need too much protection. Your job is to protect my son."

I nodded.

"Stay by his side day and night. There's no telling where an assassin might lurk. Just because we whipped their butts doesn't mean they won't try something. Alexandros's mission is to convince them to come over to our side. Your mission is to keep Alexandros in one piece, so he can complete his mission. Got that?"

"Yes, sire!"

"I'm told you're a hell of a fighter and I know you're a hell of a smart guy. So, don't let me down."

"I won't, sire."

We set out before dawn the next day. It was a surprisingly short train. Only eight wagons were required to carry the cremated remains of a thousand warriors, plus six more wagons for our gear. Each wagon had its team of horses, a teamster, and two helpers. And then there was our squadron of four dozen cavalrymen, resplendent in full armor, accompanied by a modest troop of servants, grooms, and auxiliaries, all on horseback. It was a notable display of something — whether courage or foolhardiness or arrogance or self-confidence, it was hard to know – to send such a small force into the heart of the enemy empire.

****

Alexandros rode at the head of the column, side by side with Antipatros and Hephaistion. I made a point of riding directly behind them. Truth be told, I was more excited than concerned. From my knowledge of history, I was pretty sure Alexandros would survive this trip. Of course, there was always a small chance that something I might've done could've altered the flow of time but I'd been very careful not to violate the Prime Directive. And thus far, I hadn't noticed any deviations or anomalies. On the other hand, a chance to visit ancient Athens was the opportunity of a lifetime. *The risk was small,* I told myself, *and the opportunity to observe and learn essentially unlimited.*

Nevertheless, I took my assignment to protect Alexandros seriously. I assumed Philippos had given the same assignment, and the same pep talk, to several other riders in the squadron but I took it personally. I'd grown to like Philippos and was somehow anxious to please him. Plus, I kept reminding myself, my passage to Egypt would be facilitated by staying in the good graces of both Philippos and Alexandros.

Our wagon train was met outside the city walls, in the middle of Keramaikos cemetery, by a disconcertingly large horde of people, consisting mostly of women, children, and old men, but with a substantial number of able-bodied men of fighting age mixed in. These were presumably the fighters who'd managed to get away in the aftermath of the battle or whom Philippos had recently released, as part of his general amnesty.

At the head of the grieving throng came some of the leading lights of Athenian society: Philippos's foremost undercover agent in Athens, Demades, and Philippos's greatest antagonist, Demosthenes, walking cheek by jowl; the outstanding general, Phokion, who had – fortunately for us – been relieved of his command just before the battle of Chaironeia and the capable but smarmy politician, Aischines, not far behind.

It didn't take me long, after my arrival in Athens, to find out more about these men. Demades, it turned out, had been in Philippos's pay for years and, being an honorable scoundrel, had proved to be a tireless advocate for Macedonian interests in the Athenian Assembly. Demosthenes, by contrast, was in the pay of the Persians but his hatred of all things Macedonian, and especially of Philippos personally, was genuine and heartfelt. The Persian bribes were just a nice bonus. Phokion was an incorruptible politician and an outstanding military commander. As a result, his warnings carried no weight whatsoever with the Assembly. His reward for his sound counsel had been to be relieved of his command. Aischines, although not exactly incorruptible, was honest and capable enough. He and Demosthenes were bitter rivals, Demosthenes representing the democratic party and Aischines speaking for the oligarchs. In foreign affairs, Aischines always understood that Macedonia represented the future of Greece. Demosthenes was unshakable in his belief that the Macedonians were the greatest threat to the independence of Athens. In due course, they both proved to be correct.

Keramaikos cemetery, just outside Athens's walls, was an immense city of the dead, far larger than any living city in Macedonia. However, on the day we arrived, the cemetery was in disarray. Many of the stelai were lying flat on the ground or missing altogether; marble crypts partially torn down; elaborate monuments disassembled, their statuary toppled and strewn about, plinths destroyed and mostly gone.

"What in Haides happened here?" Alexandros asked.

Our guides looked at each other. Finally, Phokion stepped forward. "We were using the tombstones to reinforce the city walls."

"What else have you done?"

This time the silence was even longer. Finally, Demades spoke up. "By the time I arrived with your father's generous peace terms, they'd armed our women and slaves for a final, desperate stand. Believe me, sire, when I saw my wife armed to the teeth, it was all I could do to stop myself from running back to Chaironeia to surrender to your father for a second time."

The laughter broke the tension. Alexandros didn't laugh but he let the subject drop. "Athenians," he cried out, sitting tall astride Boukephalas, "my father Philippos, king of Macedonia, archon of Thessaly, hegemon of the Amphiktyonic League, and victor at the Battle of Chaironeia, sends his greetings."

He was met with sullen silence.

"We come to you not as conquerors but as friends." Some muttering in the crowd. "It was not our choice to engage your husbands, fathers, and sons on the battlefield." Isolated catcalls. "We're all Greeks." Outright laughter, but Alexandros pressed on, undeterred. "You may find this difficult to believe but, when Xerxes overran Athens and destroyed your temples, he desecrated the houses of our gods. We all worship Zeus, Athena, Nike. The destruction of the temples of Athens was a sacrilege committed against all Greeks." They were starting to listen.

"My father has spent his entire adult life trying to unify all Greece for a sacred war against Persia, in order to avenge their insult to the dignity of all Greeks; in order to exact reparations from Persia for the damage done to Athens; in order to restore the greatness of Athens." *His rhetoric had raced beyond the bounds of all credibility*, I thought, but his audience was listening with rapt attention. "Won't you join with us in a great expedition against the barbarians who destroyed your city, plundered your treasures, ravaged your lands, and desecrated your temples?

"To prove our friendship, notwithstanding the recent struggle between us, my father has released all Athenian prisoners of war," I thought I heard a cheer, "without preconditions, without ransom, without rancor, and without delay. He made this decision simply in the hope that, in the next battle, your brothers and ours will fight side by side. Greek gods – our gods – want us to stand united. If we do, they'll assure our victory over those heathens." There were scattered cries of approbation throughout the crowd.

"It's a terrible waste for Greeks to be killing Greeks when we need all of our fighting men to take on the great, evil empire to our east. My father regrets all loss of life at Chaironeia, whether Macedonian lives, or Athenian lives, or other Greek lives. It was a terrible, unnecessary waste.

"After the battle, we made sure your fallen warriors were treated with the utmost dignity, were afforded all military honors, were cremated in accordance with the ancient rituals of our people. It's with great sadness that I return the remains of your fellow citizens to you but secure in the knowledge that we've carried out all of our obligations to the gods – and to our fellow Greeks – honorably, meticulously, and conscientiously."

And with that, he reached into the first wagon and handed an ash-filled amphora to the archon of Athens. The crowd was once again silent but now perhaps more sad than sullen.

"Great speech, sire," I told him. *Not bad for an eighteen-year-old*, is what I thought.

Demosthenes rose to respond to Alexandros, clambering atop the lead wagon. "All Athenians extend their thanks to King Philippos for the courtesies shown to our dead," he started. "Now is not the time to debate the origins of the dispute between us, the causes of all this destruction, the culpability for all this death. Now is the time to pay homage to our fallen heroes." His voice was high-pitched, clear, and strong.

"As Perikles said on a similar occasion, almost seventy years ago, these men sacrificed their lives not in defense of their homes and possessions but in defense of an ideal, in defense of a way of life. Athens is not just a collection of houses and shops and temples. It is, rather, the city whose inhabitants overthrew the tyrants and invented democracy. It is the city whose citizens defeated the Persian invaders, on land and on sea, at Marathon and at Salamis, thus preserving the freedom and independence of Greece. It is the city that has produced the greatest builders, artists, poets, playwrights, lovers of knowledge, and teachers of the young, that the world has ever known.

"With all due respect, the greatness of Athens predates the ascent of King Philippos to his current position of military preeminence; it predates the assumption of the Macedonian throne by King Philippos; it predates even the birth of King Philippos; and yes, it predates the founding of the Argead Royal House of Macedonia; it predates the arrival of the Macedonian tribes to the lands that they currently occupy." It was now Demosthenes's turn to push his rhetoric beyond any acquaintance with reality but his audience was spellbound.

"The greatness of Athens, although achieved under the guidance of our patroness Athena Promachos, was achieved by the talents, hard work, and selfless sacrifice of the citizens of Athens. It did not happen by accident; it was not handed to us by outsiders; and it will not be taken away from us by force of arms or the artifice of diplomacy." He was thundering by now.

"The greatness of Athens is the result of the high regard in which we hold each and every one of our citizens. It is the result of the combined efforts of generations of individual Athenians. It is the result of the farmer who faithfully tends to his fields and provides us with nourishment. It is the result of the citizen hoplite fighting ferociously on the battlefield and protecting our freedom. It is the result of the contributions of our neighbors, of our friends, and of strangers whom we met in the agora just the other day, but whose presence enriches our city. It is the result of our wives and mothers, who bear and raise and educate our young, and then send them off to defend our liberties. It is the result of our boys and girls, who will carry the flame of Athenian greatness forward to generations yet unborn. But most of all, it is the result of this one simple idea: We respect each and every one of us; we appreciate the individual worth of every citizen and resident of Athens; we value the individual enterprise of every person who lives in this city. It is this mutual respect of the polity for its individual constituents that has made Athens great. And that's the reason why these urns that you have brought back to us are such a wrenching loss." His voice was barely above a whisper, yet such was the silence of the crowd that he was easily heard at the far edges of the assembled multitude.

"These men, whose ashes we welcome to their final resting place today, sacrificed their lives knowingly, and willingly, for their city. Their wives, mothers, and children, who kissed them farewell a few scant days ago, weep at their loss. All of us here grieve at our loss. But these wives, mothers, children, brothers and sisters, all of us assembled here today, can – and do – hold our heads high. Athens expects her sons and daughters to do their share for the survival of their city, for the survival of this idea that is Athens, and these men have done more than their fair share." He was thundering again.

Prime Directive

"Each of us here today has made a great sacrifice. Each of us suffers great pain and anguish, which the passage of time may assuage but never extinguish. But, despite this pain and anguish, I ask you always to remember that these citizen soldiers, whose remains we accept today, died in defense – the successful defense – of Athens, in defense of our common way of life, in defense of our common birthright and legacy of greatness. As long as there is a single Greek living and breathing anywhere in this land, the memory of these brave and faithful fighters shall not die." He finished amidst a great upswell of sound, yet could still be heard above the roar of the crowd.

He turned to us. "We thank you, Alexandros, for returning these remains to us but now, please take your extra wagons and take your men and proceed to the city, so that we can bury our dead in peace."

The crowd returned to silence. There were tears rolling down many of the faces. I looked at Alexandros and was surprised to see that his eyes were brimming as well. Without a word, he wheeled Boukephalas and started walking toward the city. The rest of us scrambled, as usual, to catch up to him.

******

We entered Athens through the Thriasian Gate, which the natives all called the Dipylon, on account of its two gates. *Just as well we don't have to storm it*, I thought, looking at this formidable structure, consisting of an outer gate, flanked by massive square towers, and an inner gate, about half a stadion beyond the outer gate, flanked by two more towers. The area between the two gates was enclosed by monumental walls, forming a courtyard about a hundred and twenty yards long and sixty yards wide. This was, as we had been taught at the Academy, a killing zone. The idea was to permit a besieging army, thinking that it had breached the city's defenses, to pour through the outer gate and then become trapped in the courtyard, whereupon it could be destroyed at leisure by the Athenian defenders from the towers and walls above.

Although we'd come in peace, on a diplomatic mission, and with the implicit protection of Philippos's victorious army only a day's march away, I couldn't help but feel uneasy as we traversed the courtyard. *All it would take is one assassin, up there on the wall.*

Fortunately, on this particular day, all the assassins had apparently gone to the funeral, leaving nary a soldier on the walls or in the towers. There was the usual crush of travelers, hawkers, and hangers-on in the courtyard itself but they seemed harmless enough, as they parted respectfully to get out of our way. We tried to maintain a tight cordon around Alexandros and to keep moving. Unfortunately, our efforts were hampered by Alexandros's insistence on taking full advantage of his visit. He carefully inspected the construction of the walls, estimated their height and thickness, and assessed their vulnerability to sapping. Then he noticed a fountain house in the southeast corner of the courtyard. To our general consternation, he dismounted and waded into the crowd, making his way to the small structure. We had no choice but to jump off our horses and follow his lead.

The fountain house was nothing more than a lean-to, anchored against the back wall of the courtyard, its tiled roof supported by plain Doric columns on the sides, sheltering a large water-filled marble basin in its cool, shady, damp interior. An arching stream of water, issuing from the penis of a small Eros, kept the basin filled to the brim. Alexandros was delighted. He leaned over the basin so as to catch the stream of water in his mouth. "Delicious," he declared. "Try it!"

I thought of all the water-borne, disease-carrying organisms floating invisibly in Eros's stream. *Remember the Prime Directive,* I thought. *If he wants to drink, let him drink.*

"You don't know what's in that water," is what I actually said. After all, I had promised Philippos to keep his son safe. "Please drink our own watered wine instead."

"Nonsense," Alexandros replied. "Everybody take a drink!"

And we all did. He was right, of course. The water was cool, fresh, delicious. Time would tell whether it was also potable.

Finally, Alexandros was ready to proceed. We remounted and tried to make our way to the center of the city. It should've been an easy ride. We'd been told to follow the Panathenaic Way from the Dipylon to the agora. This was a wide and fairly straight street, especially when compared to the mad scramble of narrow, winding alleys diverging from it at every other step. On this particular day, however, each alley and lane seemed to be discharging a stream of people, all of whom coalesced into a sea of humanity in the midst of which we were attempting to move forward. On the whole, the people seemed more curious than hostile and Alexandros appeared to be enjoying their attention. Still, from a security standpoint, the teeming crowd was a nightmare.

"Stay close to him," Antipatros yelled helpfully. "And watch the roofs."

Finally, we arrived at the agora. We entered from the northwest corner. The street of the Panathenaia continued on to the akropolis but there was no hope of our getting through this public square any time soon. Besides, as I understood our plans, we were expected to stop by some of the municipal buildings that surrounded the agora before proceeding any farther.

"We will pitch our tents here," Alexandros announced. I looked around. The famous agora of Athens was simply a grassy plain, roughly rectangular in shape, a little more than a stadion long, a little less than a stadion wide, crisscrossed by a maze of paths worn into the grass over the years. A few ancient plane trees afforded a bit of shade here and there. There were a number of statues, in several groupings, scattered throughout. The west and south sides of the agora were lined with official-looking buildings; on the east and north sides were bordered by a mixture of public buildings, shops, and private houses. But mostly, there was an unbelievable crush of people. Every wife, maid, and house slave in Athens had apparently chosen that moment to go shopping. Old men stood around, chatting and staring at young women. Soldiers, perhaps just returning from the front line, were rushing to unknown destinations. Hordes of panhandlers, loiterers, and homeless people, went about their daily activities. As far as I could tell, everyone who lived in Athens was in the agora that afternoon.

"We're supposed to be quartered in the homes of our hosts," Hephaistion reminded Alexandros.

He was overruled. "No, we'll bivouac right here, in the agora."

"But, sire, this is an indefensible position," I objected.

"There's nothing to defend against, Ptolemaios."

We proceeded to pitch our tents, much to the amazement of the populace. Before we'd finished, the dignitaries arrived from the cemetery.

"What are you doing?" Demades demanded. "You're going to be staying with me, Alexandros."

"A simple tent's all a Macedonian soldier needs. We've brought our own accommodations, victuals, and arms. We require nothing of you, except the opportunity to address your leaders. How soon can you arrange it, Demades?"

"It's all set, sire – tours of the city, official receptions, dinners for everybody, symposia, perhaps a bit of 'private' entertainment as well. Just leave it to me. But please take down these ridiculous tents."

Alexandros was unperturbed. "The tents are staying up. Now let's get started with your program."

****

Our first stop was the Bouleuterion, right there on the side of the agora. When we pushed our way into the building, we found ourselves facing the four hundred leading citizens of Athens, constituting the Boule. As far as I knew, the Boule was in charge of running the day-today affairs of the city, although the precise details of their administrative arrangements escaped me.

The noise in the hall was tremendous. Every man there was talking simultaneously and, in an ever-escalating competition to be heard, they were all shouting at the tops of their lungs. Finally, somebody noticed that armed men had entered the building and the din quickly subsided. Although we looked somewhat out of place, wearing our mud-splattered armor among all these citizen politicians wrapped in their sparkling, colorful chitons, Alexandros appeared relaxed and confident as he found himself being introduced to various dignitaries, each of whom looked old enough to be his grandfather.

We were quickly surrounded by a welcoming committee. It turned out that the Athenian Assembly had been persuaded by Demades not only to accept Philippos's generous peace terms but also to bestow honorary citizenship on both Philippos and Alexandros. The archon performed the ceremony right then and there, placing a symbolic golden wreath on Alexandros's head. There were a few speeches, which failed to capture my attention, preoccupied as I was with trying to keep Alexandros safe in this scrum of people, none of whom had been searched for weapons beforehand. But everyone else, including Alexandros, seemed to revel in this impromptu opportunity to rub elbows. Alexandros was all smiles and charm, his manners and his language impeccable, as he pressed the Athenians to support a pan-

Hellenic invasion of Persia. The Athenians, in turn, appeared pleased, in their condescending way, to make their acquaintance with this callow youth, who presumed to lecture them on moral imperatives, religious duties, and the destiny of Greece. For my part, I couldn't wait to get back out into the agora.

Alas, Demosthenes was lying in wait when we emerged. "Let me show you around." For a sworn enemy, he seemed inordinately accommodating. Alexandros, ingenuous to a fault, eagerly accepted Demosthenes's offer and our small group set out for a tour of Athens. Alexandros was particularly anxious to visit the various temples.

There were no temples in the agora itself; however, immediately beyond the western edge of the agora rose Market Hill, topped by the magnificent home of Hephaistos, the god of fire and protector of all metalsmiths. And up ahead, looking southeast, no more than two or three stadia away, soared the akropolis itself, crowned by the Parthenon, a gleaming jewel box of white marble columns, topped by a colorful ribbon of friezes, shimmering against the cerulean sky.

"Let's go up there." Alexandros was like an eager puppy.

Demosthenes readily agreed. We set out along the western edge of the agora, with our guide lecturing as we walked along. On our right, we passed two colonnades:

The Royal Stoa, also called the Basileios, and then the newer Stoa of Zeus.

Demosthenes was in his element. "While they have covered walkways in other Greek cities, stoas have always struck me as a peculiarly Athenian institution. Most of our public life seems to take place in and around them. We use them to socialize ..."

"... you mean to argue," Aischines interjected.

"... to buy and sell merchandise," Demosthenes continued, ignoring the interruption, "to recruit students for the gymnasion or the palaistra ..."

"... to find clients or buy witnesses for the law courts ..."

"... and to engage in politics."

"I always had the impression," Demades joined in, "that some Athenians practically lived here. In fact, here is one of those creatures now." He pointed to a man in rags, sprawled against the side wall of the Basileios, sharing his blanket with a mangy dog. He was picking fleas off the dog's coat.

"This is Diogenes," Demosthenes told us with some distaste. "Each city has its share of embarrassments."

The object of the great orator's aspersions seemed unperturbed. "Ah, Demosthenes – a savage in debate, a pussycat on the battlefield."

Alexandros was delighted. "Hey, I like this guy. Is there anything I can do for you, my man?"

"Yes, kiddo. You can step out of my sun."

We moved on. Before we could leave the agora, Alexandros spotted a large group of statues, representing the twelve Olympian gods, clustered on the opposite side of the square. Each statue, standing by itself, would have been a breathtaking work of art but assembled all together their impact was a bit overwhelming. In fact, they almost made one another look pedestrian. *Who would want twelve gods sticking their noses into his affairs? One or two should be more than enough.* But Alexandros was fascinated, gazing enraptured for what seemed like an hour.

After we circled the Olympian gods, we finally made our way to a gap between the Stoa of Zeus and the Bouleuterion, occupied by nothing more than a row of stone benches. Evidently, the Athenians chose to leave an empty space between these buildings in order to provide an unobstructed view up to the temple of Hephaistos. Alexandros once again brought our procession to a halt, as he stared up the hill toward the impressive shrine.

"What we like to say," Demosthenes mentioned casually to Alexandros, as he tried to nudge him along, "is that the agora of Athens is the axis of the Kosmos. All else revolves around it."

For some reason, Antipatros seemed to take offense. "You'd only think that if you got really, really drunk, Demosthenes. Of course, in that case, no matter where you stood, you'd think the entire Kosmos revolved around you."

Demosthenes merely smiled in response. "We all suffer our delusions." He continued to point out buildings as we walked. Beyond the Bouleuterion stood the round Tholos, where various committees of councilors conducted their meetings and enjoyed their communal meals. Beyond the Tholos was the Strategion, which housed the Athenian military command. Facing the Tholos was another statuary group, that of the ten eponymous heroes. These were the ten mythical figures who gave their names to the ten tribes into which all Athenian citizens were divided for various administrative purposes.

Demosthenes once again strayed from our route. "I want to show you something." He led us to yet another tableau in the middle of the square, consisting of two figures. "These are the tyrannicides, Harmodios and Aristogeiton."

The two statues, executed in bronze, were slightly larger than life size. The younger figure, apparently Harmodios, his right arm holding a raised sword, seemed poised to strike. The older figure, Aristogeiton, had his left arm outstretched, as if to shield his companion during the attack.

Demosthenes was in full lecture mode. "Almost two hundred years ago, these two men assassinated Hipparchos son of Peisistratos. Although Harmodios and Aristogeiton paid for their courage with their lives, they freed Athens from the yoke of tyranny and permitted her to flower under democratic rule. The grateful citizens of Athens erected these statues to them, to stand among the gods and heroes of legend. Their act of killing the tyrant has made them truly immortal."

"Unfortunately," Aischines added, "these statues by Kritos and Nesiotes are only replicas. The originals, done by Atenor, were taken by the Persians when they sacked Athens during the archonship of Kalliades."

"I will get them back for you," Alexandros promised without missing a beat. Everybody within earshot smiled. He looked and sounded exactly like what he was, a bedazzled eighteen-year-old country bumpkin, standing in the middle of the Athenian agora, talking nonsense.

Of course, I knew for a fact he was talking nonsense because I knew how the Macedonian invasion of Persia would end; that's not what was worrying me, though. I was struck, instead, by Alexandros's apparent infatuation with everything he was seeing. *I've seen eager young teenagers getting seduced before but this is ridiculous.*

"Well, thank you, sire. Athens, and all freedom-loving people everywhere, will be eternally grateful." It was hard to separate the sarcasm from the condescension in Demosthenes's voice.

His tone seemed impudent to me but Alexandros didn't seem to mind. "It'll be my privilege. But can we go see the Parthenon now?"

"Right this way, sire." Demosthenes set off at a brisk pace across the agora. To accommodate Alexandros's eagerness, we practically ran up the Panathenaic Way as it wound its way upward, toward the akropolis. Despite the steepness of the climb, Alexandros continued to pick up speed. His pace began to take its toll. First, the portly Demades started to lag, then Aischines, then Demosthenes. Only Phokion was able to keep up with us; even he, however, was breathing hard. In the meantime, Alexandros and those of us guarding him were enjoying a relaxing jog, despite being weighed down with armor. All those miles around Mieza were paying off.

We stopped at a set of steps just below the top of the climb. Alexandros looked back at the gasping men behind us, smiling broadly. "No wonder those guys lost the other day."

The steps, carved right into the bedrock, at an extremely steep pitch, led straight up to a beautiful little temple, built on an outcropping high above.

"That's the home of Athena Nike – Victorious Athena." Demosthenes was panting by the time he finally caught up to us.

"Let's run up there." Alexandros took off without waiting for a response.

"We'll wait for you down here, sire," Demosthenes yelled after him.

Alexandros hesitated for a moment and then skipped lightly back down the steps. We resumed our jog up the Panathenaic Way.

Within moments, we reached the Gateway House, or Propylaia. I imagined that, once upon a time, when the akropolis still functioned as a military redoubt to which the (much smaller) population of Athens retreated in times of danger, this was simply a gate, barring the roadway that was the only practical means of access to the akropolis. Over the years, the character of this gate changed. It was now an elaborate building, serving to welcome worshipers, rather than to keep anyone out, and to remind all visitors that they were about to enter hallowed ground. As a result, what was once a simple, functional building had become a magnificent edifice in

226

its own right, much more impressive than any temple in Macedonia.

The roadway itself, consisting of bare rock worn smooth by a myriad processions and countless individual pilgrims who had been visiting this spot for more than a thousand years, entered the building through a huge middle gate, flanked by two pairs of smaller gates on either side. There were marble steps leading to the four smaller doors, with a level marble floor beyond them. However, the roadway in the center simply continued, unpaved, wide and sharply inclined, up through the building. An elegant entablature above the doors topped off the front of the building. The Propylaia were further enhanced by two large wings, on either side, framing the entry of the road into the Gateway House, and used to display secular paintings and sculpture.

While our guides were simply breathless, Alexandros was breathless and agog, staring at the ceiling high above us. "Look at that!" The ceiling, supported by nothing more than three slender Ionic columns on either side of the roadway, spanned a space fifty feet wide and almost forty feet deep. It was coffered and built entirely of marble panels, covered by shining gold stars and floral patterns painted against a background of heavenly azure. The entire entrance building was solemn, spacious, and airy. On the far side, at the upper end of the roadway, there was another flight of four steps on either side, beyond which lay the five inner doors, opening up onto the akropolis itself. "What a wonderful temple."

"Sire, this is only the Gateway House. We haven't gotten to any temples yet."

Alexandros was unfazed. "Well, let's get going then."

We made our way to the far end of the Propylaia and emerged into the brilliant sunlight of the akropolis. It took a moment for our eyes to adjust to the glare and for our minds to take in the grandeur of the prospect before us. Our entire field of view from one side of the large, gently sloping plateau to the other was filled by a suite of striking structures, each more majestic than the next, and each carefully sited so as not to overlap or hide its neighbor. Instead, each building flowed gracefully into the next one. Arrayed from right to left were the sacred precinct of Artemis Brauronia, the Chalkotheke, the temple of Athena Parthenos, the altar of Zeus, the temple of Erechtheus, and finally the dwelling of the Arrephoroi.

Each building, standing alone, would have been extraordinary. Arranged all together, and with innumerable statues and stelai scattered throughout the open areas, the impact was overwhelming. Atheist though I was, I still found myself rooted to the spot, daunted by the prospect of entering into this domain of immortals. Our entire group seemed to hesitate, either too winded or too overawed to proceed.

Prime Directive

As if reading our thoughts, Demosthenes urged us forward. "Since the expulsion of the tyrants, only the gods reside on the akropolis; however, mortal worshippers are always welcome to visit."

All of us, except Alexandros, began walking up the central pathway toward the temple of Athena Parthenos or Virgin Athena. Alexandros was too frenetic to walk. He was running from side to side, anxious to see all the sights at once.

In the middle of the pathway, half way between the Gateway House and the Parthenon, stood the heroic statue of Athena Promachos. True to her name, as the Champion of Athens, she appeared perfectly capable of defending her city. She was about fifteen feet tall, armed with a long spear and an old-fashioned shield. The golden tip of her upright spear, set off against the grayish green flanks of Mt. Hymettos far in the distance, was hurling little bolts of reflected sunshine in our direction. Because the ground continued to slope gently upward from the Propylaia toward the plinth of her statue, she seemed to be looking down on us as we walked toward her. There was a pronounced note of confidence in her relaxed stance. "Don't mess with Athens," was the implicit message.

Demosthenes, trying to stay on schedule, kept herding us forward. "It takes a lifetime fully to appreciate the akropolis of Athens, but our time is limited, so why don't we move ahead."

We put the truculent Athena Promachos behind us as we continued our walk toward the temple of her less pugnacious personification as Athena Parthenos. The Parthenon, up ahead and slightly to our right, was a large, commanding building, ringed by heavy, closely-spaced Doric columns, yet it seemed to soar with lightness and grace. I felt a bounce in my step just looking at it. The temple was built entirely of marble. On this particular afternoon, the fine-grained, almost translucently white Pentelic marble radiated an ethereal gleam, further enhanced by the colorful glow of the painted architectural features.

Three marble steps led up to the stylobate. We bounded up, eager to get a closer look. The peristyle consisted of seventeen columns on each side and eight columns on each end. Above the columns, and above the architrave, ringing the entire perimeter of the building, were ninety-two large metopes or marble panels, carved in high relief, depicting various battle scenes. Each individual frame was a masterpiece of representational art. First, the sculptor had carved white marble figures that were fairly bursting with life. Then the painter had painted these figures in subtle, naturalistic colors. The background surface of each metope was painted a pleasing shade of sapphire, which made the carved and painted figures pop out, as if floating in space. These marble men of myth looked more strikingly alive than our bedraggled group of bedazzled visitors.

Each panel was a window into famous confrontations of legend, myth, fable, and perhaps history. We witnessed the Olympian gods toppling the Titans; we relived the story of the Trojan War; we gawked curiously at the legendary Argonauts skirmishing against the formidable Amazons; we witnessed innumerable battles between Greek heroes and assorted daimons and demigods sprung into life.

"Who's going to win?" Alexandros wondered mischievously.

Phokion spoke up. "The Greeks win every time." If the man had a sense of humor, it was too dry to be discernible.

Alexandros continued to press his inquiries. "How long can they hold those impossible positions?"

"Oh, they can hold them for a long time." Demosthenes reclaimed the tour guide mantle. "The Parthenon was dedicated exactly a hundred years ago."

"And may it stand another thousand years," Phokion chimed in.

"Who built it?"

"Well, the Athenian people built it, of course." Demosthenes refused to be displaced. "If you're asking me who the architects were, some of the work was directed by Iktinos and some by Kallikrates. All of the sculptures were done either by the great Pheidias himself or to his design and under his supervision. And the moving spirit behind the entire enterprise, as I'm sure you know, was Perikles. But let's walk around to the east end of the building, where we can enter the naos."

As we made our way around the temple, I took a good look at the two large pediments, situated above the band of metopes and below the roofline at the two ends of the building. These triangular spaces were filled with free-standing, painted statues of unsurpassed beauty. We were told that the backs of the statues, which could only be seen by the gods, were finished as meticulously as those aspects visible to us mortals.

We looked at the west pediment first. In the middle, at the highest point of the triangle, we saw Athena and Poseidon locked in combat over possession of Attika. As Poseidon draws back to the right and Athena to the left, both hoping to inflict the decisive blow, two pairs of horses, hitched to chariots filled with gods and standing on either side of the combatants, rear up in alarm. The gods and goddesses, in and around the chariots, are caught in various stages of reaction, as the impact of the struggle gradually radiates outward to the farthest reaches of the pediment.

On the east end, we saw an equally stunning scene, depicting the emergence of Athena, fully armed, from the brow of Zeus. Again, the assembled pantheon of gods appears to be gradually reacting as news of this momentous birth washes over them.

Looking between the columns, we could glimpse a frieze running high up around the entire perimeter of the building itself, inside the peristyle. We were all craning our necks, this way and that, trying to follow the story told in marble. For once we all looked like Alexandros, with our heads held askew. The frieze portrayed the great Panathenaic procession. At first glance, it looked to me as if the entire population of Attika was on the move. From the west end, two streams of marchers set out, one along the north side of the building, the other along the south side, destined to meet around the corner of the building, at the east end. The procession was led by noble youths on horseback, followed by chariots filled with dignitaries. Then came the sacrificial animals, accompanied by their handlers, then the priests, followed by young girls carrying various tools and utensils for the sacrifice. Then, as we approached the east end of the building, we saw the new peplos of Athena, which was intended to replace the old cloak she had been wearing for the past quadrennial, being carried as a sail on a warship rolled along on wheels. Finally, after the frieze rounded the corner to the east, we saw the Olympian gods relaxing in conversation, awaiting the arrival of Athena's new robe.

Having followed the stone celebrants to the east end of the Parthenon, we were ready to enter the sacred enclosure itself. Although I would have thought that my capacity for amazement had been exhausted for the day, my first look inside literally stopped me in my tracks. Alexandros, walking by my side, emitted an audible gasp of surprise before he could resume breathing normally again.

What we saw was an enormous enclosed space, perhaps sixty feet wide, a hundred feet deep, and forty feet high. The floor was paved with large marble squares, polished to mirror-like perfection. Slender Ionic columns, on the sides and at the back of the hall, carried a balcony, with its own set of columns. These, in turn, supported the coffered ceiling, covered with intricate floral designs.

And the enormous naos was simply the setting for the figure in front of us. Standing some thirty feet tall, Athena chose to disregard our presence, gazing with detached superiority straight ahead, far above our heads, through the huge, open door, and out at the Attika countryside. She was standing on a marble pedestal, some five feet high, decorated with countless gilt figures, carved in shallow relief.

As we approached the base, I found myself looking at Athena's sandals, which were just about at my eye level. I backed up in order to get a better view. The skin of Athena, where it was visible – on her face and neck, on her arms and hands, and on her toes, which peeked out from beneath her chlamys – was carved ivory. The rest of her, that is to say her clothing, her hair, and her headgear, was clad in gold. Her right hand, resting on a column, held a small statue of Nike in her palm. Small, of course, was a relative term, since the statue of the goddess of victory alone was larger than life size. It was only slightly larger, however, than Athena's hand. Nike was a chryselephantine figure as well.

In her left hand, Athena held the top edge of a shield, the bottom of which rested on the pedestal next to her left foot. Curled on the inside of the shield was a huge snake, representing Erechtheus, the old god of Attika, whom Athena had evidently subdued.

Although monumental in size, this Athena was actually a beautiful woman. Her ivory face was clear, unclouded by even a hint of concern. She held her head high, despite the fact that her neck had to support a tiara upon which were seated three stylized sphinxes, each taller than a man. Her golden chlamys, over her golden chiton, hung in elaborate folds, the perfection of which only Pheidias could have achieved. The flowing gown revealed just a hint of the voluptuous body underneath. Her pose was insouciant and entirely natural, with most of the weight of her body supported by her right leg, while her left knee flexed slightly forward. The massive, colorful peplos, embroidered with such care over a period of four years by two specially selected Athenian maidens, was carefully draped over her shoulder. Unfortunately, it was barely visible from my vantage point because of the monumental size of the sculpture.

Had I been inclined to hear voices, as many of my fellow soldiers were, Athena would have spoken to me for sure; that is, I would have heard her voice inside my head. As it was, she spoke to me in a powerful way but only figuratively. I did not actually hear her voice. Looking at Alexandros, I was not sure that the same could be said about him. He was literally enthralled by the sight, unable to move.

Eventually, Antipatros and I grasped his arms and gently led him out of the naos. As he backed toward the door, he continued to stare at Athena, his moving lips reflecting an animated internal dialogue. Finally, he bowed to the goddess one more time and we were out of the hall, back in sunlight and fresh air. Despite our sluggish, almost dreamy pace, Alexandros was actually panting by the time we had negotiated the few steps down from the stylobate.

We stopped to give Alexandros a chance to catch his breath. When I looked up, I finally understood what Pindaros had meant, calling Athens a violet-wreathed, glorious, god-favored city. The jumbled rooftops of the city below were mostly hidden from our view by the parapet that ringed the entire perimeter of the akropolis. Instead, visible above the parapet was a band of forested hills and mountains, interrupted at one point by a gap, beyond which shimmered the Aegean. With the setting sun in front of us, the entire diadem of mountains ringing Athens acquired a reddish-purple cast, held together by the golden clasp of the sea below. The scene was beautiful, tranquil, deceptively benign. It was easy to forget that we were in the heart of enemy territory.

"Time to move on," Demosthenes informed us. I thought I'd caught a triumphant, albeit fleeting, smile on his lips, which he hadn't succeeded in suppressing quite fast enough. "There's lots more to see."

****

As it turned out, there was barely enough daylight left to permit a quick, superficial tour of the remaining sites on the akropolis. Twilight was deepening rapidly as we retraced our route down the Panathenaic Way, back to the agora, and then on to a private house for the evening's festivities. After we'd had a chance to wash up, after our feet were ceremonially washed by the servants, and after we were settled on our assigned couches, our host appeared and welcomed us to his humble abode. That's when we discovered that our symposion host was to be Demosthenes.

"We can't stay, sire," I told Alexandros, loudly enough for everyone to hear.

Alexandros frowned at me in disapproval. "Keep your voice down, Ptolemaios."

I joined him on his couch. "Spending the evening in the house of our sworn enemy is a security threat," I whispered.

"Stop worrying so much, Ptolemaios. Trust me, they aren't going to try to poison me. Besides, you're going to taste everything before I eat it, aren't you?" He laughed at his own joke.

"It's not a good idea, sire." I persisted but he just waved me off.

Demosthenes settled himself on the thronos at the head of the elongated circle of couches. Alexandros, with me hovering beside him, was assigned the seat of honor immediately to the right of his host. The rest of the couches were occupied by our small delegation and, interspersed among us, reclined an exceedingly thin slice of the Athenian elite. Evidently, neither Demades nor Aischines nor Phokion had made the cut. There would be no one there to blunt Demosthenes's domination of this evening.

"As our guest of honor, Alexandros, won't you please perform the libation?" There was nothing Demosthenes could have asked to ingratiate himself more deeply with his guest. Alexandros spilled the wine, intoned the prayers, led us in the singing of the paean. He was clearly in his element and our oleaginous host was happy to indulge him.

After Alexandros had finally finished, Demosthenes supervised the cutting and pouring of the wine, followed by the arrival of the food. To give the venal demagogue credit, there was plenty to eat and drink. (In hindsight, he probably didn't need any credit, having received ample funds from the Persians precisely for these purposes.) Bread with olive oil, lamb stews and fish dishes, olives, figs and apples, goat cheese and sweet cakes – the silver platters kept on coming. And to help wash it all down, a never-ending torrent of wine.

When we had all finished eating, the serving girls cleared away all the leftovers, brought us some bread for cleaning our fingers, collected the dishes, swept the floor, refilled our goblets, and disappeared for good. It was time to commence the real business of the evening. What that was depended on one's point of view. The Athenians believed that the point of a symposion was to improve the mind, through discussion, debate, defamation, and derision, with a little wine on the side to lubricate the verbal virtuosity. The Macedonians' objective was to consume prodigious amounts of wine, accompanied by bawdy singing, ribald joking, and salacious story-telling, to aid digestion and prepare for the libidinous escapades to follow.

Demosthenes was an Athenian and he was the host. "Let me raise a cup to the eternal friendship between Athens and Macedonia." While the guests drank in approval, he held his cup at a safe distance from his lips and continued to talk. "The gods have showered Athens with their bounty and we Athenians have tried to repay the gods, in our small, humble, insignificant way, by worshipping, exalting, and sanctifying them. We have sacrificed to them, fed them, housed them, clothed them, and entertained them. But most importantly, we have glorified their names throughout the civilized world by the achievements of our athletes, soldiers, mariners, poets, architects, and thinkers. It has indeed been a blessed union between the immortals who protect, inspire, and guide us, and us mortals, who serve them, carry out their commands, and spread their renown."

"Hear, hear," cried out several of the local guests. Alexandros was silent, but I could tell, simply by looking at him, that Demosthenes was playing him like a master lyrist strumming his favorite strings, plucking out just the right chords.

"It has pleased the gods," Demosthenes continued, "to bring us now to the brink of a new partnership between the timeless loftiness of Athens and the rising prominence of Macedonia. Nothing would make us happier than to see a victorious consummation of this partnership on the battlefields of Persia."

I thought I heard a few appreciative chuckles at the breathtaking audacity, not to say mendacity, of this declaration. However, Alexandros was not among the scoffers.

"Before there can be a successful partnership, however, there must be inspired leadership." Demosthenes was beginning to hit his stride. He was indeed a mesmerizing speaker. "Any leader of a joint expedition must be someone who combines not only Macedonian military prowess but also Athenian refinement and culture. No Athenian – nay, I say no Greek – will voluntarily follow into battle an uncouth ruffian, a schemer and a womanizer, a boorish barbarian."

This was too much for the assembled Macedonians. "Shut up, you windbag! Go piss in your hat." But Alexandros quickly hushed the dissenting voices. "Let the man speak!"

"We have here among us a rising star, who has demonstrated his bravery, intelligence, piety, and refinement. I raise my cup in your honor, Prince Alexandros of Macedon."

Everyone, except Demosthenes, took a deep gulp but that was probably a tribute to the quality of the wine, rather than approbation for the content of the speech.

Alexandros, who was mildly inebriated by this point, rose to respond. "Thank you, Demosthenes, for your hospitality and your kind words. I've heard, seen, and learned a great deal in the course of this day. I intend to put to good use everything I've learned and I hope you and your fellow leaders will likewise do everything in your power to advance this sacred cause upon which we are embarked."

More speeches and toasts followed. The high-minded tone of the discussion gradually degenerated, in inverse proportion to the steadily increasing levels of intoxication. Little eddies of conversation developed here and there in the room. I found myself in the eye of one such discussion, with passionate, if illogical, arguments swirling all around me. The disputants were yelling over one another, ignoring my presence in their midst, which was fine with me. I was busy communing with the dregs of wine at the bottom of my cup.

Some of the men started to disappear, singly or in pairs. I assumed they were answering the call of nature but then realized that most of them hadn't come back.

Demosthenes materialized in front of our couch. "Would you like to avail yourself of some entertainment, Alexandros?" Alexandros indicated that he would. "Do you prefer women or boys?" Alexandros chose women. "In that case, you're in for a treat. Have you ever heard of our enchanting Thais?"

"The most famous hetaira in Athens?" Hephaistion cut in from an adjoining couch, his interest suddenly aroused.

"The very same," Demosthenes affirmed. "She's agreed to grace my house tonight but only for a private chat with Alexandros. She's not a porne, you know."

"In that case, we can't keep her waiting." Alexandros rise unsteadily to his feet. I jumped off the couch as well, intending to fulfill my bodyguard duties.

Demosthenes intercepted me. "It's not necessary for you to follow, young man."

"Oh yes, it is. Wherever he goes, I go. You're not taking him anywhere by himself."

Hephaistion stepped between us. "That's fine, Ptolemaios. I'll go with him. You can find some other girl to screw."

Before I could protest the purity of my motives, Alexandros and Hephaistion set off for the back door, with Demosthenes in close pursuit.

If I were willing to have sex with somebody in this era, it wouldn't be some prostitute in Athens, I thought indignantly, and silently, as I returned to my dregs.

******

If Lanike thought her life would get easier with Alexandros out of town, she was sadly mistaken. Compared to his mother, Alexandros was a prince. At least he was relatively sane. By contrast, Olympias was growing increasingly paranoid. When news of the great victory at Chaironeia reached Pella, she found time, amidst the general rejoicing, to cavil at everything Lanike did. The morning porridge was too runny, the chamber pot too stinky, the mice fed to her pet snakes too skinny. Her real complaint was that her husband was being given the lion's share of the credit for the triumph, short-changing – at least as far as she was concerned – the achievements of her son.

The same day Macedonian troops, led by Alexandros and Antipatros, marched into Athens, Olympias invaded the palace kitchen and proceeded to smash all the earthenware pots and jars she could lay her hands on. No one ever found out the precise offense the unfortunate crockery had given to deserve summary execution but it was left to Lanike to clean up the mess. And the head lady-in-waiting had very little patience for the queen's petulance; she had bigger fish to fry. For one thing, she was trying to figure out, for the thousandth time, what was wrong with her peculiar friend.

Perhaps he prefers boys, Lanike thought. *Or perhaps he simply doesn't like me.* She rejected those conjectures immediately. She knew beyond peradventure that the young man with the strange accent and mysterious past loved her as much as she loved him. And any concerns about his homosexual tendencies were belied by the little tent she could see rising at the front of his tunic every time she touched his thigh. Having ruled out the most obvious explanations, however, didn't advance her search for a more plausible rationale. She reviewed all the possible hypotheses she had considered many times before and was once again forced to admit that they ranged from implausible to improbable to incredible. *No matter*, she finally resolved. *If he comes back to Pella alive, he'll either take me or I'll dump him.*

******

I, oblivious to Lanike's ruminations in faraway Pella, continued to stare at the bottom of my silver cup. I missed the one person in this world with whom I could converse thoughtfully, freely, and affectionately. *It's not fair to Lanike*, I thought, *to keep our relationship in a state of suspended animation. If my sacrosanct directive renders me a virtual eunuch, then, in all decency, I need to let her get on with her life.* It was a depressing thought.

"Do you need any help reading your future, sire?"

I looked up. A comely lass had somehow materialized in front of my couch. "Yes." I was glad for the interruption.

"Then give me your hand, sire."

I willingly complied, assuming she was a practitioner of palmistry. To my surprise, she took hold of my arm with both hands and started tugging, trying to dislodge me from my perch. "We can't do it here," she chided when I resisted.

"Do what?"

"Read your future, of course," she laughed, "while you read mine." She leaned forward to provide a more ample display of the text I was expected to decode.

Having finally caught on, I shook my head. "I'm afraid I'm not interested," I said, with a tinge of regret.

"Oh, come on, sire. I'm already paid for."

In the end, I relented. *I'm only doing my duty*, I told myself, *staying close to Alexandros*. We entered a long, narrow, dark hallway. I felt like a spelunker diving into an underwater cave of concupiscence. There were many doorways on either side of the corridor, some faintly illuminated by the feeble flicker of an oil lamp within, others completely dark. As we felt our way through the shadows, my senses were inundated by the sounds and smells of copulation. Apprehension and lust enveloped me in equal measure. With my right hand, I sought the hilt of my dagger; with my left, I fingered my other, rapidly hardening cutlass, before sheepishly snatching my hand away.

Prime Directive

The animalistic vocalizations emanating from the one brightly lit doorway at the end of the passageway caught my attention. *I know those grunters.* I raced ahead, leaving my surprised companion behind. When I reached the end of the corridor, I found myself staring at a windowless room, with several oil lamps glowing along the walls. The only items of furniture were a raised couch, positioned in the middle of the room and covered by a colorful linen sheet, and a small table off to the side, holding some cups, pitchers, and towels.

Positioned across the couch lay a naked young woman servicing two men at once. When I managed to raise my gaze, I did a double take. (Perhaps it was a quadruple take.) Fortunately, Alexandros and Hephaistion were far too engrossed in their task to notice my leering visage in the doorway. Swiftly, silently, and shamefacedly, I backed away from the doorway, causing my would-be paramour to collide with me from behind.

"That's the beautiful and cultured Thais," she whispered, trying to reach around my waist.

"Yes, I guessed as much. And that is the bashful and inexperienced Alexandros," I whispered back as I extricated myself from her grasp. "I've got to get some fresh air."

I was back in the dining room by the time my persistent and coquettish pursuer finally caught up to me. "Are you also bashful and inexperienced?"

"Look," I said, exasperation creeping into my tone, "we're not going to have intercourse."

"But we can talk, can't we?" Without waiting for an invitation, she clambered up next to me. "Why d'ya call him bashful and inexperienced?"

There was no harm in talking, I decided. What else did I have to do while waiting for Alexandros and Hephaistion to return? "Well," I began, "from my personal observations, Alexandros is neither bashful nor inexperienced; just the opposite. But I have overheard the chambermaids at the palace in Pella retailing a rumor, the upshot of which was that his mother, Olympias, felt that the educational curriculum prescribed for Alexandros by his father neglected certain important interpersonal skills. This was back, some four years ago, when the prince was fourteen. Anyway, Olympias allegedly retained the services of an alluring and experienced Thessalian courtesan, Kallixeina, to do for Alexandros's sexual development what Leukonides and Aristoteles were supposedly doing for his physical and mental advancement. 'After all,' she had argued, 'Alexandros is fourteen already and still a virgin.' How she knew he was still a virgin was never explained in these rumors. In any event, it was said that Alexandros rejected Kallixeina, which is what gave rise to the story that the prince was bashful and inexperienced."

"That's outrageous," the conversationalist by my side exclaimed. "The poor boy. What youngster would want to have sex with a porne procured for him by his mother?"

"She was more like a hetaira," I interjected.

"Whatever. I don't blame the kid for rejecting her. Far from proving shyness around women, his refusal to have intercourse with this Kallixeina demonstrated a healthy independence. It's the same as trying to force your child to eat all those rank vegetables he hates. Better to let him figure out for himself what he likes."

"Well, judging by what we've just seen, Alexandros seems to have figured it out by now."

"That he has; that he has. And how about you, my love?"

"I don't think so." I lifted her hand, which had somehow wormed itself onto my groin. "Why don't we just have some more wine?"

I'm pretty sure I successfully fought off her advances, although at some point the wine had its way with me. My next clear memory is of finding myself on the floor next to the couch, all alone, with my clothes in disarray, badly in need of a chamber pot.

****

I awoke at dawn the next morning, back in Alexandros's tent, in the middle of the agora. My recollection of how my charge and I and the rest of our delegation made our way from Demosthenes's house back to the agora, in the waning hours of the night, was fairly hazy. However, given the amount of wine I had consumed, I felt remarkably well.

"Get me some wine, Ptolemaios, will you please," Alexandros croaked upon rousing. "My head is about to explode."

After a quick sip, he washed his face in the water basin. "Last night was pretty great." He changed into clean clothes.

Thinking he was referring to his adventures with Thais, I found myself at a loss for words. "I'm sure it was," I finally muttered.

"I've gained a real understanding of Demosthenes," he continued, "and I think he's got a better appreciation of us."

I was instantly wary. "What do you mean?"

"Well, isn't it obvious? Athens has such a great heritage, so much history, such intellectual firepower. You can see why they look down on us. On the other hand, we have the military power now and they don't. But together, we can really achieve great things."

"Last night he didn't sound like he was ready to join us."

"Oh, he'll come around. The real problem is my father."

"Your father's the problem?"

"Yes, of course. Don't you see? He's so primitive, uncouth, vulgar. He's backward beyond belief. There is no way Greeks like Demosthenes, who are so far ahead of him, will ever agree to follow his lead."

"Your father is a visionary, Alexandros. Demosthenes is a reactionary. He wants to resurrect an Athens that disappeared a long time ago and that's not coming back. He hates Macedonia, because Macedonia has supplanted Athens as the leader of the Greek world, because Macedonia represents the future, while Athens stands for the past. He hates your father simply because your father is a Macedonian. And he hates you for the same reason."

"No, he doesn't." Alexandros was indignant. "He likes me. And he'll help turn the Athenian Assembly around to support us. They voted us honorary citizenships just the other day, didn't they? No, the problem is not Macedonia; the problem is my father."

You have been brainwashed, you idiot, I wanted to scream but, instead, I remembered the Prime Directive.

Stop messing with the future! I told myself. So, rather than trying to set him straight, I meekly mumbled another, "Yes, sire," and went back to the tent I shared with the rest of the squadron leaders.

We left Athens the next day, relieved of our urns of ashes but weighted down with more ominous baggage. I, for one, couldn't shake the feeling I had failed in my assignment, even though Alexandros was demonstrably hale and hearty. But it was Alexandros who was carrying the truly deadly psychological burden. I wished there had been something more I could've done to protect him from this invisible and invidious infection.

Chapter 8 – Scatter Pattern

The pinnacle of fortune is a better destination than dwelling place. After the victory at Chaironeia, a lot of people in Pella were walking on clouds, seeking to occupy the singular summit of success. Alas, there was not room enough for all; they started bumping into one another, with unhappy consequences for each.

Like elementary particles colliding in an accelerator, the egos of Olympias, Philippos, and Alexandros clashed in the wake of the Macedonian triumph. And just as the resultant scatter pattern in a cloud chamber reveals the structures of, and the interactions among, the colliding particles, so did the conflict of these titans of the Macedonian court expose their characters and interpersonal dynamics. The fortunes of war had raised each to unprecedented heights. They could have rejoiced in their mutual success; it could have brought them closer together; it might have fused them into a formidable team. Instead, it broke them apart.

My first inkling of trouble was an unexpected late-night visit from Alexandros. "You've gotta come'n help me," he said in lieu of greeting.

He was flushed, breathless, agitated. I couldn't imagine what the threat might be, at that hour of the night, in the middle of the sleeping palace, but my job as his bodyguard was to follow orders, not to ask questions.

"You're not going to need that," he added, when he saw me pick up my dagger. "Just put on a clean chiton."

By the time I had splashed some water on my face and changed my tunic, he was running out the door. We crossed the courtyard, after which our jaunt took an odd turn. I realized we were heading up the stairs to the women's quarter.

I stopped mid-flight. "You're sure you need me for this?"

"It's not what you think. We're going to see my mother. She's in a state. You've gotta help me calm her down."

If that explanation was intended to get me moving again, it failed to do the trick. "I'm the last person in the world you want to bring along to calm your mother," I protested desperately. Although a great deal had changed since my first day at the palace, my level of trepidation in Olympias's presence had remained constant. "I don't think your mother is a particular admirer of mine."

"No, really, I need your help, Ptolemaios."

"How could I possibly help you?"

"You could explain to my mother that my life was never in danger when we went to Athens. She's convinced that my father sent me to Athens to get me killed."

"Well, to tell the truth, Alexandros, I think your life *was* in danger while we were in Athens. We were just lucky nobody got close enough to take a swipe."

"What are you talking about? If those great warriors of the Sacred Band couldn't kill me, how could some Athenian amateur do me any harm?"

"You've got a point there," I had to admit. "But trust me, your mother isn't going to listen to me. Anything I say, she'll believe the opposite."

"Don't worry about it. Let's just talk to my mother and set her mind at ease."

Olympias was effusive in her welcome. "Well, if it isn't the fake Dionysos," she spat as we entered her reception chamber. "Always a pleasure to be reminded of unfinished business."

"Mother, Ptolemaios is my bodyguard. He can answer any questions you may have about my safety. Why don't you give him a chance?"

"Why not indeed. Have a seat, Dionysos." She pointed to a bare spot on the floor.

I remained standing. "Alexandros was in no danger in Athens."

Olympias laughed. "You're an amazing specimen, Dionysos. Everything you do, you do badly. You're an unpersuasive actor, a gregarious hermit, a transparent spy, an ignorant tutor, an inoffensive soldier, an impotent bodyguard. And now it turns out you're an unconvincing liar."

Even Alexandros had to smile at the flow of his mother's invective. But Olympias was not done yet. "An immortal god indeed. A god has abilities far superior to ordinary men. Your lack of ability makes you far inferior to the grooms in my husband's stables. No, I've got that wrong. Your lack of ability makes you far inferior to the horses in my husband's stables. In fact, you're inferior to the flies that the horses in my husband's stables swat with their tails. You're the opposite of a god."

She turned to Alexandros. "Son, from now on, we'll use a more precise name for your friend here." She assumed a solemn air as she turned back to me. "Henceforth, you shall be known as Ptolemaios

Antitheos. We'll make sure everybody calls you that from now on."

Alexandros rose to my defense. "He's not impotent." Of all the epithets his mother had just applied to me, it was an odd one to fasten on.

Olympias laughed. "How would you know?" She pondered the question for a moment. "You're not buggering this boy, are you?"

"No, we're not molesting each other." Alexandros maintained his patience. "Now, mother, will you please listen to him."

"No, you listen to me. Your father sent you to Athens because he wanted to get you killed – you got that? How do I know? Because he sent Ptolemaios Antitheos here to protect you. I mean, sending this bungler as your bodyguard was as good as sending a town crier to the agora to announce that you were coming in unarmed and defenseless."

She was on a roll. "Seriously, there was no reason on Earth to send you to Athens as his ambassador, when he had so many other sycophants anxious to go. And to send you, without an adequate contingent of soldiers, in the wake of what our army had just done to them, into the heart of enemy territory, knowing what we all know about the hatred of Athenians for our family – that wasn't just tempting fate; that was an all-out effort to get you killed."

"They don't hate our family; they only hate my father. And besides, why would my father want to get me killed?"

"Because he's jealous of you, that's why. Because you upstaged him at Chaironeia. Everybody knows you won that battle, that you're already a greater soldier than he ever was. He just couldn't stand it."

Her paranoia struck me as pathological. I knew for a fact that Philippos took inordinate pride in the accomplishments of his son and was doing his utmost to prepare him to take over the throne when the time came. But I refrained from contradicting her. *Remember the Prime Directive,* I told myself but, in reality, I was simply too chickenshit to argue with the queen.

"It's true I won the battle." Alexandros turned pensive. "But he seemed pretty happy about it at the time."

"Of course, he was happy. He knew he was going to steal all the credit for the victory from you. And then, when he realized that some people had noticed your contribution, he decided to send you to Athens. ... With this jerk as your bodyguard."

"I was never in any danger in Athens, mother. Just ask Ptolemaios."

"Ptolemaios Antitheos," his mother corrected. "And I couldn't care less what this jackass has to say. Open your eyes, son. The two of you are now rivals. And your father doesn't tolerate rivals."

Alexandros remained silent for a moment. "I'll admit this much. Greece will never unite behind us, as long as father is in overall command. The people who matter simply don't respect him. He's just so uncultured."

Olympias gave him a funny look. "It's not about culture, son. It's about who's got the biggest army. But you're right about one thing. He will never let you be in command. So how long are you willing to play second fiddle?"

"Not too long, that's for sure."

"And he knows that. Which is why he sent you to Athens."

This time, Alexandros did not contradict her.

"You may leave us, Antitheos." The queen favored me with an icy smile. "But — terrific job advocating my son's position ... pretty much in keeping with your usual level of competence."

Alexandros laughed and nodded for me to leave. I was only too glad to oblige. Mother and son remained closeted for a long while and continued to meet nightly thereafter but, much to my relief, I was not asked to attend any more of their discussions.

****

Lanike and I arranged to meet after sunset in the wooded precinct of Artemis, within a short walk of the palace. It was dark enough so that we had to feel our way. I stood, waiting at our rendezvous spot, when she touched me from behind. A frisson of electricity sent me spinning toward her. In the gathering gloom, her smiling face was a beacon of hope and expectation. Her lips quivered a little, whether from the cold or desire or defiance, I couldn't tell, at least not without covering them with my own. After a firm, moist, blissful moment, I broke it off. "I shouldn't have done that, Lanike. I'm sorry."

"Why?" she demanded. "That's all I've wanted to do since you left town and you're sorry? What's the matter with you?"

I sought in vain to strike my usual note of wisecracking levity. "Well, you know, I was worried we'd smother each other in our enthusiasm."

She appraised me with a searching, searing, sad look. We both knew what was at stake in this meeting.

Finally, and I couldn't tell whether in anger or in resignation, she changed her tone. "Look at you," she exclaimed, "you've become a real warrior. Was it tough killing people?"

"I don't think I killed anybody," I said quietly, "but at least I prevented others from killing me."

She had brought a borrowed animal skin along, which she now unrolled under a sheltering elm. "You're good at preventing things," she observed as she sat down. She patted the hide by her side, inviting me to join her. "But why are you so afraid of reaching out and grabbing what you want?"

"That's not true," I protested, knowing all the while that she had somehow managed to hit my predicament right on the nose.

"Well, never mind. Tell me about Athens."

We sat under the dark canopy of trees on a moonless night and talked, as it grew colder and colder. I described in detail all the spectacular wonders of architecture I had observed. She drew closer to me, in fascination and for warmth. I recounted, almost verbatim, the speeches I'd heard, my breath wreathing us in dew. I provided thumbnail sketches of the great men I'd met, while she insinuated her freezing hands between my thighs.

"We attended a symposion at Demosthenes's house the last night we were there," I told her, rubbing her arms to ward off the chill.

"Were there many hetairai?" she wanted to know.

"Some," I admitted, "but I was more interested in the conversations swirling about me. At one point, an argument broke out about the nature of love."

"How about pornai? How many of them were plying their trade?"

I ignored the interruption. "There was one elderly man who was making a lot of sense. He was quoting some books of Platon for the proposition that love is really a longing for the one thing that we can never attain."

"And what's that?" Lanike asked. Her hands, now reasonably warm, started to move further up.

"Immortality, of course. According to this man, we seek sexual intercourse in order to procreate, because that's the one sure means of perpetuating ourselves." The orbits traced by my hands had gradually expanded to encompass more or less Lanike's entire torso. Neither one of us seemed to be cold any longer.

"Of course, there are other avenues for achieving immortality," I hurriedly added, but it was too late. Her hands had seized my personal portal of immortality. "We should pursue higher, purer forms of love," I croaked, but she seemed intent on sticking to the carnal form and I, unfortunately, started to lose the thread of my argument.

We pawed and caressed and kissed and murmured and lost track of time. More than once, Lanike attempted to guide me inside her. Each time, I managed to resist, but at the cost of some physical as well as psychic pain.

Finally, she gave up. "Have it your way," she said, more in sorrow than chagrin. She rose to her feet, yanked the hide out from under me, and left me there, on the frigid, raw, sodden ground. "Just stay away from me," she cried over her shoulder as she stumbled back to the palace.

****

A few days later, I overheard Alexandros grousing that there would be nothing left for him to conquer by the time he inherited the throne but I thought nothing of the comment. I had interpersonal troubles of my own to address. Lanike had clearly failed to grasp the concept of platonic love and continued to run the other way every time I attempted to approach her. My friendship with Kleitos had suffered a setback as well, not only because he naturally took his sister's side in our dispute, even though he likely knew very little about the source of our discord, but also because he was apparently growing increasingly jealous of me. He thought I had close personal relationships with Philippos and Alexandros and Lanike. That was one or perhaps two too many, as far as he was concerned. I, on the other hand, resented Kleitos because he had become the favorite of every soldier and every serving girl in the palace. He had that rare ability to be instantly liked by everyone he met. *I may not be the opposite of Dionysos but maybe I'm the opposite of Kleitos.* I desperately wished for at least one close, personal friend.

The bitter truth was that, despite my rapid rise and my numerous interactions with the leading lights at the court, I was slowly drifting back to my customary state of splendid solitude. *Lucky you*, I told myself. *Now you have less chance of violating the Prime Directive and more time to devote to writing your travelogue.* Of course, I had not written a word, but then, I was still in the midst of gathering material and making preparations.

Speaking of preparations, during all this time, Philippos, along with most of his general staff, was traversing the length of Greece on a diplomatic campaign aimed at consolidating the gains achieved on the battlefield at Chaironeia. As he saw it, before he could launch his invasion of Persia, he had to make sure that, back in Greece, no challenges arose to Macedonian supremacy while he was away. Beyond that, to the extent that he could obtain any active logistical support for his invasion, in men and materiel, from his putative Greek allies, all the better. In theory at least, the invasion was supposed to be a pan-Hellenic effort.

"If we neutralize the big three," he had told me before our mission to Athens, "the rest of the small fry will fall into place." By the "big three" he meant Athens, Thebes, and Sparta. He had a slightly different approach for dealing with each.

In Athens, which was after all still a democracy, he concentrated on swaying public opinion. Of course, nothing is as persuasive to the average citizen as a thorough defeat on the battlefield, but Philippos followed up his victory at Chaironeia by dispatching Alexandros and Antipatros to woo the Athenian voters, Demades to bribe them, Aischines to bamboozle them, and Phokion to reason with them. Ironically, only Demosthenes, who had never refused any proffered Persian bribes, managed to withstand Philippos's blandishments. Nevertheless, Philippos's multifaceted campaign was an unqualified success. The Athenians were grateful, humbled, and docile. It would be a while before they would become once again susceptible to the cajolery of anti-Macedonian demagogues.

Thebes was different. It was ruled by an oligarchy of entrenched, wealthy, treacherous, and militaristic families. Philippos remembered them well from his years as a young hostage. He didn't hate them. He had been well treated and had acquired a sound education, especially in military matters, during his stay in Thebes. No, he didn't hate them; he understood them.

After the thorough defeat of the Theban army at Chaironeia, Philippos worked assiduously to break permanently Thebes's economic and military capacity. His army had managed to kill Thebes's finest troops on the battlefield. He then depleted the Theban treasury by insisting on a substantial ransom payment for each captured Theban soldier. Next, he made sure that Thebes would not be able to replenish its coffers by restoring the independence of all Theban client cities and by dismantling Thebes's little empire, the Boiotian League. He also brought back all exiled Theban leaders and expelled the ruling oligarchs, thus guaranteeing political turmoil for years to come. Finally, just to be on the safe side, he installed a Macedonian garrison on the Theban akropolis, the Kadmeia.

Moving on to Sparta, the capital of Lakonia, in the southeast corner of the Peloponnese, Philippos tried diplomacy first. He dispatched an embassy to ask the Spartan kings whether he should come as friend or foe. "Neither," was the Spartans' laconic reply. Philippos came anyway and deployed a three-pronged attack: He destroyed Sparta's economy by liberating its slave state, Messenia, which had supplied Spartans with free labor for centuries; he stripped Sparta of its arable land by transferring most of its Lakonian holdings to anti-Spartan cities such as Argos; and, most wounding to the superstitious Spartans' psyche, he desecrated – at least in the Spartans' view – the hallowed grounds of Olympia.

Spartans considered the sacred precinct of Olympia – the most ancient and venerable religious site in the Greek world and home of the quadrennial Olympic games – to be their own preserve, existing under the patronage and protection of Sparta. Philippos, having previously become the official protector of the sanctuary at Delphi, now decided to leave his imprimatur on Olympia as well. He commissioned the construction of a circular building, similar to the famous tholos at Delphi, dedicated to the exaltation of Philippos and his family. The Philippion, as it came to be known, was a relatively small but sumptuous edifice, located adjacent to the Temple of Hera and only a few steps away from the Temple of Zeus. Under its elaborate roof, and within its two concentric circles of columns, in the space normally reserved for a cult figure of the patron god or goddess, Philippos installed instead chryselephantine statues of himself, Olympias, Alexandros, and his parents, Amyntas and Eurydike.

In the eyes of the Spartans, the audacity, not to mention sacrilege, was breathtaking. In Philippos's view, the propaganda value was priceless – and the thumb in the Spartans' eyes, just a small added benefit.

After his productive sojourn to the Peloponnese, Philippos returned to Korinthos, on the isthmus between the Peloponnese and mainland Greece, roughly halfway between Sparta and Athens, where he convened a peace conference. Although it would take the delegates a few months to ratify the final charter, Philippos left clear suggestions on what he wanted to be done. His suggestions were adopted in due course. The result was the League of Korinthos, a confederation of participating Greek states, all of which agreed to a mutual non-aggression and defense pact. The League was to act through a Synhedrion, to which each member state would send delegates in proportion to its size and military might. The Synhedrion was to meet annually, with the site and date of the meeting rotating among the four pan-Hellenic festivals at Olympia, Delphi, Nemia, and the Korinthian isthmus. In between the general assembly meetings, there was to be a permanent security council, consisting of five representatives sitting in Korinthos and authorized to act on behalf of the League when the Synhedrion was not in session.

Macedonia was not a member of the Korinthian League. Instead, as its first official act, the League entered into a treaty with Macedonia, and with Philippos and his heirs, pursuant to which the League and Macedonia agreed to support each other in any military action that either one might undertake. In addition, the League also agreed to name Philippos as its permanent and hereditary hegemon and strategos, or chief executive officer and commander in chief, which positions happened to coincide with his existing job description as king of

Macedonia. Although theoretically it was Philippos's responsibility to carry out the policies of the League, it was clear to everyone that Philippos was going to lead and the League members were going to follow and support whatever actions their hegemon and strategos chose to undertake.

****

On his way home from the Korinthos peace conference, Philippos received an extended dispatch from one of his informants at the Persian court. After he finished reading it, he was unable to conceal his delight. "The stars are lining up," is all that he would say to his travel companions. "When we get back to Pella and I've got everybody together, you'll find out why I'm smiling."

Philippos arrived crowned in glory. There was peace in Greece; Macedonia was secure, prosperous, and powerful; Philippos was the military master who prevailed at Chaironeia, the diplomatic genius who engineered the League of Korinthos, and the visionary leader who would avenge the Persian invasions of Greece.

He's only forty-four years old, I thought, as I watched him enter the palace to a tumultuous welcome. *Twenty years ago, he was the leader of a small, impoverished, strife-torn nation on its way to extinction. If they had held a contest back then, he would have been voted the leader most likely to be assassinated next. And look at him now.* I could only shake my head in wonder.

269

"There'll be a feast tonight," Philippos announced, to boisterous approval. "Everybody's invited."

Turning to Antipatros, he said more quietly. "Get my general staff assembled in the armory right now. We need to do some planning."

Antipatros deputized a number of his aides to fan out and round up the officer corps for the meeting. Alexandros was invited, of course, and I attached myself to his hip, acting as if it were only natural for me to attend as well. No one objected when we entered the packed room together. All the leading lights of Macedonia were in attendance. The only missing notable was Olympias, but then, there were no women present at all. This was, after all, supposed to be a military briefing.

Philippos swept into the large hall. "Friends! I come bearing good news." He recounted in detail his disposition of Greek affairs. His command of Greek history, of recent political and military upheavals, of the strengths, weaknesses, and available resources of each town, city, and region, of the agreed upon diplomatic arrangements and military alliances, and of the tactical benefits and strategic significance of the peace settlement created by him, was simply astonishing.

He spoke without notes, without pauses, and without any interruptions from the attendees. When he finally stopped speaking, there was a moment of complete silence, followed by a spontaneous, explosive, tumultuous, and sustained outburst of cheering.

Philippos soaked in the approbation for a goodly interval but finally gestured for quiet. "Friends," he cried over the subsiding acclamation. "Friends, please settle down. I have one more bit of good news to share with you." Finally, the men settled down.

"Some important intelligence reached me just days before our arrival here." Philippos paused for dramatic effect. "Artaxerxes Ochos is no more!" There were gasps in the room. After all, Artaxerxes Ochos – barbarous, brutal, and bloodthirsty though he might have been – was the established and effective emperor of the preeminent enemy of the entire Greek-speaking world and the presumed commander of the army that Philippos was preparing to confront in the epochal struggle between East and West.

"What happened? When? Tells us about it." Several voices erupted in the room.

"Listen to this," Philippos resumed with gusto. "He was poisoned by his own physician who was put up to it by his grand vizier Bagoas. Goes to show, if you appoint a eunuch to be in charge of your affairs, expect to get your balls chopped off in the dead of night." Philippos was gleeful.

"And that's not all. After killing Ochos, Bagoas decided to imitate the dead despot by killing all of his sons, nephews, cousins – anybody with a plausible claim to the throne. He didn't stop until the only survivor was Ochos's youngest son Arses who'll presumably be putty in Bagoas's rapacious hands.

"So, gentlemen, let's get ready to take on an army commanded by a kid and led by a steer." Philippos's merriment was contagious. The room dissolved in laughter. Finally, Philippos raised his hands and shouted over the prevailing hilarity. "We'll launch our invasion early next spring. Parmenion and Attalos will lead the expeditionary corps. Once they establish a beachhead, the rest of us will follow.

"As usual, while we're away, Alexandros and Antipatros will stay in Pella, in charge of things here – and in the rest of Greece," he added with a wink.

I looked at Alexandros. Evidently, he had failed to appreciate the confidence his father had just reposed in him; all he heard was an order of battle that had left him behind. If Olympias was Medusa, then Alexandros, at that moment, was a worthy son of hers. His look of naked hatred, had Philippos glimpsed it just then, would have instantly congealed the king's pulsing arteries into crystalline veins of ruby-red quartz. Instead, Philippos – surrounded by acolytes, animated, and very much alive –

continued to gesticulate and dance, imbibing the adulation of his admirers.

"Everybody, let's get ready to feast!" the king yelled, breaking through the circle of his disciples and striding out of the room. *What happened to his limp? He must be flying on air.*

****

The limp returned, I noticed, toward the end of the feast, when Philippos laboriously made his way out of the dining room. As usual, a great deal of wine had been consumed, with Philippos leading the way, and he was no longer flying on air; more like swimming through molasses. Still, it was clear from the leering expression on his face that he was on his way upstairs for his long-anticipated reunion with Olympias.

We soon discovered that he was disappointed at his reception. Evidently, instead of an amorous encounter, there ensued a frank and vociferous exchange of views between king and queen. Although their discussion took place behind a series of closed doors, it was sufficiently raucous to permit at least snatches of their respective contentions to filter out. Alexandros's name was mentioned several times. Eventually, the king himself was exfiltrated from the queen's quarters, with his tail between his legs.

Philippos promptly found release in the arms of two of the serving girls cleaning up after the feast but the next morning, refreshed and none the worse for the tribulations of the previous night, he paid a call on his newly favorite general, Attalos the Adder. Evidently, the two of them had been talking during the diplomatic trip through Greece, because within hours there was an announcement of another feast. This was going to be a wedding feast to celebrate the union of Philippos and Kleopatra, Attalos's niece and ward. We all knew her, of course. She was known as Luscious Kleopatra around the court, to distinguish her from Little Kleopatra, who was Alexandros's younger sister.

There was a certain irony in Luscious Kleopatra's salacious sobriquet. She was a timid little girl, only a year older than Philippos's own daughter of the same name. At seventeen, Luscious had the voluptuous curves of an overripe pomegranate and the mental development of a slow-witted titmouse. She was sweet, inoffensive, and a pawn in the power politics of the palace.

Unlike Philippos's first six wives, Kleopatra promised to bring nothing but trouble to the marriage. The rivalry between the highlands barons and the noble families of the Macedonian plain had ancient roots but the suspicion and enmity between the two cliques reached new heights after Chaironeia. The highlands clans were already feeling aggrieved, not only because Philippos had moved his seat of government from the ancient capital of

Aigai to the lowlands Pella, but also because the explosive growth in wealth, trade, and commerce experienced by Macedonia during Philippos's reign had disproportionately benefitted the region around Pella, to the comparative detriment of the outlying fiefdoms.

On a personal level, Parmenion and Attalos represented two of the leading lowlands families. Parmenion had been Philippos's leading general from the outset of his reign but the Adder, although only ten years Parmenion's junior, had been laboring in the grand old general's shadow. All that changed after Attalos's notable success at Chaironeia. The Adder then solidified the alliance between the two families by marrying one of Parmenion's daughters. And now, not only had Philippos selected Parmenion and Attalos to be the joint leaders of the vanguard of the Macedonian invasion of Persia but he was also proposing to enter into his own marriage alliance with the Attalids. The ascendance of the two lowlands families rankled the highlands chieftains.

His six previous marriages brought more power to Philippos; this one threatened to subtract from his sway. It was a particularly puzzling decision in light of Philippos's consistent record of shrewd, calculating, strategic marriage alliances. He had spent the previous years of his reign working hard to keep the highlands barons happy. In fact, his marriage to Olympias was arguably part of the effort to cement the allegiance of the highlands aristocrats. Although Epiros was considered an independent kingdom and had never been a part of Macedonia, the leading Epirote families were geographically, temperamentally, and by kinship much closer to the highlands barons than to the aristocrats of the plain. In a single stroke, Philippos was threatening to destabilize the entire carefully balanced platform on which his throne rested.

Olympias herself was livid, which might very well have been the primary objective of the entire exercise. She certainly understood the strategic stupidity of the move but her outrage was much more personal. Philippos was marrying a girl half her age, a quarter of her intelligence, and an infinitesimal fraction of her independence, but a girl who was pretty, nubile, and submissive. She was, in short, a complete and tangible rejection not only of Olympias but of the very essence of everything that Olympias had brought to her own marriage with Philippos. And Kleopatra threatened to produce potential rivals to her son in the line of succession, a prospect bound to appear especially threatening to Olympias in light of the apparent ascendancy of the lowlands clique at the palace.

Philippos insisted on being the first one to break the news of his impending marriage to Olympias. In hindsight, this might have been a tactical mistake. Perhaps he enjoyed watching the procession of colors on Olympias's face after he had made his announcement – first, she turned an appalled white, followed by a breathless blue, then a jealous green, and finally an incandescent raging purple – but it certainly was not worth the subsequent price.

That night, the snakes emerged. A little after the third watch, we were awakened by the screams of a maid who had discovered one of the cold and creepy creatures sharing her bed. True to my training, and without knowing the cause for the alarm, I bounded up to the women's quarter, sword in one hand, dagger in the other, only to trip – and practically castrate myself – over a large whipsnake. By the time I captured the snake (I knew better than to kill it), I had been joined in the women's common room by half a dozen other soldiers, most of them holding a snake or two, and a large clutch of squealing, frantic, semi-naked serving girls, pointing at many more slithering shapes lurking in corners and crevices.

We could all make a shrewd guess as to the source of this sudden plague, having become acquainted with Olympias's snake-filled ménage, either from personal observation or habitual bawdy banter, but none of us was willing to give voice to our suspicions. Although the queen herself was nowhere to be seen, we were all cognizant of her penchant for materializing suddenly out of thin air and wreaking vengeance on anyone giving offense. We silently corralled as many of the snakes as we could, stuffed them into their baskets, and went back to sleep.

Not surprisingly, a few of the sinuous sneaks managed to get away. For the next day or two, I kept seeing flashes of scaly movement out of the corner of my eye. Luckily, most of the snakes were not particularly poisonous. As an added benefit, all the rats, mice, and other vermin disappeared. The chickens in the courtyard were more skittish than usual but otherwise unharmed. The maids upstairs were silent, sullen, and sleepless. Olympias remained unseen. But not unheard.

Two days after the night of the snakes came the night of the broken furniture. Philippos had evidently attempted to restore matrimonial harmony with Olympias, which turned out to be a serious miscalculation on his part. Instead of amatory adventure, there ensued a long screaming session. The entire court froze in a posture of breathless eavesdropping. Eventually, Philippos beat an ignominious retreat. It quickly became evident, however, that Philippos had chosen to depart before Olympias had finished elucidating her position because, the minute he had stepped out, we started hearing the shrill sonorities of shattering wood. By the time Olympias finished her demolition derby, I could distinguish the dull thud of a club smashing a bed from the high-pitched squeal of a sword splintering a door.

Despite the uproar, Philippos continued with his preparations, undeterred and unbowed. He made no further attempts to mollify Olympias. He remained oblivious to the rising resentments and fears of the upland aristocracy. He ignored the tittering at court. He made no effort to explain his course of action or future plans to Alexandros. He was too busy fluffing the pillows on the bridal bed.

To further enhance the prevailing atmosphere of convivial bonhomie, an ugly rumor started to make the rounds at court. Even though I wasn't a member in good standing in any of the gossip-mongering circuits and was therefore always the last to hear these things, I did eventually run into Lanike who was so anxious to share the latest rumor with me that she forgot she wasn't speaking to me.

"Can you believe what they're saying about Alexandros?"

"What are they saying about Alexandros?"

"You haven't heard? Where have you been the last few days? They're saying Alexandros is a bastard."

"What do you mean, a bastard?"

"What d'ya think I mean? That he's illegitimate; that Philippos isn't his father."

"That's ridiculous."

"I know it is but that's all anybody's talking about."

"Who's saying that?"

"Everybody."

"What's Olympias have to say?"

"You think I'm going to ask her?"

We both laughed. "Nah, I guess not."

"But she has been spending a lot of time talking to Alexandros behind closed doors," Lanike continued.

"You mean there're still some doors she hasn't smashed yet?"

"There's a standing order for carpenters to bring in a couple of new doors every morning."

"Seriously?"

"No, not seriously, you doofus." Lanike slapped my shoulder playfully. "And here I thought you were a smart guy."

"What would give you that idea? Would a smart guy fall in love with you?"

"Yes, a smart guy would, so that's another piece of evidence you're not as smart as people think."

I felt an irresistible urge to grab and kiss her but instead I just stood there, smiling foolishly, as usual. "So, who's the father supposed to be?"

Lanike seemed confused for a moment. "Oh, you mean Alexandros's father. Nobody in particular. Just not the king."

"Alexandros is almost nineteen years old and the heir apparent and nobody noticed that he was a bastard until now?"

"Maybe it's because he's the heir apparent that they noticed it now," Lanike said innocently.

We were veering into dangerous territory. "Let's go for a walk," I suggested.

We strolled down into the streets of Pella and into the olive groves beyond. After a little while, ever so subtly, I surreptitiously took her hand in mine. She pretended not to notice. We spent a long time talking about nothing, enjoying each other's company. When we finally re-emerged from among the trees, Lanike extricated her hand and ran off. "See you around," she called back. I floated, in complete defiance of gravity, all the way up to the palace.

****

The wedding reception to celebrate the union of Philippos and Luscious Kleopatra took place early next spring. It was a remarkably tense affair. Despite the king's efforts to make the seating arrangements as diplomatically harmonious as possible, practically each couch in the dining hall became a little redoubt for one court clique or another.

The Adder was given the seat of honor to Philippos's right. Alexandros arrived late, scowling, eyes to the floor, heading straight for his customary seat. He was only steps away when he noticed that his place was already occupied by Attalos. Philippos discretely signaled with his head toward the couch on his left. Alexandros slunk over to the indicated seat, his mood deteriorating with each step.

"I'll make sure my mother invites you to her next wedding," he announced loudly, upon taking his assigned place.

There was a stunned silence in the hall as everyone awaited the king's riposte. Instead, Attalos – never distinguished by his tact or judgment – plunged into the breach, jumping to his feet and raising a cup of wine. "A toast to the happy young couple." He tottered a bit but his lungpower was undiminished. "May their union finally produce a legitimate heir to the Macedonian throne."

Before the echo of the toast finished reverberating in the hall, Alexandros had crossed the space between his and Attalos's couch, a dagger glinting in his right hand. *Attalos is a dead man,* flashed across my mind. For an inebriated man of fifty-three, Attalos reacted with remarkable alacrity. He was running across the hall, toward the exit, as Alexandros's dagger whistled through the air.

Philippos, who was even more drunk than his newly-minted uncle-in-law, attempted to come to Attalos's aid. Unfortunately, in his rush to get from his couch to the other side of the hall, he fell flat on his face.

"And this is the man who's supposed to lead us from Europe to Asia." Alexandros's voice was drenched with contempt. "He can't even cross the floor from his couch to the door." And with that, the former heir apparent strode out of the hall.

I helped Philippos back to his feet. "Go follow him," Philippos told me, "and make sure he doesn't do anything stupid."

****

I caught up to Alexandros at the top of the steps leading to the women's quarter. "My mother and I are leaving Pella." Alexandros seemed preternaturally calm. "Do you want to come with us?"

It was clear from his tone that he would not be deflected from his chosen course. My choices were to stay with Philippos in the palace or accompany Alexandros and Olympias to wherever it was they decided to go. Either way, I'd be declaring my allegiance to one side and making an enemy of the other.

I played for time. "How soon are you planning to leave?"

"We set out before dawn. If you wish to come along, be at the gate, with all your gear, at the end of the third watch."

I nodded and left, lost in thought. *Whatever you do,* I told myself, *do not interfere.* On the other hand, sitting on my rear end and doing nothing might turn out to be even more radical interference. Plus, it would be perceived as a betrayal by both sides.

I decided to pay Philippos a visit. I found the king in his study, his head in his hands, snoring. But, displaying his remarkable talent for quick recovery, he was instantly awake, and almost sober, as soon as I cleared my throat to rouse him. "Just a bad headache," he told me, when I asked him how he felt.

I told Philippos that Alexandros and Olympias were intent on leaving the palace before dawn.

284

"I think it's best I let them go." Philippos was too weary to fight. "They'll come back after things have calmed down. In the meantime, go with them. Remember, it's still your job to keep Alexandros safe." He dismissed me with a wave.

I packed my gear, retrieved my horse, and made my way to the gate. I was early. The place was deserted but for the two sentries. On a sudden impulse, I asked them to hold my horse and ran off.

Lanike was asleep when I reached her chamber. I gently shook her awake. "What's up?" she asked.

When I explained what had happened, she was silent for a long moment. "I guess we should say goodbye. We may not see each other again."

"Nonsense," I protested. "They'll all make up in a week."

"I don't think so. Philippos may be ready to forgive and forget but the queen is not the forgetful type and, when it comes to a threat to her son, she will never forgive. I don't think you guys are ever coming back."

"You'll see," I tried, and failed, to project an air of confidence in my prediction.

I reached over and tried to kiss her but she pushed me away "They'll be waiting for you." She was determined not to cry. "Better get going."

Reluctantly, I started moving toward the door. "Please give my regards to Kleitos. Tell him I'm sorry I didn't get a chance to say goodbye but we'll be drinking and carousing together soon enough."

"I'll tell him. Now take care and godspeed." And with that she turned to the wall, her shoulders shaking ever so slightly.

I resisted the urge to get down on my knees and comfort her. Instead, I tiptoed out of the room and slowly made my way back to the gate.

By the time I got there, three members of the Mieza cohort – Nearchos, Erigyios, and Harpalos – were already waiting. Evidently, Alexandros had asked them to join our little group of exiles. They stood around, stomping their feet in the cold, wondering what the future held. I, of course, had a vague idea of the general outline but the details remained hazy.

Alexandros and Olympias arrived, trailing a small entourage of loyal servants, numerous horses and carts, and loads of gear. *Amazing how fast it all got organized. Unless it's something they've been planning for some time.*

Prime Directive

We rode out as the sentries of the fourth watch arrived to relieve their comrades. No one tried to stop our departure and no one raised the alarm.

It took us two weeks to reach Epiros. We left Olympias with her brother Alexandros, the Epirote king, along with her entourage, her baggage train, and her dreams of return and revenge.

Three further weeks of travel through some of the most rugged mountains I'd ever experienced brought the remnants of our exiled group to the camp of King Langaros of the Agrianians. Alexandros was exhilarated by the thought of spending the next few months, or perhaps years, living with these nomadic barbarians.

The first night after our arrival, as we settled down on our straw mats, thoughtfully provided by King Langaros, Alexandros was in an expansive mood. "These Agrianians will make wonderful soldiers when we return to Macedonia. Not that it'll matter anyway, because no Macedonian soldier will fight against me. If it's a choice between Philippos and me, who do you think they'll follow?"

"Go to sleep." I was too busy trying to stop our bedmates from sucking me dry to answer his question and he had no further rejoinder to add.

"The fleas and lice have certainly made their choice," I observed under my breath but Alexandros was already asleep.

Chapter 9 – A Nuptial Paroxysm

In the spring of 250 Z.E., Olympian gods competed with each other in bestowing their bounty on the king of Macedonia. Certainly, that was Philippos's own perception of his status in the world, which assessment he was happy to share with anyone willing to listen. "I'm practically a colleague of theirs, don't you know," he liked to joke. "No surprise they hold me in high regard."

The pretensions to divinity were not meant to be taken seriously but, as with all such jokes, there was an aspirational undercurrent to Philippos's humor. And there was no gainsaying Philippos's winning streak. On the geopolitical front, his control of Greece was firm and unchallenged and his invasion of Persia was finally under way. An expeditionary force of ten thousand, including a thousand cavalry, under the overall command of Parmenion and Attalos, had crossed the Hellespont and disembarked on the Troad coast. Better yet, no opposition from the Great King had materialized, possibly because of the ongoing turmoil in Persepolis.

Arses, the kid emperor of Persia, lasted less than two years on the throne. Selected for his malleability by the puppeteer Bagoas, Arses made the fatal mistake of attempting to slip his master's strings. The venomous vizier would have none of it. Proceeding in the usual pleasant Persian fashion, he poisoned Arses and then, even before the young emperor's final convulsions had subsided, he had all of Arses's relatives put to death.

Next, Bagoas installed yet another would-be marionette, a 44-year-old soldier named Kodomannos, who claimed that his grandfather was a brother of the father of the previously poisoned Artaxerxes Ochos. Evidently, the blood-thirsty Bagoas had been so thorough in his purges of the royal family that Kodomannos, who might have been a distant offshoot of a junior branch of the royal family or who might have been nothing more than the bastard son of a royal chambermaid with an active imagination, became the most plausible candidate available for the throne. Upon his accession, Kodomannos assumed the name of Dareios Tritos, to give himself at least a veneer of respectability.

Once in power, however, Dareios turned out to be a recalcitrant puppet. Unlike Arses, Dareios was a grown man, a proven soldier, and an accomplished infighter. His first act, upon obtaining his position, was to expropriate Bagoas's inexhaustible inventory of toxic potions and to force the great poisoner to savor some of his own stock. With Bagoas out of the way, Dareios then proceeded to secure his control of the empire in the customary way but he was not quite finished with the process of killing every potential rival when the Macedonian expeditionary force crossed the Hellespont.

Parmenion and Attalos, taking advantage of the temporary state of distraction in Persepolis, acted swiftly to take control of the Troad, to establish supply dumps and lines of communication, and generally to prepare the ground for the main Macedonian army, expected to invade, under Philippos's personal command, later that year. Then, having made quick work of their primary assignment, the old commander and his almost equally old son-in-law marched their forces down the coast toward the Persian-occupied Greek cities of Ionia. Once again, there was no Persian opposition and the Greek-speaking citizens of these former Greek colonies welcomed the Macedonian soldiers as liberators. The cities of Erythrai, Ephesos, and the island city of Chios all opened their gates in welcome. In Ephesos, the grateful citizens set up a statue of Philippos alongside the cult figure of Artemis herself in the goddess's fabulous, world-famous temple. Clearly, the Ephesians were well-informed about the Macedonian king's latest proclivities.

On the domestic front, Philippos was enjoying a similar run of luck. Luscious, having delivered a baby girl precisely nine months after her marriage to Philippos, was pregnant once again. The delighted Philippos was certain that this time she would produce a baby boy who could serve as the backup heir he had been seeking prior to his departure for Asia.

The king visited his blooming bride every day, bringing bouquets of flowers plucked fresh that morning on the hillsides outside of Pella. Unlike the musty, moldy smell of the rest of the palace, the women's quarter exuded a bucolic, sylvan aroma, mixed with just a hint of the expectant mother's emesis and the baby girl's excreta. During each visit, Philippos would spend the majority of his time playing with his baby Europa, which was perfectly fine with Europa's beaming mother. The grateful Kleopatra, basking in her husband's attentions, selected a few particularly choice flowers from each day's haul, weaving an impromptu wreath that the old goat would proudly wear around his neck for the rest of the day.

During this same time frame, Philippos's second son, Alexandros, also returned to Pella. Whether Alexandros believed it or not, he had never ceased to be the primary heir – a position he had occupied in his father's heart since the day of his birth. After Alexandros's hasty departure, following the unfortunate incident at the wedding feast, Philippos had dispatched a steady stream of emissaries to track Alexandros down and persuade him to return. Philippos's persistent importuning, plus the even more persistent fleas, plus Alexandros's own sense of missing out on things, finally combined to persuade the impetuous prince to return home, although the relationship between king and heir remained rather frosty. Nevertheless, the return of his hot-headed son was, for the king, another source of familial warmth in those balmy days of blue skies and endless sunshine. (The threatening black cloud on the horizon – the specter of Olympias, who had not been asked to return – was still safely out of lightning-bolt range, at her brother's court in Epiros.)

Even Philippos's eldest son, the half-wit Arrhidaios, although he would never be an heir, was proving useful as marriage bait in cementing a strategic alliance that his father, ever the crafty diplomat and marriage broker, was cobbling together prior to his departure for Persia.

Karia was an old, small, independent kingdom squeezed between the Persian-occupied Greek cities of Ionia and the Persian-occupied kingdoms of Pisidia and Phrygia. It was ruled, at that moment, by a Grecophile king of Karian descent named Pixodaros. The Karian royal family had always been careful to maintain cordial relations with Persia, in whose giant shadow they were obliged somehow to maintain their independence. Pixodaros himself had been quick to marry off his eldest daughter to a Persian nobleman named Orontobates in order to demonstrate his loyalty to all things Persian. At the same time, Pixodaros was also not averse to hedging his bets by sending out feelers of friendship to Macedonia, the rising power on the other side of the Aegean Sea. Philippos, sensing a kindred spirit and seeing an opportunity to cause trouble in Persia's back yard, proposed to Pixodaros a marriage between his eldest son Arrhidaios and another of the Karian king's daughters. Pixodaros was thrilled by the offer. Arrhidaios's lack of mental capacity made no difference as far as he was concerned. What mattered was that, with a Macedonian army rampant in Ionia and the Persian court in turmoil, Karian independence would be protected, whichever side ultimately prevailed.

The nuptials were in the final stages of negotiation when the first, tiny, imperceptible thread began to unravel from Philippos's carefully woven fabric of treaties, alliances, betrothals, and conquests. It all started to go wrong in the most foolish way imaginable. Alexandros, recently returned to Pella but still inordinately resentful and suspicious, caught wind of Philippos's most recent matrimonial maneuvering. Instantly, and idiotically, he apprehended a conspiracy designed to usurp his position as Philippos's primary heir. Alexandros must have believed that, by marrying the Karian princess, his older half-brother Arrhidaios (he was the offspring of Philippos's third marriage, to Philinna of Larissa) would somehow grow the fully functioning brain that he had failed to acquire at birth. Admittedly not a rational explanation but I for one was unable to devise a more cogent theory to account for Alexandros's actions.

Behind Philippos's back, Alexandros dispatched his friend, the actor Thettalos, to Karia to ask for the princess's hand for Alexandros, instead of Arrhidaios. Philippos found out about his son's plot within days after Thettalos had boarded a ship bound for Halikarnassos but not in time to intercept Alexandros's envoy. Pixodaros accepted the proposal with alacrity, thrilled by the prospect of becoming the father-in-law of the Macedonian heir apparent, as opposed to a Macedonian half-wit unlikely ever to amount to anything, albeit a royal Macedonian half-wit.

Philippos's initial reaction to this sequence of events was characterized by uncontrollable convulsions of laughter. His merriment, however, quickly turned into cold fury. "What the fuck were you thinking?" he screamed at his son upon barging into his room. "Do you think that the daughter of a mere Karian, who's nothing more than a vassal of the barbarian king, is suitable marriage material for the future king of Macedonia?"

"But she's good enough for Arrhidaios?" Alexandros protested weakly.

"He's a retard, you fucking moron," Philippos thundered. "And you used to be such a bright boy. Who else knew about this?"

"Nobody."

"Sure – nobody," Philippos snorted. "You're confined to quarters. There'll be an armed guard posted on your door and, if you try so much as to take a piss beyond the threshold, they'll chop your dick off, you dumb prick."

With that, he marched out of Alexandros's room and headed straight to mine. "Did you know about this?" he yelled as he burst through the door.

"Know about what?"

"Don't play the fool with me, Ptolemaios. I know you better than that."

"I have no clue what you're talking about, sire."

Philippos explained it all to me. My first reaction was to laugh but the king was not in a jovial mood. "Pack your things, round up your buddies – Nearchos, Erigyios, and Harpalos – and be out of Pella before nightfall."

"What did we do?"

"It's what you didn't do. And besides, I can't exile my own son, so his support group will have to do."

"That makes no sense, sire."

"Sure it does. I want to cut him off from everybody he knows."

"Well, I know what that feels like. But how's that going to pour more sense into Alexandros's head? Besides, we're not even his inner circle. He's got much better friends than us."

"Yes, but you guys aren't Macedonian, are you? What's the point of exiling somebody whose family lives half a day's ride out of town? You four are all outsiders, so you four are getting tossed. Got it?"

"Yes, sire."

"Don't spend too much time worrying about it. Just make sure you're out of here before nightfall, you hear?"

And so, Alexandros became a prisoner in his own home and the four of us made our way back to King Langaros of the Agrianians. Luckily, Alexandros's confinement, and our exile, didn't last long. Philippos's fury subsided quickly and he recalled us within two months.

It was only a few weeks later, while pondering his next steps, that Philippos hit upon his ultimate matrimonial masterstroke. The highlands barons had been restive ever since his marriage to Luscious Kleopatra and the subsequent emergence of the flatland junta of

Parmenion and Attalos. Something had to be done to mollify the highlanders before they could all march off, unified and cohesive, into Asia. The obvious answer was another strategic marriage or two but Philippos was not looking forward to taking on another wife. It was clear to him, at least in hindsight, that he had reached the limits of his conjugal juggling abilities when he married Luscious. One more wife could easily cause his balls to come crashing down.

Luckily, he had one more offspring available for matrimonial diplomacy, his daughter Kleopatra. (His remaining three daughters, Kynane, Thessalonike, and Europa were off the market, although for very different reasons. He had, somewhat rashly, given away his oldest child – the headstrong, willowy, exotic, half-barbarian Kynane, issue of his first marriage to the Illyrian princess Audata – to Amyntas the Nephew, partly in gratitude for the young man's graceful acquiescence to having his rightful claim to the throne of Macedonia usurped by his uncle Philippos, all those years ago, and partly as a means of creating, in the person of Amyntas, another back-up heir, just in case. On the other hand, Thessalonike, his daughter with the Thessalian beauty Nikesipolis, and Europa, his daughter with Luscious Kleopatra, were, at eight and one years of age, both beautiful, precious, adorable, and delicious, but also too young to be married off just yet.) So Little Kleopatra was, at least for the moment, the last remaining card in his deck of daughters eligible for diplomatic deployment.

Philippos was determined to derive the maximum possible benefit from arranging her betrothal. His dilemma was choosing one of the restive highlanders as the lucky recipient of Philippos's nuptial bounty. "They're all pygmies," he confided to me in an unguarded moment, "and to choose one is to slight all the others."

That was when he had his stroke of genius. Instead of marrying Little Kleopatra to one of the undistinguished upper kingdom chieftains, he would send her off to a man whom all of the highlanders admired and with whom they all had bonds of affinity and kinship: Alexandros, the king of Epiros. Besides, a marriage to an actual king was the least that Little Kleopatra deserved. At the same time, such a merger should not be overly offensive to the lowlands barons, especially after they had received the previous trophy in the form of Philippos's wedding to Attalos's niece. In addition, this union would also neutralize Olympias's grievances; after all, Alexandros of Epiros was her brother. As a final benefit, Alexandros of Epiros possessed a sizeable military force in his own right, at least a part of which he could lend to Philippos for the Persian expedition.

So what if Little Kleopatra was obliged to marry a significantly older man and a man who happened to be her uncle? Sacrifices had to be made for the sake of the family, for the sake of Macedonia, and for the sake of the great pan-Hellenic invasion of Persia. The betrothal negotiations were speedily concluded and a wedding date set. Only then did Philippos inform his daughter of his decision. She accepted her fate with equanimity. "Well, at least he's family."

Philippos set about making the necessary arrangements with his usual verve. While in the midst of preparations for the greatest military adventure since the Trojan War, he took time out to organize the most lavish and elaborate wedding ceremony ever witnessed in Greece. And he didn't neglect his familial and religious duties, either. He was there, in the room, when Luscious gave birth to a beautiful baby boy whom they named Karanos. At the same time, he also dispatched a messenger to the Oracle of Delphi with the following question for the Pythia: "Will I succeed in defeating Dareios, the Great King of Persia?"

He was careful to craft as clear a question as possible. He didn't want to make the same mistake as Kroisos had made, some 210 years earlier, when he asked the Oracle whether he should invade Persia. In response, the Lydian king was told that, if he attacked Persia, he would destroy a great empire. Kroisos attacked and a great empire fell – his own.

When the response from the Delphic Oracle arrived, Philippos assembled his commanders in the armory for a public reading of the prophecy. "The bull is garlanded. All is ready and the sacrificer is at hand," he read aloud.

Prime Directive

"Well, it was sporting of Apollon to call Dareios a bull," Philippos observed with a wink. "I think of him more as a steer but, either way, I'm glad to hear that he's garlanded and ready to be sacrificed because we're on our way to administer the fatal blow."

He clapped his hands, slapped his thighs, hopped and twirled. He was literally dancing for joy. I hadn't seen him this giddy since the immediate aftermath of Chaironeia. "Back to work," he finally said. "We start marching to the Hellespont right after the wedding of my Little Kleopatra."

****

The wedding turned out to be an affair to remember. Macedonia had become the leading political and military power in Greece and Philippos wanted to show off its new wealth, stature, and sophistication to all those scoffing snobs from the South. Any personal propaganda value that he might derive from the extravaganza was simply an added bonus.

Philippos chose to stage his showcase in Aigai, Macedonia's ancient capital, taking advantage of its cool summer climate and the natural beauty of its environs. Although the official celebration was scheduled to last three days, many visitors were expected to arrive early and stay late. In addition to participating in the festivities, athletic contests, and musical and theatrical performances, and in addition to partaking of the nightly feasts, visitors were also expected to tour the ancient royal palace, to admire the weathered beauty of venerable temples and other hoary architectural marvels, and to visit the royal tombs holding the remains and favorite possessions of all past Macedonian kings, from Karanos, the legendary founder of the Argead dynasty, all the way to Philippos's father Amyntas and his brothers Alexandros and Perdikkas, each of whom had worn the diadem prior to Philippos. "We've been here for a while," was the subliminal message Philippos was hoping to convey.

On the first day of the festival, Philippos and Kleopatra received a parade of ambassadors from Greek city states and barbarian neighbors alike, each presenting ostentatious presents to the bride and making declarations of eternal friendship and support to her father. Curiously, the Athenian ambassador, after presenting a heavy gold crown to Philippos, made a long speech of support, ending with the ringing declaration that anyone who plotted against the Macedonian king and then sought asylum in Athens would be captured and returned to Macedonia. Did the Athenians know something that Philippos didn't or were they just expressing their usual hope for turmoil and instability in Macedonia?

The afternoon program featured athletic contests and musical performances starring the foremost competitors, singers, and bards that money could buy. In the evening, there was a sumptuous banquet, held under a sparkling, cloudless sky, with many courses of exotic delicacies, a torrent of wine, a dramatic recitation by one of Greece's foremost tragic actors, and an endless string of drunken toasts and insincere felicitations. It was almost dawn when the last of the stragglers left the party.

Those stragglers presumably headed straight to Aigai's refurbished and newly opulent amphitheater, which was to be the site of the primary events of the second day. Before dawn, every available seat in the greatly expanded outdoor arena was taken. A special section in the front was cordoned off for the families of the groom and bride and for the king's official guests. Even that section was filling up fast. Prominent in the first row was Olympias, back in Macedonia for the first time since her exile. As the mother of the bride and sister of the groom, she couldn't very well have been denied an invitation. Sitting to her right was the bride herself, modestly concealed beneath a veil. Seated around them were the other surviving wives of Philippos, all but Kleopatra. Luscious, with two babes in arms, managed to find for herself a seat on the opposite side of the arena, amidst a bunch of noble women from Lower Macedonia.

The cavalcade set off from just outside the royal palace promptly at sunrise. The twelve Olympian gods led off the procession, in the form of gorgeous, larger-than-life sculptures, exquisitely executed in naturalistically painted white marble, with generous applications of gold foil. Each god stood in his or her own chariot, pulled by a pair of matching white horses, and led by an imposing groom, outfitted in a Macedonian hoplite's parade uniform. And there was a thirteenth chariot, identical to the preceding twelve, carrying a larger than life statue of the thirteenth god – Philippos.

Behind the chariots came a pair of huge, perfectly white sacrificial bulls, each wearing a splendid garland of wild flowers. The bulls were pulled along by their handlers and followed closely by shit-shovelers, carrying their spades and buckets. Behind the shit-shovelers marched the priests, resplendent in their ceremonial robes, each holding the tools of his trade: A large mallet to stun the bull and a curved butcher knife to slit its throat.

The priests were followed, after a decent interval, by Philippos himself, striding alone, dressed in a gold-embroidered white cloak over a plain, white, ankle-length chiton. The only splash of color was the flowery wreath around his neck, plaited for him the night before by Luscious herself. In his hair he wore a narrow gold diadem but was otherwise unencumbered by any jewelry, or weapons, or other tokens of his station. He walked in regal isolation, his bodyguards having been instructed to march discretely in the background, a good stadion behind their charge. The beloved king of Macedonia did not require protection from his own people.

Marching in the gap between Philippos and his bodyguards were the two Alexandroi, the prince of Macedonia and the king of Epiros. After the troop of bodyguards marched an entire phalanx of Foot Companions, carrying their full complement of weapons, including their swords, breastplates, and gleaming silver shields, lacking only their sarissas. Prancing behind them came a squadron of the Companion Cavalry, each trooper astride a matching, massive, chestnut stallion. The riders were equipped in golden helmets, cuirasses, and greaves, with their brown cloaks billowing behind them. They were armed with their traditional swords at the waist and short javelins in their left hands.

Behind the cavalry came the athletes who were to participate in that day's contests, each equipped for his sport. Musicians, dancers, acrobats, magicians, priests, sages, soothsayers, and assorted riff-raff completed the procession.

The entire route from the palace to the amphitheater was lined with wildly cheering folks, standing three or four or five deep. As he walked, Philippos turned his head from side to side, acknowledging the cheers with a wave and a smile. The rest of the marchers remained rigidly in step, staring straight ahead.

To enter the theater itself, the procession had to pass through a long, dark tunnel built under the stands.

The statues of the gods, riding in their chariots, emerged one by one from the mouth of the tunnel, each receiving an admiring cheer. As soon as each statue entered the arena, it was swiftly unloaded by a team of men and placed on its pedestal, arrayed at the outer perimeter of the playing field. When the thirteenth statue arrived, it was greeted by a stunned silence. After a long, pregnant pause, some of Philippos's more fervent supporters, seated at the top of the stands, managed to work up a burst of polite applause.

Philippos in the flesh strode out from the tunnel, blinking in the glare of the rising sun. His appearance triggered an uproarious explosion of noise, the offending statue instantly forgotten. Philippos paused, drinking in the ovation.

Still in the tunnel, the two Alexandroi stopped as well, waiting for Philippos to move on. The bodyguards, having just entered at the far end of the tunnel, drew nearer to the Alexandroi and then waited for the marching to resume.

The ovation rolled on and on, fading momentarily, only to erupt again with renewed vigor. Philippos stood, smiled, raised his arms. The two Alexandroi waited. The bodyguards waited.

One of the bodyguards, a man named Pausanias, emerged from the troop and loped forward, almost unnoticed in the darkness of the tunnel. When he emerged from the mouth of the tunnel, carrying a curved Celtic sword in his right hand, the noise was still deafening. Pausanias ran up to Philippos and said something in his ear, which Philippos couldn't hear. He looked at Pausanias quizzically, leaning his head closer to the bodyguard's mouth. As he did so, Pausanias thrust his sword into Philippos's abdomen, just below the ribs, sinking it into the king's torso up to the hilt.

Philippos looked at him with surprise, a thin rivulet of blood emerging from the corner of his mouth. Pausanias withdrew the sword, causing Philippos's body to crumple to the earthen surface of the arena, a huge scarlet flower blossoming on the front of his white tunic. The spreading sanguinary stain coordinated grotesquely with Kleopatra's bright garland, still resting intact and inert on Philippos's chest.

Pausanias took off running toward an exit located on the opposite side of the oval. Philippos never uttered a word. Really, he never moved at all from the moment the Celtic sword penetrated his abdominal cavity; his body simply acquiesced to the remorseless pull of gravity as he collapsed to the ground. By the time the two Alexandroi ran up to him, Philippos was dead, his remaining eye sightless, glassy, and dull. His son tore at the tunic, attempting to stanch the blood, but the flow was already slowing of its own accord, most of Philippos's blood supply having oozed out of his body, creating a sticky, crimson lake around his pristine white garments.

I averted my eyes, fighting off waves of nausea. I had seen a great deal of carnage on the battlefield, undoubtedly more gruesome than the scene unfolding in the arena, and I had certainly anticipated Philippos's demise, but I was still not prepared for the ghastly sight of a man at the height of his powers slaughtered like a sacrificial animal in the midst of what should have been a splendid celebration. His death, in its singularity, was somehow more final, more real, more shocking, than the aggregate butchery I had witnessed before.

For the first few seconds after the assassination, an eerie silence gripped the amphitheater. Then pandemonium broke out. The Companion Cavalry rode in on their horses, followed by the Foot Companions, brandishing their swords. The spectators were screaming, cursing, wailing, praying. The vast majority of attendees rushed for the exits, trampling those unfortunates who lost their footing. A few people jumped down from the stands onto the playing surface but were quickly pushed back into the seats by the soldiers. Some people sat stunned, staring, motionless. Luscious stood uncertainly amidst the swirling mass of people, trying to keep her babies from looking at the grisly scene in the arena. The statue of Philippos was knocked off its pedestal in the stampede and was lying face down in the muck.

Three bodyguards took off after Pausanias – Leonnatos the Lynkestian, Perdikkas from Orestis, and Squeaky Attalos. Pausanias made it out of the theater unmolested and was headed for a nearby stand of trees, where four horses had been tied up, waiting for him. The gap between Pausanias and his three pursuers remained fairly constant, rendering it unlikely he would be caught before making good his escape.

Just when Pausanias was on the point of reaching the tree to which the first horse was tethered, he tripped on a root and went sprawling. Before he could regain his feet, Perdikkas ran him through with his javelin. Leonnatos and Squeaky then fixed him to the ground with their spears, and the three of them proceeded to hack him to pieces, just as I ran up, screaming, "Don't kill him; don't kill him!"

Perdikkas turned and looked at me, smirking. "You're a bit late, Metoikos; this bastard got what he deserved. But you go right ahead and clean up the carcass, if you're so inclined." And with that, the three of them walked away.

Alexandros, surrounded by other bodyguards and covered in his father's blood, rushed up next. He turned Pausanias's body over with a compact kick to the ribs and confirmed that the man was indeed dead, notwithstanding the quizzical expression on his face. Without a word, Alexandros twirled on his heels and walked back to the arena. The bodyguards, including me, followed behind.

By the time we returned, the amphitheater was almost empty, although Olympias and Little Kleopatra were still in their seats. Alexandros jumped up to them, gave each a hug, leaving them both bloodstained, and exchanged a few words of comfort with his mother. Kleopatra seemed genuinely stupefied but Alexandros and Olympias were preternaturally calm. Alexandros then jumped straight onto the back of Boukephalas, who had magically materialized in the arena and was being held next to the railing by one of the cavalrymen.

He turned to the mass of soldiers milling around the playing field and swiftly sorted them out. A group of bodyguards was detailed to return the body of the king to the palace while funeral arrangements were being made. Another group was dispatched to retrieve the assassin, whose badly damaged corpse was to be nailed to a cross and left as carrion for vultures and other scavengers. The remaining bodyguards were told to escort Olympias, her daughter, and her new husband Alexandros to the palace and keep them under protection there. Alexandros also made provision for Luscious and her children, on the opposite side of the arena, to be taken into protective custody.

The commander of the Foot Companions was told to deploy his troops to maintain order in the amphitheater and in the rest of Aigai as well. A few of the cavalrymen were ordered to get off their animals and join the Foot Companions, making their mounts available to a group of Alexandros's friends who had gathered in the middle of the arena. I was told to get on a horse as well.

Prime Directive

Once the orders had been issued, Alexandros rode off with his augmented squadron of Companion Cavalry to meet the rest of the army, leaving the corpse of his father behind.

****

I gazed at Philippos for one last time. He didn't look like a man who had raised Macedonia from the brink of oblivion to its current status as the leading nation in the Hellenic world, a man who had imposed his will on his country and on all of Greece, a man who had unquestionably been Macedonia's greatest monarch. No, he looked small, older than his forty-six years, and dead before his time.

In twenty-three short years, Philippos had brought Macedonia to the forefront of Greek and European power not simply by personal bravery on the battlefield but, rather, by revolutionary innovations in military doctrine and armament, by visionary understanding of geopolitical trends, by masterful and ruthless exploitation of strategic advantage, by personal tact and deft diplomacy, and, not least of all, by marrying well and often. But, looking at his lifeless and bloody corpse, it seemed highly unlikely that he would be joining his immortal colleagues on Mt. Olympos any time soon.

What a shame, I thought. *To come so close to leading his pan-Hellenic expedition against Persia, only to be struck down on the point of crossing the Hellespont.* Of course, without knowing all the sordid details, I had been generally aware all along of what fate held in store for the Macedonian king. Nevertheless, at that moment I was hard-pressed to fend off the waves of melancholia lapping at my psyche.

Despite understanding, on an intellectual level, the inexorable and impersonal forces that determined our fortunes, I was finding it difficult to accept the evident lack of control any of us could exert over our destiny. And, despite knowing and accepting the prohibition against all personal attachments, which lay at the core of the time travelers' code of conduct, I couldn't escape my dawning awareness that I would miss my occasional rhetorical exchanges with the great man. He had been the only person in my adopted era who had come close to figuring out who I really was. With his death, I was more keenly aware than ever of being an isolated outsider, sojourner from elsewhen, resident alien, and sole representative of my kind in this young and tumultuous age.

Banishing these thoughts as best I could, I concentrated on catching up to Alexandros, who was at that moment hurtling toward his fateful meeting with the army, which would determine the future course of Macedonia.

Chapter 10 – Aftermath

Ruthless. That word kept reverberating in my brain as we thundered toward Aigai's western gate. The assassination had been executed with ruthless efficiency, but why had Pausanias done it and, more importantly, had he acted alone? I had no answers and the one man who could have provided them – the assassin himself – had been eliminated with equally ruthless dispatch.

It took us perhaps ten minutes to ride from the amphitheater to the parade grounds just outside the city wall. By the time we arrived, the army was assembled, fully armed, arrayed in phalanx formation, and standing at attention. *How the hell did they get here so fast?*

Antipatros was strutting on his charger, inspecting the troops, when we rode up. "The troops are ready, sire," he called out for all to hear.

"At ease!" Alexandros smiled. "You can put your sarissas down and draw a bit closer, so you can all hear me."

"Sarissas down! Two steps forward!" Antipatros yelled. His order was repeated in turn by each squadron commander down the line. Then, on a signal, all 20,000 foot soldiers moved as one, dropping their pikes and stepping forward. There was no sound, except for two discrete thuds as the men stepped forward in unison. Two more orders and the men were standing shoulder to shoulder, chest to back, in a compact cluster.

At that point, Alexandros took over. "Now relax and listen up. And you cavalry, why don't you close in, behind these men, as tight as you can."

Despite all these efforts, the assembled army still covered quite a bit of ground but Alexandros had no trouble being heard by the farthest soldier. "As you all know, I lost my father today. No," he corrected himself, "we all lost our father today." The men listened silently.

"Only two short years ago, my father led us to the greatest victory ever achieved by Macedonian arms. Our victory at Chaironeia was but the culmination of our long struggle to attain our rightful place among Greek states. But my father was more than a victorious general. He was the savior of our nation. The gods allowed my father twenty-three years in the saddle, twenty-three years at the head of this splendid army, twenty-three years as the leader of our country.

"He used his time well. He made each of us a better soldier. No, he made each of us the best possible soldier we could be. He turned us into the best fighting force the world has ever seen.

"My father brought us fortune, victories, prosperity, and fame. But his work's not done. That's the true tragedy of his untimely death. As we stand here today, mourning our loss, we must carry on. We're duty-bound to complete the mission he left us." The men were nodding now.

"We've been chosen by Zeus, Apollon, Herakles, and the other immortals to lead all of Greece in avenging the sacrilege committed against our gods by the Persian hordes. We've been chosen to liberate our Greek brothers who have been enslaved by the godless tyrants of Persepolis. We've been chosen to rid the world of these effete eunuchs and barbarian bastards." A few snickers.

"Are you ready to carry on the mission left to us by the immortal Philippos?" Roaring approbation and the beating of swords against shields signaled the men's assent.

"But first, we need to elect a new leader of this army, a new king for our nation."

There was an immediate, overwhelming response from the men. "We want you, Alexandros; Alexandros is our king; Alexandros, Alexandros, Alexandros."

Antipatros raised his arms to bring the tumult under control and then shattered the resulting silence with his powerful voice. "Long live King Alexandros of Macedonia!"

The twenty-year-old youngster was elected by unanimous acclamation. As he sat on Boukephalas, smiling, waving, acknowledging the renewed, sustained, and unceasing uproar, various commanders began dismounting and approaching Alexandros to pay homage and pledge their personal allegiance and loyalty, led of course by Antipatros. He was followed by one of his sons-in-law, Alexandros of Lynkestis. The entire Mieza clique came next, including me, presumptuous as that might have been. The other nobles, chieftains, and commanders approached the new king in turn. After the notables, ordinary soldiers walked up to Alexandros. He patiently accepted their oaths, their congratulations, and their good wishes. He exchanged a few words with many of them, sometimes asking after their fathers or brothers. It was surprising how many soldiers he knew by name.

The sun was beginning to set and the line of soldiers was still unending. Finally, Alexandros cocked an eyebrow toward Antipatros, who was sitting next to him. Antipatros roared into action, ordering all to resume their stations. In moments, the soldiers were arrayed once again, standing at attention.

"There will be a feast tomorrow evening," Alexandros yelled. "Join me! We'll eat, drink, and remember my father. Until then, get some rest because very soon now we're marching to Persia."

With that, Alexandros rode off to the palace, borne along on waves of cheering. At the palace, another endless line awaited, snaking its way from the entrance to the reception hall, across the principal courtyard, through the main gate, and into the square in front of the palace. Alexandros managed to enter the reception hall from the back, mostly unseen by the many well-wishers, courtiers, and supplicants awaiting his return. Ignoring the throng gathered outside the hall, he met with his military commanders first. He confirmed Antipatros as the ranking officer for Macedon-based military forces and as the regent for the kingdom in his absence. He confirmed Parmenion and Attalos, in absentia, as the commanders of the expeditionary corps in Asia. He named seven members of the Mieza clique as his royal bodyguard, including Hephaistion, Lysimachos, Aristonous, Peithon, Arybbas, Demetrios, and ... Ptolemaios. Yes, amazingly enough, he actually mentioned me by name. Several other people, some of them holdovers from Philippos, most of them friends of Alexandros from Mieza days, were assigned to various commands and offices.

After making his staffing arrangements, Alexandros was almost ready to receive the folks lined up outside the reception hall. But first, he asked to see his mother. Olympias promptly appeared, illuminating the room as she entered, resplendent in a bright green, flowing, floor-length chiton, her hair, bosom, and fingers festooned in gold and flashing with precious stones, her bearing triumphant, imperious, haughty, and exultant. For a widow in mourning, who had witnessed the murder of her beloved husband only hours earlier, she had made a remarkable recovery.

Seeing her son seated on the throne, Olympias rushed up to him, fell to her knees, and attempted to kiss his hands. Instead, Alexandros jumped up, raised his mother to her feet, and embraced her. He whispered something in her ear and they retired, hand-in-hand, to an adjoining meeting room, making sure to bar the door before anyone else could follow. They remained ensconced in their private conclave for what seemed to the rest of us like an eternity, although it probably lasted no more than half an hour.

Finally, Alexandros emerged, mussed but happy, leaving his mother behind. He asked to see his sister Kleopatra and her new husband, Alexandros of Epiros. When they entered, his first act was to reaffirm, in his new capacity as head of family and head of state, the marriage between the two, seeking to remove any possible doubt as to their marital status. He then had a long, private discussion with the new groom about the logistics of the upcoming Persian campaign and the support that he could expect to receive from the Epirote king. Having received fulsome assurances of assistance, Alexandros wished his new brother-in-law (and uncle) a safe journey back to Epiros and moved on to his next audience.

His older half-sister Kynane came into the hall. She was pregnant, disheveled, and distraught. She seemed genuinely upset about the death of her father but, when she tried to convey her condolences to Alexandros, he cut her short. "Where's your husband?" he barked.

Her husband, Amyntas the Nephew, whom she had married less than a year earlier, was actually a cousin to both of them. He was the son of Philippos's brother Perdikkas, who had been king until he lost his life in a battle against the Illyrians, led by Kynane's grandfather, King Bardylis. In fact, Amyntas himself had been, while a child, at least in theory and for a short time, king of Macedonia, known as King Amyntas Tetratos, before being eased aside by his uncle, the regent Philippos.

"He left ... two days ago. They went hunting ... in Lynkestis ... with Heromenes and Arrhabaios," Kynane stammered, shaken by the violence of her brother's inquiry. Heromenes and Arrhabaios, the two elder brothers of Alexandros of Lynkestis, were well-known figures at the court.

"Why wouldn't he stay for Kleopatra's wedding?"

"I have no idea, sire. It's something they do every year. Now is the best time to hunt for boar."

"He should've been here. There's absolutely no excuse." Alexandros was furious.

"But he's your cousin and your friend, Alexandros," Kynane pleaded. "You're both commanders in the Companion Cavalry, for gods' sake. He's always going on about how much fun you guys have. And he's always worshipped your father. He'll be devastated when he finds out what happened. He'll be back as fast as his steed can carry him, I'm sure. Please, brother, don't be mad."

"That's enough." Alexandros cut her off again. "Get back to your rooms, now!"

Kynane stared at him, speechless.

"When is the baby due?" Alexandros asked, relenting a little, as he watched her shuffle out of the room, clearly shaken.

"Take care of yourself," he advised, after being told that it would be another two months or so. "Better stay in your rooms for now."

As soon as Kynane was gone, Alexandros ordered Kassandros the Frog Killer to take a squadron of

Companion Cavalry and hunt Amyntas down. "I want him here in the palace tomorrow morning."

Aside from his mother, Alexandros did not bother meeting with Philippos's surviving wives. He did take time, however, to give explicit orders for their dispositions. He was especially insistent that Luscious Kleopatra and her two infant children be taken back to Pella immediately and confined to their rooms in the palace, under guard, with no visitors allowed.

Next, he met with various officials and made arrangements for the funeral and the feast scheduled for the next day. Finally, he was ready to meet everybody else. The doors were thrown open and the masses poured in. Alexandros spoke with each well-wisher and supporter, whether aristocrat or ordinary citizen, cordially albeit briefly. His recall of names and knowledge of affairs was encyclopedic, his patience astounding. It was well past midnight by the time the last of the visitors had left and we were able to retire for a few quick hours of sleep.

******

Except in my case, sleep would have to wait. When I got back to my cubicle, Lanike was already there. Exhausted though I may have been, I was happy to see her. That was before I noted her grim expression.

"My father's given me to Andronikos," she said, without preamble.

"Who's that?"

"He's one of my father's drinking buddies but what's the difference? Don't you get it? I'm getting married. Once I'm jailed in my husband's house, we may never see each other again."

Hadn't thought of that. I'd been perfectly happy with our current platonic arrangement, where we would meet from time to time for our relatively chaste chats, enjoy each other's company, and dream of wonderful things to come, without ever getting particularly specific. I really enjoyed having someone with whom I could speak freely, safely, and intimately and had assumed that Lanike felt the same. "Can't you simply refuse? Explain to your father that marriage would jeopardize your position at the court."

"The short answer is no. A daughter can't refuse a marriage arranged by her father. But the longer answer is that I don't blame my father. I'm amazed he's waited this long; I'm way past marriageable age. Undoubtedly, he kept hoping I'd find a suitable bridegroom in Pella and send him to my father to make the necessary arrangements. Frankly, I thought I'd found one but somehow it never came to pass."

I decided to take refuge in my usual flippancy. "I didn't know you had your eye on somebody." But she had no patience for my shenanigans. "We've known each other for almost eight years. I was a child when I first laid eyes on you, pretending to be Dionysos. And I've loved you every single day since. I've wasted my best childbearing years waiting for you!" Tears were rolling down her cheeks and my eyes seemed to be drowning as well.

"I'm sorry, Lanike. I really am."

"It's not too late! You could still go see my father. He'd take you over Andronikos without a second thought. You are a big man at the court, now bigger than ever, having been named one of the king's bodyguards. That's big enough for him to overlook your nickname. Won't you go see him?"

"What nickname?"

"Metoikos. Ptolemaios Metoikos. Or haven't you noticed that's what people call you?"

Of course I'd noticed. It was practically my surname. "It means traveler, doesn't it?"

"Not really. More like an outsider."

That struck a bit too close to home. "What do you mean, an outsider?"

"That's what the word means. It's more than just a traveler. It's an alien, stranger, outsider. That's what you are, aren't you?"

That's exactly what I was. What's more, I knew it in my bones. I'd simply chosen to suppress my awareness. Now it all came flooding back. *You're supposed to be an outsider, you idiot! Remaining an outsider is practically a corollary of the Prime Directive.* Try as I might, I couldn't talk myself out of my disappointment. Somehow, it was deeply wounding to find out the connotations of my nickname.

"It's funny, you know. I've always been an outsider, even before I came here to Macedonia. It's who I am. And most of the time, I like it that way. You could say I'm almost proud of it. But every once in a while, when I let my guard down, a little prick of something sneaks in. You could call it loneliness but it's more than that. It's a need to belong to something, to some group, to be part of a team."

"Luckily, we women never have that problem. We always belong to somebody. First, it's our fathers, then it's our husbands. Sometimes it's our brothers, sometimes it's our sons, but somebody always owns us." A note of bitterness had crept into her words but she swiftly suppressed it. "The good news is that I have a solution for both of us. If you marry me, you needn't be lonely ever again and I can at least belong to somebody I like."

"I wish it were that simple, Lanike. I really do. But we can't get married."

"Why not?" The pain in her voice was palpable. I sat down on the bed next to her and tried to ease her anguish. "Don't touch me!" she yelled when I reached for her hand. "Just tell me what's wrong with me and I promise never to bother you again. ... Not like I'm going to have much choice in the matter."

"There's nothing wrong with you, Lanike. I love you."

"Then why won't you marry me?"

There was a long silence, while I sought an answer. Even in the dim light of my oil lamp, Lanike could see echoes of my inner struggle on my face. She just gazed at me, hope, pain, sadness alternating in her eyes.

Remember the Prime Directive! In truth, there were two reasons why I couldn't possibly marry her. The Prime Directive was one of them but the fact that I had every intention of returning to my own era as soon as the emergency escape hatch materialized was almost as important. How could I marry this lovely girl, knowing I intended to vanish from her world a few years hence? And worst of all, I really couldn't tell her the truth. Our instructors at the Academy repeatedly drummed into our heads the truism that a secret, as soon as it's shared with one other person, ceases to be a secret.

"I can't marry you because soon I will have to go home, leaving you behind forever."

"What are you, crazy? Every woman who marries a soldier know that she'll be a widow soon enough. And until that happens, chances are she'll only see him when he drops in to beget another child."

"So why would you want to marry a soldier?"

"I don't want to marry a soldier; I want to marry you."

"It breaks my heart, Lanike, but I can't marry you and I can't even explain to you why."

"Is it some religious thing? Did some oracle pronounce a curse on you? What is it?"

I started to tell her I was an atheist and didn't believe in any silly superstitions but then I thought better of it. *How is my rigid, unquestioning adherence to the Prime Directive any different from an article of religious faith?* Many a man has given up his religious beliefs for a beautiful woman. Why shouldn't I? But there was a difference. The Prime Directive was not about me.

I said nothing. I took Lanike's hand and we cried together. "Can't you at least give me a baby?" she asked at last.

"In fact, I am cursed," I whispered softly. "And giving you a baby is exactly the one thing I'm forbidden to do."

Prime Directive

There was nothing more to say. She rose and left, more evanescent than a ghost receding in a dream. Except there was no waking from this nightmare.

****

Despite my exhaustion, I couldn't fall asleep. I tried to distract myself by thinking of anything but Lanike. I replayed in my mind the events of the day, starting with the horrendous image of Philippos's white tunic turning scarlet as Pausanias withdrew his sword. I could still see the surprise on Philippos's face and the calm countenance of his killer. Pausanias didn't give the impression of a madman nor did he act as someone committing suicide.

As I thought about it, it became crystal clear that what I'd witnessed was a carefully planned assassination. To start, Pausanias's weapon was not standard issue. It was, however, easier to conceal than a normal sword and particularly well-suited for his intended purpose. Moreover, he must have known that Philippos would be walking alone and unarmed and he must have known the route of the procession well enough to realize that the dark entrance tunnel into the arena was the perfect opportunity to make his murderous move.

And what about the horses waiting at the stand of trees just beyond the outer wall of the amphitheater? Pausanias couldn't have been acting alone. There was simply not enough time for him to pre-position four horses that morning, while simultaneously mustering with his cohort of bodyguards prior to the start of the parade. Plus, a lone assassin didn't need four horses to make his getaway. Who were the other three accomplices and what happened to them? Why didn't they meet Pausanias at the stand of trees, as planned?

They did meet him at the stand of trees, I realized. There were in fact three men running right behind Pausanias toward the horses at the copse – Leonnatos, Perdikkas, and Squeaky Attalos. Only they didn't join him on the horses; they killed him instead.

I immediately rejected the thought. Those three couldn't possibly have been part of a conspiracy to assassinate Philippos. They were, after all, three of Alexandros's closest friends. Which was kind of odd, now that I thought about it. Of all the people present in the arena that morning, the three guys who reacted the fastest and ended up chasing the assassin first were three of Alexandros's closest friends. *Goes to show Alexandros has a good eye for talent.* He certainly liked quick thinkers. There couldn't possibly be anything sinister in the coincidence of the three men reacting fastest also being three of Alexandros's best friends.

On the other hand, the fact that the three of them proceeded to kill Pausanias on the spot, when they could have just as easily captured him, did appear a little suspicious, at least in hindsight. Certainly, anybody as

328

quick-witted as those three should have realized the importance of capturing the assassin alive.

Still, it was difficult to believe that Leonnatos, Perdikkas, and Squeaky Attalos could have been part of a conspiracy to kill Philippos. If they had been, Alexandros would've gotten wind of it and would've stopped it.

Or would he have? Without a doubt, a great deal of tension had existed between father and son. Still, the idea that Alexandros could've acquiesced in the murder of his father was simply too much to swallow. He'd been the apple of his father's eye. Philippos had devoted more time and attention to Alexandros's upbringing and preparation for kingship than he had to his military campaigns. He'd lavished more love on the boy than he had on all his wives and mistresses combined. Surely, no one would repay a lifetime of devotion by extinguishing its source.

All the more surprising then how preternaturally calm Alexandros had been during the immediate aftermath of the assassination. But then again, his mother had been equally unperturbed. Perhaps it was simply an inherited trait.

I'm sure there'll be an investigation, starting tomorrow, and we'll find out for sure, I thought as I finally drifted off to sleep. *Unless, of course, Alexandros himself was part of a successful conspiracy to take over the monarchy.* Even falling asleep I remembered the favorite maxim of my old history professor: "When it comes to a coup d'etat, there is no such thing as a successful conspirator; there are only dead conspirators and new kings."

****

I was awakened way too early, perhaps only a few minutes after I'd finally fallen asleep, by a commotion in the king's quarters. When I went to check on the source of the noise, I discovered two men, bound, shackled, and chained to a ring in the guardroom wall. I could empathize with their predicament. Upon closer inspection, the two men turned out to be Heromenes and Arrhabaios.

Before I could approach them, Alexandros walked in, accompanied by Kassandros and some of his men.

"Where's the Nephew?" Alexandros wanted to know.

"He got away; somebody must've warned him. But we managed to catch these two."

Alexandros turned to Heromenes and Arrhabaios. "Where's Amyntas?"

"We don't know," Heromenes answered. "He left last night, before your men showed up. Right after we got the news. He said he had to get back for the funeral."

"Well, he must've gotten lost, because nobody's seen him come back to Aigai."

"I'm sure he'll turn up before noon," Arrhabaios assured the king.

"That might be too late for you two," Alexandros advised him calmly.

"What do you mean?"

"What I mean, Arrhabaios, is that our investigation has uncovered evidence showing that you and your brother and your friend Amyntas conspired with Pausanias to kill my father, the king. Now you two face a choice. You can confess to the conspiracy and tell me where we can find Amyntas, in which case I promise you a quick and relatively painless death. Or you can keep lying to me, in which case you will still confess to the conspiracy and tell me where we can find Amyntas, but your death will be neither quick nor painless. So, which will it be?"

"But, sire, that's absurd," Heromenes protested. "We were in Lynkestis, hunting. We know nothing about any conspiracy. The first we heard about the tragic death of the king was last night. We had nothing to do with it. We were crushed by the news. We would have returned with Amyntas but had to take our gear home first, which is where your men grabbed us. We're in mourning, with the rest of Macedonia."

"Amyntas isn't in mourning, I assure you. He's busy trying to tell my troops he's the rightful king of Macedonia. Now, for the last time, confess to the conspiracy and tell me where I can find Amyntas and we'll go easy on you."

"Sire, in your grief you're imagining things. None of us had anything to do with your father's death. Amyntas loved your father. He was a loyal subject for more than twenty years; all of his life, really. You know that. You served together in the Companion Cavalry. Why would he now, all of a sudden, after all these years, decide to kill your father?"

Alexandros was unmoved. "Take them away and get the truth out of them."

Before Heromenes and Arrhabaios could be dragged away, Alexandros of Lynkestis rushed in. "Sire, what's going on? Why are my brothers in chains?"

"They're traitors. The only reason you're not joining them is because Antipatros vouched for you. But I wouldn't push my luck if I were you."

"Please, Alexandros, show some compassion. We've all been loyal supporters of your family our entire lives. This is a preposterous accusation. Tell me who made it and I'll deal with him."

"I made it. Now, you can either leave on your own or you can be dragged away with your brothers. Which will it be?"

Lynkestis rushed out, distraught, undoubtedly hoping to enlist Antipatros in the effort to save his brothers' lives. Alexandros nodded to his men, telling them to proceed with their work.

About an hour later, Antipatros and Lynkestis found Alexandros in his chambers, getting dressed for the funeral. "You have to let them go," Antipatros told him. "They're innocent."

"You're too late. They've confessed. Here, you can read their confession."

Antipatros didn't even bother to look. "People will confess to anything if you torture them enough."

"That's not true. No matter what we did to them, they refused to reveal the Nephew's whereabouts."

"Maybe that's because they don't know where he is."

"Listen, Antipatros. You have served my father loyally for many years and I hope you'll do the same for me. As a personal favor to you, I won't execute your son-in-law along with his brothers. But don't tell me they're all innocent. Amyntas thinks he's entitled to the diadem and

333

he recruited them to assist in his conspiracy to kill my father. They've said so in their written confession. Now, if you'll excuse me, I have to get ready for the funeral."

****

It seemed as if the entire population of Macedonia turned out that afternoon on the plain surrounding the tombs of the kings. Overnight, Philippos's sepulcher, located on the southern edge of the cemetery, had been prepared to receive his remains.

It was astonishing to see what the workmen had been able to accomplish in less than twenty-four hours, even if Philippos had been preparing for his own funeral since the day he became king and even though the structure itself had been erected some time ago. The tomb was a vaulted building, perhaps fifteen feet wide, thirty feet long, and fifteen feet high at the top of the arched ceiling. It contained the main burial chamber and an antechamber. Except for the facade, the entire structure was constructed from cut and fitted limestone blocks. The facade was all marble, with marble doors, framed by two marble Doric columns, and topped off by an entablature, consisting of an architrave, a frieze, and a cornice.

Centered inside the main chamber stood the sarcophagus, its lid still off, awaiting Philippos's corpse. On the stone floor of the chamber and all around its walls were arranged various objects belonging to the king, mostly military gear, some of it made for Philippos, some captured in his many campaigns. The antechamber was empty, awaiting the remains of his seven wives. In due course, after all the wives had been properly interred, the entire structure would be sealed and, with the passage of centuries, end up covered by layers of debris, dirt, and soil, destined to become just another grass-covered tumulus in the choppy sea of undulating mounds comprising the burial grounds of the Argead dynasty, awaiting the prying picks and spades of future archaeologists.

Standing off to one side stood the army. Shortly after noon, Alexandros appeared, in full military dress, riding Boukephalas. He was flanked by his bodyguard and assorted other officials, all mounted. The bodies of two men were being dragged behind this small group of riders – Arrhabaios and Heromenes. They were not dead yet, simply unable to walk, because the bones of their legs had been broken. Their faces were unrecognizable, their bodies covered with charred and bleeding wounds.

We headed straight for the neat, orderly array of the army cohorts. Alexandros had decided that the trial of the traitors had to be concluded before his father's funeral could proceed. In Macedonia, cases of treason were decided by a vote of the army. Luckily, this was to be a short trial.

As soon as we arrived, the two accused prisoners were placed between our small group of riders and the front rank of the foot soldiers. Alexandros himself pronounced the charges. The confession of Arrhabaios and Heromenes was read next. They were given an opportunity to respond to the charges but chose to say nothing. The army then condemned them by a voice vote. They were immediately put to death by swords thrust through their chests, possibly to their relief. Alexandros ordered that their corpses be mounted on either side of Pausanias's remains for the edification of the public. And with that, he was ready to proceed with his father's funeral.

I couldn't help a sardonic thought: *Efficient and ruthless as always. The ostensible murderers caught, tried, and executed. No additional suspects and no loose ends. And all this before the body has had a chance to get cold.*

The assembled multitude was treated to an endless succession of religious rituals. Animals were slaughtered, their entrails inspected, their flesh burnt on a stone slab. Priests chanted, yelled, repeatedly prostrated themselves and jumped up again, and generally implored the gods to welcome Philippos among them. There were dancers and acrobats. Finally, a small procession stepped forward, bearing the shrouded body of the departed monarch and many of his possessions, all of which were duly placed inside the tomb.

Prime Directive

Alexandros made another trenchant speech. He promised the army and the people that he would continue his father's policies. He announced that all taxes levied against the citizens of Macedonia would henceforth be abolished. Their military obligations, on the other hand, remained in effect. They were still subject to indefinite conscription but all their equipment would be provided at state expense. He invoked the gods and spoke of his personal destiny. In his peroration, he drove home his main point: Under his leadership, Macedonia would march from triumph to triumph, achieving heretofore unimaginable greatness, prosperity, and peace. By the end of his speech, he had moved, at least rhetorically, beyond the accomplishments of his father.

His audience liked the speech. They interrupted him repeatedly to voice their approval and gave him a long, enthusiastic ovation at the end. Afterward, everybody adjourned to the funeral feast in surprisingly cheerful spirits.

Tables had been set up throughout the palace courtyard and in the fields outside the palace walls. It was a lucky coincidence that Philippos had planned a great banquet for this evening to celebrate the consummation of the marriage of Little Kleopatra and Alexandros of Epiros. His planned extravaganza was simply repurposed by the new king.

By the end of the evening, almost everyone in attendance was roaring drunk. Alexandros himself was only moderately inebriated. He chose this moment to conduct his audience with the visiting ambassadors who'd come to town to witness a magnificent wedding and ended up staying for a changing of the monarchs.

The ambassadors once again declared the eternal friendship of their cities and states with Macedonia and their unwavering support for Alexandros, as the new Macedonian king. They also took their measure of the new ruler. What they saw was a twenty-year-old, somewhat inebriated, relatively short stripling. He was clean-shaven and wore his hair long, in the latest Athenian fashion. In his sumptuous robes, he looked unprepossessing, like a kid playing dress-up. They duly reported to their governments that the new king of Macedonia was inexperienced, weak, not terribly intelligent, and incapable of maintaining his hold on his own army and people, much less exerting any influence over the affairs of Greece.

Chapter 11 – Quelling Greek Unrest

In Athens, Demosthenes received a report of Philippos's assassination and Alexandros's accession, delivered to him by private courier, the night before the government messenger, carrying the official dispatch of the Athenian ambassador, arrived in town. Although Demosthenes was still in mourning for his daughter, who had died the previous week, he rose early the next morning, put on his most festive garb and a jubilant mien, and hurried off to the Assembly.

"Citizens, citizens," he yelled upon arrival. "I bring you joyous tidings. I have had a wonderful dream. I dreamt last night that I was an ox, yoked to a cart, driven by Philippos of Macedon. But then, as I struggled to pull the cart up the muddy, rutted road, through a terrible storm, Zeus unleashed a stroke of lightning from his seat on Mount Olympos and smote Philippos dead. The yoke fell away from my neck, the storm clouds dispersed, the sun came out, I was transformed back to a man, and I sauntered home, free as a lark. Don't you see what this means?"

"It means you've lost your mind," Aischines interjected. "Aren't you supposed to be in mourning for your daughter? Is this how you honor her memory?"

"No, my dream is a message from Athena, which I must share with my fellow citizens. This message is the gods' way of honoring my daughter. Her memory will now be forever linked, in the minds of all Athenians, with the news of our liberation."

"What are you talking about?"

"Don't you see? The uppity upstart from up north is dead. We're free of the tyrant once again."

While Demosthenes and Aischines were bickering, a messenger arrived at the amphitheater and made his way to the archon, handing to him the Athenian ambassador's dispatch from Aigai. The archon read it and rose at once, interrupting the debate between Demosthenes and Aischines.

"My fellow citizens!" He waved the scroll in his hand. "An official message from our ambassador to Macedonia. Let me read it to you.

"'Yesterday morning, during a wedding celebration, King Philippos Amyntou Makedonios was stabbed to death by one of his own bodyguards. The king of Macedonia is dead. He has been replaced by his son Alexandros, a youngster of no proven accomplishment or ability. In the wake of the assassination, the new king has pledged to continue his father's policies but it is reasonable to assume that he will find it difficult to maintain control of his own army, much less exercise any influence abroad. We expect numerous challenges to the legitimacy of his claim to the throne from men with superior pedigree and less doubt as to their parentage. We will continue to monitor the situation and send further reports as events warrant.'

"So, my fellow citizens," the archon continued, "Demosthenes's dream was indeed a message from the gods, utilizing Demosthenes as their prophet."

There was an understandable uproar in the Assembly. People were shouting, laughing, cheering, dancing, celebrating. Demosthenes struggled to regain control. Finally, when he was once again able to be heard, he proposed that a gold crown be awarded to the assassin, whoever he might be, and that he be declared an honorary citizen of Athens. His motion was adopted unanimously, without further debate.

Other speakers rose to praise the divinely inspired Demosthenes and to denounce and vilify Philippos, the last man – prior to his unnamed assassin – whom they had declared an honorary citizen, less than two years earlier. No one recalled the gratitude they had felt to the Macedonian king for his lenient and magnanimous treatment of Athens in the aftermath of the defeat at Chaironeia. Instead, the Assembly cancelled all further business for the day and declared a day of thanksgiving for the death of the tyrant.

Celebrations broke out all over the city. Athenians wore garlands, made sacrifices to the gods, sang triumphant songs of victory as if they themselves had struck the fatal blow, got roaring drunk, and bedded their spouses or any other available partners.

****

While his fellow citizens were busy celebrating, Demosthenes returned home to compose a message to Attalos, at his campaign headquarters in Ionia. Demosthenes advised the Adder that he was prepared to raise a large volunteer army, funded by the Persians and manned by mercenaries from all over Greece, anxious to invade Macedonia and overthrow Alexandros, whom he labeled a callow imbecile. The only missing ingredient, Demosthenes wrote, was a new leader to take over the Macedonian throne, once the invasion had been successfully concluded. Demosthenes pointed out that the Adder was the nearest living male relative of Karanos, the son of Philippos and Kleopatra, and the only legitimate heir. Unfortunately, Karanos was only an infant who would require the assistance of a regent for some years to come. Attalos, given his proven military and political experience, was just the man to assume the post, according to Demosthenes. Would he accept the job, the Athenian rabble-rouser wanted to know.

It took less than two weeks for Demosthenes's message to reach Attalos. Attalos showed the message to Parmenion and discussed his options with his father-in-law. After turning the matter over in his mind for a day, the Adder concluded that betting his life on the reliability of Demosthenes was a poor gamble and decided to forego any thought of rebellion for the time being. He forwarded Demosthenes's letter to Alexandros, accompanied by his own cover letter, professing his shock and dismay at the duplicity of the Athenian provocateur and recommending that Alexandros take the most severe possible measures to punish the inveterate agitator. He closed by pledging his continued and unwavering support of, and loyalty to, his new king.

****

Ambassadors from every city in the Greek world, not only Athens, had traveled to Aigai at Philippos's invitation and they all hastened to report to their governments the assassination of the fearsome king and their assessment of his inexperienced successor. Reactions to their dispatches were fairly uniform throughout Greece. In Thebes, the citizens rose up and drove out the Macedonian garrison stationed on the

Kadmeia. Insurrections broke out in Argos and Sparta. Another Macedonian garrison was sent packing in Ambrakia. There was unrest in practically every member city of the Korinthian League, resulting in the expulsion of many Macedonian garrisons and the deposition of several pro-Macedonian governments.

Reports of uprisings erupting throughout Greece began to filter back to Pella within a week after Philippos's funeral. Alexandros conferred with Antipatros and his other generals to determine an appropriate response. His advisors unanimously recommended caution and diplomacy. Alexandros thanked them for their counsel and ordered immediate military action.

The entire army, except for two divisions of foot soldiers, whom Alexandros left home with Antipatros, marched south three days after the first reports of rebellions had reached Pella.[11] Before leaving, Alexandros also detached a small contingent of two dozen picked men, under the command of Hekataios, and sent them off to Ionia, ostensibly to serve as liaison between his forces and the expeditionary corps under Parmenion and Attalos.

I was riding with my squadron, in the vanguard of the army, when we reached the southern border with

---

[11] See Map 3 at AlexanderGeiger.com to trace the route of Alexandros's travels, as described in this and the four subsequent chapters.

Prime Directive

Thessaly (of which Alexandros was nominally the archon, having inherited that position upon the death of his father), when we found our path through the Tempe Pass, located between Mount Olympos and Mount Ossa, blocked by a formidable force of Thessalian troops. Given the local topography, it was obvious to me that any attempt to force the pass was doomed to failure.

Alexandros, accompanied by a handful of bodyguards, rode ahead and was met by a small delegation of local dignitaries. When he told them he had no quarrel with Thessaly and was simply marching through to cities further south, they advised him to settle down and wait, while the national assembly met and deliberated the issue of granting permission to the Macedonian army to march across Thessalian territory. Alexandros, saying nothing in response, smartly spun Boukephalas around and rode back to his army, with the rest of our small group riding in his wake.

As soon as we returned, Alexandros called upon all the sappers, masons, and stonecutters in the ranks to report for duty. Perhaps four hundred men stepped forward. He told them to set out immediately toward Mount Ossa and chisel out a staircase up its precipitous northern flank, sufficiently wide to permit the rest of the army safely to climb up the mountain and back down the other side. "And by the way," he added as the men were leaving, carrying their tools, "I want the army to be on the other side of the mountain by tomorrow morning."

When the Thessalian troops, massed in the Tempe Pass, awoke the next day, they were treated to an excellent view of the rear end of our army, on the wrong side of the pass, marching away from them and toward the now defenseless heartland of Thessaly. The same delegation of local dignitaries as the day before hurried to catch up to Alexandros, riding at the head of our column. When they came abreast, they extended a fulsome welcome to the Macedonian monarch and his troops and competed with each other in their expressions of friendship and loyalty. Alexandros smiled quietly and asked whether it would be convenient for the national assembly to meet with him the following afternoon. He was assured that the delegates were already on their way to Larissa and would be eagerly awaiting his arrival.

The cream of Thessalian society, scared out of its wits, was in fact duly assembled in Larissa when Alexandros arrived. The national assembly confirmed him as archon of Thessaly. They turned over to his command their entire cavalry, renowned throughout the Greek world for its horsemanship and the quality of its mounts. They made a substantial monetary contribution to aid in the Macedonian war effort. And they invited us to a feast to celebrate the reaffirmation of the bonds of friendship and alliance between the two nations.

Alexandros politely accepted the title of archon, took the Thessalian cavalry and money, and declined the invitation to the feast. He and the army, reinforced now by Thessalian cavalry, were on our way out of town before nightfall. We didn't pause until crossing the Hot Gates three days later.

We encamped on the far side of Thermopylai, where Alexandros convened a meeting of the Amphiktyonic Council. The councilors, somewhat surprised to see the young man so far south and in the company of so many troops, confirmed him as hegemon of the Amphiktyonic League, a position which he claimed by right of inheritance from his father, with as much grace as they could muster.

While still in camp, a breathless delegation from Ambrakia caught up to him. They blamed the expulsion of the Macedonian garrison on a misunderstanding and begged the king's forgiveness. Alexandros, who had no time for detours (Ambrakia was just to the south of Epiros), accepted their apologies, imposed a stiff fine, and sent the delegation home, accompanied by a new, larger Macedonian garrison.

We continued south, arriving at the gates of an astonished Thebes less than a week later. Alexandros's army, including soldiers marching on foot, covered more ground in a day than most men were able to travel riding a horse. Leaving the army outside the walls, Alexandros rode into town, accompanied only by his bodyguard, all smiles and charm. He had a pleasant chat with the ruling oligarchs. The Thebans apologized profusely, acknowledged him as hegemon, paid a huge fine, and requested an opportunity to welcome back, and to provision, a much larger garrison on the Kadmeia. Alexandros reluctantly accepted their proposals but reminded them that this was their second anti-Macedonian rebellion in the last two years. He warned them not to make the same mistake a third time.

As soon as the agreement was concluded, Alexandros and his army set out toward Athens, where panic reigned. The tombstones in Keramaikos were once again uprooted; women and slaves were once again armed; Demosthenes was once again denounced as a dangerous demagogue. Alexandros rode in, leaving the army once again encamped outside the city walls, and met with his old friends at the Bouleuterion. An agreement was swiftly concluded, along the lines of the Theban surrender, except Alexandros, like his father, couldn't bring himself to station troops on the akropolis. The citizens of Athens, relieved and grateful, ratified the agreement in the Assembly that afternoon. Alexandros declined their offer to make him an honorary citizen twice over.

****

In the meantime, Hekataios and his men arrived at the expeditionary headquarters in Ionia two days after Attalos's messenger had left for Greece, bearing Demosthenes's letter and Attalos's accompanying note to

348

Alexandros. Hekataios brought routine orders from Alexandros to the joint commanders of the invasion force, which he handed over upon arrival. Parmenion and Attalos read their orders, which basically reaffirmed Philippos's previous dispositions, and then invited Hekataios to share a meal with them.

That night, just before the break of dawn, while everyone was asleep, Hekataios snuck into Attalos's tent and cut the Adder's throat. He then entered Parmenion's tent, woke the old man, and presented him with a further, secret message from Alexandros, which made it clear that Hekataios had acted pursuant to Alexandros's orders in eliminating Attalos.

Parmenion considered, for a moment, whether to arrest Hekataios, put him on trial for murder, and lead a rebellion against Alexandros, but then rejected the thought. The old general regretted losing his son-in-law but judged that he himself, and his sons, would advance further under Alexandros than against him. Even if they could count on the support of Persia, Athens, Thebes, Sparta, and various other Greek city-states in any attempt to overthrow the king – support they would all undoubtedly promise but might fail to deliver – he had his doubts as to the ultimate likelihood of success of any such venture. Unlike the many hotheads in the Greek world, Parmenion had actually seen Alexandros in action. And besides, he and his family had served Macedonian kings for generations and he was not a traitor.

In short, Parmenion accepted Hekataios's secret message, implemented the changes requested by Alexandros, appointed as many of his own relatives and supporters to key command positions as he could, and sent Hekataios back to Alexandros with a message urging the young king to join him in Asia at the first opportunity, because he didn't expect the Persian king to remain quiescent for much longer. Hekataios and his men set off for the return trip to Pella the next day.

****

Alexandros wasted no further time in Athens. As soon as the Assembly ratified the city's latest surrender, we were on the march again, heading for a meeting of the Hellenic League in Korinthos. After watching developments in Thessaly, Boiotia, and Attika, member states sent delegates with unusual alacrity. Once the conference convened, Alexandros wasted little time presenting his proposals. He was elected hegemon of the Korinthian League "in perpetuity," he was designated strategos of the pan-Hellenic campaign against Persia, and he was urged by the delegates to depart for Asia as soon as possible. His proposals to the League exceeded his father's program in one respect. He was not content to accept a reaffirmation of the mutual non-aggression and defense pact his father had shepherded through the Synhedrion. Instead, he presented a detailed list of requirements to the member states, specifying what personnel and materiel each member state was expected to contribute to the war effort. The delegates approved the list without demurrer.

Sparta was the one significant city-state that was not a member of the Korinthian League, didn't attend Synhedrion meetings, and didn't pledge its support for the campaign against Persia. On the contrary, the Spartans made it clear they intended to pursue their own policies, without regard to the wishes of the Macedonian upstart. Fortunately for them, Alexandros didn't wish to expend either the time or the resources required for an extended Peloponnesian campaign. Winter was fast approaching and he was anxious to return home. As a result, he was content, for the time being, to hem Sparta in as much as he could, by appointing puppet regimes in Sparta's neighboring communities, such as Messenia and Archaia, leaving the ultimate resolution of the Spartan problem for another day.

In two short months, Alexandros had reaffirmed the alliance between Macedonia and Epiros, had reasserted Macedonian control over Thessaly, had reinstated Macedonian garrisons at strategic points throughout Greece, had been reappointed hegemon of the Amphiktyonic and Korinthian Leagues, had overawed all would-be opponents in Greece, and had left an extensive requirements list with Macedonia's putative allies. He was, at the time, twenty years old.

Chapter 12 – Training Exercise

Having done what he could to counter the impression that he was a callow imbecile, Alexandros started the march back north. There was, however, one more stop he was anxious to make along the way. As his father before him, he wished to consult the priestess of Apollon at Delphi to determine whether his projected campaign against Persia would meet with success.

Unfortunately for Alexandros, by the time we arrived in Delphi, the Pythia had closed up shop for the season. Even when Alexandros offered, through the subsidiary priests who attended to the Pythia's needs, a substantial donation to Apollon, the head priestess would not be moved. She sent word that Alexandros could resubmit his query when the oracle reopened for business once again next spring.

Alexandros was not so easily deterred. He barged into the old woman's dwelling, grabbed her around the waist, and proceeded to drag her to the cave from which she normally issued her pronouncements. Finally, the priestess capitulated and agreed to walk to the cave. "You're invincible," she told him, as she struggled to get free.

"That's good enough for me." Alexandros released her. "Thanks for answering my question."

He left behind a generous donation to Apollon, as promised, and departed with his army and with a new nickname. For the rest of his life he would be known as Alexandros Aniketos, the Invincible Alexandros.

****

Along the route from Delphi to Pella, the messenger, who had been dispatched from the expeditionary headquarters in Ionia some weeks earlier, finally found us. He delivered to Alexandros Demosthenes's perfidious manifesto, along with Attalos's cover letter, professing the Adder's undying loyalty to the new Macedonian monarch.

Alexandros was bemused. "Too late now, you old snake," he remarked to no one in particular. "Truth is, even if I'd gotten this earlier, it wouldn't've made any difference. You've been a dead man for some time now. I do hope, though, that you enjoyed making that toast at my father's wedding feast."

Once back in Pella, and after confirming with Antipatros, Hekataios, and his many other agents that all was in order, he gave the army, not including us bodyguards, a well-deserved furlough. "Be back by next full moon," he told them. "And rest up. When you get back, we'll start our training in earnest."

****

Lanike was nowhere to be found. Everyone I asked at the palace reported that she had left to get married and was not expected to return. "It's a great match for her," Kleitos told me when I finally managed to corner him. "He's a nobleman, believe it or not. I can't imagine how our father managed to pull it off."

"You're being too modest, Kleitos," I chided him. "Your sister is the head lady-in-waiting to Olympias and you're a commander in the Companion Cavalry. Any man would be proud to marry into such a family. Besides, Lanike told me he was one of your father's drinking buddies. She never said anything about his being a nobleman."

"She told you about her upcoming marriage?" Kleitos was surprised. "I didn't realize she went around blabbing to strange men about her personal affairs. Not to say you're a strange man, of course."

"Of course not."

"Well, on second thought, you are pretty strange, Ptolemaios." He broke into one of his contagious laughs. "Did she tell you the prospective bridegroom's name?"

"Yeah, she did. I think it was Andronikos but it didn't mean anything to me. I've never heard of the guy."

"Actually, chances are you probably do know him. I'm surprised you didn't recognize the name."

"Why would I recognize the name? Who the hell is he?"

"He's one of us! He's a member of the Companion Cavalry. You've probably seen him a hundred times but for some reason nobody's ever bothered to tell you his name. I guarantee he knows who you are. I'll introduce him to you the next time we see him."

"That's alright," I said quickly, "don't bother. I don't want to do anything that might interfere with your sister's happiness."

Kleitos gave a queer look. "Why would anything you do interfere with my sister's happiness? To tell you the truth, I don't think she's too happy about this match," he added after a short pause, "not that it makes any difference. Being happy is not her job. She's got plenty of other responsibilities to worry about."

"Why wouldn't she be happy about the match?" I tried to make the question sound as innocent as possible.

"I shouldn't be telling you this but we're friends and I know this will go no further."

"You bet," I assured him.

"Well, he's a widower, much older than she is. He's got a bunch of kids already, the two eldest sons almost as old as their new stepmother. It's going to be hard for Lanike to settle down to the life of a mistress of an old, mostly empty, out-of-the-way castle, with an absentee husband, after all the excitement she's been through here. I think she was hoping for a younger man. But then, she's no spring chicken herself, is she?"

"What do you mean an absentee husband?"

"Haven't you been listening, Ptolemaios? Andronikos is in the Companion Cavalry. How much time do you think he'll be spending at home? Plus, he's an ambitious nobleman, like they all are. You can bet he's going to make sure he's included when we cross over to Asia. Chances are his two oldest sons will come along as well. My sister will be lucky to see him a couple of months each year. Of course, maybe she'll prefer it that way," he added with a wink.

I was too stunned to respond. Somehow, hearing all the domestic details awaiting my lovely Lanike finally drove home into my thick head all the ramifications of our last parting.

"This just can't be the end," I muttered, too softly for Kleitos to make out my words.

"Hey, want to come along for the wedding feast? I'm sure neither my father nor my sister would object."

"That would be wonderful," I lied. "When is it?"

"Oh, there's no date yet. Depends on when Andronikos can get away. Which will be the same time you and I can get away. I'll let you know once the date is set."

"Great, I'm looking forward to it," I said, realizing as soon as the words left my lips that nothing good could possibly come from my attending Lanike's wedding feast.

****

We spent the winter doing forced marches through deep snow, beating the hell out of each other with wooden stakes, executing endless close order drills, and generally building unshakable bonds of camaraderie. For our final exercise, as the winter finally receded, Alexandros decided to launch a nice little war against some of the northern barbarian tribes. The bellicose neighbors had been acting up lately; the borders had to be secured prior to departure for Asia in any event; and there was no training as effective as a taste of the real thing.

The training turned out to be a bit more intensive than Alexandros had intended. It all started out encouragingly enough. Because the lands of the Agrianians lay along the route of the march toward the hostile barbarian tribes, Alexandros decided to make a slight detour and visit his friend, King Langaros of the Agrianians, whose guest he, and a few of us, had been only recently, during our exile from Pella. King Langaros extended to the visiting monarch and his army as lavish a welcome as his resources allowed. He threw a beer- and wine-saturated party for all and he even offered to accompany Alexandros on his expedition to clean out the rebellious barbarians with some of his best troops. Alexandros gratefully accepted the offer. That was the easy part of the training exercise; after that, the going became tougher.

First, we were confronted by the prospect of a difficult transit of the Shipka Pass, strongly defended by a Thrakian tribe, entrenched behind a line of heavy wagons. However, Alexandros used this challenge as a teaching opportunity. He correctly surmised that, when our infantry approached, the Thrakians would roll the rock-filled wagons down toward them, in the hope of killing and maiming as many of our soldiers as possible. He instructed the troops simply to separate ranks when the wagons approached and let them roll harmlessly through the resulting channels. More easily said than done, especially when confronted with the fearsome sight of massive, stone-laden wagons hurtling toward heavily armed men wearing cumbersome armor and constricted by the narrow and rugged terrain of the defile. But all those close order drills paid off. The men did as they had been told; the wagons rolled harmlessly through; not a single man was injured. A nice, practical illustration of the benefits of discipline. Needless to say, the Thrakians panicked upon seeing their clever stratagem come to naught and were easily routed in the subsequent battle.

The next exercise involved the Triballians, a fairly peaceful tribe living on the banks of the Danube. Upon seeing the arrival of Alexandros's army, they retreated into the woods, with the intention of picking off our troops with arrows and stones from their blinds in the trees, as the phalanxes marched by. Alexandros didn't afford the Triballians an opportunity to implement their preferred tactics. He sent his Agrianian archers forward to smoke the enemy out of the woods and then let loose his cavalry to cut them to pieces when they emerged from their sheltered positions.

The subsequent arrival of the army at the Danube represented something of a logistical triumph. In a test of an alternative provisioning strategy, Alexandros had dispatched, months earlier, a fleet of supply ships to sail east, along the Thrakian coast of the Aegean, then up north, through the Hellespont and into the Black Sea, and then back west, up the Danube River, to the rendezvous point. This operation was rendered all the more difficult by the fact that no Macedonian army had ever travelled as far as the projected meeting place, meaning that both the supply ships and the ground troops were operating in what was, for Macedonians, virgin territory. Yet, all the supply ships and all the troops arrived at exactly the right place at exactly the right time. Another militarily-useful capability successfully mastered.

For the next challenge, Alexandros felt a sudden urge to cross the Danube, which was a wide and swiftly flowing river at that point, especially when swollen by the spring snowmelt. He decided to take the opposite bank, which was strongly defended by a large force of savage Getai. A portion of the army executed a night-time crossing, utilizing the supply ships that were already on the scene. But the capacity of the ships was quite limited. As a result, fifteen hundred of us cavalrymen, with our horses, floated across on makeshift rafts. The infantry were told to sew up their tents, fill them with straw, and use them as improvised flotation devices. Their equipment was ferried across in dugout canoes. Four thousand infantrymen and their gear made it safely across the river using these techniques.

The pink streamers of early next dawn found the yawning Getai still dutifully guarding the riverbank and a small but classically equipped Greek army, both cavalry and hoplites, lurking in the tall grass behind them. When the astonished Getai suddenly noticed the orderly ranks of Macedonians emerging from the rushes, our shiny armor glinting in the rising sun, the fierce warriors ran away.

Alexandros and his detachment stayed on the far side of the Danube long enough to plunder some of the Getai settlements and to conduct a service of thanksgiving. An elaborate stone altar, half a dozen sacrificial victims, and the normal compliment of priests and handlers were all ferried across the Danube for the purpose. Alexandros was meticulous in his observance of the requisite rites. The sacrificial animals were washed, garlanded, and ritually slaughtered. Their entrails were inspected. The choicest cuts were burnt on the altar, generously infused with aromatic resins and spices. The priests recited their incantations and blessings. Alexandros made a long speech, making sure to express his appreciation and gratitude to all deities who might conceivably exercise jurisdiction over the land of Macedonia, the army, the royal family, the current military expedition, the local area and its geographic features, and his own martial prowess. He thanked Zeus, Herakles, Apollon, Ares, and the rest of the Olympians, but he didn't stint any of the local gods, singling out Istros, the divine ruler of the Danube, for particular praise and a generous portion of the incinerated flesh. The expeditionary force then settled down for a quick feast, dispatching whatever meat was left over after the gods had consumed their share, along with the usual porridge and vegetables, all washed down with the weak and sour local brew.

His longing to project Macedonian power beyond the mighty Danube having been duly satisfied, Alexandros and his detachment returned to the bulk of the army, waiting patiently on the southern bank of the river. We brought back with us whatever meager loot we had managed to plunder from the Getai, the effort required to ferry it across the river far outweighing its value, but the troops enjoyed the trinkets. They served as emoluments, mementos, and medals, all in one, regardless of what their intrinsic value might have been.

****

After the Getan exercise, the army started to make its way back to Macedonia. We carried out an uneventful crossing of the Shipka Pass, leaving the Triballian territory behind, and turned west, toward the lands of the Agrianians, with the intention of dropping off King Langaros and his troops at the hilltop village that served as the capital of Agriania. But two days short of our destination, Alexandros received reports of troublesome developments farther west along Macedonia's northwestern border, in Illyria.

Specifically, those pesky Illyrians were once again in revolt. Except this time, the insurrection appeared better organized and more formidable than usual. The lands controlled by the Illyrians stretched from

Macedonia in the east to the Adriatic in the west, and from Epiros in the south to the Danube and beyond in the north. Both in territory under occupation and in population under arms, the potential military capacity of the Illyrians far exceeded the resources of Macedonia. Fortunately for the Macedonians, the weapons and tactics of the Illyrians were far inferior to those implemented in the Macedonian army during Philippos's reign. In addition, the incessant internecine warfare among the various Illyrian tribes made the Greek city-states look like a close-knit family of pacifists by comparison.

This time, however, undoubtedly inspired by news of Philippos's death, the Illyrians appeared determined to reverse the tide of losing engagements that had seen them pushed back from the Macedonian frontier. King Kleitos of Dardania, one of the Illyrian states – he was the son of the late King Bardylis and the brother of the late Princess Audata, Philippos's first wife – had entered into an alliance with King Glaukias of the Taulantians, another Illyrian state, as well as with the chieftain of the Autaratians, another primitive and bellicose tribe of Illyrians. For once, all the Illyrians appeared united in their opposition to Macedonia.

The training exercise suddenly became deadly serious. Alexandros met with his commanders to determine upon a course of action. King Langaros offered to deal with the Autaratians on his own, using his battle-tested Agrianian light troops, while Alexandros, with the Macedonian army, responded to the challenge posed by the Dardanians and Taulantians. Alexandros accepted Langaros's suggestion and we set off immediately, across rugged terrain, toward Pelion, Kleitos's fortress capital.

Pelion controlled the road from Illyria to Macedonia and was a formidable stronghold. It was surrounded by impassable mountains on three sides, with a valley and a small river, the Apsos, on the fourth side. The wall facing the valley appeared impregnable. The road itself led through a narrow mountain pass, down into the small valley, across the Apsos, past the menacing fortress wall, then across another ford, and back up into yet another mountain pass.

Thanks to its customary celerity, the Macedonian army arrived at Pelion before the stronghold could be reinforced by Glaukias and his Taulantian troops. That was the good news. The bad news was that, having assessed the fortifications of Pelion, it became clear to the Macedonian commanders that the investment of Kleitos's fastness would require a lot of time and equipment and more troops than Alexandros had at his disposal. Furthermore, any attempt to continue marching along the road, toward Macedonia, would subject Alexandros's troops to a withering barrage of arrows, stones, bolts, and assorted other projectiles as we passed beneath the fortress walls, resulting in massive casualties, not to mention the attendant loss of face. The third alternative of turning around and marching away, back into barbarian territory, would do nothing to quell the Illyrian uprising and would simply subject Alexandros's army to future attacks along our difficult route of retreat, at a time and place of the enemy's choosing.

While Alexandros and his commanders debated these alternatives, their choices were narrowed considerably by the arrival of Glaukias in our rear. The Taulantians occupied the pass through which we had entered into the Apsos valley earlier in the day and then spread out into the foothills surrounding the valley. As night fell, the campfires of the Taulantians encircled our camp like a blazing pearl necklace, with Kleitos's fortress serving as the clasp.

Alexandros told his foot soldiers to get a good night's rest, because the next day they would be called upon to demonstrate their close order drill. And in fact, the next morning, after an unhurried breakfast, Alexandros ordered his troops to line up in parade formation. He also told them to maintain absolute silence during the subsequent drills. And then, for the better part of the day, Alexandros put his infantry through their paces, right there in the small valley beneath Pelion's walls. The phalanxes marched, turned, extended their lines and shrunk them, raised their sarissas and dipped them, made ninety degree turns and abrupt about-faces. The entire corps moved in unison. There was never a foot out of sync, never a spearpoint out of alignment. And it was all executed in total, eerie silence.

The Illyrians had never seen anything like it. It was as if someone who had spent his entire life living in caves was suddenly ushered into the Parthenon. The barbarian warriors slowly crept closer and closer to the valley, their mouths agape, their bulging eyes shining brightly.

When the Taulantians had inched in close enough, Alexandros gave the signal for the final maneuver of the day. Suddenly, and in unison, 20,000 troops shattered the silence, raising a mighty roar, beating their swords against their shields, and charging at the nearest barbarians. The startled savages dropped their weapons and ran. We in the cavalry set off in close pursuit. Many Taulantians died. The rest scattered into the surrounding hills. Alexandros struck camp and marched away, back into the barbarian country from whence we had come.

The surviving Taulantians – and most of them had survived – gradually made their way back into the valley in front of Pelion and then they celebrated. As far as they were concerned, they had won. No one would admit that they had been so overawed by the Macedonian display that they had let the enemy escape from their grasp. It was enough that they had forced the Macedonians to retreat.

Alexandros, who had halted his troops a short distance from the Apsos valley, waited three days while the Illyrians celebrated, danced, and drank. On the third night, his army turned around, marched back, and slaughtered the sleeping and inebriated celebrants, whose commanders had neglected to erect any defensive fortifications or even to post any sentries. Glaukias and a few of his Taulantians managed to make their way into Kleitos's fort as dawn broke while most of their brethren lay dead or dying in the valley and the surrounding foothills.

When Kleitos, the Dardanian king, heard the news and assessed the killing ground beneath the fortress walls with his own eyes, he took the only action that appeared logical to him under the circumstances – he burned Pelion to the ground and escaped with his troops to Glaukias's mountain fastness deep in the forests of Taulantia. Neither he nor Glaukias ever bothered Alexandros again.

Chapter 13 – Object Lesson

The Macedonians didn't pause to celebrate. Alexandros was anxious to find out how his friend Langaros was faring in his struggle against the Autaratians. He needn't have worried. The two allied armies met three days later. When the two commanders saw each other, they leapt off their horses, raced to each other and embraced, laughing and slapping the other's back.

Langaros brought good news. He had easily scattered the Autaratians and opened up the road back to Macedonia. He also brought some bad news. Apparently, Alexandros's movements through the wilderness had been shadowed by an entire cadre of spies deployed by various Greek cities.

When reports emerged about the alliance between Kleitos and Glaukias and when Alexandros's predicament under the walls of Pelion became known, these spies didn't await the outcome of the battle. It was obvious

368

that, with Kleitos in front of him and Glaukias in his rear, Alexandros's position was hopeless. Anxious to steal a march on their competitors, the spies rushed off to report Alexandros's defeat without waiting for the actual battle to take place. After all, the outcome was a foreordained certainty.

When these spies arrived with their stories in various Greek cities, they set off wild celebrations. The news spread like wildfire and it grew better as it went along. By the time it reached Thebes and Athens, the breathless reports had Alexandros killed beneath the walls of Pelion, more Hektor than Achilleus, and his army destroyed.

In Athens, Demosthenes outdid himself. No prophetic dreams this time. Instead, he produced an ostensible eye witness, a bandaged and bloody barbarian, who gave a vivid account of the destruction of the Macedonian army and the ignominious death of Alexandros. The Athenian Assembly, whose hopeful optimism always outpaced any healthy skepticism and obliterated all collective memory, declared three days of celebrations.

In Thebes, the restless renegade elements, which had been suppressed after the last rebellion, once again rose to the fore, expelled from their government the collaborationist oligarchs appointed by Alexandros, and led the rabble against the Macedonian garrison on the

369

Kadmeia. Several Macedonian soldiers were killed, including the two Macedonian commanders, and the rest of the garrison was trapped and under siege in its elevated citadel.

These were the reports that Langaros brought with him when the Agrianian and Macedonian armies met on the road between Pelion and the Macedonian frontier. One additional short dispatch caught Alexandros's attention: Amyntas the Nephew had been spotted in Larissa. It was said that he was meeting with representatives of several Greek cities who were conspiring to use him as a figurehead to replace Alexandros on the Macedonian throne.

If Alexandros had in fact been killed, of all his potential successors, Amyntas the Nephew would have had the best claim to the diadem. After all, he had been elected king once before, albeit as a child, with Philippos designated as the regent. Despite the fact that Philippos eased him out of his monarchy before he had a chance to rule, Amyntas nevertheless retained a decent argument that he was the legitimate king. Beyond that, Philippos had sired only two legitimate sons, not counting Alexandros: Arrhidaios the halfwit and Karanos the infant. Neither one of those two was currently capable of ruling. Finally, if any further argument were required, Amyntas could point out that he was married to Philippos's daughter (and Alexandros's half-sister)

Kynane, providing further support for his claim to the throne.

Of course, Alexandros was not actually dead. His coloration was livid, however, as he read the report from Larissa. Without pausing to consider whether the report was accurate or not and whether, if accurate, it reflected an erroneous assumption on the part of Amyntas and the Greeks that could be easily corrected, he flew into a rage instead. He sat down and wrote a coded note to his mother in Pella, entrusting it to Hekataios and his two dozen cutthroats, who took off immediately. Alexandros then had a brief meeting with Langaros, in which he thanked his friend for all his support, borrowed some of Langaros's best archers, and sent the Agrianian king back home, along with handsome presents and the promise of marriage to Alexandros's half-sister Kynane, although technically Kynane was not yet a widow. Finally, he ordered his own army to be ready to march in two hours.

For the next ten days, we marched from Illyria to Thebes, traveling faster than the news of our progress. The first notice the startled Thebans had of Alexandros's continued presence among the living was seeing his unmistakable figure, astride Boukephalas, prancing outside the Elektra Gate.

****

Olympias was thrilled to receive her son's message. Although she had never given any credence to the rumors of his demise, she was nevertheless anxiously awaiting reports of his inevitable triumphs. She quickly decoded the message and proceeded to carry out Alexandros's instructions with her typical, ruthless, hands-on efficiency.

She sent Hekataios and his men to Larissa; Amyntas the Nephew, the likeable young man who should have been king but had never contested Philippos's usurpation, was never seen again. A few days later, Olympias, accompanied by two of her bodyguards, stopped by the rooms where Kleopatra and her children were being held. Without a word to Luscious, she picked up a pillow and smothered the infant Karanos in his crib, while her guards restrained the screaming mother. Then, exceeding in her enthusiasm the task assigned to her by Alexandros, she grabbed little Europa by the neck, lifted the toddler off the ground, and throttled her. When the little girl stopped kicking, she relaxed her chokehold, letting the lifeless little body thud to the ground like a sack of potatoes.

At that point, Olympias reached behind her and one of her guards placed a length of rope, with a noose already fashioned at one end, into her open hand. Olympias threw the rope at the heaving chest of the disconsolate Kleopatra, spun on her heels, and strode out of the room, past Kleopatra's guards still impassively manning the door, her head held high, a satisfied smile breaking through her stern countenance. Throughout her brutal foray she had uttered nary a word.

Luscious Kleopatra took the hint. When the guards checked on her the next morning, they found her lifeless body twisting slowly at the end of the rope thoughtfully provided by Olympias. Her body was not interred in Philippos's tomb. At Olympias's insistence, it was thrown out with the kitchen offal instead.

That same night, a terrified Kynane, who had given birth to Amyntas's child only weeks earlier, fled with her baby girl Adeia, and little else, to her uncle Kleitos in Dardania. Olympias, who had undoubtedly received notice of the escape, let them go.

****

While his mother was implementing, or perhaps overimplementing, his instructions back in Pella, Alexandros was awaiting the Thebans' response to his ultimatum. Cloaking himself in the mantle of hegemon of the Korinthian League, he had demanded that the Thebans stop violating their treaty obligations, acknowledge him as the duly elected leader of the League, and surrender the two chief instigators of the insurrection.

To deliver their reply, the Thebans dispatched a town crier to the top of the city wall, from which perch he could be heard not only by Alexandros but also by all of his soldiers, encamped just outside the walls. The Thebans declared themselves prepared to negotiate with Alexandros but only if he agreed to surrender Antipatros and Philotas to them first. Anticipating that this demand would not meet with Alexandros's approval, the Thebans then proceeded to issue an invitation to all freedom-loving Greeks to join them in throwing off the yoke of the Macedonian tyrant.

Sitting in his tent, listening to the Thebans' response, Alexandros was not a happy camper. He had no wish to expend money, time, or Macedonian lives on a protracted siege of Thebes. His training exercise had already taken more time than he had expected and the window of opportunity to cross the Hellespont with his entire army, during the current fighting season, was quickly closing. On the other hand, this was the third time the Thebans had rebelled against Macedonia; they served as a focal point of Greek opposition against the planned invasion of Persia; and they were intolerably impudent.

As a thirteen-year-old youngster in Mieza, Alexandros had projected a preternatural sense of self-confidence. He had implicitly believed that he'd been chosen by the gods to accomplish great deeds on the battlefield. What was more, he'd been able to persuade others that he was destiny's darling. But, at that time, it had all seemed to be a subconscious personality trait, almost an accidental affectation. At some point since then, however, perhaps reading the Iliad or listening to Aristoteles or watching his father at Chaironeia or assessing his own successes during his recent jaunt through barbarian territories, he'd come to the conscious realization that the expectation of success, the projection of inevitability, the appearance of invincibility, actually mattered. He realized that the Thebans' insolence couldn't be allowed to stand.

Alexandros once again flew into a rage. Except this time, it seemed to be a coldly calculated furor. He ordered siege engines to be constructed, earthen ramparts erected, and wall-sapping operations commenced. He also invited the other cities of Boiotia, all of which harbored hoary historical hatreds for their dominant and domineering neighbor, to live up to their League obligations and send troops and supplies in support of the siege. The Boiotian cities responded in direct proportion to the weight of their accumulated grievances. The more aggrieved they considered themselves to be, the more wholehearted was their response to Alexandros's call.

Demosthenes was busy in the Athenian Assembly, trying to organize a relief force to come to the aid of Thebes. However, the enthusiasm he commanded in the immediate aftermath of his theatrical production featuring the bloody and bandaged barbarian had diminished greatly when it turned out that the report of Alexandros's demise had been somewhat premature. In the end, the Athenians decided to sit on their hands and await the outcome of the siege of Thebes, safely ensconced behind their own city walls.

The Thebans, on the other hand, observing the beehive of activity under their walls, decided to go on the offensive. Their phalanxes, which had been undefeated until Chaironeia and which were still considered the best in Greece, came pouring out of the city gates and attacked the soldiers busily engaged in siege operations. The tide of victory appeared to be flowing in their favor, too, despite the best efforts of Alexandros's hardened veterans, until Alexandros noticed that, in their enthusiasm, some of the Theban soldiers assigned to guard one of the postern gates had rushed over to join the fight. He ordered Perdikkas to detach two companies of Silver Shields and crash the gate, which Perdikkas was able to accomplish, despite sustaining a serious wound himself. Once inside the wall, the Silver Shields fought their way to the Kadmeia and linked up with the garrison, which had been held hostage in their citadel. The combined forces then turned about and attacked the civilian population of the city.

Once the Theban phalanxes, which had been on the verge of victory only moments earlier, realized that the city wall had been breached, their discipline began to waver. Some of the hoplites began to retreat toward the city gates, while others continued to hold their positions. Alexandros, sensing their indecision, threw all of his remaining reserves into the fight. The Thebans began a wholesale retreat toward the Elektra Gate, while the Companion Cavalry did its best to prevent them from reaching their objective.

Scores of Theban foot soldiers were trampled to death, either by the hooves of the Companion Cavalry or the feet of their fellow soldiers. The Elektra Gate became clogged with bodies and couldn't be closed. The Macedonian cavalry poured in, followed by the Macedonian infantry, and then by the soldiers from the neighboring towns.

At some point, the Theban soldiers stopped retreating. Small clusters of them stood their ground and fought. But they had no chance against the overwhelming force of the Macedonian advance. In a matter of minutes, almost all of the Theban fighters lay dead or dying, carpeting the field outside the Elektra Gate, stacked several bodies high in the Gate itself, and lining the streets and alleys radiating from the Gate.

And then the savagery commenced in earnest. Old men were dragged from their houses and slaughtered. Women had their clothes torn off, were raped repeatedly, and were finally cut down as they ran screaming through the streets, naked and bleeding. Children cowering in their bedrooms had their brains bashed in.

There was no sanctuary. Every temple was plundered, all those inside slaughtered. Every house was looted, ravaged, and eventually torched. Anything that moved, from people to horses to chickens, was killed. The paving stones of the streets were slick with gore; the fountains in the public squares ran crimson with blood; human body parts festooned doorways, roofs, and trees.

Tough Macedonian veterans, nauseated by the carnage, refused to continue. But the solders from the neighboring towns insisted on exorcising the accumulated grievances of centuries of oppression.

Alexandros was fully aware of the butchery as it proceeded. He retained complete control, at least of his own troops, throughout but he did nothing to stop the bloodbath. He was not, however, oblivious to the great cultural heritage of Thebes. He issued strict orders that the house of the legendary Theban poet Pindaros was not to be damaged nor any of his relatives who might be found within harmed. The house was certainly spared; however, for one reason or another, no one was left alive within its walls.

When the slaughter finally ended the next morning, Alexandros convened a meeting of the League Council, in order to maintain the fiction that he was acting on its behalf and carrying out its policy in the sack of Thebes. As many delegates as could be rounded up on short notice were present, mostly representing the neighboring cities. They were asked to determine the ultimate fate of Thebes.

Alexandros maintained punctilious procedural protocol. Each delegate was given an opportunity to speak. Even a Theban survivor was brought in to address the delegates. His appeals fell on deaf ears. The delegates gave vent to centuries of resentment. In particular, they recalled that, during the Persian wars, Thebes had fought on the wrong side of the conflict. There was no need for Alexandros to speak; his wishes were well known to the delegates.

The ultimate vote was unanimous. Thebes was to be razed to the ground, although the temples, public monuments, and the house of Pindaros were allowed to remain standing. All personal property found within the city walls constituted spoils of war, rightfully belonging to the armies that captured it. All inhabitants of Thebes who survived were to be sold into slavery, with all proceeds paid to Alexandros to defray his military expenditures. All Theban refugees who had eluded capture were banished from Greece. Any Greek who offered shelter or assistance to a Theban fugitive made himself subject to exile. The Macedonian garrison on the Kadmeia was reinstated. All the lands and possessions of Thebes were parceled out among her neighbors.

The orders of the League Council were carried out forthwith. The ancient city of Thebes, once ruled by

King Oidipous himself, a city that rivaled any Greek community, including Athens, in antiquity, cultural heritage, military might, and historical importance, the fabled city of seven gates and some fifty thousand inhabitants, passed into legend.

More than ten thousand people died on the day the walls were breached. An additional thirty thousand people were sold into slavery, at an average price of 88 drachmas per head, netting 440 badly needed talents for the Macedonian treasury. The remaining inhabitants of the city disappeared from the pages of history without a trace.

In other Greek cities, celebrations of Alexandros's demise came to an abrupt halt, as the brave citizens trembled at the thought of a visit by the young and very much animate ruler. Trepidation and lamentation replaced jubilation. In Athens, the Assembly repudiated Demosthenes and lavished awards on Demades, who succeeded once again in dissuading the Macedonian monarch from meting out to Athens its just deserts. Throughout Greece, Macedonian garrisons were welcomed with open arms, Macedonian visitors received honorary citizenships, and Macedonian policies were praised in public fora. Smoldering resentments undoubtedly continued to bubble beneath the surface but there were no further open uprisings, which was just as well. The time for training exercises and object lessons was over; the crossing of the Hellespont awaited.

Prime Directive

****

Neither Kleitos nor I had participated in the sack of Thebes. I always had the Prime Directive as a handy excuse. Kleitos didn't need an excuse. "I didn't enlist to become a butcher," he said. "Today I'm glad they call me Metoikos," I replied.

The campaign had changed all of us. The troops had gained skill, self-confidence, and toughness. They had also lost some of their humanity, which, for an army seeking to maximize its effectiveness, was presumably an improvement. Alexandros had confirmed his beliefs as to the benefits of speed, propaganda, and terror. And I had discovered I really missed being at the Academy.

In the end, we were all anxious to get on with the invasion of Persia, the troops in hopes of further conquests and additional loot, Alexandros in pursuit of his destiny, and I hoping to get closer to the day of my return to my former life. Unfortunately, the leaves on the trees were turning to rust and gold, the fighting season was over, and our crossing of the Hellespont would have to wait until next spring.

When we returned to Pella, Kleitos told me that Lanike's wedding feast had been scheduled a fortnight hence. After a sleepless night, I told him I wouldn't attend. I didn't send a wedding gift either. Perhaps a bit of Alexandros's ruthlessness had rubbed off on me.

Chapter 14 – Crossing the Hellespont

Alexandros stood in the prow of the trireme, in full parade armor, the white plume of his helmet whipping in the wind, his polished breastplate spraying showers of reflected sunshine, a short cavalry spear poised in his right hand. Standing behind him were a number of senior officers, including his second-in-command Parmenion, flanked by sons Fast Philotas and Nuts Nikanoros. And standing behind them were the king's bodyguards, including Kleitos and me.

Just as the keel of the ship started to scrape against the rising seabed of the approaching shore, Alexandros reared back and threw his javelin a good stadion up the beach, into the accumulated debris at the edge of the high tide line. "I hereby claim Asia by right of conquest," he exclaimed over the pounding roar of the rolling breakers. As he turned toward us, his arms raised, his head held high, his mien triumphant, he managed to give the impression of someone who had actually conquered something. Then he turned once again and leapt into the foamy surf.

We all rushed over to the railing to observe our leader's progress as he struggled to make his way onto dry land in his soggy armor. I glanced over at Kleitos who was trying hard to suppress a smile. "Why does he do stuff like this?" I whispered in his ear. Kleitos shrugged and jumped over the rail. I followed suit.

The ritual conquest of Asia by spear was Alexandros's third religious or symbolic performance of the day. Earlier that morning, just before boarding the lead ship of the little flotilla assembled by Nearchos for our crossing of the Hellespont, he had gathered us all at the ostensible tomb of Protesilaos, the legendary hero, described in the Iliad as the first man to leap onto Asian soil when the Greek fleet arrived at Troy and as the first Greek to die in the conflict. *An odd choice of role model,* I thought, *for someone intending to take on the successors of Troy.* But then again, maybe Alexandros had a premonition of his fate.

The ceremony at the cult site was mercifully brief as we were all anxious to get on our way. Alexandros merely poured some wine on the gravesite, said what was for him a short prayer, and made a donation to the local shrine. Then we were off to our ships.

In mid-channel, as our galley was bobbing on the waves, Alexandros once again brought our progress to a halt in order to conduct a full-fledged rite of thanksgiving and propitiation. A bull was sacrificed to Poseidon, right there, shipboard, and its flanks burnt on an altar erected immediately in front of the helmsman's wheel. Libations were poured from golden chalices, after which the chalices themselves were hurled into the waves. Alexandros then thanked not only Poseidon but all twelve Olympian gods as well as the local gods of the Hellespont and its adjoining shores. He promised generous gifts and everlasting worship to them all and prayed for their support not only during our crossing but also throughout the great military venture upon which we were embarked. Only after the conclusion of the ceremony was the flotilla permitted to proceed.

We were able to land our ships in the vicinity of Abydos and disembark without any Persian opposition because the advance expeditionary corps that Philippos had dispatched two years earlier still controlled this portion of the Troad. On the other hand, by the time of our arrival, even control of this small corner of land was a fairly close thing.

During the previous year, shortly after the murder of Attalos the Adder, Dareios finally succeeded in consolidating his power in Persepolis and began to address various festering irritants in the many far-flung corners of his empire. The Macedonian expeditionary corps operating in the Troad, Aiolia, and Ionia was one of those irritants.

Prime Directive

Dareios turned to one of the many Greek mercenary generals in his employ, Memnon of Rhodos, to deal with the Macedonian nuisance. Memnon set out with a force of 5,000 Greek mercenaries. His first objective was to relieve Pitane, a small town on the coast of Aiolia, which was, at that moment, being besieged by Parmenion. Before reaching Pitane, however, Memnon received a message from Dareios, asking him to march instead to Kyzikos, a port on the Sea of Marmara, which was about to be sacked by another part of the Macedonian expeditionary corps. Memnon duly diverted his forces but arrived too late to save Kyzikos for the Persian side.

Having learned from this failure, Memnon stopped to re-evaluate, from a strategic point of view, what his primary mission should be. He concluded that his job was to take control of the landing sites that the combined Macedonian and Greek army was most likely to use when the principal invasion came. Therefore, he marched into the Troad and recaptured Lampsakos, a strategically important port at the northern end of the Hellespont. Next, he took aim at Abydos, which being held at that moment by a small Macedonian force under the command of Attalos's successor, Kalas. Kalas sent a desperate message to Parmenion, asking for relief. Parmenion immediately raised the siege of Pitane, gathered all the remaining expeditionary forces, and raced to Kalas's aid. He arrived just in time to save Abydos for the Macedonian side. Parmenion was sufficiently concerned, however, to send a message to Alexandros, urging an early invasion of Asia by the main force of the pan-Hellenic army.

Unfortunately, when Alexandros received Parmenion's message, he was deeply enmeshed in his training exercise and unable to do anything about the old general's request. The invasion would have to wait until the next spring, he advised his commander. In the meantime, he instructed the expeditionary corps to dig in and hold as much of the Troad as they could. He also ordered Parmenion himself to leave the army in charge of Kalas and return to Pella for consultations. The veteran soldier obeyed, in spite of what must have been a certain level of trepidation, given the fate of his co-commander Attalos the Adder. In the end, Parmenion proved indispensable and was named second-in-command for the principal invasion.

Over the winter, Alexandros conferred with Antipatros, Parmenion, and the other senior commanders (they urged caution, which advice Alexandros ignored, as they knew he would) and made preparations for next spring. As soon as the snows melted, Alexandros set off. His army numbered some 37,000 men, which seemed to be a fairly formidable force, especially when added to the expeditionary corps already on the Asian side of the Hellespont, until one looked more closely at the composition of Alexandros's army.

Only 13,800 of Alexandros's troops were Macedonian, 12,000 heavy infantry and 1,800 cavalry. Before departing Pella, the young king had felt compelled to leave about half of his Macedonian troops behind with Antipatros, just in case trouble arose once again after his departure, either in Greece or among the barbarians. He hoped that his demonstration projects, at Pelion and in Thebes, would leave a lasting impression but he couldn't be sure.

On the plus side, Alexandros's army was enlarged by levies contributed by Greek city-states and barbarian tribes alike. These foreign forces not only augmented the fighting strength of his army but they also served as convenient hostages guaranteeing the good behavior of their fellow citizens or tribesmen left behind. The Korinthian League supplied 7,000 heavy infantry and 500 cavalry soldiers; the Thessalians contributed 1,800 cavalry; the Illyrians and other barbarian tribes supplied another 7,000 light-armed troopers and 500 mounted scouts; his friend King Langaros sent 1,500 Agrianian archers and skirmishers. Finally, Alexandros was able to recruit some 5,000 mercenaries from all over Greece.

In addition to the fighting men, Alexandros's army also included sappers, engineers, surveyors, administrators, seers, soothsayers, priests, scholars, scientists, and campaign historians. Aristoteles's influence was evident in the heterogeneity of this latter group. No previous military force, in the long and sanguinary history of human conflict, had ever incorporated such a large and organized contingent of people whose sole function was to collect data, advance the frontiers of human knowledge, preserve for posterity a record of the army's achievements, and create and disseminate propaganda. Not entirely coincidentally, the expedition's chief historian was Aristoteles's nephew, Kallisthenes.

Conversely, Alexandros severely limited the number of camp followers. His soldiers were expected to fend for themselves. There were to be no servants, squires, wives, or ladies of easy virtue. Sexual services could be procured locally, along with victuals and other necessities of life, as far as Alexandros was concerned.

Only a small portion of this host was able to traverse the Hellespont with us during the first crossing of the flotilla. Alexandros's entire fleet comprised only 160 ships, which meant that ferrying the entire army across the channel, along with the horses, armor, equipment, and the entire baggage train promised to be a long and tedious operation. Alexandros was far too impatient to stand by and watch. As soon as we had disembarked from our ship, he entrusted the rest of the operation to Parmenion, while he, accompanied by a small contingent of cavalry, set off to reconnoiter the countryside.

****

His first stop was to Ilion, the ostensible location of Troy. I, for one, was disappointed by what we saw when we got there. On the purported site of the legendary metropolis, there stood only a small, dilapidated, dusty village. It was immediately obvious to me that the sole occupation of its inhabitants was the exploitation of gullible visitors. In the first place, the location of the village was spurious. I knew from my studies that the actual remnants of Troy were buried beneath layers of rubble, debris, soil, and turf several miles to the southwest of the location of the village but that evidently made very little difference to the tourists, because everything else in the village, in addition to its location, was phony as well. There were bogus archaic relics, fraudulent antique weapons, sham ancient documents, fake primordial trinkets, fictitious archeological sites, and ersatz tour guides.

Alexandros, to all outward appearances, had just entered the Elysian Fields. He swallowed the tall tales of our quack guides whole. He bought every relic, trinket, and memento on offer. He visited a decrepit little temple of Athena, where he was shown some weathered armor that had allegedly once belonged to Achilleus. He immediately traded in his own fine armor for the crumbling remnants of a corroded cuirass and a pair of dented greaves.

He never stopped to consider the improbability of any actual artifact surviving from the Trojan war. The stirring events recounted by Homeros had taken place more than 800 years earlier but to Alexandros, who had been reading the Iliad daily since childhood, it had all happened just yesterday.

The putative priests of Athena in their decaying little temple gratefully accepted Alexandros's offer to make a donation to the goddess and hastily arranged a complete religious service for his benefit, inviting their gullible new patron to officiate. It was well past midnight by the time we managed to find our way back to Abydos but Alexandros was still too excited to fall asleep. Although I was too tired to keep up with him, I wondered whether he had managed to catch any sleep at all that night.

******

When we awoke early the next morning, the weather was still fine. Almost half the army had already crossed the channel during the previous day. Assuming our luck continued to hold, it seemed likely that the entire operation could be completed in two more days.

"The gods like it better when you sacrifice to them, rather than whip them," Alexandros observed with a smile. He was referring to the story in Herodotos, according to which, when Xerxes attempted to cross the Hellespont in the opposite direction, some 146 years earlier, a terrible storm blew in and destroyed the pontoon bridge built by Xerxes's engineers for the traversal. The Persian emperor, in his fury, not only had the hapless engineers decapitated but he also ordered that 300 lashes be administered to the sea itself.

"Let's go hunting," Alexandros called out. "Parmenion will see to the rest of the ferrying operations."

He quickly assembled most of the old Mieza contingent and we were soon off and running. (Well, we were actually riding horses this time.)

"They told me yesterday at Ilion that there are still lions in the hills beyond the village," an excited Alexandros yelled over his shoulder as we rode away from the shore at breakneck speed. I kept my doubts as to the veracity of this intelligence to myself. "We'll pick up a guide and some bush beaters along the way."

The hunt was a complete fiasco, of course. Even if there had been a dozen prides roaming the hills of Ilion, we would never have caught a glimpse of a single solitary cub. The din and the dust and the stench created by our horses and our bush beaters would have caused even a deaf, lame, anosmatic, and terminally senescent lion to swim across the Hellespont in terror, long before it came within our sight.

What surprised me was that we saw no signs of any animal life at all. Admittedly, the hills were mostly scrubland, dominated by dense but short shrubs, with an occasional stunted pine peeking over the shoulders of its hunched brethren, but there were some open meadows, with lots of spring flowers, aromatic herbs, and succulent leaves. Surely, there were shrews, mice, voles, squirrels, weasels, foxes, and even a few deer and antelopes making their homes amidst all this vegetation. Thanks to our bumbling guide and noisome bush beaters, we successfully avoided running across any of them.

After spending half a day chasing phantoms, Alexandros and I became separated from the rest of the group. "I think they went thataway." Alexandros pointed in the opposite direction from where we had last seen our fellow hunters. "Let's see if we can catch up to them."

We continued riding until it was certain we were alone and no one would find us any time soon. Then we stopped in a pleasant, sun-dappled meadow, letting our horses graze, while we sat in the grass, eating our bread and drinking watered wine.

"I miss my father," Alexandros said.

I must have looked startled by his comment, coming out of the blue and without context, because he felt the need to explain. "There's no one I can talk to, you know; nobody wants to follow a leader who's got doubts ... or who cries for his daddy."

"Except me, I guess."

"You're different, Ptolemaios."

"Tell me about it."

"No, I mean it in a good way. You're different, it's true, but that's why I can trust you. You won't go blabbing to the others."

"When I first arrived, as a dirty, starving stranger in rags, your father used to talk to me, too. I guess I'm kind of an inherited talisman."

Alexandros laughed. "I never realized how much I had inherited from him. I wish I could still ask him for advice."

"Should've thought of that before." The words had blurted out before I could stop them.

"Before what?" Alexandros flared up.

I said nothing, staring him in the eyes, trying to read his thoughts.

Alexandros averted his gaze. "Mind you, there had to be a change," he finally whispered. "The Greeks, and especially the Athenians, were never going to follow him."

"Like they're following you now?"

"There were a lot of things I didn't understand before. Like what a maggot that Demosthenes was. But still, it was my destiny to lead this invasion; don't you see that?"

"Who told you that, your mother?"

"Leave her out of it."

I tried to change the subject. "He was a great man, you know."

"I'm beginning to see that now. Which is why I miss him. I'd apologize to him, if I could. And ask for some advice." He paused. "It's been a tough couple of years."

"Your father did it for twenty-three years."

He seemed lost in thought. "The toughest part is keeping my mask on, every minute of every day." He was murmuring, more to himself than to me, staring at the brush shadows shivering in the breeze. "I don't know which is tougher. Being on stage all the time, having to project confidence and certainty, or being always alone, unable to speak frankly to anyone."

"But you *are* certain and confident."

He laughed ruefully. "See what I mean. Even you bought it."

I chose not to argue with him.

"Do you have any idea how desperate our situation is?"

I did in fact have some idea but said nothing.

"To begin with, we've got a relatively small army, perhaps 48,000 men, if you add the troops that were already here to the ones we're bringing over. And we really can't expect any reinforcements any time soon. Those accursed allies of ours are sitting back, hoping we get wiped out, not appreciating that we're fighting their fight too. If the Persians win, what do they think will happen to mainland Greece next?

"In the meantime, the Persians have unlimited resources and unlimited manpower. They could field a hundred thousand men against us, if they wanted to, or two hundred thousand, or three.

"In a way, though, it's lucky I've only got 48,000. I can't even pay that many. Do you realize the men haven't been paid in a month?"

"Didn't help matters when you abolished all the taxes."

"Had to be done. Can't expect farmers to pay taxes if you're taking all their labor away."

"So, why have you dragged us all here? And why don't we turn around?"

"I can't, man. I've got to follow my destiny. Plus, when the gods give you a job, it's not like you can say no. At least not if you have any sense of arete."

"The gods have given you this job?" I was skeptical.

He nodded.

"How do you know?" I persisted.

"I've known since I was a little kid. I know the way you know that you're right-handed or that you've got a hooked nose."

"Is that why you're so scrupulous in observing all the rituals?"

"Well, as far as the rituals go, I figure it can't hurt. Might even help a bit. You never know what motivates the gods but you certainly don't want to piss them off."

He fell momentarily silent. "But it's not the rituals that matter. It's the thread of life that the Fates have spun for you that determines your destiny."

"So you have no control over what happens?"

"Oh no, you've still got to do all the heavy lifting yourself. It's just a question of whether it'll pay off in the end. The thread is spun but where it leads only the gods know for sure."

He changed the subject once again. "In the short run, though, we've got to win a battle soon. We need some loot *now* to pay the men and to keep feeding them. But most of all, we need to win a battle *now* to keep them believing in me."

"Do you think we'll have a battle soon?"

He laughed. "Well, I'm going do everything I can to provoke one."

Abruptly he turned serious again. "Sometimes, as I lie awake, asking the gods for a sign, I get a bad feeling about this coming battle."

"What do you mean?" I kept my voice noncommittal.

"It's almost like a premonition, you know. It feels like the end of the line, sometimes."

I said nothing, afraid to breathe. *You've got no idea,* I thought. I couldn't help feeling sorry for this earnest, complicated, talented, doomed young man. *His fate will be whatever it will be but for you it'll just be a transition point.* I tried in vain to chase away my melancholy thoughts.

Alexandros barged into my reverie. "Do you think we'll win?"

"What do you mean?"

"When we get our battle with the Persians, do you think we will win?"

"Why are you asking me? How should I know?" I was starting to panic.

"But you do know, don't you?" This was more an assertion than a question. "So, stop stalling, Ptolemaios, and tell me. Do you think we'll beat the Persians when we meet them or not?"

He was more right than he realized. Of course, I knew the answer but I wouldn't have told him, even without the constraints of the Prime Directive. He was barely able to resist the forces crashing in on him as it was. The last thing he needed to know was the outcome of the battle. *It's better not to see the blow that kills you.*

Unbidden, a certain feeling of kinship to this troubled young man intruded into my thoughts. In truth, neither he nor I knew where our respective threads, woven for each of us by the Fates, would lead. The fact that I had a pretty good idea where his thread would end didn't change our shared ignorance of our own ultimate destinations. Nor did his identity as a king and mine as a marooned traveler change the fact that we were both lonely, isolated outsiders, struggling through unknown terrain.

I physically shuddered, trying to shake off my present train of thought. *You're nothing like him,* I silently reminded at myself.

I looked at Alexandros. He was still glaring at me, waiting for an answer.

"The Pythia told you you're invincible. What do you need my prognostication for?"

"Yeah, well, sometimes it's hard to know what the Pythia means. You, on the other hand, always seem to know what you're talking about."

"Thank you, sire," I demurred with false modesty, "but mostly I've got no more clue than the next guy."

He didn't believe me but let the matter drop. "I guess we'd better go find the others."

We never did find the rest of the hunting party and ended up riding, just the two of us, in silence, all the way back to Abydos. For the second night in a row, it was well past midnight when we finally arrived at our tents. But this time, it was I who had trouble falling asleep.

****

Two days later, when the ferrying operations were finally completed, the army set out for the closest strategically important city that Alexandros could find, which happened to be Daskyleion, the seat of Hellespontine Phrygia, the satrapy that comprised the Troad, Mysia, and Bithynia. Alexandros reasoned that the Persians would not tolerate a threat to their provincial capital and would therefore offer a set piece battle, rather than risk even a symbolically damaging siege. Events eventually confirmed his calculation.

The first city we reached, en route to Daskyleion, was Lampsakos, which had welcomed Parmenion and Attalos as liberators less than two years earlier but had then been reconquered by Memnon and subjected once again to Persian rule. If Alexandros expected that he too would receive a liberator's welcome, he was disappointed. In their three-hundred-year history, the Lampsakenes had found themselves under the sway of Lydia, Persia, Athens, Sparta, Persia, Macedonia, and then Persia again, and had evidently grown weary of their frequent tergiversations. When Alexandros's army approached the city walls, a philosopher named Anaximenes emerged and conveyed to Alexandros an offer from the city elders to pay Alexandros a substantial sum of money, if his army would skirt the city and keep on going. Alexandros gladly accepted the offer. At that moment, his need for ready cash (and Lampsakos was renowned for its gold coinage) far exceeded his desire for another conquest.

Next, we came to a small town named Kolonai. The city fathers, having observed the successful resistance of Lampsakos, also came out to greet Alexandros and to ask him to bypass their town. Unfortunately, Kolonai couldn't match the wealth of Lampsakos and the city fathers had no money to offer. Nevertheless, Alexandros left Kolonai alone, free of charge. He couldn't afford to waste time or provisions on unimportant sieges.

The next city along our route of march was Priapos, which was apparently controlled by more enterprising merchants. Unlike their neighbors, the leaders of Priapos welcomed Alexandros into their city and offered to resupply his army – for a price, of course. Alexandros took advantage of their offer, with the last of his remaining cash, to the mutual benefit of both sides.

****

While the invading army was making steady progress toward its objective, the local Persian satraps, whom Dareios had deputized to deal with this nuisance, were conferring with the mercenary general Memnon to determine their strategy. The three Persian leaders were Arsites, satrap of Hellespontine Phrygia, Arsamenes, satrap of Kilikia, and Spithridates, satrap of Ionia and Lydia. They met at Zeleia, just east of the Granikos River, which lay athwart Alexandros's route to Daskyleion.

Memnon, who had maintained his Greek contacts despite years of service at the Persian court, had received detailed reports of Alexandros's recent exploits in Greece. He also deployed spies in the Troad who provided him with a steady stream of detailed dispatches. All this intelligence enabled him to formulate an accurate assessment of Alexandros's capabilities and proclivities. At the Zeleia conference, Memnon advocated a strategy of passive resistance. He explained to the satraps that Alexandros, while a dangerous adversary on the battlefield, lacked adequate logistical support to sustain a prolonged campaign on foreign soil. All they had to do was wait him out.

The Persian leaders were incredulous. Were they expected simply to stand by while this annoying primitive from the wilds of Thrake ravaged their lands, they wanted to know. No, Memnon explained patiently, they were expected to ravage their own lands before Alexandros reached them, in order to deprive the invading army of necessary provisions. They were also expected to shelter their populations behind the ramparts of their walled cities and they were expected, at all costs, to avoid a pitched battle with the primitive from Thrake.

At that point the satraps laughed, thinking that Dareios's Greek servant had taken leave of his senses. "We Persians do not hide from some gnat that's trying to bite us on the ass. We slap him dead. What's this youngster ever done to scare us? And how exactly do we explain to Dareios that we failed to stop this insolent, impotent interloper from ravishing the king's lands and killing his people, without even putting up a fight?"

Memnon tried to explain, as diplomatically as he could, that the Greek infantry phalanx was superior to anything the Persians could field; that it was a mistake to underestimate the Macedonians; that he was as anxious to defeat the enemy as they were. "We'll defeat the invaders either way," he assured them, "but my way minimizes our risks and casualties."

"I've got 5,000 hoplites," Memnon continued, "and Alexandros's got 28,000 heavy infantry alone, not counting his light-armed troops and skirmishers. My mercenaries are the best but they're not good enough to overcome six to one odds."

"Wait a minute," Arsites exclaimed. "We have 18,000 cavalry and he's only got maybe 4,500 combined, counting all the Macedonian, Thessalian, and allied horsemen. How's that for odds? Plus, you forgot that we have our own allied infantry, numbering more than 30,000 men. Those men, combined with your mercenaries, should be more than a match for his infantry."

Memnon was unmoved. "With all due respect, sire, the conscripts whom our great king has impressed into the Persian infantry are no match for a Greek phalanx. They'll cut and run at Alexandros's first thrust, at which point only my Greek hoplites will stand in the enemy's way."

"But you're ignoring the cavalry," Arsamenes repeated with rising irritation. "The odds are overwhelmingly in our favor when it comes to mounted warriors. Our cavalry is much better armored and, don't forget, our cavalry is comprised almost exclusively of the sons of Iranian nobility. If we can turn this coming battle into a cavalry engagement, surely we can carve those underarmed savages into fine Persian stew."

"With all due respect, sire, it's infantry that wins battles. Cavalry is good for protecting the flanks and for chasing down fleeing foot soldiers but against a well-ordered phalanx, cavalry is impotent."

"So, let's leave the infantry out of it. You're telling us that this Alexandros is a hothead who likes to attack. Let's get him to attack us with his cavalry and then hit him back with ours. We're sure to overwhelm him, cavalry to cavalry. We'll have superior numbers, better armor, and the best knights in the world. And don't bother telling us his cavalry is tougher than ours because we know better."

"Well, that's a fine idea, but just how do you propose to pull it off? Despite his immature years, this Alexandros is not an idiot. He isn't likely to forget his infantry while he engages in a purely cavalry engagement."

"We have a plan." Spithridates proceeded to lay out the satraps' stratagem. Even the skeptical Memnon had to concede that it was a brilliant plan.

"So, are we all agreed?" Arsites asked. Everybody nodded. A couple of the satraps were rubbing their hands.

"And one more thing," Spithridates added, just before they broke up. "Let's make sure we kill the insolent youngster as early in the battle as we can. After that, it'll be just a mopping up operation. And we certainly want to make sure that we don't have to deal with this infestation of gnats again."

****

As the pan-Hellenic army approached the Granikos from the west, Alexandros received reports from his scouts that the Persian army had taken up position on the other side of the river. He ordered his army into battle formation and rode forward, at the head of a squadron of Companion Cavalry, to reconnoiter the situation for himself. What he saw gave pause even to the impetuous Alexandros.

The Granikos was broader, deeper, and swifter than he'd been led to believe because it was still swollen by the recently melted snowpack of the surrounding mountains. Moreover, at the point where the Daskyleion Road reached the river, the west bank sloped gradually toward the ford but the opposite bank was tall, steep, and slippery. Swimming across the rushing, whirling, roaring torrent and then clambering up the treacherous slope on the far side would've been a daunting proposition for any army under the best of circumstances. On this particular afternoon, however, any thought of an attempted crossing was rendered absurd by Memnon's 5,000 hoplites, standing in battle order, shoulder to shoulder, shields resting on the ground, spears pointing straight out, staring at the small group of Macedonian riders on the other side of the river. It was obvious that, short of divine intervention, it was not possible for us to take the other bank.

"Well, it won't be easy," Alexandros finally conceded, "but we'll have the element of surprise on our side." Seeing our blank expressions, he explained. "They'll never expect us to cross against them here. And if we do it right now, it'll surprise the living daylights out of them."

Somebody laughed, taking Alexandros's comment for a joke, but most of us knew he was in deadly earnest.

Parmenion cleared his throat. "Sire, just looking at them over there on the other side, does it really look like they're going to be surprised?"

"Yes, it does." Alexandros was firm. "And we will attack now, this afternoon, before the sun sets."

"Sire, anybody who attempts to cross now will be killed. It makes no sense to waste men on an attempt. Let's think of a better plan."

"First of all, I'm going lead the first squadron across the river, so we know at least somebody's going to make it to the other side without getting killed. And second, we'll attack with our cavalry first. While the cavalry has Memnon's infantry pinned down, you can lead the infantry across. They won't know what hit them."

"That's ridiculous, sire, with all due respect. Against an organized phalanx, cavalry has no chance, and those boys over there look pretty organized to me. Trying to do it after getting all waterlogged in the river and while climbing up a muddy, slick hill, with no footing, is insane. It's late in the day; it's going to be dark soon. Let's bring the entire army up to the river and put on a show for them to admire, while we still have some light. With any luck, we'll scare them enough so they'll sneak away during the night."

Alexandros lost his patience. "That's just the point. We can't take a chance they'll sneak away. We've got to have a pitched battle right here and now." He spun on his horse and started to ride back to the rest of the army, issuing orders as he went.

"My scouts have found another crossing place, further downstream," Parmenion yelled after him but Alexandros pretended not to hear.

In a matter of minutes, all thirteen squadrons of the Companion Cavalry attacked across the river, with Alexandros in the lead, as always. We were met by a hailstorm of javelins, arrows, bolts, and stones. Those horses that managed to swim across found it impossible to obtain any purchase for their hooves on the silt and mud of the other side. Neither horse nor man could get up the far bank. The two or three who succeed were quickly impaled on the thicket of spearpoints awaiting their arrival at the top of the embankment.

After a while, most of us stopped struggling and just sat there, waiting to die. Realizing the hopelessness of our predicament, Alexandros did the unthinkable. He turned around and returned to the west bank. The rest of us followed his lead. When we emerged from the river, we saw that the infantry had never moved.

Parmenion stood there, watching us, as we climbed out, wet, muddy, and blood-covered. Alexandros refused to meet his gaze, busying himself with the wounded. The entire engagement had taken less than ten minutes. We'd lost twenty-five of our best men.

"Erect tents, light campfires, and grab something to eat," Alexandros ordered, "but don't fall out. As soon as it gets dark, we'll start marching."

Turning to Parmenion, he added more quietly: "We'll go see about that crossing further downriver that you talked about."

Parmenion nodded. Alexandros looked at him and said nothing further. If Alexandros's glare had the power to kill, Parmenion would've been a dead man.

****

We rode under cover of darkness. Even though we had no clear idea where we were going and even though it was impossible to see anything on a moonless night, our horses somehow managed to maintain their footing and we reached the downriver ford well before sunrise. The rest of the army was marching behind us. Only the tents and burning fires were left to mark the site of our previous, disastrous engagement.

With the first glimmerings of dawn, Alexandros sent scouts across the river. They returned, reporting nary a soul on the other side. Alexandros quickly issued orders to all his commanders. Evidently, we'd fooled the Persians into believing we would attempt another frontal assault in the morning and they'd failed to follow our progress downriver during the night. Therefore, the Companion Cavalry would cross immediately and take control of the eastern bank. While the cavalry shielded the ford, the infantry would swim across and form up as soon as they reached dry land. He expected the entire infantry to be lined up, in battle order, covering the entire plain, from the eastern bank of the Granikos to the foothills of the adjoining mountains, by the time the sun rose above the horizon. The Thessalian cavalry would protect the rear and cross last.

By the time he finished issuing orders, the first units of the infantry began arriving. Surprisingly, they'd been able to march, in the dark, almost as fast as we'd managed to ride.

When Alexandros saw the infantry vanguard, he gave them a jaunty salute, spun on his horse, and set off for the ford. The rest of us in the Companion Cavalry followed, plunging into the icy water for the second time in less than twelve hours.

"Today will determine the future," Alexandros yelled to the soldiers behind, before his remaining words were swallowed by the roar of the rushing river.

When we emerged on the far side, the sky above the nearby mountains was just beginning to blush. Peering upriver, we could barely make out the black silhouettes of Persian cavalrymen, approaching in the distance.

Chapter 15 –Granikos

An idyllic, peaceful scene awaited us as our horses emerged from the freezing water. Once we had clambered up the muddy bank, we found ourselves gazing at a lush green expanse of arable land, planted with spring wheat, beginning to tiller. The entire plain between the riverbank and the mountain foothills to the east, perhaps a mile away, was mantled in a thin mist, rising gently with the morning sun. The Persian knights trotting silently, placidly toward us shimmered like a mirage in the haze. The battlefield where thousands would die later that afternoon was bathed in a tranquil silence as the two armies mustered for mortal combat.[12]

I found myself lost in thought. In my mind's eye, I could see exactly how the battle would unfold. This time, it was more than a simple premonition. After all, we had all learned about the Battle of Granikos in school. Alexandros, believing that he had spotted a weakness in the enemy line, would launch a cavalry thrust, leading his

---

[12] For an animated depiction of the Battle of Granikos, see Battle 2 at AlexanderGeiger.com.

Companion Cavalry from the front, as usual. A fierce cavalry battle would ensue during which Alexandros would be fatally wounded. As word spread of the king's death, the Persian infantry would attack across the entire width of the plain. The disheartened Macedonians would continue to resist in a desultory fashion but by the end of the day, almost the entire pan-Hellenic army would be either dead or in captivity. Only a few hundred survivors would manage to make their way back home to spread word of the appalling disaster.

I expected to be one of the survivors but, if so, I intended to head the other way. My plan was set: At the appropriate moment, perhaps after playing dead until nightfall, I would strip off my armor, make my way into the Phrygian mountains, and hide out in the primordial forests for several weeks. After that, I would arrive – presumably emaciated and in rags – in Daskyleion, impersonating a Persian conscript from a faraway land who'd managed to survive the battle and then endured a long sojourn in the wilderness. After a suitable period of recuperation and assimilation, I would begin the next stage of my journey home, this time as a subject of the Persian Empire.

Forcing my attention back to the real world, I saw the Persian cavalry approaching in slow motion, lapping against our advanced units like a gentle yet implacable flood tide, arriving, wave after wave, in their glittering coats of mail, stopping just short of effective weapons range, taking our measure, and then calmly falling back in formation. It was almost as if they were on a sightseeing excursion, gawking at an exotic, albeit lesser, form of life. And they did indeed look much more impressive than we did. Even their horses were clad in armor. The riders wore tight-fitting trousers, made of some sturdy-looking textile, and long, fitted, fabric tunics, complete with long sleeves. Around their loins, they were protected by a girdle made of leather and metal plates, to which they attached their short cavalry swords and curved daggers. Their shins were covered with highly polished steel greaves and their torsos, front and back, were protected by steel, chainmail cuirasses, sparkling in the morning sun. On their heads, they wore a felt headpiece, with ear and neck flaps, cushioning the round steel helmets, which came complete with visors, cheek plates, and mouth coverings. In their hands they carried two spears each, a javelin for throwing and a short pike for stabbing. I had to admit that, compared to them, we looked like semi-naked savages.

Did they seem so impressive to me because mentally I was already switching sides? I rejected the thought. I sincerely regretted having to take leave of my comrades. Outsider or not, I certainly felt much more kinship to the Macedonians than to the Persians. I had spent nine years living among them and had formed some close attachments. I even permitted myself to believe that I might have forged a few friendships. But none of that could alter the inexorable flow of events. Very few of my fellow soldiers would leave this seemingly serene field alive, uninjured, and free. I, on the other hand, was determined not only to survive but also to make my way back to my own time, bringing with me the accumulated treasure of my experiences in, and observations of, this ancient world.

Strangely, the Persian cavalry had done nothing to oppose our crossing of the Granikos. Surely, even if they had been somehow fooled by our nighttime march downriver, they would have surmised our intentions very early the next morning. Their cavalry, had they wished, could have prevented our taking the east bank, just as they had done the night before. But, as I learned later, the Persian high command had something else in mind. They were as eager for a set piece battle as Alexandros was. They wanted to put an end to this Hellenic invasion once and for all and to exterminate the expeditionary army to the last man, if possible. They had no desire to deal with the threat of another invasion from Greece at some point in the future. On the contrary, they were already making plans for the counteroffensive in the opposite direction, which would result in the permanent incorporation of all Greek-speaking people into the ever-expanding Persian Empire.

To achieve their objective, the Persian commanders were determined to make sure that the battle against the invaders would be fought on their terms. First, and most importantly, it would be primarily a cavalry battle. After all, the knights were the elite arm of the Persian army, both socially and militarily. And on this day, they would outnumber all of the cavalry available to Alexandros, including the Thessalian and other allied mounted troops, 18,000 to 4,500. The infantry would only come into play after the battle was won and Alexandros lay dead. Then Memnon's mercenaries, assisted by the Persian conscripts, would attack the demoralized Greek infantry and destroy them in detail. Second, the battlefield chosen by the Persians, the plain to the east of the Granikos River, was ideally suited for a cavalry engagement. It was flat and wide, devoid of obstacles that could hamper sweeping cavalry maneuvers. Third, the battle would be fought primarily by ethnic Iranian horsemen, not by Greek mercenaries or the impressed infantry of various subject nations. To the Persian aristocrats, there was always something ludicrous about the Greeks' view of them as effete and effeminate, especially given the Greeks' own reported sexual mores, but on this day the Persians would bury any epicene stereotypes once and for all.

The Persians were well aware of the Macedonians' efforts to ford the Granikos downriver from the previous day's attempted crossing. After waiting patiently for Alexandros's Companion Cavalry to complete its crossing, a few squadrons of Persian horse feigned an attack, intended mostly to fool Alexandros and his commanders into thinking that they had forced their way across, rather than been invited into the Persian trap.

When the Companion Cavalry counterattacked, the Persians calmly withdrew, permitting the remaining Greek soldiers to complete their transit of the river essentially unopposed.

By mid-morning, both armies were drawn up in battle order, facing each other in lines perpendicular to the Granikos River and stretching across the adjoining flatland, all the way to the foothills of the eastern mountains. On the Greek side, the Companion Cavalry was arrayed on the right end of the line, nearest the mountains, under Alexandros's personal command. The middle of the line was occupied by phalanx after phalanx of Macedonian and allied heavy infantry. The left end of the line was held down by Thessalian and other allied cavalry, under their own commanders. Parmenion had overall command of the infantry and allied cavalry.

The Persians arranged their forces in a somewhat less orthodox fashion. Their infantry was arrayed across the middle of the plain, without the protection that contact with the river and the foothills would have afforded against being outflanked. Memnon's mercenaries were placed dead center in this rather short, but deep, line of infantry. However, the Persian infantry was invisible to the Greeks because it was completely shielded by the Persian cavalry, drawn up, squadron after squadron, across the plain and in front of the Persian infantry. Any attack against the Persian infantry would have to get through the Persian cavalry first.

The Persian cavalry in the center of the line launched a flanking attack against Alexandros's wing of the Greek line, leaving the center of the Persian cavalry line thinned out. Alexandros immediately counterattacked, taking most of the Companion Cavalry with him, hoping to create a gap in the weakened Persian center, which the infantry units under Parmenion could then exploit.

The Persian cavalry was prepared for Alexandros's counterattack. Just as Alexandros arrived, leading a flying wedge of Companion Cavalry at the apparent Persian soft spot, the most elite Persian cavalry unit, led by Dareios's son-in-law Mithridates, suddenly materialized in front of him. Other elite Persian units, led by the satraps personally, were closing in on the Macedonian salient from the sides. A truly desperate engagement ensued.

Those of us who had managed, more or less, to keep up with Alexandros as he galloped across the battlefield now found ourselves amidst a sea of Persian mounted warriors, cut off from any immediate support by either the remaining elements of our cavalry or any of our infantry units. Not since the Trojan War had there been a comparable clash, with the leading commanders of the opposing forces engaged in personal, hand-to-hand combat against each other.

The first salvo of Persian lances was triggered by Mithridates who threw his javelin directly at Alexandros, at close range, and with great force. Alexandros saw the missile coming and attempted to deflect it with his small cavalry shield but the shield proved inadequate to the task. The metal head of the spear punched right through the shield and penetrated into Alexandros's cuirass. We couldn't tell immediately whether it had sunk into his flesh or not. It certainly didn't penetrate far enough to stop Alexandros.

He yanked out the javelin with a violent jerk, tossed it aside, and then thrust his own spear into the breastplate of Mithridates who had been closing in on him the entire time. Mithridates's armor was stronger than the Macedonian spear, which broke upon impact. Mithridates shrugged off the assault and drew his sword. Alexandros, displaying his customary composure, rammed the remnant of the spear left in his hand into Mithridates's face, forcing the Persian off his horse.

Before he could finish Mithridates off, however, another Persian nobleman, Rhosakes, rode up on Alexandros from behind and hit him over the head with his sword, slicing his helmet in two and penetrating the skin beneath, causing the suddenly visible blond hair to turn pinkish red. Alexandros, clearly dazed and unsteady on his horse, still managed to spin and slash wildly with his own sword, catching Rhosakes in the face and killing him instantly.

Prime Directive

At that moment, a Persian knight, not more than three or four feet in front of me, let out a screech and threw his lance. I was barely able to lean out of the trajectory of the flying shaft and, by the time I regained my seat, he was on top of me, swinging his sword. Falling back on old habits, I dispensed with my weaponry and grabbed his sword arm with my hands instead, dislocating his shoulder in the process. He cursed and broke off his attack, only to be replaced by another charging Persian.

Several seconds elapsed before I was able to return my attention to Alexandros, whom it was theoretically my job to protect. I looked up just in time to see Rhosakes's brother Spithridates, the satrap of Ionia and Lydia, charging at Alexandros from behind. Alexandros, his face covered in blood pouring from his scalp wound, sat slumped forward, holding on to Boukephalas's mane. It was hard to tell whether he was still conscious. Spithridates arrived silently behind the king's back, raised his sword, and was about to end the short, eventful career of this gifted, and flawed, young man with one last downward swing.

Although I had expected this denouement, had known that it was coming, and had prepared for its arrival, I still found it difficult to watch. It was not my head that was about to be splintered, but still, it was my life that flashed in front of my eyes, featuring mostly highlights from my years in Macedonia. I saw the ladies whirling at the wild Dionysia all those years ago; I saw

Kleitos come bounding to me as I lay delirious near my cave; I recalled my early conversations with Philippos; I remembered my first face-to-face meeting with Lanike; I relived the exhilaration of my first combat at Chaironeia; I saw the Parthenon once again; I experienced again and again the thrill of surviving one barbarian attack after another. Odd how the brain reacts in times of extreme stress.

All these scenes flickered across the virtual screen of my mind in less time than it would have taken for my eyelids to descend and rise again, had I had time for a blink. But the interval, although seemingly endless, was too short for an eyelid flutter. All I could do was stare wide-eyed at the tableau in front of me, waiting for the fatal stroke to descend, when a second sword appeared and slashed downward instead. The second sword, being wielded by Kleitos Melas, swung almost simultaneously with Spithridates's saber, perhaps a split second earlier. Certainly, Spithridates's weapon was descending when Kleitos's sword hit his shoulder, slicing cleanly through Spithridates's rotator cuff and severing his humerus from his clavicle. Spithridates's detached arm, still holding the sword, fell harmlessly onto Alexandros's back. The mortally wounded satrap didn't utter a sound. He simply rode away, a bright, crimson fountain of blood spurting from the spot where his right arm used to be.

It took more time for me to comprehend what I'd just witnessed than it had taken for Spithridates to raise his sword arm and for Kleitos to slice it off. *Alexandros didn't die.* My thoughts seemed to be moving in slow motion. *And it was Kleitos who saved his life.* I resisted the implications of those thoughts for as long as I could. Luckily, before the new paradigm could set in, the situation at hand spun wildly out of control.

Although Spithridates's arm and sword hit Alexandros's back with no more force than a lover's gentle pat, the impact was enough to dislodge the king from his perch. He collapsed to the ground, motionless. I immediately positioned my horse to shield the king's body, as did Kleitos and several other bodyguards. We formed a tight little ring around our fallen leader, while a much larger ring of Persian knights closed in around us. There were hundreds of Persians, jostling against one another, fighting for the privilege of claiming the enemy commander's head and hands. Of course, they had to kill us first but that didn't appear to be an insurmountable obstacle at that moment.

I almost didn't mind. In the heat of the battle, I was no longer an outsider, an alien traveler, a stranger in this wonderful, vital time. I was closer to the men fighting next to me than I'd ever been to another human being. They were more than brothers to me; we were offshoots of a single, living, breathing, desperately fighting organism. A life and death struggle is a marvelously unifying, uplifting, almost addictive experience, especially if it doesn't have a fatal conclusion. And dying never crossed my mind.

Unbeknownst to us, the rest of the pan-Hellenic army wasn't simply standing still, awaiting the outcome of our desperate little scrum. Taking advantage of the fact that the Persian cavalry screen had been rent at several points as a result of our cavalry thrust, the Macedonian heavy infantry poured through the gaps and engaged their Persian counterparts. It was an unequal struggle. At the first brutal, shocking, overwhelming impact of the Macedonian front rank against the Persians' infantry lines, the inexperienced and inadequately armed Persian foot soldiers gave way, retreated, and soon turned to run. Only Memnon's mercenaries in the center continued to hold their ground.

Our other allies did what they could. The Agrianians were especially effective. They simply waded into the huge melee surrounding our position, darting beneath the bellies of the Persian horses, hamstringing them as they went. The Thessalian cavalry joined in, riding down the escaping Persian foot soldiers and killing them midstride. Those members of the Companion Cavalry who were not trapped in the middle of the scrum with us did their best to fight their way in from the outside in order to save us.

If any of our cavalry comrades suspected Alexandros's dire state, they certainly didn't let any doubts slacken their efforts. On the contrary, they fought like men out to save the life of their beloved leader and, even though they were greatly outnumbered, their efforts were beginning to tell. The pressure around us gradually eased and one of the bodyguards was able to jump off his horse and kneel down next to Alexandros, wiping the blood off his face. The king sat up and then rose, unsteadily, to his feet. Somebody else grabbed Boukephalas who had been gallantly standing by, riderless but undaunted, waiting for his master to remount. We lifted Alexandros onto his horse's back, which seemed to revive him. He raised his arms and smiled. Somehow, every Macedonian on the field of battle saw him and let out a wild cheer.

There was a corresponding loss of morale among the Persian knights. They stopped pressing against us and began to pull back. Moments later, they were in full retreat, pursued by elements of the Companion Cavalry, creating eddies of mayhem in the concentric waves of fleeing knights, spreading like ripples in a pond from the spot where Alexandros sat once again astride Boukephalas.

Remarkably, Alexandros had resumed command of his army, ordering the cavalry to break off pursuit and concentrate on consolidating control of the battlefield. In truth, there was only one pocket of resistance left – Memnon's mercenaries. The entire might of the Macedonian phalanx now came to bear against their fellow Greek hoplites, while the Macedonian cavalry surrounded them on all sides, making sure that none could escape.

The Greek mercenaries sent an envoy, asking for quarter, offering to join Alexandros's side in any future battles. Alexandros rejected their request. "Any Greek who fights for the Persians forfeits his right to live," he observed tersely.

The Macedonians butchered about 3,000 mercenaries, at which point the remaining 2,000 threw down their weapons and surrendered, thereby delaying their deaths for a little while longer, because the Macedonian soldiers refused to slaughter unarmed men. Instead, Alexandros had them clapped in chains and shipped back to the Pangaion Hills in Thrake where they were put to work in the mines until they died. On the average, the process took about four months.

When the last of the fighting ended, Alexandros took stock of the casualties. In addition to the Greek mercenaries, the Persians had lost perhaps a quarter of the subject-nation levies. This did not trouble them greatly. Of much more concern was the loss of about 2,500 ethnic Iranian knights, including many leading noblemen. Dareios's son-in-law Mithridates was dead, as was his son Arbupales, as was Spithridates, the satrap of Ionia and Lydia. Arsites, satrap of Hellespontine Phrygia, survived and fled to Daskyleion, where he committed suicide two days after his arrival. Memnon somehow managed to get away.

On the Macedonian side, the casualties were surprisingly light, especially given the ferocity of the fighting in Alexandros's vicinity. Only a few dozen men were dead and perhaps as many as two hundred lay wounded. Alexandros insisted on speaking personally to each wounded soldier in his army, making sure he was being cared for properly and asking about the circumstances of each injury. He listened patiently to the answers, no matter how exaggerated and fantastic some of the wounded soldiers' stories might have been. Only after all the Macedonian wounded had been treated did Alexandros submit to the ministrations of his personal physician. The victory feast was postponed for another night. No one was in a mood to celebrate just yet. We all knew it had been an exceedingly close call.

I knew more than that. I knew that Alexandros was supposed to be dead, along with most of his army. There was only one reason why Spithridates had not delivered his fatal blow – Kleitos's timely intervention. *Kleitos wouldn't've been here if you hadn't saved his life, way back when,* I reminded myself unnecessarily.

What the implications of this change in the fabric of the space-time continuum were, I couldn't begin to fathom, but it was certainly clear that everything I'd learned about the history of this era, from this point forward, was no longer valid. I was condemned to live, at least for the next few years, through an alternate historical narrative and could only hope that the inertial tendencies of the temporal stream would reassert themselves at some point, that the reverberations of my thoughtless interference, at the edge of that meadow in the highlands of Macedonia, traveling down the river of time, would eventually dampen out. How long that would take, there was no way to tell. But I consoled myself with the knowledge that the escape hatch would materialize, on the Mediterranean coast of Egypt, near the Nile delta, a little more than a decade hence, no matter what. And as long as the river of time returned to its original banks before reaching my native era, all would be as I'd left it before departing for my ill-fated trip.

I intended to keep my rendezvous with that escape hatch. And until then, I would spend whatever time I could spare from trying to survive on tormenting myself with the knowledge that my violation of the Prime Directive had indeed changed the course of history. The extent and duration of the change remained unknown.

I tried to envisage what the future held but for once my imagination failed me. For the first time in a long time I had no idea what would happen next.

Prime Directive

Author's Note to Revised Second Edition

Ptolemaios, known to English-speaking historians as Ptolemy I, was born circa 364 B.C.E. (the date is disputed) and died circa 282 B.C.E. He left behind a memoir recounting his adventures with Alexander III of Macedonia. Unfortunately, this memoir is now lost. However, a distant echo of Ptolemaios's history continues to reverberate in our collective memory because it was utilized as original source material by ancient historians writing during Roman imperial times, such as Lucius Flavius Arrianus (Arrian), Quintus Curtius Rufus (Curtius), and possibly Lucius Mestrius Plutarchus (Plutarch[13]), whose works are still extant today. Modern histories of the period covered in this book are in turn based largely on these ancient Roman accounts.

This novel is an attempt to reconstruct the first part of Ptolemaios's lost memoir. Of necessity, some of the narrative, much of the characterization, and almost all of the dialogue were invented by the author. The spelling of the characters' names, however, is authentic. On the other hand, there is no historical evidence to suggest that Ptolemaios was a time traveler or that anyone ever called him Metoikos.

---

[13] By coincidence, Plutarch was born in Chaironeia, some 384 years after the battle described in this book. It is tempting to speculate that his childhood visits to the battlefield resulted in a life-long interest in history.

The author has received a great deal of helpful and constructive feedback since the original publication of this work in 2013, which feedback has resulted in a good many changes (and, it is hoped, improvements) in this revised edition. The author is indebted to all those readers who took the time to send in their comments.

April 15, 2019

Alexander Geiger

Additional Materials

Additional materials, including sources, illustrations, maps, battle depictions, an author's blog, and descriptions of upcoming volumes, are available at AlexanderGeiger.com

About the Author

The author is a history buff who has always wished he could travel back in time to visit some of his favorite historical figures, places, and events. The entire Ptolemaios Saga is an account of one such extended trip, intended to witness the dawn of the Hellenistic world. The men and women who lived, strived, fought, and loved during this seminal age didn't know their ideas, exploits, and accomplishments would reverberate all the way to the present day but, boy oh boy, did they leave a mark. Imagine being able to see, through the eyes of Ptolemaios Metoikos – who was actually there – all the adventures, sights, and colorful figures of that vibrant, memorable, and thrilling era. It's the author's hope that you will enjoy the ride.

In real life, the author is a graduate of Princeton University and Cornell Law School and a retired commercial litigator. He lives with his wife in in Bucks County, PA.

Please email all comments, questions, suggestions, or requests for author interviews and appearances to Alex@AlexanderGeiger.com.

Made in the USA
Monee, IL
12 December 2019

18494684R00246